THE HOSTAGE

SUSAN WIGGS

THE HOSTAGE

MIRA®

MIRA®

ISBN 0-7394-0996-4

THE HOSTAGE

Copyright © 2000 by Susan Wiggs.

Visit us at www.mirabooks.com

Printed in U.S.A.

For Lisa and Bruce, with love

ACKNOWLEDGMENT

Thanks to Barb, Betty, Alice and Joyce for reading
and critiquing—you were right, as usual; to
Alicia Rasley and Jill Barnett for particular insights;
to Martha Keenan for superb editing; to the diva,
Emilie Storrs, for extreme diva-tude; and to the
Chicago Historical Society for information and technical
assistance. Making up a story is so much easier
than getting the facts right!

Part One

And the wind raging, and the fire burning,
and London and Paris and Portland outdone, and
no Milton and no Dante on earth to put
the words together.

—*Chicago Tribune*
(burned before distribution)

Part One

Prologue

Chicago
8 October 1871

It was the hottest October anyone could remember. Less than an inch of rain had fallen in three months. Livestock died of thirst, their bloated carcasses splayed beside sun-baked mudholes. The unseasonable warmth made women regard baking day with special loathing and small children cranky with prickly heat. Laboring men paused in their work, looked up at the sky and remarked to each other that they'd surely welcome a breath of winter.

Drought and dry windstorms kept the fire companies frantically busy; engineers and pipemen were called on to put out as many as six fires a day, battling the flames that fed on unpainted frame cottages, rickety shanties with roofs of tar and shake, and the endless supply of wood-chips from Chicago's lumber mills.

Into the restless stream of hot prairie wind floated a single spark.

Later, some would say the spark came from a stove chimney. Many believed the gossip that the unfortunate placement of a lantern near a cow in Mrs. O'Leary's barn had caused the mayhem. Others would swear, in the terrible aftermath, that the hand of God himself started it all, while still others accused the Devil. Some even blamed a hail of comets that rained from the night sky. In the great charred ruin of the city, fingers would point and recriminations would echo across courtrooms, in the city hall and at hearings before the Board of Fire.

But the fact was, a single spark, dipping and swirling like a drunken ballerina, rode an updraft of wind that night. It sailed high over a neighborhood of wood frame houses, barns packed with timothy hay, sheds full of coal and wood shavings for tinder, sidewalks constructed of knotty spruce and pine-block roadways.

The West Division neighborhood was a rabbit warren of narrow, miserable alleys and makeshift shanties, a place no respectable person would ever visit. But it was home to day laborers and women with too many babies, to shopkeepers and immigrants, to drunks and dreamers, loose women and strict Catholics. And in the tacked-together neighborhood they bore their children, worshiped, ate, drank, fought, loved and buried their dead.

The dry, blowing heat prompted some folks to find their beds early, while others tried to drown their discomfort in drink and song. The thin, lively whine of fiddle music and the thump of hobnail boots on plank floors emanated from some of the cottages. Noise flooded through open windows and caused flimsy walls to reverberate with the hectic celebration.

And high in the wild night sky, the spark looped and changed direction, pushed along by the wind blowing in from the broad and empty Illinois prairie.

The spark entered a barn where five milk cows and a horse stood tethered with their heads lowered, and a calf lay curled on a bed of straw.

The tiny ember dropped onto a store of musty hay, and when the wind breathed on it, a small circle of orange appeared.

No one saw the pool of flame spread like spilled water,

dripping down and over the stacked hay, igniting the crisp, dry wood shavings from Bateham's Planing Mill. No one saw the river of fire flowing along the worn plank floor. No one noticed the horse's nostrils dilate in fear or heard the animal emit a high-pitched whistle of alarm.

Finally, a drayman with a wooden leg, who happened to be loitering across the street, noticed the deep-toned, unnatural light and headed clumsily for the barn. The cows, tied by their halters, stood unmoving even when Pegleg Sullivan came crashing into the barn and untied them. The calf, with its hide on fire and its tether hanging in the wood shavings, plowed into Pegleg and half dragged him out into the yard.

Tall, graceful fronds of flame bloomed at the side of the barn. Stark orange light licked across the beaten earth of the yard between house and shed.

Finally, a man's voice broke the night. "Kate, the barn's afire!"

In Box Number 342, at the corner of Canalport Avenue and Halsted Street, the first alarm sounded.

And over the sleeping faces of the children in the West Division of Chicago, a strange and rusty glow of light flickered.

One

"What's the matter with Deborah?" asked Phoebe Palmer, standing in the middle of a cluttered suite of rooms at Miss Emma Wade Boylan's School for Young Ladies. Lacy petticoats and beribboned unmentionables littered the divans and ottomans of the fringed, beaded and brocaded salon. "She won't even let her maid in to attend her," Phoebe added.

"I'll see what's keeping her." Lucy Hathaway pushed open the door to an adjoining chamber. Deborah's dress, which she had worn to Aiken's Opera House the previous night, lay slumped in a heap of tulle and silk on the floor. A mound of sheets lay scattered over the bed, while the smell of expensive perfume and despair hung in the air.

"Deborah, are you all right?" Lucy asked softly. She went to the window, parting the curtain to let in a bit of the waning evening light. In the distance, some of the taller buildings and steeples of distant Chicago stabbed the horizon. The sky was tinged dirty amber by the smoke and soot of industry. But closer to Amberley Grove, the genteel suburb where the school was located, the wind-swept evening promised to be a lovely one.

"Deborah, we've been pestering you for hours to get ready. Aren't you coming with us tonight?" Lucy persisted. Though the engagement bore the humble name of an evangelical reading, everyone knew it was simply an excuse for the cream of society to get together on the Sabbath. Though weighty spiritual issues might be discussed, lighter matters such as gossip and romance would be attended to with appropriate religious fervor. Tonight's particular social event had an added drama that had set tongues to wagging all week long. The intensely desired Dylan Kennedy was looking for a wife.

"Please, dear," Lucy said. "You're scaring me, and ordinarily *nothing* scares me."

Huddled on the bed, Deborah couldn't find the words to allay her friend's concern. She was trying to remember what her life had been like just twenty-four hours ago. She was trying to recall just who she was, tallying up the pieces of herself like items in a ledger book. A cherished only daughter. Fiancée of the most eligible man in Chicago. A privileged young woman poised on the threshold of a charmed life.

Everything had fallen apart last night, and she had no idea how to put it all back together.

"Make her hurry, do," Phoebe said, waltzing in from the next room with a polished silk evening dress pressed to her front. "Miss Boylan's coach will call for us in half an hour. Imagine! Dylan Kennedy is finally going to settle on a wife." She preened in front of a freestanding cheval glass, patting her glossy brown hair. "Isn't that deliciously romantic?"

"It's positively barbaric," said Lucy. "Why should we be paraded in front of men like horses at auction?"

"Because," Kathleen O'Leary said, joining them in Deborah's chamber, "Miss Boylan promised you would all be there. Three perfect young ladies," she added with a touch of Irish irony. She reached for the curtain that shrouded the bed. "Are you all right, then, miss?" she asked. "I've been trying like the very devil to attend to you all day." The maid put out a pale, nervous hand and patted the miserable mound of blankets.

Deborah felt assaulted by her well-meaning friends. She wanted to yell at them, tell them to leave her alone, but she had no idea how to assert her own wishes. No one had ever taught her to behave in such a fashion; it was considered unladylike in the extreme. She shrank back into the covers and pretended not to hear.

"She doesn't answer," Lucy said, her voice rising with worry.

"Please, Deborah," Phoebe said. "Talk to us. Are you ill?"

Deborah knew she would have no peace until she surrendered. With slow, painstaking movements, she made herself sit up, leaning against a bank of Belgian linen pillows. Three faces, as familiar as they were dear to her, peered into hers. They looked uncommonly beautiful, perhaps because they were all so different. Black-haired Lucy, carrot-topped Kathleen and Phoebe with her light brown curls. Their faces held the winsome innocence and anticipation Deborah herself had felt only yesterday.

"I'm not ill," she said softly, in a voice that barely sounded like her own.

"You look like hell," Lucy said with her customary bluntness.

Because I have been there.

"I'll send for the doctor." Kathleen started toward the door.

"No!" Deborah's sharp voice stopped the maid in her tracks. A doctor was unthinkable. "That is," she forced herself to say, "I assure you, I am not in the least bit ill." To prove her point, she forced herself out of bed and stood barefoot in the middle of the room.

"Well, that's a relief." With brisk bossiness, Phoebe took her hand and gave it a friendly, aggressive tug. Deborah stumbled along behind her and stepped into the brightly lit salon.

"I imagine you're simply overcome because you'll be a married woman a fortnight from now." Phoebe dropped her hand and smiled dreamily. "You are so fabulously lucky. How can you keep to your bed at such a magical time? If I were engaged to the likes of Philip Ascot, I should be pacing the carpets with excitement. The week before my sister married Mr. Vanderbilt, my mother used to joke that she needed an anchor to keep her feet on the ground."

Deborah knew Phoebe didn't mean for the words to hurt. Deborah was a motherless daughter, the saddest sort of creature on earth, and at a time like this the sense of loss gaped like an unhealed wound. She wondered what a young woman with a mother would do in this situation.

"So," Lucy said, "let's hurry along. We don't want to be late."

Through a fog of indifference, Deborah surveyed the suite cluttered with combs, atomizers, lacy underclothes, ribbons, masses of petticoats—a veritable explosion of femininity. It was the sort of scene that used to delight her, but everything was different now. Suddenly these things meant nothing to her. She had the strangest notion of being encased in ice, watching her friends through a wavy, frozen wall. The sense of detachment and distance hardened with each passing moment. She used to be one of the young ladies of Miss Boylan's famous finishing school, merry and certain of her place in the glittering world of Chicago's debutantes. It all seemed so artificial now, so pointless. She felt alienated from her friends and from the contented, foolish girl she used to be.

"And what about you, dear Kathleen?" Phoebe asked, aiming a pointed glance at the red-haired maid. Phoebe took every chance to remind Kathleen that she was merely the hired help, there at the sufferance of more privileged young women like herself. "What do you plan to do tonight?"

Kathleen O'Leary's face turned crimson. She had the pale almost translucent skin of her Irish heritage, and it betrayed every emotion. "You've left me a fine mess to be tidying up, miss. And won't that keep me busy 'til cock-crow.'' Saucy as ever, she exaggerated her brogue on purpose.

"You should come with us, Kathleen.'' Lucy, whose family had raised her to be a free thinker, didn't care a fig for social posturing, but she knew that important people would be attending. The politicians, industrialists and social reformers were valuable contacts for her cause—rights for women.

"Really, Lucy,'' scolded Phoebe. "Only the best people in town are invited. Dr. Moody's readings are strictly for—''

"The invitation was extended to every young lady at Miss Boylan's,'' Lucy, who was both wealthy and naive enough to be an egalitarian, reminded her.

"Stuff and nonsense,'' Kathleen said, her blush deepening.

"Perhaps you *should* attend,'' Phoebe said, a calculating gleam in her eye. "It might be fun to surprise everyone with a lady of mystery.''

The old Deborah would have joined in the ruse with pleasure. Lively, intelligent Kathleen always added a sense of fun to the sometimes tedious routine of social climbing. But it was all too much to think about now, and she passed a shaking hand over her forehead. The celluloid hairpins she hadn't bothered to remove last night exaggerated the headache that made her grit her teeth. The pain hammered so hard at her temples that the pins seemed to pulse with a life of their own.

"Phoebe's right, Kathleen,'' Lucy was saying. "It'll be such fun. Please come.''

"I've not a stitch to wear that wouldn't mark me as an imposter,'' Kathleen said, but the protest failed to mask the yearning in her voice. She had always harbored an endless fascination with high society.

"Yes, you have.'' Deborah forced herself out of her

torpor. "You shall wear my new dress. I won't be needing it."

"Your Worth gown?" Phoebe demanded. At her father's insistence, Deborah's gowns all came from the Salon de Lumière in Paris. "For mercy's sake, you've never even worn it yourself."

"I'm not going." Deborah kept her voice as calm as she could even though she felt like screaming. "I must go into the city to see my father." She wasn't sure when she had made the decision, but there it was. She had a matter of utmost importance to discuss with him, and she could not put it off any longer.

"You can't go into the city tonight," Phoebe said. "Don't be silly. Who would chaperone you?"

"Just come with us," Lucy said, her voice gentle. "Come to the reading, and we'll take you to see your father afterward. Philip Ascot will be in attendance, won't he? He'll be expecting you. What on earth shall we tell him?"

The name of her fiancé rushed over Deborah like a chill wind. "I'll send my regrets."

"You aren't yourself at all." Lucy touched her arm, her light brush of concern almost powerful enough to shatter Deborah. "We shall go mad with worry if you don't tell us what's wrong."

Phoebe stuck out her foot so Kathleen could button her kid leather boot. "Was it last night's opera? You were fine when you left, but you stayed in bed all day long. Didn't you like *Don Giovanni?*"

Deborah turned away, a wave of nausea rolling over her. The notes of the Mozart masterpiece were forever burned into her.

"It's your bloody flux, isn't it?" Kathleen whispered, ignoring Phoebe's boot. "You've always suffered with the heavy pains. Let me stay behind and fix you a posset."

"It's not the flux," Deborah said.

Lucy planted her palm flat against the door. "This isn't like you. If something's wrong, you should tell us, dear."

Nothing's wrong. She tried to eke out the words, but they wouldn't come, because they were a lie. Everything was wrong and nothing could ever be the same. But how did she explain that, even to her best friends?

"It's of a private nature," she said faintly. "Please. I'll explain it all when I return."

"Oh, so you're going to be mysterious, are you?" Phoebe sputtered. "You're just trying to make yourself the center of attention, if you ask me."

"No one asked you," Lucy said wearily.

Phoebe sputtered some more, but no one was listening. Though she had come up through school with the rest of them, Phoebe had set herself apart from the others. Nearly as rich as Deborah and nearly as blueblooded as Lucy, she had concluded that the two "nearlys" added up to much loftier status than her friends enjoyed. She was a terrible and unrepentant snob, generally benign, though her remarks to Kathleen O'Leary sometimes brandished the sharp edge of malice. Phoebe alone understood that one did not simply abandon an exclusive social event. But this merely proved the inferiority of a girl like Deborah Sinclair. New-money people simply didn't understand the importance of attending the right sort of functions with the right sort of people.

"I'd best go ring for my driver," Deborah said.

Lucy moved away from the door. "It won't be the same without you."

Deborah bit her lip, afraid that the sympathy from her best friend would break through the icy barrier she had painstakingly erected between control and madness. "Help Kathleen with the gown," she said, hoping to divert everyone's attention to the masquerade.

After sending for her coach, Deborah buttoned on a simple blue serge dress and tugged a shawl around her shoulders. Pushing her feet into Italian kid leather boots, she didn't bother with the buttoning. Instead, she wound the ribbons haphazardly around her ankles and then jammed on a hat.

In the main salon, the others dressed more carefully. Eyes shining with forbidden pleasure, Kathleen stepped into the French gown, her homespun bloomers disappearing beneath layers of fancy petticoats. The gown of emerald silk and her Irish coloring gave her the look of a Celtic princess, and her face glowed with an excitement Deborah could no longer share.

Before leaving, Deborah stepped back and surveyed the scene, seeing it for the first time through the eyes of an outsider. Over her father's protests she had left his opulent, gilded mansion for the solid gothic halls of Miss Boylan's. Her father believed the very best young ladies were educated at home. But once he learned a Hathaway and a Palmer would be in attendance, he had relented and allowed Deborah to complete her education with finishing school. She looked with fondness upon Lucy, Kathleen and Phoebe, who were her closest companions and sometimes, she thought, her only friends. The four of them had shared everything—their hopes and dreams, their broken hearts and romantic triumphs.

Finally Deborah had encountered something she could not share with her friends. She could not. It was too devastating. Besides, she must tell her father. She must. Please God, she prayed silently. Let him understand. Just this once.

"Have a wonderful time this evening," she said, her hand on the door handle. "I shall want to hear all about Kathleen's debut when I return." She forced the words past a throat gone suddenly tight with terror.

Kathleen rushed to the door. "Miss Deborah, are you certain that—"

"Absolutely." The word was a mere gust of air.

"Let the poor thing go," Phoebe said in a distracted voice. She lifted her arm with the sinuous grace of a ballerina and drew on a silken glove. "If you stand around arguing all evening, we'll be late."

She and Lucy launched into a squabble over how Kathleen should wear her hair, and Deborah took the opportunity to slip out into the tall, cavernous hall and down to the foyer, where her driver waited. Outside, she saw the school's large, cumbersome rockaway carriage being hitched to four muscular horses. The school crest adorned the black enamel doors.

Deborah's private Bismarck-brown clarence, with its gleaming glass panes front and rear, waited at the curb. Thanks to her father's habit of flaunting his wealth, the expensive vehicle, with its experienced driver and Spanish coach horse, was always at her disposal. Within a few minutes, she was under way.

She gripped a leather strap at the side of the interior of the coach, bracing herself against the rocking motion. As they pulled away from the school, with its ponderous, pretentious turrets and wrought iron gates, she felt like Rapunzel escaping her tower prison. Small farms sped past, squat houses hugged low against the prairie landscape of withered orchards and wind-torn cornfields. Lights glimmered in windows and the sight of them pierced her. She pictured the families within, gathering around the table for supper. She had only seen such families from afar, but imagined they shared an easy intimate warmth she had never felt growing up in the cold formality of her father's house.

She cast away the yearning. All her life she had enjoyed the advantages most women never dared to dream about. Arthur Sinclair had crafted and aligned his daughter's future with the same precise attention to detail with which he put together his business transactions. His rivals vilified him for his aggression and ambition, but Deborah knew little of commerce. Her father preferred it that way.

The drive into Chicago was swift. Jeremy, who had served as her personal driver since she was three years old, drove expertly through the long, straight roads that crisscrossed the city. Jeremy lived in a garden cottage along the north branch of the Chicago River. He had a plump wife and a grown daughter who had recently wed. Deborah wondered what Jeremy did when he returned home to them, late at night. Did he touch his sleeping wife or just light a lamp and look at her for a moment? Did she awaken, or sigh in her sleep and turn toward the wall?

Deborah knew she was using her meandering thoughts to keep her mind off the ordeal to come. She shifted restlessly on the seat and cupped her hands around her eyes to see through the glass as Chicago came into view. Ordinarily, the air was cool closer to the lake, but this evening, the day's heat hung well past sundown.

The whitish fuzz of gaslight illuminated the long, straight main thoroughfares. The coach crossed the river, rolling past the elegant hotel where the reading party was to take place. Well-dressed people were already gathering. Liveried doormen rushed to and fro beneath a scalloped canvas awning that flapped in a violent wind. Huge potted shrubs flanked the gilt-and-glass doorway, and inside, a massive chandelier glowed like the sun. The gilded cage of high society was the only world Deborah had ever known, yet it was a world in which she no longer felt safe. She couldn't imagine herself walking into the hotel now.

Traditionally set for the second Sunday of the month, the lively readings and discussions ordinarily held a delicious appeal for her. She loved seeing people dressed in their finery, happily sipping cordials as they laughed and conversed. She loved the easy pleasures of glib talk and gossip. But last night the magic had been stolen from Deborah.

No matter. Tonight she vowed to reclaim her soul.

She shivered, knowing that skipping the social engagement was only the first act of defiance she would commit tonight. She had never before carried out a rebellion, and she didn't know if she could accomplish it.

As the carriage wended its way up Michigan Avenue, Jeremy had to slow down before an onslaught of pedestrians, drays, teams and whole family groups. They seemed to be heading for the ,Rush Street bridge that spanned the river. Despite the lateness of the hour, crowds had gathered at the small stadium of the Chicago White Stockings.

Rapping on the curved windshield, Deborah called out, "Is everything all right, Jeremy?"

He didn't answer for a few moments as he negotiated the curve toward River Street, heading for the next bridge to the west. They encountered more crowds, bobbing along in the scant illumination of the coach lamps. Deborah twisted around on the cushioned bench to look through the rear window. The pedestrians were, for the most part, a well-dressed crowd, and though no one dawdled, no one hurried, either. They resembled a dining party or a group coming out of the theater. Yet it seemed unusual to see so many people out on a Sunday night.

"They say there's a big fire in the West Division," Jeremy reported through the speaking tube. "Plenty of folks had to evacuate. I'll have you home in a trice, miss."

She knew Kathleen's family lived in the West Division, where they kept cows for milking. She prayed the O'Learys would be all right. Poor Kathleen. This was supposed to be an evening of pranks, pretenses and fun, but a big fire could change all that.

She wondered if Dr. Moody's lecture would be canceled because of the fire. Probably not. The Chicago Board of Fire boasted the latest in fire control, including hydrants, steam pump engines and an intricate system of alarms and substations. Many of the stone and steel downtown buildings were considered fireproof. The city's elite would probably gather in the North Division to gossip the night away as the engineers and pumpers brought the distant blaze under control.

She stared out at the unnatural bloom of light in the west. Her breath caught—not with fear but with wonder at the impressive sight. In the distance, the horizon burned bright as morning. Yet the sky lacked the innocent quality of daylight, and in the area beyond the river, brands of flame fell from the sky, thick as snow in a blizzard.

Apprehension flashed through her, but she put aside the feeling. The fire would stop when it reached the river. It always did. The greater problem, in Deborah's mind, was getting her father to understand and accept her decision.

The coach rolled to a halt in front of the stone edifice of her father's house. Surrounded by yards and gardens, the residence and its attendant outbuildings took up nearly a whole block. There was a trout pond that was used in the winter for skating. The mansion had soaring Greek revival columns and a mansard roof, fashionably French. A grand cupola with a slender lightning rod rose against the sky. A graceful porch, trimmed with painted woodwork, wrapped around the front of the house, with a wide staircase reaching down to the curved drive.

"You're home, miss," Jeremy announced, his footsteps crunching on the gravel drive as he came to help her down.

Not even in a moment of whimsy had Deborah ever thought of the house on Huron Avenue as a home. The huge, imposing place more closely resembled an institution, like a library or perhaps a hospital. Or an insane asylum.

Squelching the disloyal thought, she sat in the still swaying carriage while Jeremy lowered the steps, opened the door and held out his hand toward her. Wild gusts of wind pushed dead leaves along the gutters and walkways.

Even through her glove she could feel that Jeremy's fingers were icy cold, and she regarded him with surprise. Despite a studiously dispassionate expression, a subtle tension tightened his jaw and his eyes darted toward the firelit sky.

"You'd best hurry home to your wife," she said. "You'll want to make certain she's all right."

"Are you sure, miss?" Jeremy opened the iron gate. "It's my duty to stay and—"

"Nonsense." It was the one decision she could make tonight that was unequivocal. "Your first duty is to your family. Go. I would do nothing but worry all night if you didn't."

He sent her a grateful bob of his head, and as he swept open the huge, heavy front door for her, the braid on his livery cap gleamed in the false and faraway light. Deborah walked alone into the vestibule of the house, feeling its formidable presence. Staff members hastened to greet her—three maids in black and white, two housemen in navy livery, the housekeeper tall and imposing, the butler impeccably dignified. As she walked through the formal gauntlet of servants, their greetings were painstakingly respectful—eyes averted, mouths unsmiling.

Arthur Sinclair's servants had always been well-fed and -clothed, and most were wise enough to understand that not every domestic in Chicago enjoyed even these minor privileges. To his eternal pain and shame, Arthur Sinclair had once been a member of their low ranks. So, though he never spoke of it, he understood all too well the plight of the unfortunate.

She prayed he would be as understanding with his own daughter. She needed that now.

"Is my father at home?" she inquired.

"Certainly, miss. Upstairs in his study," the butler said. "Would you like Edgar to announce you?"

"That won't be necessary, Mr. Marlowe. I'll go right up." She walked between the ranks of silent servants, surrendering her hat and gloves to a maid as she passed. She sensed their unspoken questions about her plain dress and shawl, the disheveled state of the hair she had not bothered to comb. The stiff, relentless formality was customary, yet Deborah had never enjoyed being the object of the staff's scrutiny. "Thank you," she said. "That will be all."

"As you wish." Marlowe bowed and stepped back.

With a flick of her hand and a jingle of the keys tied at her waist, the housekeeper led the others away. Through the doors that quickly opened and shut, Deborah could see that valuables were being packed away into trunks and crates. A precaution, she supposed, because of the fire.

Standing alone in the soaring vestibule, with its domed skylight three storeys up, Deborah immediately and unaccountably felt cold. The house spread out in an endless maze of rooms—salons and seasonal parlors, the music room, picture gallery, dining room, ballroom, conservatory, guest suites she had never counted. This was, in every sense of the word, a monument to a merchant prince; its sole purpose to proclaim to the world that Arthur Sinclair had arrived.

Dear God, thought Deborah. When did I grow so cynical?

Actually, she knew the precise moment it had happened. But that was not something she would reveal to anyone but herself.

Misty gaslight fell across the black-and-white checkered marble floor. An alabaster statue of Narcissus, eternally pouring water into a huge white marble basin situated in the extravagant curve of the grand staircase, greeted her with a blank-eyed stare.

Beside the staircase was something rather new—a mechanical lift. In principle it worked like the great grain elevators at the railroad yards and lakefront. A system of pulleys caused the small car to rise or lower. Her father had a lame leg, having been injured in the war a decade ago, and he had a hard time getting up and down the stairs.

To Deborah, the lift resembled a giant bird cage. Though costly gold-leaf gilding covered the bars, they were bars nonetheless. The first time she stood within the gilded cage, she had felt an unreasoning jolt of panic, as if she were a prisoner. The sensation of being lifted by the huge thick cables made her stomach lurch. After that first unsettling ride, she always chose to take the stairs.

The hand-carved rail of the soaring staircase was waxed and buffed to a high sheen. Her hand glided over its satisfying smoothness, and she remembered how expert she had been at sliding down this banister. It was her one act of defiance. No matter how many times her nanny or her tutor, or even her father, reprimanded her, she had persisted in her banister acrobatics. It was simply too irresistible to prop her hip on the rail, balance just so at the top, then let the speed gather as she slid down. Her landings had never been graceful, and she'd borne the bruises to prove it, but the minor bumps had always seemed a small price to pay in exchange for a few crazy moments of a wild ride.

Unlike so many other things, her father had never been able to break her of the habit. He governed her sternly in all matters, but within her dwelt a stubborn spark of exuberance he had never been able to snuff.

Deborah started up the stairs. The study housed Arthur Sinclair's estate offices, and he worked there until late each night, devoting the same fervor to his business as a monk to his spiritual meditations. He regarded the accumulation of wealth and status as his means to salvation. But there was one thing all his money and influence could not buy—the sense of belonging to the elite society that looked down on his kind. Acquiring that elusive quality would take more than money. For that he needed Deborah.

She shuddered, though the house was overly warm, and took the steps slowly. She passed beautifully rendered oil portraits in gaudily expensive gold-leafed frames. The paintings depicted venerable ancestors, some dating back to the *Mayflower* and further. But the pictures were of strangers plucked from someone else's family tree. She used to make up stories about the stern-faced aristocrats who stared, eternally frozen, from the gleaming frames. One was an adventurer, another a sailor, yet another a great diplomat. They were all men who had done something with their lives rather than living off the bounty of their forebears.

She would never understand why her father considered it less honorable to have earned rather than inherited a fortune. She had asked him once, but hadn't understood his reply. "I wish to have a feeling of permanence in the world," he had said. "A feeling that I have acquired the very best of everything. I want to achieve something that will last well beyond my own span of years."

It was a mad quest, using money to obtain the things other families took generations to collect and amass, but he regarded it as his sacred duty.

She reached the top of the stairs and paused, her hand on the carved newel post. She glanced back, her gaze following the luxurious curve of the banister. Through the inlaid glass dome over the entryway, an eerie glow flickered in the sky. The fire. She hoped the engineers would get it under control soon.

But she forgot all about the fire on the other side of the river as she started down the hall toward her father's study. A chill rippled through her again, carrying an inner warning: One did not contradict the wishes of Arthur Sinclair.

Two

Tom Silver arrived in Chicago with murder on his mind. Heaved up by wind-driven waves, the deck of the steam trawler shifted under his feet. He knew it would be hard going to get to shore in the dinghy, but he didn't care. He had a job to do.

Yet when he saw the city in flames, he paused in putting spare cartridges in his belt loops and gaped at the fiery orange dome over the sky. The unnatural arch of light and flame was so eerie that, just for a moment, he forgot everything, including the deadly purpose in his heart.

"Hey, Lightning," he called, thumping his foot on deck to summon his companion, who was in the engine room. "Come have a look at this."

The lake steamer *Suzette* chugged toward its final destination at Government Pier. Its point was marked by a lighthouse beacon, but Tom had a hard time keeping his mind on navigation. The sight of the burning city clutched at his gut, made his heart pump hard in his chest. He couldn't help thinking about the tragedies that would strike tonight with the swift, indifferent brutality of fate. Fire was like that—random and merciless.

And damned inconvenient, given his purpose tonight. He had come hundreds of miles, from the vast and distant reaches of Lake Superior, to hunt down Arthur Sinclair. He wouldn't let a fire stop him.

The smell of steam and hot oil wafted up through the fiddley, and the clank of machinery crescendoed as a hatch opened. "What the hell is going on, eh?" asked Lightning Jack, emerging through the narrow opening. He shaded his eyes and squinted at the city. "*Parbleu,* that is one big fire."

"I guess I'll get a closer look tonight," Tom said, making his way down to the engine room.

Drawing back on a lever, he tamped down the boiler and then climbed abovedecks to help Lightning Jack drop anchor in the deep water. Though it was late, he had to shade his eyes against the light of the conflagration. People had gathered on the long fingerlike pier. Boats shuttled between the mouth of the river and the long dock. At the Sands, the fire reared so close that people drove wagons into the lake to escape the leaping flames. But their backs were all turned to the lake. Like Tom, they were mesmerized by the spectacle of the city in flames.

The skeletal tower of the Great Central elevator, surrounded by smokestacks, threw a long black shadow on the churning water. The fire tore across the city with the prairie wind, hot and muscular, feeding on the close-set structures.

Tom had seen any number of fires in his lifetime, but never one like this. Never one in which the wind seemed to bear the flames in its arms. Never one that moved with such furious speed. Flames covered the homes and businesses like blankets, building by building, block after block. He could see the deadly veil of crimson covering the West Division and pushing relentlessly at the edge of the river.

Tom Silver did not know Chicago well, for he had spent little time here, but it was the largest city he had ever seen. It was shaped by the lakefront and the branches of the river, which were constantly busy with commercial traffic. Ten railroads converged on Chicago, sixteen bridges spanned the river and canal, and hundreds of thousands of people made their home there.

Now its heart was on fire. This was the inferno, like the dreaded one in the Old Testament stories he used to read to Asa.

The thought of Asa brought Tom's grim purpose back into focus. Tonight he would have his revenge. Nothing— not even the flames of hell—would stop him.

"You going to wait this out?" Lightning Jack asked, seeming to read Tom's thoughts.

"Makes no sense to wait," Tom pointed out. "If the fire spreads to the North Division before I get there, I'll lose him for sure."

"Then you had best be quick. It could be a convenience, eh? If the house burns, you won't have to worry about evidence being found."

Tom studied his oldest friend, his mentor, the man who had raised him. Lightning Jack duBois had found Tom, a five-year-old abandoned in a cabin in the north woods, sitting blank-eyed next to the stiff corpse of his mother. She had died of starvation, and Tom's fate was not far behind, except that the tough old voyageur had intervened.

Since that long ago day, Tom had given Jack all his loyalty and trust. Just as Asa had trusted Tom.

"What is that look, eh?" Lightning Jack made a face. "You want to abandon the plan?"

"You know better than that." Tom felt hard, driven. The killing would be a purification ritual, a way to wash his soul clean of the black rage that consumed him. At least, that was what he kept telling himself.

Lightning Jack's brow drew down in a scowl. "It is no crime, but retribution."

Arthur Sinclair was a murderer, though no doubt his soft white hands were unsoiled, even in his own eyes. He employed underlings to do his work for him, but he was just as guilty as if he had slain seven souls with his bare hands.

"I still think you should let me go with you," Lightning Jack said, resting his hand on the handle of his hunting knife.

"No." Tom buckled on his cartridge belt. Truth was, Lightning Jack lacked a cool head. He tended to let passion get the best of him, and rage made him reckless. He despised Arthur Sinclair with a virulence that poisoned his heart, for his heart was the thing Sinclair had taken from him.

Tom's hatred for Sinclair was different. Colder, more precise. The clarity of his hatred made him better equipped to kill. Lightning Jack was too volatile. He wore his grief for Asa like a hair shirt, and it made him wild and vulnerable.

"Shipping traffic's heavy," Tom pointed out. "You'd best stay here and look after the *Suzette*."

"Spectators, I'm guessing," Lightning Jack said. "Refugees. Like ants swarming in a flood. They have nowhere to go."

Tom scanned the shoreline, picking out a train depot by a breakwater, towers and smokestacks, all pulsating in firelight. People trapped at the lakeshore waved their arms, signaling to the passing boats.

Lightning Jack watched as Tom holstered the Colt police revolver they'd bought at the Soo Locks. "Do you have enough cartridges?" Lightning asked.

"Jesus, how many times do you want me to shoot him?" Tom opened his buckskin jacket to reveal the row of ammunition in his belt loops.

"Seven," Lightning said as Tom tied the thin leather strap of the holster around his thigh. "Go now. Time is short. I'll keep the *Suzette* ready to weigh anchor."

Tom lowered the dinghy into the water and began to pull toward the shore. The lake boiled with wind-whipped waves that crested and sloshed over the sides. Some of the boats he passed were gearing up to rescue refugees from the fire. If he were a better man, he would join the rescue effort. But he wasn't here to save anyone. He was what circumstances had made of him, and in his heart there was no room for anything but hatred.

Every now and then he glanced over his shoulder at the waterworks north of the river. The structure still seemed to be intact, its gothic spire a black arrow against the noxious orange sky. Maybe the tower was close enough to the lake to survive the fire. So long as the pumps and bellows of the waterworks remained safe, the flames could be brought under control.

Yet he could not help noticing it was a losing battle. The high wind howled and stormed with hellish fury. Firebrands rained harder and thicker from the sky, sparking up blazes each place they touched. By the time he found the Sinclair mansion, the fire would not be far behind.

Tom tied up at a rubble-built bulkhead, securing the dinghy beneath an outcropping of rock. Under the circumstances, he had to be cautious. A panicked victim of the fire would not think twice about stealing a rowboat, and it was a long swim back to the steamer.

He hauled himself out and scrambled up the embankment. Emerging onto a brick-strewn street, he immediately felt a blast of the fire's hot breath. His caribou hide shirt and trousers would protect him from the flying sparks—for a while, at least.

A couple of distant explosions startled him as he made his way along the north bank of the river. He passed banks and hotels, McCormack's Reaper Works, shops and theaters, parks and boulevards. People looked out the windows of nearly every tall building, their gazes turned toward the fire. Eerily, the night grew lighter with each passing moment. He could pick out street signs and people standing in groups, talking excitedly. A short distance away, tugboats on the river screamed for the bridges to be turned to let them through, but the huge crowds gathered on the shore prevented the bridge operators from doing their job. The fire from the west blew toward the forest of masts and rigging. Good thing Lightning Jack had agreed to lay-to offshore. There was no safe place in the city tonight.

This was unfamiliar territory to Tom, but he knew where Sinclair lived. He had studied the location on a map, and the route was branded on his memory.

He had not reckoned on having to navigate a sea of humanity, though. Men, women, children and livestock surged along the main thoroughfares, pushing toward the lake. Overloaded carts, drays, mule trucks and express wagons clogged the roadways. In his entire life, Tom hadn't seen so many people. Some were dressed in nightclothes, others in evening wear. Carts and carriages clattered past with little heed for the safety of the pedestrians. Men dragged trunks behind them; women clutched quilts and kettles and drawers stuffed with belongings. People fled, their arms filled with books and mementos, bundled clothes, odd-shaped bags and even a metal safe or two.

What did a person save when faced with losing everything? Tom wondered. Priceless antiques, irreplaceable photographs, quilts and curios made by the hands of loved ones long dead. And money, of course. There was always that.

The rumble of collapsing buildings drowned out the shouting and caused children and horses to panic. Everywhere he looked, Tom saw carts running out of control or crashing into buildings or trees and left abandoned. One carriage, with a crest on its door that read "The Emma Wade Boylan School," lay on its side, the team still struggling in its traces.

Three young women, dressed in silks and lace, quarreled on the boardwalk near the fallen carriage.

"I say we leave them," the brown-haired woman said.

"We'll not abandon the horses," the black-haired one retorted. "We must—"

"Move aside." Tom yanked his bowie knife out of the top of his boot. Feminine gasps greeted the sight of the glittering blade, and they fell back, clearly horrified. He sliced through the traces that bound the horses to the coach, then slapped the beasts' rumps to drive them off down the street.

The well-dressed woman gaped at him. "He...you... the horses!"

Her companion said, "*Now* what shall we do?"

The redhead lifted her gaze to the flaming sky. "Pray," she said.

Tom didn't wait around to see the outcome of the argument. He had a job to do.

As the crowd and the smoke pressed upon him, he felt a sharp hunger for the harsh, empty majesty of the north woods wilderness. Soon, he told himself. In just a short while, he would be back where he belonged. But first he had to find his target—the house on Huron Avenue. Then he could head home to Isle Royale. There, he would try his best to endure a life that had been irrevocably changed by Arthur Sinclair.

He wondered what it would feel like to kill the man who had killed Asa. Would his heart exult in dark, cleansing joy? Would he be filled with pure glee? Would the satisfaction of revenge drive away the loss and betrayal that had consumed him since the disaster? Perhaps he would feel nothing at all. He would welcome the numbness. Feeling nothing would be a blessing after the months of suffering through soul-killing grief.

Tom had killed in the war. As a courier, he'd been used by General Whitcomb of the 21st Michigan in the way a hunter used bloodhounds. But being in the war had not given him a taste for murder.

He pressed on harder, faster, seared by the blowing heat. He passed a lanky boy burdened with a shaggy dog that kept trying to escape its young master's arms. The boy was about fourteen, the age Asa had been when he died. Tom tried not to see the struggling youth, tried not to hear the kid saying "Easy, Shep. Take it easy. I'll keep you safe." He tried not to remember the way a boy's rounded face could look so damned earnest and protective. Tom felt relieved when the youth and his dog veered off toward the lake.

If he had lived, Asa would have been fifteen in the spring. He would have had his birthday in March, and maybe Tom would have given him a bowie knife or deer rifle to mark his step toward manhood. The two of them would have sat by the stove, tying flies or playing checkers. Even now, months after the accident, Tom could picture the complete absorption in Asa's face when he worked on a fishing fly. He could still hear Asa's laughter in his heart.

I miss you, Asa.

Turning down a nearly deserted side street, he walked faster, breathing hard as anticipation built, tasting smoke and ash in his throat. The smell of burning timber and the sight of falling cinders reminded him of being in the thick of battle. He never should have gone to war. Lightning Jack had warned him that it would steal his spirit.

Just as he had warned Asa about working at the mine.

Asa hadn't listened any better than Tom had, in his youth. Bored by the routine of island life and winters spent under the tutelage of a demanding scholar, Tom had run away to join the fighting. What he had seen and done during those dark years had turned his soul to ice. Only the gift of Asa had dragged Tom back into the light. Now that Asa was gone, there was nothing to keep him from falling into darkness once again.

Firebrands and cinders rained thickly over the streets, and each brand ignited a new fire. Men posted on rooftops tried to defend some of the larger buildings, but the bright dervishes of flame made a mockery of their efforts. Distant explosions pocked the night, each greeted by frightened screams.

At a broad street, the crowd flowed northward, following a long strip of green space bordering the lake. Family members shouted at one another to hurry. Tom broke off from the surging refugees and headed in the opposite direction.

"Hey, mister," someone hollered in a hoarse voice. "You don't want to go that way. The fire crossed over the North Branch."

Tom ignored the warning, though the news startled him. Only a fire of demonic proportions could cross a river as wide as the branches of the Chicago. The fire department would have no hope of stopping it now. He wondered if he would be able to reach the Sinclair mansion before the fire did.

He felt mildly startled to find himself alone on a deserted street. The fire raged through buildings on either side—one appeared to be a woodworking mill, the other a brewery. Strange, he thought dispassionately. The city was burning and no one was sticking around to defend it.

He passed into darkness as he headed north, away from the fire, and sensed a change in the atmosphere as he emerged onto Dearborn. The wide boulevard, flanked by stone pilasters and tall wrought iron fences, lay in perfect splendor, though smoke lay thick in the air. Broad lawns, some with coach houses and outbuildings, surrounded the opulent mansions. The homes resembled majestic fortresses with handsome gables and half-wheel windows three storeys up. Skylights and cupolas graced the rooflines. Through a broad bay window he saw a family sitting in a parlor, playing cards while a woman played piano. At some of the other houses, people gathered at the windows to watch the fire.

Yet the sky behind the sedate facades glowed with that ominous and unnatural orange tinge, spangled by flying sparks. These fine houses were not long for this world. He hoped like hell he'd have no trouble finding Sinclair's house, and that his quarry would be at home. He had to consider the possibility that Arthur Sinclair had evacuated his house, but there was a good chance the wealthy industrialist might stay put. Judging by the spectators watching out the windows of the grand mansions, the rich felt safe from the flames. Men like Sinclair thought they were invincible, that their money could buy them anything, even protection from death.

Stupid fools.

Three

"**D**eborah, what the devil are you doing here?" Arthur Sinclair demanded, looking up from the large metal safe in the wall of his office. Grasping the open door of the safe, he stood, lurching a little on his bad leg as he turned to face her. His cane rested against the broad wall map behind the desk. The map depicted the Great Lakes and surrounding territory, with markers where his mines and timberlands were located. Standing before the map, he resembled a king surveying his realm. "It's late," he added. "You had an engagement tonight."

"Hello, Father," she said, crossing the plush carpet of Persian silk. Like everything else in the house, his estate office was self-consciously ornate and filled with antiques that were supposed to look as if they had been in the family for generations. The long Regency period bookcases housed leather-bound volumes he had never opened. The artwork on the dark green walls depicted hunting scenes in places he would never be invited. And the Louis XIV desk was littered with the work of a man who intended to muscle his way into society by brute strength rather than privilege of birth.

He was depending on Deborah to vault him to the next level of acceptance. And that was precisely what she had come to talk to him about.

She embraced her father lightly, kissing his cheek and then stepping back. As always, he smelled of bay rum and cigars. The scent evoked the feeling of security she always associated with her father and made her heart squeeze with fondness for him. Lord, she didn't want to disappoint him. That was not what she wanted at all.

"I'm sorry I interrupted you," she said.

He gestured at the open satchel on the floor that was stuffed with greenbacks and negotiable securities. "Getting my stock and insurance certificates together in case the worst happens."

"The fire, you mean."

"Yes. If they don't get the blaze under control soon, I'm driving up to the lake house." His handsome, craggy face creased into a scowl of disapproval as his gaze swept over her. "What the devil are you wearing? Was Dr. Moody's appearance canceled due to the fire?"

"I don't know," she said, braiding her fingers together. Though accustomed to managing servants, maids, drivers and tradesmen, she doubted her ability to stand up to her father, who had been known to crush railroad magnates and mining barons in order to get his way. "I decided not to attend tonight. I needed to see you instead. To tell you—"

"Your fiancé's already been to see me," he said.

Her mouth went dry. All the blood seemed to drain out of her hands, leaving her fingers cold and numb. "Philip was here?"

Her father's eyes held the sharp blue chill of shattered ice. "Earlier this evening. So I imagine I already know what you're going to say."

Dear God. What had Philip told her father?

Bile rose in her throat, and she could not speak until she managed to swallow. "What did he tell you?"

Arthur spread his hands. "He told me about the way you behaved at the opera last night. I'm ashamed of you, Deborah. Purely ashamed."

This was the last thing she had expected. She hadn't imagined Philip would complain to her father, of all things. She gaped at him, then found her voice. "Ashamed of *me?* But what did I—"

"Philip says he's willing to overlook your outrageous behavior, thank God," Arthur said. He turned away from her and began pulling boxes of bills and certificates out of the safe.

"*My* behavior?" she asked. She tried to cling to a sense of outrage, but in spite of her resolve, shame crept in. She had no idea what to say. All her life she had been provided with the best governesses, tutors, teachers and companions in the country. Yet not one of them had prepared her to deal with her own father.

"Your immaturity and foolishness are going to cost me dearly," he blustered. "He wants me to double your dowry settlement. And I have no choice but to do as he asks."

She forced out a dry, bitter laugh of disbelief. Philip Ascot IV had laid waste to her dreams last night, and as a reward, he expected twice the bride price he and her father had settled on. "Then you will be pleased to know that you won't have to pay him a cent," she said, keeping her voice firm even though she wanted to die. She loved her father, honored him, on occasion felt close to worshiping him. The times she had crossed him were few and far between, but now was one of those times.

"What in tarnation do you mean by that?"

"I've decided not to marry Philip," she stated.

That got his attention. He froze in the midst of ramming notes and certificates into the leather satchel and turned to face her. "That's not amusing, Deborah."

"I'm not trying to be amusing. I'm trying to—" She paused. What *was* she doing? Her future, indeed her entire existence had been defined by the fact that she was going to be the wife of one of the most socially prominent men in the country. Without that, who was she? Until now, that question had never occurred to her but suddenly the answer seemed vital. Closing her eyes, she took a leap in the dark. "I won't marry Philip Ascot."

"You're getting cold feet before the wedding," her father said reasonably, his face softening with an indulgent smile. "Common enough in a bride, or so I'm told."

She tried again. "It's not a matter of cold feet. My mind and my heart have changed. Irrevocably. Until yesterday...I thought marrying Philip was the future I wanted. I didn't know any better. I...I'm sorry."

"The wedding will go forward as planned," he snapped, his temper pushing through fatherly indulgence. "You'll learn to govern your infantile tantrums and behave like a true woman. Everything is settled. The guest list includes everyone up to Mrs. Grant herself. You don't simply tell the First Lady—"

"I'll tell her myself," Deborah promised, though the prospect terrified her. "We're talking about the rest of my life, Father. I won't live it with Philip Ascot."

Anger blazed in his eyes. "You'll live your life as I say," he stated. "I have always acted in your best interest."

"I know you believe you have," she conceded. "But this time, I must trust my own judgment."

"You will trust *me*. Haven't I always given you the best of everything? Haven't I spent a fortune turning you into the sort of young lady a man of quality dreams of marrying?"

"What about my dreams?" she asked, but she spoke so softly that he didn't hear.

"You have no understanding of what your life would be if I simply let you have your way," he went on, his face flushing a deep, unhealthy red. "You'd be hopeless, no better off than a saloon girl or a farm wife. Thanks to me, you'll never know struggle, never know hardship. Your children will have the world at their feet. But only if you provide a proper family background—as an Ascot."

Deborah began to pace the long, carpeted room. "You arranged this marriage with no regard for my wishes. Do you realize I was never asked? You and Philip met over brandy and cigars, and the next day I was presented with this." She held up her hand, pale in the gaslight, a very large diamond winking obscenely.

"You seemed perfectly delighted," he pointed out.

"Because you were, Father. I should have objected long ago." But she hadn't. She had been as dazzled by Philip's good looks and charming flattery as her father had been by his social standing. "Don't you see that when human hearts are involved, you can't simply make things happen?"

"Balderdash. What are they teaching you at that school?"

"Clearly not enough to help me make you understand," she said.

"Arranged marriages are the hallmark of a civilized society. Love doesn't happen overnight. You must show patience and understanding, and above all, obedience to those who know what is best for you."

"I will never love Philip. Ever."

"The opportunity to marry into the Ascot family doesn't arise very often. Philip's an only child, and he has no cousins. You need this marriage, Deborah."

"No, *you* need it. And Philip needs it. For all his blue-blooded pedigree, he is nearly destitute. He has the name. You have the fortune. Together the two of you have everything you want. I can't imagine why you even need me. Just make him your son and be done with it." The words burst from her, and the moment they were out, she wished she could catch them from the air and somehow make them disappear. But it was too late.

Her father stood staring at her, and his face bore the

shocked expression of a man who had just been stabbed in the back.

Although he would never admit it, Arthur Sinclair had always felt inferior because his money was considered "new" by the upper crust. And to her father, the opinions of the socially prominent mattered greatly. He yearned for the one thing his money could not buy—the patina of generations-old gentility. In his mind—and in the minds of those he strove to impress—there was a particular quality to inherited wealth that was lacking in the fortunes of a self-made man. He would never be able to achieve that quality, but he could take a step closer by marrying his only daughter and heir to the flawlessly aristocratic Philip Widener Ascot IV.

They had never spoken of this, of course, and the fact that Deborah had brought it up was a measure of her desperation. Remorseful for having hurt him, she said, "You're a good man, Father. The best there is. Whether or not I marry Philip will not change that."

Slowly his coloring returned to normal. He no longer looked harsh or angry, just immeasurably disappointed.

"Father, I didn't come here to quarrel with you," she said quietly.

Moving as if his bones hurt, he lowered himself to his chair. When Deborah looked at him, she always saw a titan of industry, a man who was larger than life, larger than legend, even. Yet tonight, something was different. He simply looked like a man worn down by weariness. She couldn't tell if the change was in her, or in him.

"Did I ever tell you what your mother said to me the day she died?" he asked after a long pause.

Deborah didn't follow the sudden switch in topic, but he seemed calmer now. She owed it to him to let him make his point. "You've said so little of that day," she said. "I know it must have been painful for you."

She had been just three when her mother died giving birth to a stillborn son. Deborah had exactly one memory

of her mother. It was just a flash of awareness, not really
a full-blown memory. She had been too young for that.
But that made the faint, flickering awareness all the more
important to her.

Sometimes, when Deborah closed her eyes and emptied
her mind, she could call up that memory, achingly vivid
and scented with violets. She could feel the gentle touch
of her mother's cool hand on her brow, could recall being
awash in her mother's love. Even now, so many years
later, she remembered the sweet whisper of a soft voice,
saying, "Go to sleep, my precious girl. Go to sleep."

And there it ended. Perhaps the moment had never really happened, perhaps Deborah had fabricated it out of
her own yearning for just one tender memory of the
mother she had never known. But no matter. She believed
the moment had happened, and would never let the memory go. She held it clasped to her heart, stubbornly and
tightly, like a pearl in a closed fist.

Her father had not remarried because, by then, pride
and ambition held him in their grip. He would only accept
a wife of the highest social distinction...yet such a woman
would never have him, a vulgar upstart. Frustrated, he put
all his energy into raising Deborah to achieve the one
thing he never could—class. He never asked her if she
wanted it; he just assumed she craved social prominence
as intensely as he did.

He and Deborah only had each other. He regarded her
as his most priceless ornament, and would settle for no
less than a fourth-generation Ascot for her husband.

"What did she say, Father?" she asked gently.

"She knew she was...going," he said gruffly, turning
back to the safe. "She was...bleeding. The last thing she
said to me was 'Make her life perfect. Make everything
perfect for her.'"

Deborah's vision blurred with tears. She tried to imagine what those final moments had been like for her
mother, holding her stillborn son and knowing she would

never see her small daughter grow up. And all the while, her father had stood vigil, suffering the loss of his wife and only son.

"That's all I'm trying to do," Arthur explained. "I'm trying to make everything perfect for you, trying to give you the life your mother wanted for you. And by God, I intend to see it done."

Gaslight hissed gently into the silent house. Deborah knew her father meant well, but she also knew she could not marry Philip Ascot or anyone else, for that matter. She must make her father understand and, in time, possibly even forgive her. After a lifetime of existing only to please Arthur Sinclair, crossing him in this one all-important matter would daunt even strong-willed Lucy or sturdy, practical Kathleen. Phoebe would be just as appalled as Deborah's father, for she could not imagine anything more perfect than marrying the handsome, dashing heir to one of the oldest families in the country. Part of the marriage arrangement specified that the famous Ascot residence, Tarleton House in New York City, would be restored as their principle residence. Everyone at Miss Boylan's thought it sounded like a dream come true, so much so that Deborah had forgotten to ask herself if it was what *she* wanted.

Deborah had no allies in this struggle of her will against that of her father. "Please," she said. "Can we just discuss—"

"Certainly not," he said, speaking brusquely. "I have said all I have to say on the matter."

The look that crossed her face prompted him to add, "Go to bed, my dear. We're both tired. In the morning you will apologize to Philip and pray he forgives you for being such a ninny." Drawing the buckles tightly around his important papers, he walked to the door of the study. "Now, if you'll excuse me, I must dismiss the help early tonight on account of the fire."

*   *   *

A loud blast, like a gunshot, exploded in the night. Deborah sat up in her bed, already screaming before she was fully awake.

Her gaze darted to the lace-draped French windows. Judging by the angry scarlet glow of the sky, she thought morning had come. But then the sky flickered uneasily, and she remembered the fire. Dear heaven, hadn't it been brought under control yet?

"Father," she shrieked, leaping from her bed and yanking open the door.

To her relief, she spied him rushing down the hall toward her, satchel and cane in hand and kerosene lamp held high.

"What was that terrible noise?" she asked, shaken.

Gripping the head of his cane, he strode to the window. "The gasworks substation. Coal gas," he added, his hand shaking just a little as he moved the drapes aside. "Highly explosive. I'm sure that was it, because there's no gaslight in the house."

Deborah joined him at the window and caught her breath in shock. The fire, which had caused her only a glimmer of concern earlier, had made hideous progress. Everything to the south and west was a sea of flame.

"Dear God," she said. "It's crossed the river. The whole city is on fire." The incessant shriek of ships' whistles pierced the roar of the wind. Boats crowded behind the bridges, demanding to be let through. The clear *bong* of a bell tolled a steady alarm. Shouts and the clatter of hooves could be heard in the neighboring streets. She pressed her fingertips to the window pane; the glass felt unnaturally warm.

"It's that infernal wind," her father said. "I went to bed thinking it couldn't possibly spread the fire across the river, but there you are. It's in the North Division."

Whirlwinds and swirling gusts carried flaming brands from one building to the next. Structures ignited as if a torch were being touched to each, one after another. Dervishes of flame spun across rooftops with furious speed. The pine-block roadways and boardwalks fueled the inferno. In the main thoroughfares, people fled on foot or in overloaded conveyances manned by frantic drivers.

A shattering sound drew her attention to the upper-storey windows in the house across the street. As she watched, the windows blasted open, one after another, all in a row. It was as if someone had taken a gun and shot them out. Then, from an alley behind the house came a teamster, beating the horses of a cluttered cart, and as the team roared past, she could see that the very contents of the cart were in flames.

Huron Avenue itself lay in a shroud of smoke. Deborah turned to her father, clutching his sleeve. "This is a nightmare," she said. "We must go!"

"Of course." He glared out the window. If his ill temper could not douse the flames, nothing could. "The phaeton's waiting in the mews behind the house. I had it readied before sending the hired men home tonight. Can you be ready in five minutes?"

"Less," she said, already snatching her dress from the upholstered clothing stand in the corner. "Where will we go, Father?"

"To Avalon," he said, referring to his summer estate in Lake View as he hurried out to ready himself.

Deborah had rarely dressed without help. On formal occasions, her corset was so stiff and tight that she couldn't even bend to do up her own shoes. Tonight, the sense of impending danger made a mockery of the vanity that used to delight her so much. Her white batiste nightgown served as chemise and petticoat, for she tugged the dress right over the garment. She left her hair in its untidy braid, pulled on stockings and shoes, and grabbed her shawl.

Her nerves wouldn't settle until she reached Avalon. Situated on the north shore overlooking the lake, the estate would provide a tranquil oasis from the flames, where they could wait out the fire. Perhaps, in the calm after the firestorm, she could bring her father to see reason in the matter of her marriage.

Firelight streamed through the windows, illuminating the suite of rooms where she had spent her childhood. All her costly, beautiful things were here, in a chamber redolent of verbena furniture polish and fresh-cut flowers. What if this magnificent house burned to the ground, and all its contents with it? She found, to her surprise, that she felt curiously indifferent about the notion of never seeing it again.

What sort of person was she, Deborah wondered as her father reappeared at her door, that she could be so calm about losing everything?

She noted that he had donned his best Savile Row suit and kid leather spats. Even in the face of disaster, he seemed determined to keep up appearances. He held his cane and the bulging case containing his most important documents. "Are you ready?" he asked.

"Yes, let's go," she said briskly. "And I'm glad we're together," she added.

They hastened to the door, and her father stopped. He put out his hand and cupped her cheek. She froze in surprise, for he rarely touched her with affection.

"I'm pleased that you came to see me tonight," he said with the gruff tenderness that never failed to remind her that she was all he had in the world. "This matter with Philip—we'll find an accord. You'll see that marrying him is the proper course of things. The proper course indeed."

"Oh, Father." She bent her cheek into the cradle of his hand. "We really must go."

She stepped out of the room and he turned, his hand on the door handle. A look of pure and utter desolation settled over his craggy face. In that moment, she realized that, although there was nothing for her in this house, nothing for her to clutch to her chest and go running through the streets with, it was different for Arthur Sinclair. This vast mansion was his dream, his place in the world, built by his own hard work and ambition.

"Come," she said gently. "This pile of wood and stone isn't worth your life."

Together they went to the head of the main stairway. Then Deborah stopped and glanced over her shoulder toward her private suite of rooms.

"What is it?" Arthur asked. "Did you forget something?"

"Mother's lavaliere," she replied, suddenly remembering the one thing she wanted to keep. "I know just where it is. Wait for me outside, Father. I'll be right behind you."

He nodded and went to the elevator cage. Deborah dashed back to her suite and hurried to the dressing room. She had no need of a lamp, for the ominous glare of the fire turned the darkness to unhealthy noon. An entire large chamber was devoted to her wardrobe, a forest of Worth gowns and Brussels lace bodices on wire forms, cuffs and collars of every description, stacks of bandboxes containing hats. In a tall narrow armoire that smelled of lavender sachets, she found what she sought—her mother's lavaliere in a red velvet pouch tied with silken cords. Stuffing the treasure into her bodice, she rushed back to the stairs.

Her father waited in the foyer, brightly illuminated by fireglow streaming through the skylight. Arthur Sinclair looked as neat and precise as the black-and-white checkerboard pattern on the floor. It was hard to believe that outside this elegant sanctuary, throngs of Chicagoans ran from the fire. But the clanging of alarm bells and shouts from the street hinted that the flames were racing ever closer.

"I'm ready, Father," she called.

Just then, the heavy front door slammed open.

Deborah froze at the top of the steps, one hand on the newel post. A huge man, covered in soot, with blackened holes burned into his fringed buckskins, stood at the threshold. Behind him, the blaze flared up and roared with an inhuman howl. The wild man burst into the house, crossing the foyer with long, purposeful strides. Even from a distance, she could see the fury in his eyes and the smoke that rose from his smoldering garments.

A looter, she thought, her stomach clenching.

His relentless stride, his swirling dark hair and the gun in his hand made him the most frightening spectacle she had ever seen. She could not even manage to scream.

Arthur Sinclair didn't move, but stared at the five-shooter in the stranger's huge hand. Her father did not look up at her, and it took her only a second to realize why. He didn't want her to make her presence known to the looter.

She bit her lip to keep from calling out.

"See here now," her father said sternly. "If thieving's your aim, you'll find baubles a-plenty throughout the house. No need to harm me or— No need to harm me."

"I'm not here to rob you, old man." The looter's voice was low and harsh.

Deborah's father gestured with his brass-tipped cane. "The liquor and wine are kept in the basement. Just take what you want and be gone."

"I want you to look at me, Sinclair," the looter said. "I come from Isle Royale."

Her father stiffened, and his knuckles whitened as he gripped the handle of his cane. His jaw began to tic as he clenched and unclenched his teeth. He took an uneven step toward the narrow hallway that led to the alley in the back, where the phaeton waited. "Look," he said, "if it's about the copper mine, my claims adjusters will settle—"

"Yes, that's why I'm here." The man took a step closer, planting himself between the stair rail and Sinclair. "To settle with you. And it's not about money."

He planted his feet wide and brought his arm up, pointing the revolver at Arthur's chest.

Sinclair raised the satchel like a shield. "Don't be a fool. I can pay—"

"With your blood, you son of a bitch."

Deborah didn't give herself time to think. As nimble as she had been as a little girl, she propped her hip on the gleaming, waxed stair rail and shoved off. The much-polished surface was as slick as grease. In the blink of an eye, she zipped down the rail, seeing things only in flashes of awareness: her father's astonished, openmouthed face, the man half turning, even as the gun went off.

She felt a terrible blow as her body collided with that of the intruder, and all the air rushed out of her lungs. The glass skylight over the vestibule shattered with an explosion of noise. The gun went sliding across the floor, then spun like a top in the middle of the foyer. Arthur grabbed a marble cherub from the statue in the curve of the stair and brought the white stone down on the intruder's head. The wild man gave an animal bellow of pain and rage, then sank with a groan.

"By God, you saved my life," Arthur said, regarding Deborah with astonishment.

"Father," she said, gasping for air as she picked herself up off the floor. "Do you think you killed him?"

"It would be no more than he deserved. May he burn in hell." Moving quickly despite his infirmity, he headed for the rear of the house.

Deborah put a hand to her bodice, and with a sense of dismay discovered that it was empty. There, at the foot of the stairs, lay the velvet pouch with her mother's lavaliere. She went to snatch it, then moved to follow her father out to the phaeton.

But she felt a tug of resistance. Looking down, she saw the hamlike fist of the wild man clutching the hem of her skirt.

Four

His head pounded like a fist-sized heartbeat. The ringing agony made him want to puke.

The woman with the yellow hair stood like Joan of Arc over him. Her image blurred and melted around the edges, and for a moment he thought he was going blind from the blow to the head. He squeezed his eyes shut, then opened them again and let out a shuddering breath. His vision was sharp and clear once again, but he didn't like what he saw. The woman's mouth formed a red *O* of abject horror. This was no Joan of Arc. He could see the uncertainty flickering in her eyes, could practically read her mind. Should she scream and alert Sinclair, or keep mum so he could get away?

"Go ahead and holler for him," he said, letting go of her dress and giving her a shove. "You'd be doing me a favor." She stumbled back against the stairs, lost her footing and fell like a broken doll, sinking in a puffy tangle of skirts.

Standing up, he grabbed the newel post as his vision swam and reeled. He forced himself to focus on his goal: retrieve the pistol, pursue Sinclair, shoot him dead.

His boots crunched over shards of broken glass as he crossed the checkerboard floor. Bad shot. The woman had slammed into him at the precise moment he had squeezed keep from pleading. "Please, let me go. I've done nothing to hurt you."

He thrust his gun in its hip holster and stalked on, showing no indication that he heard her.

"I can pay you." She tried to claw off her blue topaz bracelet. "Take my jewelry."

"Lady, I don't want your damned jewelry," he said between his teeth. The alley angled to the left. He hauled her down the center of it as stinging sparks rained down on them.

Deborah dug in her heels and leaned back, rebelling with every ounce of strength she possessed. Admittedly, that was not much, but fright and fury added power to her resistance. She had never before fought anyone for any reason.

"Woman, I'll drag you if I have to," her captor said, barely slowing his pace. "Your choice."

Her strength ebbed fast, and she went limp. Before she crumpled completely to the cinder-strewn pavement, he caught her against his rough, smoky buckskin chest. "Damn it," he said between clenched teeth. "You can come with me, or stay here and burn. What'll it be?"

"I'd rather burn in hell than go with you."

"Fine." He let go of her.

She staggered back, catching herself before she collapsed. The heat from the inferno battered her head. Sparks and cinders rained down from every rooftop. She could smell the scent of burning hair, could see small blackened holes appear in her full skirts. With the fringe of her shawl, she beat out a glowing ember. Casting a frantic glance backward, she could see nothing of the mansion that had been her father's house, nothing but rubble shrouded in a thick fog of eye-smarting smoke. On both sides of her, the buildings burned out of control, turning the alley into a tunnel of fire. Her throat and lungs filled with hot smoke.

In the roadway ahead, Paul Bunyan marched heedlessly

forward, not even looking back to watch her burn like a martyr. She hated that he didn't look back. She hated *him* for not looking back. Most of all, she hated having no choice but to flee the fire in one direction—toward her captor. After last night, Deborah reflected, she had not been able to stop shivering. She had pulled the covers over her head and, lying in the dark, reflected that she had reached the bottom of a black pit of despair. Now that she found herself confronted by a crazed murderer, she was beginning to think there were worse things than that pit.

When she reached his side, choking and sputtering on smoke and outrage, he barely acknowledged her except to seize her by the arm and yank her roughly along with him. She tried to demand what he wanted from her, what malice he bore her, but she was coughing too hard.

They emerged onto the main street, and finally she grasped the full force of the conflagration. A river of humanity flowed along the street, bobbing and surging forward like boiling rapids. She called to passersby for help, but no one responded. They were all too preoccupied with their own survival. Besides, the fire blazed with a deafening roar that made it seem almost alive. Deborah coughed and wheezed, starving for a breath of air. She staggered with dizziness, and only the oak-hard arm of her abductor held her up. Rushing people, smoke, cinders, flaming buildings, explosions—all filled her senses. But as she was pulled along, her larger view of the crowd narrowed and focused down to individual and heartbreaking detail. A mother holding a screaming baby and running down the street. A child standing on a street corner, turning in circles and crying until someone grabbed him and hurried off. A single shoe in the gutter. A tired old rag doll underfoot. Everywhere she looked, she saw the horrifying evidence of loss and destruction. A drunken man stood atop a piano, declaring the fire the friend of the poor man and exhorting people to help themselves to liquor. A thrown bottle struck him, and he stumbled and fell.

Armageddon had arrived, she thought. And Satan himself had come to escort her through the flames. To what purpose, she had no idea. Terror swept through her with the same swift and unrelenting fury of the firestorm.

Caught up in the flow of humanity, they surged with the crowd past grand buildings and residences with flames shooting out of the windows. Bundles of blankets were being dropped from upper storeys. To her horrified amazement, she realized that the hastily bound bundles of mattresses and bedding contained valuables. And some of them, insanely, contained children.

A little girl in a red nightgown fought her way free of one of the bundles and raced blindly into the street, wailing in terror. Panic-stricken, she headed into the path of a careening express wagon.

The wild man made a sound of impatience. He dropped Deborah's arm and plunged into the middle of the road, snatching up the child with a single bear-paw swipe. Moving quickly for a creature of such immense size, he bore the crying child to the walkway.

For a moment Deborah was so surprised that she simply froze, though rushing people jostled her. Dear heaven, a kidnaper. He was a deadly madman, preying upon helpless women and children.

Deborah watched as he set the hysterical child on his shoulder. With his free hand he grabbed a black wrought iron light post and stepped up on its concrete base, rising high above the throng. The girl in red waved her arms frantically, and a man with a sweat-stained face broke free of the crowd and rushed toward her.

"Poppa," the little girl squealed as the looter surrendered her to her father.

Deborah gathered her wits about her, covered her bare head with her shawl to conceal her blond hair and plunged into the thick of the crowd. She had no thought but to flee, to lose herself in the ocean of humanity surging through the streets. The maelstrom of noise thundered so loudly that her senses seemed to shut down, filtering out the chaos. Her only awareness was of the thin, high-pitched sound that came unbidden from her own throat. She had never seen a rabbit hunted down by a wolf, but knew now what the rabbit sounded like, felt like, when fleeing a predator. Two days ago she had understood her life. She had known who she was and where she fit in. And if, from time to time, she had felt a small, traitorous prodding of discontent, she had quelled it easily enough by reminding herself of all the unearned privileges she enjoyed. The past two days had disengaged her from that comfortable spot like a snail being pried from its shell. And like the snail she was uprooted, lost in an alien world, longing to crawl back into her shell but unable to find the way back.

She forced herself to look ahead to the open square of the intersection. Hurrying in that direction, she slammed into a stout, screaming woman wearing a housekeeper's black muslin dress and a white lace cap. With a feather duster clutched in her hand, she stood paralyzed by terror except for the misshapen, screaming mouth. Instinctively Deborah grabbed the woman's hand and propelled her along the walkway. She felt a strong urge to rush away, but the frightened woman clung to her. Ahead of them, a man pushing a heavily laden wheelbarrow slowed their progress.

Deborah spoke aloud, but she couldn't even hear herself. She gritted her teeth and sucked in breath after breath of the hot, filthy air. They reached an intersection where the crowd thickened. A runaway cart, driverless and pulled by a panic-stricken horse, careened into the crowd. Deborah felt the maid's hand torn from her own, and for a moment a gap separated them. Then a flood of people flowed into the gap, engulfing the lost woman, and Deborah could only go on.

She recognized the street that ran along the edge of the Catholic cemetery. Two blocks beyond that lay the lakefront park. People hurried faster, eager to reach the safety of the water. Deborah kept her head down, the shawl pulled up over her hair. She darted glances here and there, praying the wild man would not see her. Perhaps she had managed to elude him. If so, it was the only lucky thing that had happened to her in days.

She wondered what in heaven's name the man could have been thinking. What would prompt him to burst upon her father, intent on murdering him in the midst of a catastrophe? Her father had assumed the man was a looter. No doubt there was plenty of that going on in the city tonight. But the insane man had not shown any interest in robbing the Sinclair house. He seemed focused only on killing her father. He had known her father's name. Had mentioned a place...an island?

The memory of the intruder made her recoil, and bitter bile rose in her throat. She fought down the need to be sick, wishing, not for the first time in her life, that she was made of sterner stuff. No one had ever taught her how to contend with matters such as how to escape an insane murderer in the midst of a fire of Biblical proportions. Or how to find her father, borne God-knew-where in a runaway carriage. Or how to survive the night.

Each time she heard the clop of hooves or the grind of cart wheels, she checked to see if it was her father. But she never saw him. She could do no more than hope he had brought the team under control and headed toward the lake. From there, he would travel northward to his summer estate. The trouble was, the streets were clogged with fallen rubble and fleeing people. Landmarks crumbled even as she passed.

She wondered what he thought had become of her. In

the sudden confusion of the collapsing roof, the gunman and the spooked horses, he might be imagining any number of fates. She hoped madly that he had not tried to fight his way back to the house on Huron Avenue to search for her. The whole district, once a tree-lined bastion of fashionable mansions, was now engulfed in flames.

"I'll be all right, Father," she said under her breath, then nearly choked on the irony of her own words. "If tonight doesn't kill me, I'll be all right." She intended to get to the lakeshore and work her way northward. Perhaps she would find a driver to take her to the summer place. She would find her father at Avalon. She had to believe that.

She hoped he would believe it, too. But there was no reason for him to consider her capable of surviving. Arthur Sinclair had raised her to be as useless and ornamental as a rose in a corn patch. All she was and all she knew were those things useful to the wife of a wealthy man. She was known to be accomplished, according to the glowing reports from Miss Boylan's. But those accomplishments had to do with ballroom dancing or doing needlepoint or reciting poetry in French. None of which was likely to help her survive the fire destroying a whole city.

Her thin-soled Italian shoes were not made for trudging any distance, and her feet quickly grew blistered and sore on the rubble-strewn roadway. She had little sense of direction, having been chauffeured all her life, so she simply followed the general direction of the surging mob. A man leading a brace of horses thrust her aside. Something in the way he pushed at her shoulder made her jump back and scream with panic, slamming against a building. She shut her eyes as the horses passed, telling herself to calm down.

At a fork in the road, she saw people rushing along each branch of the split. A decision. She had to make a decision. What a remarkably novel notion.

She had no idea which was the quickest path to the lake. It was dark up ahead, indicating that the fire had not yet reached the north shore. For no particular reason, she took the left branch and found herself hurrying in a crowd of people, some of them in nightclothes, their arms burdened with hastily snatched possessions, their sooty faces pinched with fright. No one had been prepared for a fire of this speed and intensity.

Keeping her head down, she hurried along a street lined by older buildings that housed shops and saloons burning from the roof down. A street-level window shattered as she passed it. Ducking instinctively to avoid the flying splinters, she felt a rush of heat and the sting of stray shards of glass on her face. Choking, her eyes streaming, she wiped her bloodied hand on her skirt and moved on.

A high-pitched yelp pierced through the roar and din of the fire. She peered into the window of a dry goods shop and saw a mongrel dog scratching frantically at the glass pane. For some reason, in the midst of this rush of humanity, Deborah's heart went out to the creature.

Darkness shrouded the abandoned shop, yet at the back of the room she detected the hungry glow. Within moments, the shop would be afire. She urged herself move on, but the dog's frenzied barking caught at her. She tried the shop door and found it locked.

"Help," she said, turning to the first man who came along. "You must help this poor creature!"

The man, burdened with a clock and a bottle of liquor, glanced into the window. "It's only a dog," he said, not even slowing his pace. "Best worry about saving yourself, miss."

"Please—" she began, but he was already gone.

Deborah was not sure what to do. She had never rescued a dog from a fire before. She had never even met a dog before. Her father had commissioned her eighteen-year-old portrait to be done with her holding an ugly little pug dog, but she had posed with a porcelain model, not the real thing.

The trapped mongrel scratched at the window with undiminished vigor. Deborah gave a sob of frustration, then took off her shawl, wrapped it around her hand and pounded at the window. The panes rattled but didn't crack. The dog feinted back and cringed in confusion, then started yelping again. Nearly weeping in desperation, Deborah shut her eyes, turned her face away and whacked the window with all her might. The glass shattered and a blast of heat exploded from the building. The dog came out as if shot from a cannon. She caught it in her arms, hardly able to believe it had survived her bumbling rescue attempt.

The dog leaped out of her grasp and shied away in a panic. She put out her hand, but the creature just snapped at her finger.

''Come on, then,'' she said. The dog hesitated until a coal dray clattered past, nearly crushing it beneath an iron-banded wheel. Then the mongrel sprang back into Deborah's arms. It was a smelly, scruffy thing, but she savored its lively warmth as she struggled on through the street. She had gone a full block before she became aware that somewhere along the way she had lost her shawl. She'd probably dropped it after breaking the window.

She cast about furtively, looking for the wild man, and to her relief she did not see him. She pushed on, still holding the little dog. Nothing felt real to her. It was a night out of hell. It was what she had imagined war to be. Terror and wounded refugees and the sense that the world was being ripped to pieces. Only the hope that she might find a way to her father and their home on the lake kept her going.

At last she reached the rockbound shore of Lake Michigan. The water stretched out endlessly before her, a churning field of ink. The howling wind whipped up wavelets that reflected the towering fire. The water itself resembled a sea of flame. The lake bristled with ships' masts and the smokestacks of steamers. Hundreds of vessels had gathered to witness the spectacle. Boats plied back and forth between the lighthouse and the pier, rescuing people and belongings.

For as far as the eye could see, the lakeshore teemed with refugees and conveyances, barnyard animals and pets running willy nilly through the night. People had waded out into the water to escape the blizzard of sparks and flying brands of flame. Deborah had no idea what to do. She tried to press northward, but it was a struggle hampered by the crush of humanity, the chilly water sloshing at the shore and various landings and piers jutting out into the lake. At last she could go no farther, for the way was blocked by a jetty of sharp black rocks.

She simply stood still, hemmed in by family groups clinging together amidst an outer circle of coaches, carts and barrows. She hugged the small mongrel dog to her chest, then, lifting her face, observed the burning city with a solemn sense of shock and awe. The flames formed a vast inverted bowl of unnatural light over a huge area. There was something mystical and magnificent about the conflagration. Others around her seemed to share her hushed awe, her openmouthed silence. There was simply nothing to say. There were no words to speak in the face of a disaster so vast and so all-consuming.

What had become of her father? His beautiful mansion? His business offices in the city? What had become of the only world she had ever known?

Shaking free of the spell cast by the giant fire, she looked around, scanning the crowd for a familiar face and keeping an eye out for the murderer. She wondered who these people were, where they all came from. Chicago was a city of three hundred thousand souls. Most of them had probably lost everything. Would they simply pick up and go on? How would they ever sift through the rubble of the fallen city and find their former lives?

Like phoenixes rising from the ashes, survivors would emerge from the wreckage of the burned-out city. Criminals awaiting hanging might run free. Wives who hated their husbands might escape their torment. Rich men would find themselves suddenly penniless. A poor man might come into wealth he never imagined. In the face of a fire, everyone was equal. It put her on the same level as the criminal who had abducted her, she thought with a shudder.

A tantalizing notion came to her, subtle as a whispered suggestion. What if Philip Ascot never found her again? What if she was lost forever to Arthur Sinclair? Then she would never have to battle her father over marrying Philip.

Deborah tried to imagine what it would be like to be nothing, nobody, to belong to no one. Immediately a wave of resentment washed over her. In running and hiding from an unwanted marriage, she would forfeit her father. Her friends. Her *life*. No man should have the power to do that to her. Yet still the fantasy held a bizarre appeal. If she were to simply disappear, would she even be missed? What would it do to her father? She honestly didn't know. She had the sense that he valued her as a commodity, but as a daughter? She remembered back to their moment of connection in the study and thought perhaps he loved her in his blustering, bombastic fashion. Even so, losing her would not change the shape and color of his world. Her father would grieve for a time, then give himself over to business ventures. Philip would find some other heiress to marry. Her friends might honor her memory, but they would find paths of their own to follow.

The fact was, she was not a necessary cog in the wheel of anyone's life. Remove her, and everything would go on uninterrupted. She wondered what it would be like to be needed in the way this small lost dog needed her. To be the single element necessary for its survival was an awesome thought. She quite doubted that she was equal to the task.

She shivered, feeling a chill wind off the lake, and pulled the dog closer. She thought about her friends, Lucy and Phoebe and Kathleen. It seemed a lifetime ago that they had been getting ready for the evening's entertainment. Where were they now? she wondered. She prayed they had survived, that unlike her they had realized the danger of the fire and stayed safe away from the city.

Somewhere in the crowd, a baby cried and a woman's voice spoke in soothing tones. Gradually people began talking, planning, worrying aloud. Prayer and speculation. Arguments and accusations. The babble of voices crescendoed, became deafening. With no one to talk to, Deborah felt more alone than ever. Still holding the dog, she picked her way up and over the rock and rubble jetty, wondering how far she would be able to walk before exhaustion claimed her.

Her clothes were tattered, her feet sore, her hands bleeding. Every part of her ached, right down to the roots of her hair. She wondered when the dawn would come, and what the day would bring. Staggering along the shore, she had to make a wide bow around the mob. She found herself wading into the surf and felt lake water swamp her, swirling around her ankles, stinging and then numbing her raw and wounded flesh.

Then, through the babble of German, Polish and Norwegian, through the brogues of Irish immigrants and the flat accents of native Chicagoans, she heard her name being called in a clipped, educated voice. "Deborah! Deborah, is that you? Deborah Sinclair!"

Her head snapped up and she scanned the lakeshore drive. A tall sleek coach was parked amid the drays and farm carts. A slender man in disheveled evening wear stood on the box, a long quirt in one gloved hand, the other hand cupped around his mouth. The wind stirred his blond hair and in the sky behind him, fire blossoms glowed.

Philip.

Five

The moment Deborah recognized her fiancé, everything seemed to be sucked out of her. She stood unmoving, so wracked by dull astonishment that she had frozen solid. Unable to reason. Unwilling to feel anything. There was Philip, looking as handsome and commanding as he had—was it only Saturday night? Now he was calling to her again, ordering her to come to him.

Only seconds earlier she had been thinking of a new life, a new start, unencumbered by expectations, promises and obligations, and her own sense that she had no purpose in life other than fulfilling her father's intentions for her. Now she conceded, with a humble sense of defeat, that she had no idea how to make a life on her own.

As if in a trance, she picked her way toward Philip, her thoughts dissolving into a confused muddle. Shock and fatigue pushed her toward him, the only familiar face in a world gone mad. She felt as helpless as the dog had been, trapped behind the glass in a burning building, at the mercy of the only person willing to rescue her. The brief fantasy about disappearing swirled away; it had no more substance than the wisps of smoke hovering over the lake. It was time to go back to the life she had planned and to the man who would direct it for the rest of her days.

Chill gusts of lake-cooled wind chased after her as she moved slowly up the steep bank to the place where Philip waited, perched on the running board of a carriage. Numbing exhaustion closed over her. Lines began to blur. Resignation dulled her thoughts. Anything, she told herself, anything was preferable to the hellish night she had just endured.

At last Deborah reached him, reached this man she was scheduled to marry. This man who was regarded by polite society as the American version of royalty. This man who would give Arthur Sinclair grandchildren who would be accepted in the same circles as the Guggenheims and Vanderbilts.

Philip's handsome face, so refined it was beautiful in the firelight, was her beacon. He extended a gloved hand. "Thank God I found you, darling." He spoke in the mellifluous lazy drawl of a Harvard Porcellian clubman. "What a stroke of luck!"

She stared at the black leather hand reaching for her.

The long, elegant fingers twitched with impatience. "Come along, then," he said. "I don't intend to sit among riffraff all ni—damn!"

The small dog snapped at him. He glared at the creature, then at Deborah. "Where the devil did you get that?"

"From a shop. A burning shop..." Her mind was a screaming jumble. Disjointed thoughts flew past and disappeared before she could grasp them. She felt numb; she could barely speak.

"Never mind," Philip said. "Just get rid of the filthy creature and take my hand. There's a girl."

The screaming in her head grew louder, yet like a sleepwalker, she obeyed. This was Philip, for heaven's sake. Philip, whom she'd known since she was tiny. Who had suffered through ballroom dancing lessons with her, who had sat stiffly in her father's study and promised to offer Deborah entree into the highest circles of society in exchange for her hand in marriage—and a staggering dowry.

She thrust aside the instinctual resistance that held her back. At Miss Boylan's she had learned to dread scandal over all else—bodily injury, personal insult, wounds to the soul. Only the lowliest of breeds would make a scene. This lesson had been hammered into Deborah, so she set down the little dog. It danced about her feet and scrabbled its paws desperately at the hem of her skirts, but she ignored it, refused to look down.

Philip gave another expert flick of the whip. The dog yelped and scurried away, scampering under the carriage. Finally coming to her senses, she tried to go after the mongrel, bending low to peer beneath the conveyance. Philip reached for her, and his gloved hand closed around hers, tugging upward.

"Not so fast," said a rough and terrible voice behind her. "She's coming with me."

The madman. Wild dark hair, battle in his eyes, he towered over the crowd gathered in the roadway.

Philip dropped her hand. "Clearly you're mistaken," he said with an incredulous bark of laughter. "Stand down, man. You're in the way, and I'm in a hurry."

"Philip, this man is a menace," Deborah babbled. "He tried to murder my father!"

When the buckskin-clad man moved in closer, Philip swore and brandished the whip. The braided leather lashed out, but unlike the dog, the outlaw didn't flinch, didn't even blink. He merely put up a fist the size of a joint of roast beef and caught the whip in midstrike.

He hauled back with the motion of a seasoned fisherman, reeling Philip in like a trout. Philip spat a curse even as he fell forward off the carriage box. It was hard to tell if he collided by accident with the other man's fist, or if the man actually threw the punch that knocked him cold. All Deborah knew for certain was that Philip Ascot IV gave an unhealthy groan and crumpled to the ground like a dropped sack of feed corn.

She stared at him for a moment. The fine frock coat had twisted awry, revealing a small pearl-handled handgun protruding from his cummerbund. How odd to think of Philip carrying a gun. Yet after last night she realized she didn't know him at all. Reflexively, she reached for the gun.

A large, soot-smudged hand closed around her wrist. She cried out and tried to pull away, but her abductor's hold on her was implacable. She was a fool for not being quicker and grabbing Philip's gun when she had the chance. Not that she knew the first thing about using a handgun. But now she had nothing, not so much as a hatpin with which to defend herself.

The man pulled her away from the road and down toward the lake.

"No!" Numb inertia gave way to defiance. She dug her heels into the grassy embankment by the roadway. "Let go of me!"

He ignored her protest, dragging her along behind him with callous brute force. Dear God, what had she done? Why had she hesitated to join Philip in the enclosed safety of the carriage?

It occurred to her, in a flash of new awareness, that she'd had a third choice. She could have—should have—fled by herself. Yet she'd failed to seize the opportunity. Independence had never been an option for her.

"Help," she called to all the people they passed. "Save me! This man is trying to kidnap me!"

Some within earshot stared at her curiously but most merely shook their heads and went back to their own struggles. No doubt they had seen more bizarre sights this night than a hysterical woman.

"Please," she tried again. "I don't know this man. He's abducting me. For the love of God, please help!"

A workman in knickers and shirtsleeves stepped into

their path. The wild man said nothing, only gave him a burning look, and the man stepped out of the way. The brute's towering height and the breadth of his shoulders made him a fearsome spectacle, Deborah realized with sinking hopes. Still, she kept screaming, and a priest in a long cassock approached, rolling back his voluminous sleeves to reveal surprisingly beefy forearms.

"See here now," he said in a thick Irish brogue. "The poor lass is out of her head with fright."

"That's a fact, mon frère," said the big man. "My poor wife lost everything tonight, and she's not herself."

"Wi...wi—" Deborah was too shocked to get the words out.

"I reckon she'll be all right by and by," her abductor said, grasping her insolently around the waist. He held her so tightly she could scarcely breathe. "We could use your prayers, mon frère. We surely could." He pulled her quickly away, heading down toward a wide wooden pier that jutted out onto the lake.

"But he's not...I'm not his wife—" she called, but she was dragged relentlessly along, and the Irish priest had already vanished into the throng on the beach. Deborah opened her mouth to call out again, but before she could speak, her captor pressed her roughly against one of the wet timber piers upholding the dock. He put his angry, frightening face very close to hers. She could smell the leather and smoke scent of him—the essence of danger and strangeness.

"Quit your caterwauling," he ordered. "I'm out of patience."

She forced herself to glare up at him. He was a giant of a man. She had never seen a man so tall. She was terrified, but she had nothing to lose. "And patience is such a gift of yours, I'm sure," she spat with far more bravado than she felt. "What will you do? Sock me in the face? Shoot me?"

"Tempting offers, both of them." He took her upper

arms in a bruising grip and lifted her bodily off the ground. The sensation of being entrapped between his strong hands raised a havoc of panic in her. The blood drained from her face and dry screams came from her throat, but he didn't seem to be bothered by her protests. Handling her like a longshoreman with a timber bale, he bundled her into a small wooden dinghy tied up at the pier and cast off the ropes.

"What are you doing?" Deborah shrieked. "You can't—"

He shoved off with such force that she fell backwards, hitting her shoulder painfully on something hard and sharp. The impact drove the breath from her lungs. By the time she righted herself, he was pulling strongly out into the lake. The hot glow from the burning city made him appear more fierce and frightening than a dark angel.

He glared at a spot over her shoulder. "What the hell is that?" he muttered, laying aside his oars.

"What is what?" she asked.

"Something in the water."

She grabbed the side of the boat and twisted around. "Philip?"

"Close. I think it's a rat." He reached down, the fringe on his sleeve brushing the surface of the water, and scooped up the animal, holding the dripping, shivering creature aloft. "Yours?"

She grabbed the dog and gently cradled it to her breast. The smell of smoke and wet fur nearly made her gag, but just for a moment, she felt a flood of hope and relief. Then she looked at her captor, his huge form lit by the glare of the burning city, and the terror and confusion returned. Without taking her eyes off him, she set the dog in the bottom of the boat. The mongrel shook itself violently, spraying water. Deborah knew she had to act. Her hesitation on the shore had cost her dearly and she must not make the same mistake again.

No longer worried about the indignity of making a

scene, she seized one of the oars. Drawing back, she swung it at the big man. Being violent was harder than it looked, she realized as he ducked. Frustrated, she swung it back the other way. He put up a hand and caught the oar, wrenching it from her grasp. He never said a word, just took up rowing again.

Deborah slumped down on the hard, narrow seat. She had gained nothing by trying to fight back, yet the very idea that she had dared made her feel slightly better. Very slightly. Within moments, fright and uncertainty returned with a vengeance.

The stranger's simmering silence alarmed her far more than any tirade of threats. He had a hard look about him that frightened her, yet she found herself studying his shadowed face with something more than fright. There was a large swelling on his head where her father had struck him with the marble statue. The blow probably would have cracked the skull of any other man. His bear-paw hands gripped the oars with easy certainty, and his smooth, rhythmical strokes told her he was an experienced waterman.

She had no idea why she was speculating about this stranger, so she forced herself to stop. She held fast to the wet, smelly little dog as each powerful stroke of the oars bore her farther from shore.

Finally she couldn't stand it anymore. "What do you want with me?" she demanded.

He gave no answer, and the look he shot her made her doubt whether or not she truly wanted to know.

"Where are you taking me?" she asked. She definitely wanted to know the answer to that.

He simply kept rowing. The small boat pounded through the choppy water, riding up the crest of each wave, then slapping down in its trench, one after the other. The dog trembled in her lap.

She bit her lip, trying to hold in a rising panic. Even after all she had seen this night, she still felt no easing of her terror. With each passing second, she slipped farther and farther away from all that was familiar. She felt numb, yet beneath the numbness lay a banked hysteria beckoning her to madness. If she gave vent to it, she might never stop screaming.

Drawing in a deep breath, she asked, "Are you a white slaver?"

"*What?*"

"A white slaver," she repeated. "Is that what you are?"

"Yeah," he said, flashing her a predatory grin that was even more intimidating than his thunderous scowl. "Yeah, that's me. A white slaver."

She shuddered, resentful of his sarcasm. The idea of white slavers had been planted by the forbidden novels the young ladies of Miss Boylan's giggled over late at night. In the books, the adventure seemed to befall innocent, usually fair-haired girls, though what became of them after being taken by their brutal captors was always left to the imagination. Deborah had always envisioned a shadowy place, the air spiced with incense, exotic music emanating from the unseen corners.

The stranger brought the dinghy alongside a larger boat. The firelight picked out the low-browed profile of a small steam freighter. In the pilot house a single lamp burned, swinging with the motion of the waves.

He tied the dinghy to the stern. Without bothering to ask permission, he bent and scooped up the dog, which immediately bit him.

"Ouch! Damn it!" He brought the dog over the side, practically flinging it into the trawler. He swung around to glare at Deborah. "Climb aboard," he ordered.

She clutched the sides of the rowboat. "No."

He let out a long breath that sounded of repressed fury. "Do you really want to fight me on this?"

"I refuse to go."

"Climb aboard or I'll heave you over, too," he said.

She stared at him, all six and a half feet of him. The fringed buckskins of a savage. The dark, lank, sawed-off hair of a backwoodsman. The bear-paw hands that could snap a person in two. The reflected glints of fire and rage in his eyes. No. She did not want to fight him.

For the first time in her life, she was going to have to think ahead, to plan. She would wait for the right opportunity, and then she would act.

Bracing her hands on the hull of the trawler, she pulled herself up. The churning water made her lose her footing, but she clung tenaciously to the ladder. Her foot snagged in the hem of her skirt, and she heard a ripping sound. It crossed her mind that climbing a ladder in front of a gentleman was a risky and unladylike thing to do. Another swift glance at Paul Bunyan reminded her that he was no gentleman, and that ladylike qualms would not be tolerated.

Then a moment of utter clarity came over Deborah. She held the ladder with one hand while a wave lifted the stern end of the trawler, bringing the molten glass water up to her knees. She had it in her power to end this here, now.

Before she could change her mind, she simply opened her hand and let go of the ladder. A brief sensation of falling, then the cold shock of the water stunned her. She felt her wet skirts bell out, trapping air momentarily before pulling her down, down...

It was the worst possible moment to change her mind, but Deborah couldn't help herself. Something deep within her protested and rebelled. She didn't want to die at all, no matter how miserable she was. She wanted to live. She scissored her legs, trying to kick toward the surface, so hungry for air that she feared her chest would explode. She wasn't going to make it, she thought, seeing blackness through her slitted eyes. She'd failed at suicide, and now she would fail to save herself.

Her arm brushed something hard and rough—a floating log or part of the ship, perhaps—and felt herself being dragged up to the surface. She coughed up water, then sucked in air with explosive breaths. Only then did she realize her captor had gone in after her. Looking even more forbidding soaking wet, he grabbed the ladder with his free hand and hauled her up and over the transom, manhandling her as if she were livestock. In the open cockpit of the trawler, the wild man regarded her with disgust.

"What the hell's wrong with you, woman?" he demanded.

She knew he didn't want a response, and for a long time, she couldn't speak anyway. Her legs felt weak and rubbery with fatigue. The ecstatic dog greeted her, turning like a dervish on the cluttered deck and yelping joyfully. She felt too numb to do any more than sit down heavily amid her wet, tangled skirts and stare at nothing at all. After a while, she managed to catch her breath. "Smokey," she said, addressing the dog. "That will be your name."

The wild man secured the dinghy to the steamer. "You mean you don't even know this dog?" he demanded. "We took on a stray?"

"If you don't like strangers on your boat, then let us both go," she challenged him.

"If that critter gets on my nerves, he's cutbait," her captor promised, pulling in the ladder. Without a word of warning, he peeled off his fringed jacket and then his shirt, revealing the deep chest, narrow waist and giant arms of a lumberjack. Then he unlaced his trousers.

Deborah gasped and looked away. "How dare you? It's indecent."

"I'll tell you what's indecent. Jumping into Lake Michigan in October. On second thought, that's not indecent. Are you crazy, or just stupid?"

When she dared to look back at him, he was dressed in denim jeans and a bleached shirt, and was lacing on another pair of boots.

The big boat smelled of dampness and fish. It had a broad deck behind the raised pilot house, and rows of crates lashed along the periphery. A narrow hatch covered by wooden louver led below.

Deborah had spent plenty of time on the lake, but never in a craft like this. She had enjoyed endless summer afternoons flying along in her catboat, or long lazy days cruising aboard her father's steamer yacht, the one he had bought from Mr. Vanderbilt of New York City, just so he could have something once owned by a Vanderbilt. Sometimes they steamed as far north as the locks at Sault Sainte Marie.

But this was not a pleasure cruising boat, she knew.

The man crossed the deck with heavy, thudding footsteps. The small gray dog backed against her skirts and growled.

A thump came from below, where she imagined the cabins and the boiler room to be. As Deborah watched, the louvered hatch opened and a small, wiry man with sleek black hair emerged. He took one look at Deborah and his eyes widened, then sharpened with astonishment.

"A visitor, eh? I thought I'd heard someone," the man said. The faint flavor of French tinged his words. As he hoisted himself up and out of the hatch, Deborah saw a streak of pure white against the black strands of his hair. Though not young, he was fit and muscular. An Indian. She had never seen an Indian at such close range before.

"You are very wet," he observed, glancing from her to the pile of damp buckskins on the deck. "The fire, she is a bad one, eh?" He shaded his eyes and faced the city. "I figured it'd be out by now." He peered at Deborah. "So. Who the devil are you?"

The dog growled, and she snatched it into her arms.

"Name's Jacques duBois," the man said with a trace of Gallic courtesy that surprised her. "Commonly called Lightning Jack. Welcome aboard the *Suzette,* mademoiselle."

She stood up and cleared her throat, tasting grit and smoke. Her damp skirts hung in disgrace. "My name is Deborah Beaton Sinclair."

His congenial grin disappeared. He threw a glance at the other man. "You brought a Sinclair aboard my boat?"

"He's crazy," she said in a rush, praying duBois would understand. "He forced me to come with him, though I offered him a fortune to set me free. I am here against my will."

"Aren't we all, chère. Aren't we all."

"He abducted you, too?" she inquired.

"No." Lightning Jack gestured at the flaming night sky. "But I have no liking for Chicago. Pile of dry sticks, railroad slums and smelly stockyards. Pah." He spat over the side.

"Please. This is a terrible misunderstanding. You must take me back to shore. Your friend is not right in the head."

"Friend." Lightning Jack winked at the tall man. "Tom Silver was my foster son. Now that he is grown, he is my partner in commerce. Did he not tell you?"

"He told me nothing." She turned the name over in her mind. *Tom Silver.* A simple name for a savage man. "Has he always been insane?"

Lightning Jack hooked his thumbs into the rope sash around his middle. He regarded her with a narrow-eyed harshness that made her take a step back. "Mademoiselle, I assure you he is not insane." He moved past her to join the man called Tom Silver, who was loading wood from a tender tied to the boat. Silver moved with a peculiar ease for one so large. As he bent and straightened with the rhythm of his task, she saw that he had one vanity, something she hadn't noticed before. Within the strands of his long dark hair, he wore a single thin braid wrapped with a thread of leather. Secured to one end of the braid was a feather, perhaps from an eagle.

Looking at him, she felt an unaccustomed lurch of...not

fear, exactly. Trepidation, yes, but it was mixed with an undeniable curiosity. She was alone with two savages, and so far she had not been injured or terrorized. Perhaps they were saving the torture for later.

With a shudder, she turned to look back at the city. Her father, one of Chicago's most enthusiastic promoters, had always called it "Queen of the Prairie." But everything had changed in just one night. From the deck, she could see the whole extent of the conflagration. Nothing in her experience approached the terrible majesty of this sight. The fire raged from the southwestern reaches of the city to the north shore of the lake. It spanned the river and its branches, cutting a deadly swath through the entire city, right up to the lakeshore railroad lines. The tower of the waterworks stood like a lonely, abandoned sentinel flanked by the fire. The heart of the city had been burned out.

Flames spun upward from the high rooftops. From a distance they resembled orange tornados, the sort that sometimes whirled across the prairies far beyond the city.

Government Pier bristled with people crowded close together. Deborah imagined they were as dumbstruck and battle-weary as those at Lincoln Park had been.

She wondered about her father, and her friends from Miss Boylan's. And Philip. How close she had come to taking his hand and driving off into the night with him. She kept picturing that black leather hand reaching for her, kept hearing his refined voice, promising to take her to safety.

Instead, here she was with a skin-clad barbarian, being dragged away like a hunting trophy in his smelly boat.

Like Tom Silver, Lightning Jack wore the skins of dead animals and his hair indecently long. Unlike Silver, he wore a pleasant smile. He caught his partner's eye. "*Alors, mon vieux.* We stoke the boilers," he said and they started climbing down a hatch.

"What about me?" Deborah asked. Her voice rose on a note of hysteria.

The two men looked back at her and Tom Silver narrowed his eyes dangerously. "Don't you get it, Princess?" he asked in annoyance.

"Get what?"

"You're a hostage."

Six

"I guess you got some explaining to do, *mon copain*," said Lightning Jack.

With desultory motions, Tom checked the pressure gauges on the boilers. His head throbbed where Sinclair had hit him. "I reckon."

"So talk. Start with the devil's bastard, Sinclair. I was afraid you might lose him in the confusion of the fire."

Tom drew on a pair of hide gloves and fed wood to the fire, building up heat as they prepared to get under way. He glanced over his shoulder at Jack.

"I found him," Tom said. "I found Sinclair."

"And did you kill him?" Jack's onyx eyes glittered. The look on his face indicated that he already knew the answer.

Tom finished stoking the boilers. He slammed the steel hatch shut and rotated the dial. Then he turned to face his friend, the man who had raised him.

"No," Tom repeated, taking off the thick gloves. "I didn't kill him."

"*Merde.*" Jack believed in simple, direct justice. He had been a voyageur in his younger years. His mother was Chippewa, his father French Canadian. He had earned the nickname "Lightning" years ago when he'd been struck by lightning during a spring storm on the lake. The wound had left a permanent jagged patch along the side of his head where only white hair would grow.

Lightning Jack spoke French, English and Chippewa, and he swore now in all three, slipping easily from one tongue to the next.

"Parbleu," he grumbled. "If you found him, why didn't you shoot him?"

Tom was too bone-weary to go into detail. And maybe he didn't know the answer himself. There had been that split second, that brief hesitation, when his resolve to murder Arthur Sinclair had wavered. What had seemed so simple in the planning turned out much different in the execution.

"The city's on fire," he said to Jack. "We picked the wrong night to hunt down Arthur Sinclair."

"You found him. You had him dead to rights. Were you waiting for a formal invitation?"

Tom didn't reply.

"I should have done the deed myself. I would have slit the devil's throat from ear to ear, *comme ça.*" He traced the motion with a finger. "And what do you bring me in return? His yellow-haired runt of a daughter."

Tom took a long swig from a stoneware jug of cider, balancing the vessel on his bent elbow. Even the motion of tipping back his head to drink made him dizzy from the goose egg. Deborah, he thought. Deborah the debutante.

"I would take no joy in slitting the throat of such a one as her," Jack said.

"We're not going to kill her."

"Do you have a better idea?"

Tom thought about the huge house, filled with paintings and antiques and trophies of a rich man's toils. "We're going to get her father's fortune in ransom."

"I don't want his fortune."

"Because you don't need it," Tom pointed out. "But

what about the others? They sure as hell could use the ransom money.''

"Hostage. Pah." Lightning Jack took the jug from Tom and drained it. "What sort of revenge is that?"

"A better sort. I saw the way he lives, Lightning. I figured out what's important to him." Tom spoke the words with a new insight—some things were worse than dying. It was a hell of a thing, figuring that out, but seeing Sinclair like a king in his castle had opened his eyes. Tom wasn't surrendering his need for revenge, just changing his methods.

"Sinclair's failed mine left folks destitute. His money could bring them some relief."

"That is not good enough." Steam drove the pistons, and Lightning Jack raised his voice over the boiling hiss. "Arthur Sinclair must suffer for what he did."

Tom didn't answer. Now that the boilers were stoked, he led the way abovedecks to the pilot house. Miss Deborah Beaton Sinclair still stood astern, holding her shaggy dog and watching the fire, her wet clothes dripping. He couldn't figure out if she had fallen into the lake deliberately or by accident. He had no idea what was going on in her head, and didn't care to know, but for some reason he kept wondering. She looked small and slight, her dress and hair bedraggled, her delicate features limned by firelight, her face vulnerable and inexpressibly sad.

She reminded him of a broken china doll. It occurred to him that the city was her home, and here she stood watching it burn. Before her eyes, her own father had taken off in a runaway carriage. She had lost all that was familiar to her. He did not want to think of this young woman's sadness, but he couldn't help it. She had the sort of fragile, melancholy countenance that evoked things he was not used to feeling. Like sympathy. Protectiveness.

It was stupid, he told himself. She was the spoiled daughter of a man who did not blink at wiping out a whole town. At Arthur Sinclair's knee, Miss Deborah had probably learned that in the pursuit of profit, there were no rules or restraints.

When she looked up at him, he noticed a smudge of soot on her cheekbone. Her hair had come loose, and there were large black-ringed holes burned in her damp dress. She kept stroking the dog with one small hand, over and over again.

He bent to the windlass at the bow and cranked in the anchor. He raised the dinghy and made it fast astern. Then he gave a whistle. The engines ground, the twin screw propellers churned and the trawler lurched forward.

The motion made Deborah Sinclair stagger back against the rail. "Where are you taking me?"

He didn't answer.

"What is your intent?" she demanded, sounding loud and testy now. "I demand to know."

Her shrill tone evaporated his sympathy. Seizing her had been an act of pure impulse. He had not looked ahead to moments like this, had not considered what it would mean to have a female aboard. They did female things. They had female needs. And this was not just any female. This one probably had a maid just to button her shoes for her. A servant to sprinkle sugar in her tea. A footman to open and close the carriage door for her.

"Well?" she asked. "Have you gone deaf or are you simply being rude?"

"Quarters are below," he said. "Follow me."

"I'll do nothing of the sort."

He gave a snort. "Fine. Spend the night on deck. Makes no difference to me."

She took two steps back and tilted up her head to look him in the eye. "I don't plan on staying," she said.

"Who was the tenderfoot with the horsewhip?" he asked, ignoring her statement.

"That was Philip Widener Ascot IV," she said. Her voice was flat, her face expressionless. "He is my fiancé."

Tom mimicked a limp-wristed parody of Ascot wielding the whip. "Charming fellow. You're a lucky young lady."

"You may be sure he will remember you from last night, and all the papers will be filled with a description of you."

"Will he remember that you refused to go with him?"

"I did not refuse. There was no time—"

"You had time. You could have grabbed his hand and jumped into his coach."

"You would have pursued me."

"Maybe," he admitted. "Maybe not. You'll never know, will you? Because you chose me."

She recoiled. "I did nothing of the sort. Why would I choose you?"

"That's a question you should be asking yourself. I sure as hell don't know what's in that head of yours."

"And you are in such trouble," she shot back. "Do you know who my fiancé is?"

"Besides a horse's ass?"

She made a sound of disdain. "He is from one of the first families of the city. He is heir to a publishing empire with ties to New York City. When he and my father find me, he will publish this account in every newspaper in the country."

"*If* he finds you, there won't be enough of him left to swab the decks with." Tom shook his head. "Believe me, having my description published in the papers won't cause me to lose any sleep."

She stared at him inquisitively.

"What?" he asked, irritated.

"You have a strange manner of speaking," she remarked. "It's a combination of backwoods ignorance and educated formality. Why is that?"

"Quit prying and go below," he ordered. He didn't want her to know a damned thing about him. "And pray your father buys your freedom soon."

She bristled imperiously. "Or else?"

"Or else you're in for a long, cold winter."

She twisted a diamond ring off her finger. "That's worth a fortune. You may have it. Just take me ashore."

He pocketed the ring without looking at it. "No."

"You can't hold me aboard this boat all winter," she objected.

"You're right about that," he said, then grasped the ladder leading to the pilothouse. "We'd best get a move on."

"You won't get away with this," she yelled.

He slowly turned to face her. "Don't you get it, Princess? I already have."

Seven

Deborah felt sick with the motion of the boat, but she willed back the waves of nausea. Shivering, chilled to the bone in her damp dress, she waited until Tom Silver disappeared into the pilothouse. The little French Indian called Lightning Jack spoke to him briefly. They seemed to be arguing about something. Then both men bent over a slanted table strewn with charts.

Good. They were paying her no heed at all. They probably assumed she would slink below to fling herself on a bunk and weep hysterically until exhaustion claimed her.

Which was exactly what she wanted to do.

But she refused to allow it, even though every instinct urged her to crumble in defeat. She tried to think what to do. Kathleen would take action. She was never one to sit still. Lucy would confront these men with righteous indignation and rail at them about the injustice of their crime. Phoebe would attempt to endear herself to them, and sweet-talk her way out of trouble.

Deborah came to a decision, the only possible course of action she could think of. Before she could change her mind, she set down the shaggy little dog and moved to the stern. She had watched covertly while Silver had hoisted the dinghy, and she thought she could figure out how to lower it again.

The eerie light from the city was bright enough to burn through the smoke and fog. But the farther they steamed away from Chicago, the fainter the light. She would have to work fast.

She found the mechanism that would release the winch and unhooked it. The chains made a terrible noise, reeling out with a metallic grating sound. The small rowboat smacked the water with a splash, then swirled in the wake of the steamer. The big boat was traveling a lot faster than she had imagined it would.

Glancing over her shoulder, she ascertained that the men in the pilothouse had not heard. She spared a thought for the dog, shivering in a corner of the deck, but it was all she could do to save herself. Then she stepped up on the transom, holding on to the ladder.

Deborah searched her soul for guidance and wisdom. She wished she could find just one measly drop of courage. She felt nothing but icy, breath-stealing terror. Before she could change her mind, she flung herself over the back and scrambled down the ladder as far as she could go. Cold mist, churned up by the propellers, showered her, nearly blinding her as she climbed into the dinghy. Wrestling with the knots, she managed to untether the small craft.

Within seconds, she was adrift on the gale-swept lake as the trawler steamed northward. She could scarcely believe it. She had escaped.

Cold waves slapped up and over the sides of the small wooden craft. Water sloshed in the hull. Letting loose with a laugh of elation, she fitted the oars into the oarlocks and began to row. The wild man had made it look easy, but the water felt as heavy as mud.

Still, her escape might have worked had she not made one critical error. She should have brought the dog.

The little beast put its forepaws on the side of the trawler and yapped piercingly into the night. She hoped the noise of the steamer would drown out the barking.

She held her breath, praying the kidnapers would ignore the racket. But she saw the trawler circle back, chugging like the Loch Ness monster toward her.

On deck, a large figure rose with a grappling hook in hand.

Damp and fog shrouded the boat and the lake surrounding it. The cramped quarters where Deborah awakened had a very small portal, and a narrow louvered vent for fresh air. It wasn't a proper stateroom and could not even be called quarters, but a storage room with a pile of blankets. She groped in the half light, finding coils of rope, a box of tools whose use she couldn't fathom, a moldering shirt and two things that puzzled her—a child's shoe and a copy of *Les Misérables* in the original French. She encountered an empty bottle, an illustrated Farmers' Almanac, a jar of shiny, opaque green stones and a chamberpot.

Moving slowly and painfully, she availed herself of the primitive facilities, then put on her dress. At some point, which she could not remember, she had peeled it off to collapse in exhaustion. Her fingers worked clumsily over the buttons, but she managed to do herself up. She found her way on deck with difficulty. Where was she? She looked out at the lake. Nothing but fog. Chicago—indeed the shore—was nowhere in sight.

She ached in every joint and limb. She felt seasick, but there was nothing in her stomach to surrender. The little dog she had dubbed Smokey cavorted in friendly fashion around her feet, but she could not even summon the strength to pat his head. *Traitor,* she thought.

Tom Silver stood in the wheelhouse, steering the trawler through the impenetrable fog, ignoring her. Lightning Jack emerged from the galley holding a thick china mug. "Tea," he said, holding it out. "It's medicinal. Helps with the *mal de mer.*"

She felt too defeated to argue, and so she took the mug, wrapping her chilly fingers around its warmth.

"How does he know where to go in this fog?" she asked. Her voice rang hollow in the thick, hazy air.

"He follows my instructions," Lightning Jack explained. "This is my boat." He jerked his silver-streaked head toward the surface of the water. "The way is posted by buoys and channel markers. Fear not. You are safe aboard the *Suzette*."

Safe. She did not even know the meaning of the word anymore.

The water appeared considerably calmer and flatter than it had been...when?

"What time is it?" she asked.

"You mean what day? You've slept for two days."

She nearly choked on her tea. Dizzy, she lowered herself onto the bench. She forced her eyes to focus on something, anything, to keep from fainting. She stared at her shoes, scuffed and worn from her ordeal. For two days she had slept in her shoes.

How strange it now seemed that Kathleen used to take her foot between her knees to do up Deborah's shoes with the button hook. She shut her eyes in despair.

There must have been some powerful drug in the tea, for everything swirled behind her closed eyelids, and then she knew nothing. With a vague, dreamlike awareness, she felt the mug taken from her hand. Powerful arms lifted her. The sensation startled her awake with a cry. Panic hammered in her chest, and she screamed.

"Shut up," said Tom Silver through gritted teeth. "I'm taking you back to your bunk."

"Put me down," she yelled, horrified at his nearness, the lake-and-leather scent of him, the way he held her in his tree trunk arms.

"Fine." He practically dumped her down the hatch. "Just don't fall asleep in the pilothouse again."

She was shaking when she returned to the cramped quarters, pressing herself back against the door. Different, she told herself, trying to still the crazed beating of her heart. This was different. This man, this Tom Silver, hated her. His hatred was supposed to keep him from touching her. She didn't want anyone to touch her, ever again.

Deborah awoke again hours—or days?—later to the rattle and churn of the trawler's engine and the murmur of masculine utterances. She lay perfectly still, trying to pretend this was not real. She refused to open her eyes. So long as she kept them closed she could pretend she was back at Miss Boylan's, in her own bed of pressed Irish linens. In a few minutes, Kathleen would come with tea and milk on a tray, and they would discuss Deborah's plans for the day.

But inevitably, the damp fishy smell of the boat and Smokey's doggy odor chased away the fantasy. Once again, she struggled to the galley, finding Lightning Jack poring over a chart.

He offered her tea again.

"Just water, please. Your tea makes me suspicious."

"You should be grateful for the sleep. This is a long and boring voyage."

"And what is our destination?"

"That is up to your father. If he surrenders to our demands, we'll put you on a train in Milwaukee."

She felt a spark of eagerness. "Have you already sent a message?"

"We'll wire from Milwaukee," he said.

"Why are you and Tom Silver making demands from my father?" she asked. "What do you want from him?"

"Justice," Lightning Jack said simply.

"I don't understand. Justice for what?"

He stared out the window, pocked with spray. "For murder."

An incredulous laugh escaped her. "You think my father murdered someone?"

"I *know* he did." Lightning Jack rose from the bench.

"You know nothing of the sort," she retorted. "My father has never harmed a soul. He's a good man—"

"He is fortunate to have a daughter who believes in him. But that does not alter the truth."

"Then tell me your version of the truth."

"Last summer—"

"That'll do, Jack." A large and ominous shadow filled the doorway, obliterating the light. Tom Silver ducked his head and stepped into the galley. "Best check on the piston drivers. Weren't you going to do that today?"

Lightning Jack nodded. He looked at Deborah briefly. "Find something to eat. You'll need your strength."

"But you—what—" Before Deborah could get the words out, he was gone. She glared at Tom Silver. "We were in the middle of a conversation."

"I heard."

"You had no right to interrupt."

"You have no rights, period."

She shot up from the table. Her vision swam, and for a horrible moment she feared she might swoon. She grabbed the edge of the table to steady herself. "I have every right to know why you took me against my will. I have every right to know why you forced me aboard this smelly boat and why you're taking me far from home. I have every right—"

"You claim a lot of rights for someone who's a prisoner."

She tried to form an answer, but lost her grip on the edge of the table. The deck raced up to meet her, and she squeezed her eyes shut, bracing for a fall. But something stopped her. A giant male hand caught her, gripped her shoulder and steadied her. She opened her eyes, and a shiver of nauseating revulsion rolled over her. His touch was harsh, impersonal. It set off a reaction within her that made her sick.

"Let go of me," she said, breathing the words through clenched teeth. "I beg you, let go."

"Don't beg. I can't stand that in a female." He gave her a shove, and she staggered back to the bench. "Do as you're told and keep your mouth shut, and we'll get along a lot better."

"Did it ever occur to you that I don't care to get along with you?"

"No, but it occurred to me that I could tie you up and gag you."

Her jaw dropped. The utter cruelty of this man stunned her. She was accustomed to the little refined cruelties of ruthless social climbers, but not to the raw force of Tom Silver's brutality.

"What's this?" he asked, picking something up off the floor.

Deborah reached for the velvet pouch. "It's mine. It must have dropped when I nearly fell just now. Oh, don't—"

But he did, of course. He opened the pouch, and out fell her lavaliere. The blue topaz prism, set in silver filigree, was not the most costly of baubles, but its sentimental value to Deborah was beyond price. "That was my mother's. Give it back," she said, holding out her hand.

"Nope." He stuck it in his pocket. "We'll send it to your father—so he knows we're not bluffing."

It was the one possession that truly meant something to Deborah. "Please," she said. "Not that. You've already taken my diamond engagement ring. That's much more valuable."

"And more likely to be stolen by the messenger."

"My father might think you simply found that in the confusion of the fire," she pointed out. Then, realizing her mistake, she covered her mouth.

"You're right," he said. "Maybe I should send an ear or a finger."

"This is a nightmare," she whispered. "This can't be happening."

He stared at her narrow-eyed for a few minutes, then took a wickedly sharp knife from the top of his boot.

Deborah gave a shriek and scrambled for the door. He grabbed a handful of her hair and used the knife to slice off a thick blond lock. "This'll do," he said, sheathing the knife.

She moaned, sinking to the bench and clutching at her ruined hair.

He left her sitting alone in the cramped galley, struck speechless and motionless by the fact that she had lost everything in the world and was bound on a journey into the wilderness with two madmen.

Eight

Smokestacks and grain elevators rose ghostlike through the mist enshrouding the city of Milwaukee. At the stern of the trawler, Tom felt the presence of the girl like the weight of an albatross tied around his neck. He understood all too well that long poem Frère Henri had studied with him one winter. A man had to wear the evidence of his deeds, and he could never go back to what he was before.

He had abducted the woman on impulse, but now she was his, totally dependent upon him. Holding the daughter of Arthur Sinclair as a hostage on the boat was sheer idiocy, but as a means of revenge it might just work. Lord knew how this would turn out. The whole damned thing made his head ache, a common occurrence since he had been whacked in the skull by Deborah's father. The swelling had subsided, but not the pain.

His hostage was in the pilothouse, pacing back and forth, stopping occasionally at a portal to look at the city. He found himself thinking of a time, when he was a boy, that he had caught a butterfly. It had been beautiful, yellow and royal blue, with long-tipped wings and antennae as delicate as a silk thread. He had put the creature in a glass jar, adding a branch of honeysuckle for it to feed on and carefully poking holes in the metal top of the jar. In the morning he'd found the butterfly dead, its wings ragged from beating against the jar, the honeysuckle wilted and brown.

Deborah Sinclair hadn't eaten in days.

He wondered why she hadn't tried to escape again. After that first attempt, she seemed resigned, defeated. Either it was a ruse, and she was biding her time, or she had surrendered. He stalked across the deck and yanked open the door of the pilothouse. When he stepped inside, she turned a cool gaze upon him. The dog she called Smokey lifted one side of its mouth in a snarl, but otherwise didn't move from its favorite napping spot on the galley bench.

"You have to eat something." Tom grabbed a canister of biscuits from a shelf, pried off the lid and thrust them at her. "You look like a broom handle."

"And you," she retorted, "have the manners of a troglodyte."

He thunked a bottle of cider down next to the biscuit tin.

With a weary sigh, she pushed the tin and the bottle away. "I am neither hungry nor thirsty."

"Eat, goddamn it." He wondered what the hell he was going to do with her. "You'll get sick if you don't."

"I'm already sick," she said with quiet contempt.

Her words raised the fine hairs on the back of his neck. "What the hell's that supposed to mean?"

She studied him for a moment. "That frightens you, doesn't it?" she said, clearly intrigued by the notion. "You're quite terrified of me dying while on your watch."

"Woman, I don't give a damn whether you live or die," he said harshly. "But we're counting on your father to care." He subjected her to an assessing glance. She had the naturally pale coloring of a blonde and the wan fragility of a hothouse orchid. In the past few days, the hollows beneath her cheekbones had deepened, and her tattered dress seemed to hang more loosely from her petite frame.

He thought of the butterfly again. "What do you mean by sick?" he demanded again.

"I suffer from the *mal de mer*."

"Lightning Jack's tea is supposed to help that."

"It doesn't help me."

"Then what will? Tell me that, Princess."

She looked him straight in the eye. "I need a proper bath and a change of clothing and an actual mattress to sleep on and something decent to eat—"

"Excuse me while I ring for the servants," he said.

"You asked," she retorted.

Tom helped himself to a biscuit, thinking it didn't taste half-bad. "What does a debutante eat, anyway? I've always wondered."

She sniffed. "I'm not some rare breed of dog that requires a special diet."

"Then eat the damned biscuit."

"No." She tucked her arms around the shaggy little mutt.

He pressed his palms flat on the chart table and leaned across it, watching his shadow sweep over her. "If you think a hunger strike is going to convince me to let you go, you're wrong."

"If I starve to death, my father will—"

"Will what?" He let a humorless smile curl his mouth. "Hunt me down and kill me? I wish like hell that he'd try."

She regarded him with a probing, blue-eyed stare that made him unaccountably nervous. "I think it's time you explained a few matters to me."

"I'll explain nothing to you."

"Then I'll eat nothing," she countered.

Biting his tongue to keep from uttering an oath that would singe her ears, he sat down on the stool across from her and held out the biscuit tin. "You eat one of these, I'll answer one question."

She squinted at him like a seasoned cardsharp. "You're

on.'' Without even looking down at her hand, she selected a soda biscuit from the tin and ate it quickly and efficiently. "First question." She dusted the crumbs from her hands. "Why do you and Lightning Jack believe my father is a murderer?"

He could tell from the way she spoke that she had a hard time even saying the word. In the silence that followed her blunt question, he heard the waves lapping at the hull of the boat, and the twang of the wind through the stay lines securing the smokestack. "Because it's true," he said. "Arthur Sinclair is responsible for seven deaths, and Jack and I witnessed them all."

"If that's so," she said, "then isn't it a matter for the authorities rather than a pair of...of..." She studied him closely for a moment. "I don't know what you are—besides a kidnaper."

"Lightning Jack is the skipper of this boat. I'm—" He paused to measure his words. What was he, anyway? He knew what he used to be. As a youngster he had worked as Lightning Jack's business partner, fishing the rich waters of Lake Superior and sending the catch to the big cities. Then had come the war years, and he had gone off in search of adventure, foolishly thinking a soldier's life would open the world to him and show him the things he had always thought were missing from his life.

What he had found instead was a nightmare beyond anything he could have imagined. He had returned from war wild-eyed and jumpy, with a soul that would not settle. Only the gift of Asa, given into his care by his dying best friend, had brought Tom back to himself. He and the boy had rebuilt their lives on Isle Royale, the rhythm of their years marked by the seasons. From spring thaw to ice-up in early December, they worked side by side at a trading post that supplied the families of the tiny harbor settlement. The easy intimacy of their relationship came to mean the world to Tom.

They spent the winters on the mainland in Fraser, in

the company of the learned and well-respected Frère Henri. The Trappist monk had tutored Tom in his time. Over many a cold, dark winter, he had sat at the robed man's knee and learned French, mathematics, the classics. The elderly churchman had been taking Asa down the same path—but thanks to Arthur Sinclair, it was a journey Asa would never complete.

"Well?" Deborah Sinclair prompted, drumming her fingernails over a heading chart. "Finish what you were saying. Lightning Jack runs this steamer. What about you?"

He nodded toward the biscuit tin. She grudgingly ate another one and washed it down with a swallow of cider.

"I used to be a fisherman out of Isle Royale. Do you know it?"

"I've seen it in my fa— on a map of the Great Lakes. I used to imagine that Lake Superior formed the profile of a giant dragon's head, and that Isle Royale was the eye."

"I operate a trading post on the island," he said. "Or I did, until recently." After the tragedy, he had pulled a mantle of stoicism around himself, tending to his business with precision but not passion, spending hours simply sitting in a fishing boat, unable to think of a single good reason to row back to shore. Then, when the wire had come from the insurance company, absolving Sinclair's company of any responsibility, rage had taken the place of inert pain. The injustice had planted the need for revenge in Tom's mind. He had begun to see it as his only chance to live with himself after losing Asa.

"So you claim my father committed murder," she said. "On Isle Royale." Before he could speak, she said, "That wasn't a question. I'm merely summarizing."

"It's not my claim," he corrected her. "It's a fact."

"Then present the facts to the proper authorities and let the law take its course," she said reasonably. "But you won't do that, will you? Because you know my father has never been to Isle Royale. He didn't murder anyone.'' She was staring at him with those blue eyes again, those strange mirrors that reflected things he didn't want to see.

She was smarter than he had expected her to be. Tom suspected it would not surprise her to learn that indeed the insurance board had ruled that the seven deaths were caused by an accident. Nor would it surprise her, he thought cynically, to discover that the ruling commissioner's pockets had been generously lined by Sinclair's cash.

"How did the victims die?" She daintily touched her lips.

He knew she was looking around for a napkin, but he couldn't offer her something he didn't have. "A mining explosion."

She shut her eyes briefly and pursed her lips, looking hurt, looking as if she cared. But he knew better than that. All she cared about was getting off this boat.

"It sounds like a tragic accident, but not murder," she concluded, opening her eyes. "My father has a lot of enemies. They make a lot of wild accusations. But that is no excuse for what you're doing." Idly stroking the fur of the dog, she added, "This isn't the first time I've been kidnaped, you know."

That jolted him. "It's not?"

"When I was much younger, a war veteran snatched me from Lincoln Park, where I was picnicking with my governess." She helped herself to a biscuit, as if she had forgotten her hunger strike. "He got as far as the Michigan Southern railroad yards and didn't even have a chance to make his ransom demand before my father's hired Pinkerton agents seized him."

"You never found out what he wanted?"

"He claimed my father was guilty of profiteering during the war."

"He was probably right."

"The soldier was insane. He had lost his mind, probably from the things he had seen in battle." She blinked slowly, and he couldn't help but notice the lavish sweep of her eyelashes. "I understand he was hanged for his troubles."

"Because he was stupid enough to get caught."

"I recall thinking he was rather…sad. Just what is it you expect from my father?" she inquired.

He sat silent and impassive.

"Oh, very well," she said, mistaking his hesitation. She ate yet another biscuit, then took another swig of apple cider. "What will you demand?"

"Restitution for the families he destroyed. Admission of his own guilt and the liability of his mining company."

"That's absurd," she said. "Even my father can't magically sweep away a tragic accident. And if he could, he wouldn't bargain with the likes of you."

"Not even for the life of his own daughter?" Tom shot back.

She crunched down another biscuit and took another drink, swallowing nervously. "Is that what Lightning Jack will send in over the wire?"

"You'd best hope you mean more to him than his precious fortune."

Suddenly she looked very small and vulnerable to him. She pulled in her shoulders and ducked her chin, as if avoiding a sudden storm. A peculiar melancholy darkened her eyes, made her cross her arms defensively. While they were talking, he had nearly forgotten she was just a little twig of a woman.

"What?" he demanded, angry at the way she discomfited him. "Do you think he would ignore the danger you're in because it's too costly?"

She didn't answer right away. The dog wriggled down from her lap and nosed the door open, letting itself out on deck. "I've never sent a wire," she said softly, as if speaking to herself. "Is it true you have to dictate the text to the clerk? If that is the case, wouldn't the clerk get a little suspicious about a ransom demand?"

"Jack knows what he's doing."

"Ah. An experienced kidnaper, then. And tell me, how will my mother's jewelry and a lock of hair travel over the wire?"

"That'll be posted by mail packet. When he gets it, he'll know we mean business." He glowered at her, trying to pull his mind away from the idea that her mother had died. "You'd just better hope your father can be found."

"The city has burned to ashes," she snapped. "I suspect not even the White Stockings stadium can be found, Mr. Silver, much less one man out of thousands of homeless. This is the most foolish of adventures. If you had the tiniest bit of sense, you would simply put me ashore and let me take the train back to Chicago. I could convince my father to forget the entire incident, and we could all go on with our lives."

He had a sudden memory of the slender, handsome man in the hack on Lakeshore Drive. Philip Ascot, her beloved publishing heir. If there was no response from Sinclair, they would try to contact Ascot, Tom decided. Though why a fellow would want to marry this skinny, stubborn, yellow-haired woman was beyond him.

"How is it that you use words like debutante and induce?" she asked suddenly, out of the blue. When he glared at her, she flushed and bit into a biscuit. "I mean, I imagine Isle Royale is a wild and unsettled land. Yet you have a curiously refined way of speaking."

"We troglodytes tend to hole up in the winter when the lake freezes over," he said. "There's plenty of time for reading and study." He suspected she'd be surprised to learn that he had studied with a church scholar, spoke three languages—English, French and Chippewa—and that late at night, by the light of a kerosene lantern, he was reading Darwin's *Origin of Species.*

"Then you should be well-versed enough in logic and law to know that your mad scheme will never work. It won't bring back the people who died. Please," she said. "Let me go, and you can get on with your life."

The trouble with going on with his life was that he didn't want to. Asa's death had left a dark and gaping hole in the middle of him that sucked in everything light and good, everything that used to give Tom joy and fulfillment.

He swore, noting that the word brought a blush to Deborah's cheeks, and left the pilothouse, thumping up on the top deck to do some chores. As he cleaned the engine housing, her words hammered at him. *Let me go. Your mad scheme will never work. It won't bring back the people who died.*

He knew that. Damn it, he knew that. But he hungered for justice. He couldn't abide the outcome of the hearings. Like a fool, he had thought the disaster claims adjusters would tell the truth, but they'd ruled the way they were paid to—in favor of Arthur Sinclair.

But that was before Deborah. She was a hell of a bargaining chip. Merely killing Sinclair would have been a mercy too great for the bastard. By kidnaping Deborah, Tom had taken from him the one thing his money could not replace.

One look at Jack's face told Tom the news. "No response from Chicago?"

"The news is bad. The fires burned for days, and the city is...gone. Simply gone. All but the West Side north of Fullerton Avenue." Lightning Jack climbed aboard. Smokey, who had taken a liking to him, leaped and yapped in greeting. *"Alors, doucement,"* Jack grumbled good-naturedly. "*Doucement, mon chou-chou.* Gently, now."

"What about the parcel?"

"I sent it on the packet. It will be held at the telegraph office until he claims it," Jack said. "That means we will not have a reply any time soon."

Tom took a grim satisfaction in imagining Sinclair opening the parcel to find his daughter's necklace and a lock of her hair. He wondered if he should have forced her to write a plea in her own hand. No, the lock of hair was enough. That pale blond silk was something rare indeed.

Jack unloaded the supplies he had taken on in Milwaukee. Food and drink, candles and kerosene, a load of wood and a mysterious cloth-wrapped bundle. "Some things for the girl," he explained, catching Tom's look. "She has been uncomfortable."

"Hell's bells," Tom said. "We're not taking her on a pleasure cruise, Lightning. She's a hostage."

"I have been wondering about that. Can she be a hostage if her father doesn't know we're holding her for ransom?"

"If he gets the wire you sent, followed by the package, he'll know."

"I heard rumors while I was ashore. Chicago is not the only place that burned Sunday night," he said. His hand made a swift and superstitious sign of the cross to protect himself from evil. Like his father before him, Jack believed in omens and portents, and in the basic malevolence of the universe.

"There were other fires?" Tom asked.

"Peshtigo, Wisconsin, burned—a lumber town. Hundreds, maybe thousands died there. The same happened somewhere in Michigan. All Milwaukee is talking about the night it rained fire. There are men wearing sandwich boards proclaiming it's the end of the world, and who are we to say they are wrong?''

Tom gestured out across the broad gray waters of the lake. ''We're still here. The world's still here.''

''Perhaps this is all that's left.''

Tom was in no mood for philosophizing. ''So where did you send the wire?'' he asked.

''A notice will be placed in the *Tribune,* which has already begun running a list of advertisements to reunite families separated in the fire. I paid extra for notices in the *Times* and the *Journal* as well. You would be proud of my wording, *mon gars.* I said 'In the matter of his daughter Deborah, Mr. Arthur Sinclair is urged to retrieve an important message from the central telegraph office.'''

Tom nodded. ''So we wait here?''

''I cannot. I must get back to the island for the last shipment of the season. The people there are depending on me.'' He pursed his lips, thinking hard. ''My friend, I think you are making a mistake,'' he said quietly.

''What?''

''I think it is best for all if you take the woman ashore and put her on a train.''

''Jesus, Lightning, I thought you were with me on this. We've taken the richest girl in Chicago, and you want to simply send her packing?''

''She is more trouble than she's worth anyway.''

''Then you haven't done the calculations, my friend,'' Tom said, hardening his heart. ''She won't say, but I think she's his only child. She's worth—literally—a king's ransom.''

''So does it all come down to money?'' Lightning Jack asked, his voice low but sharp as a blade.

''This isn't about money,'' Tom snapped. ''It's never been about money. But I know how to grab an opportunity when I find one. We went all the way to Chicago to find Arthur Sinclair. The perfect instrument has been dropped into our laps. She's a valuable commodity. He'll sacrifice anything to get her back.'' Tom paced the deck in agitation. ''When you take a man's life, he suffers but once. When you take the thing that he loves, he suffers every moment he is without her.'' Tom knew too well the truth of it.

''How do you know he loves his daughter?''

''If he didn't, he would have ditched her long ago. She's the most annoying female I've ever met.''

Lightning Jack subjected him to a long study. Under the streak of white, one eyebrow lifted in speculation. ''Is she, now?''

''I'm surprised you didn't notice.''

''So.'' He shaded his eyes and looked toward the north. It was a rare, clear autumn day, perfect sailing weather. In the distance, the bridge over the river rotated, letting out a schooner and a brig. Jack snapped his fingers. ''We compromise. You stay with her here in Milwaukee.''

The thought of looking after Deborah Sinclair on his own made Tom's stomach churn, and he shook his head in vigorous denial. He had no doubt Lightning Jack could navigate the shoals around the peninsula and get himself through the Soo Locks on his own. Jack had been making the voyage for years, but he was no longer a young man, and the trip was grueling.

''I can't stay, either.'' Only a short while ago, he would have added that he had to get back to Asa, that Asa was depending on him. Now he had nothing. Nobody. No reason to hurry back to the island, to reopen his business and get on with things. But the idea of staying in a strange city with the likes of Deborah Sinclair made him sweat. ''We'll take the girl to Isle Royale. It fits, Lightning. We'll make Sinclair fetch her from the island.''

''He has never seen the island,'' Lightning Jack mused. ''Perhaps you are on to something. But the girl.'' He puffed out his cheeks. "It would be like taking a kitten into the jungle."

Tom remembered what she was like when she got her back up. "She'll survive."

He looked toward the bow, where Deborah Sinclair sat wrapped in a plaid blanket, catching the weak autumn sun on her shoulders as she read from a battered copy of *Gulliver's Travels* that she had found in one of the bunks. The wind off the lake toyed with her hair, lifting the long, golden strands to the light. Watching her, he felt an odd twist of sensation deep in his gut.

He dismissed the feeling as suspicion. She had been watching the harbor. They lay to a good distance offshore, but she'd already made one stupid escape attempt, and she might try another.

A brisk wind brought the schooner and the brig out quickly into the main channel. The vessels plowed over the iron-gray swells. In the bow of the trawler, shielded from the wind, Deborah Sinclair paid no heed to anything but the book she was reading. A haunting melancholy seemed to hover over her like a chill mist.

The trouble with holding her hostage, Tom decided, was that he had to witness her suffering. And she was not the enemy. Yet it was Deborah and her lonely isolation he would have to face, day after day. He steeled himself. This was for Asa. Asa and the other families Sinclair had destroyed. No going soft now.

Lightning Jack seemed to read Tom's mind. "She is completely harmless, eh? She is without guile. Exactly as—" He stopped himself, but not before Tom understood.

"Ah. Now I see where you're going." The black emptiness ached inside Tom each time he thought of the boy he had lost. "You've convinced yourself that she's as sinless as Asa was. But you're wrong."

"How do you know that?"

"She's a goddamned female, and a Sinclair to boot. What more must I say?" Tom made a fist. "You mark my words. She'll betray us at first opportunity."

"And if you are wrong?" asked Lightning Jack.

"If I'm wrong, we can put her ashore at Sault Sainte Marie."

Tom offered the compromise only because he knew he was right about the frail blond woman who was his hostage. Despite the fragile innocence in her eyes, she was far from harmless.

Nine

Deborah scarcely dared to breathe as she slowly drew out the box of matches. She could feel Tom Silver's gaze studying her from the opposite end of the steamer, and she prayed he had been fooled by her innocent pose at the bow.

"Don't you say a word," she warned Smokey, who lay curled on a coil of rope nearby. "You spoiled my other chance to get away, and I won't have you spoiling this one."

The dog yawned and rested its chin in its paws.

She tugged the thick Tattersall blanket more snugly around her, but opened it in the front to make a wind break for lighting the matches. She shifted her gaze to the east, where the steeples, grain elevators and smokestacks of Milwaukee pierced the sky. Only last summer, she'd passed by this city on her father's yacht. It was a major port on the lake, and it had a railway station—her best chance of escape.

Last time she had seen this view from the lake, escape had been the furthest thing from her mind. Aboard the steamer yacht *Triumph,* she had basked like a well-fed cat in Philip's attention and her father's approval. Lucy and Phoebe had been aboard for the cruise, and she remembered thinking how perfect everything was. This past August, she had been cheerfully oblivious to any cruelty or hardship. She'd had no idea people like Tom Silver and Lightning Jack existed. When she ate grilled whitefish for luncheon, it never occurred to her to wonder where the fish had come from, who had caught and cleaned it, and what his life was like.

In just a few short days, she had discovered that perhaps the world was not the charmed and golden place she'd always experienced. She was coming to know a new side of herself, a side that had not been honed and buffed to a high sheen by the masters and mistresses at finishing school. She was learning that she had a number of less-than-admirable qualities and a capacity for deceit.

On the deck in front of her, concealed by the plaid wool blanket, lay three signal flares. She had stolen them from beneath a storage bench the night before and had been waiting for her chance ever since. With two boats clearing the harbor, the moment had arrived. When they saw a distress signal, they would assume the trawler was sinking, and they'd come to the rescue. Maritime law compelled them to respond.

Deborah would call out to the passing ships, and if she was very lucky, a shore patrol might even spot the flare and come to investigate. She had her eye on a mildewed life ring secured to the side of the trawler. If necessary, she would dive into the icy water of Lake Michigan. Never mind that her last attempt had been a disaster. She had very recently realized that some things were more treacherous than drowning.

In the afternoon sun, the hull of the distant schooner shone with a promising glitter, as if the vessel had been careened and recently painted. It sailed about a quarter mile to the south, close enough to respond quickly once she ignited the flare.

Deborah took a deep breath. It was time.

She glanced over her shoulder, noting that Tom Silver

seemed busy at the wheelhouse. Lightning Jack had gone below and the dog slept peacefully in the autumn sun.

Slowly she positioned the flare between her feet to hold it steady while she lit the match. The breeze plucked at the blanket. The match ignited with a sibilant hiss, then immediately died in the breath of the wind.

Her hand shook as she struck a second match, inhaling the noxious sulfurous smell. She gritted her teeth and cupped her palm around the burning tip of the match. This time, she leaned in close to protect the fragile flame and touched it to the fusee of the flare. The tiny, weak flame wobbled and went out.

Heart pounding, she tried a third time. She prayed incoherently under her breath.

The fusee smoldered, then caught with a small burst of sparks. Disturbed from a sound sleep, Smokey leaped to his feet and started yapping.

"Thank God," she whispered, grasping the flare, standing up and waving it in an arc over her head. Stinging sparks rained on her hand and head. With more power than she knew she possessed, she launched the fusee high into the air. With an ear-splitting hiss, the missile ascended into the sky, emitting a cloud of green smoke in its wake.

Deborah held her breath, hands trembling as she hastened to light another flare. She could not trust that one alone would attract the attention she needed. The second fusee wouldn't light, but she kept trying. *Oh, please,* she prayed silently. *Please get me away from these madmen.*

Heavy footsteps thudded toward her. Based on all that had befallen her since Saturday night, the sound of a man's hurried tread should cause her to shrink in terror. Yet the exhilaration building in her chest left no room for fear. For once in her life she was thinking for herself, acting on her own behalf. It was heady stuff for a woman who had been taught from the cradle to be a doll-like ornament capable only of following orders.

When she saw the expression of rage on his face as Tom Silver approached, she dropped the blanket and ran to the rail of the ship's pulpit. "Help!" she yelled, waving her arms at the schooner. The small gray dog kept barking and trotting back and forth at the rail. Panic and desperation pounded through her like a sudden sickness. "Help!" she called again.

The great sails of the schooner jibed in response to a shift in course. The wind filled the pale canvas, and in a few moments the sailboat was headed toward the trawler. Deborah gripped the wires of the pulpit, threw back her head and shouted with triumph. Her flare had captured their attention. She waved her arms faster, hoping they would read urgency in her gesture.

Tom Silver took hold of her wrists, gripping them hard.

"Let go of me," she said, trying to wrench herself away. "Don't touch me."

"Then quit waving your arms like a crazy woman," he replied.

"I'll quit if you let go."

"Fine."

As soon as he let loose of her hands, she started flailing again, but one look from Silver stilled her efforts. She tried another tack, reaching for the life ring. Instantly he plucked it from her hands and threw it into the cockpit beyond her reach.

"You don't really want to go into the lake again," he explained calmly. Then he spoke no more. His silence disconcerted her, for she expected him to yell at her as was his custom. Instead, he simply stood beside her, watching the schooner draw closer, until it lay within shouting distance.

Deborah drew breath to begin yelling for help. Tom Silver leaned down to ask her, "Do you really want me to shut you up?"

Lightning Jack came up through a hatch. He sat in the

cockpit like a spectator at a sporting match, watching the action.

She clamped her mouth shut, growing more and more discomfited as she waited to be rescued from the man who stood close beside her. She always had the most uncanny sense of him when he was near. He smelled of the wind and the forest, and his hulking form gave her the sensation of standing in the shadow of a rather large tree.

She flicked a nervous glance at him. "Why aren't you yelling at me?"

He kept his gaze on the schooner. "There's no need." His voice was quiet and controlled.

"Well, you can't blame me, can you?" she said indignantly. "Isn't it a rule of war that a prisoner is obligated to try to escape?"

"Is that what this is? A war?"

On the schooner across the churning water, a figure on deck lifted a bullhorn to his mouth. "Ahoy! Are you in distress, then?" he called, the sound faint in the wind.

"Help!" Deborah shrieked, jumping up and down. "I'm being held prisoner!"

A strong arm slipped around her waist, hugging her in against the long, hard length of Tom Silver. It was not a cruel touch, but felt somehow commanding. "Shut up," he said simply. "I warned you—"

Panic exploded in her head, and for a moment she couldn't breathe. "Help!" she choked out, clawing at his big hand.

"The flare, it was an accident." Lightning Jack's deep shout sang across the swells. "Begging your pardon. Please disregard."

Deborah forced down the panic. She was trapped, yes, but she wasn't helpless. Success depended on staying calm. "Please," she yelled again. "Don't listen to him. I—"

"I said," Tom Silver cut in, "shut up."

She gathered all the courage she could muster from the scant supply inside her. "I'll do nothing of the sort."

"Fine." He moved so swiftly and with such boldness that she had no idea what was happening until he took her face between his hands and covered her mouth with his.

He tasted different from Philip. He tasted like nothing she had ever imagined. For a moment, that was her only coherent thought.

Though Tom Silver's lips were curiously soft, his embrace held her immobile, imprisoned, helpless as a rabbit in a steel trap. The panic in Deborah's chest hammered its way outward, telegraphing alarm along her limbs, radiating terror to every nerve ending.

She made a sound of protest against his mouth, trying in vain to twist away from him. She beat her fists on his arms, and the bulging muscles there tightened to iron-hard masses. She pushed against his chest, but felt only an unyielding wall. Faintly, somewhere in the realm outside of her panic, she heard Lightning Jack's call to the schooner. "Ah, *l'amour*," he said good-naturedly. "You see, we celebrate young love!"

The skipper of the schooner called something that sounded less than celebratory. Deborah could scarcely breathe as she made a sobbing, frantic sound in her throat.

"You can let her go now," Lightning Jack called. "The schooner, she is turning her tack."

Tom Silver let go instantly. His surrender of her was so quick that she stumbled back and had to grasp the pulpit rail to keep from falling. He didn't seem to notice that his brutal embrace had nearly made her swoon with horror. He dismissed her as if she were an undersized trout, thrown back into the lake.

She sagged against the rail, waiting for her racing heart to slow and her breath to catch. Then, giving herself no time to be afraid, she hiked one leg, then the other over the rail. The brisk wind blew her skirts. The wire of the rail pressed against the backs of her knees. She tried not to remember how cold the water was, tried not to recall the horrible suffocating sensation of drowning.

Then she let go.

Two huge hands grabbed her by the arms, then went around her waist. Tom Silver dragged her up and over the rail. Without a word, he pulled her along the narrow walkway toward the stern. She dug in her heels and stopped. As mechanical as a locomotive, he swung her up and over his shoulder. Breathless, furious, she was whisked past Lightning Jack, seeing from her upside down perspective a mixture of surprise and concern on his face, and past Smokey, who yapped and followed them down to her tiny chamber.

Tom Silver shoved her facedown on the bunk.

Something in Deborah snapped, unleashing fury. She twisted onto her back, bringing her knee up, slamming it into his groin. He let out a bellow of pain and doubled over. She seized the moment to scramble off the bunk and head for the door. Before he could even straighten fully, his big arm reached out and grabbed her. His face was pale and wet with sweat, contorted by pain. She felt no remorse whatsoever. Who would have thought that a man the size of an ox could have such a vulnerable spot? She must remember that for the future.

Breathing laboriously through his nostrils, he seemed to find his bearings once again. He shoved her back on the bed, driving the breath from her lungs. She spat in his face, arched her back and kicked wildly, and would have scratched his eyes out if she could have reached them. Lord, it felt good to fight like a madwoman. With this insane battle, she shed the last of the polite self-control that had governed every breath she had ever taken.

Tom Silver captured her wrists and pinioned them neatly in one hand above her head. His scent of lake water and sweat swept over her. Something about the pose awakened a deep, horrified fascination inside her. She felt both drawn to him and repelled by him.

His manner was far less equivocal—crude, matter-of-fact. He treated her not as if he disliked her, but as if he simply didn't care.

Turning her and pushing his knee into her back, he bound her hands behind her. "Damn. You have more gumption than I gave you credit for. Who taught you to fight like that?"

"Let me go, you hideous insufferable lout," she said. Speaking her mind felt good, too, she realized with a touch of wonder. "Get away from me."

"Gladly. But first..." He reached into his back pocket.

She screamed, suddenly panicked by the feeling of immobility. In a minute he'd be shoving himself at her.

A folded cloth covered her mouth. He tied the bandana snugly behind her head. Finally, he attached the cord from her hands to her ankles so that she lay completely helpless on the bed. Tears scalded her eyes, but she refused to shed them. Enough of weakness and weeping. They were no help at all in a situation like this.

Tom Silver clearly didn't give a damn whether she cried or not. He stood back, regarding her with an impassive expression. "I would have let you go today," he said in a conversational tone. "Lightning Jack and I were discussing it."

Liar, she thought. *You're only saying that to torture me.*

"Yep. Our agreement was that if you behaved yourself, we'd call it quits."

Liar. If that was the case, you would have told me.

"Maybe you'd be on a train tonight if you hadn't set off that flare and tried to jump overboard. You'll never know. But you taught me something, Princess. You are your father's daughter."

The brute didn't know it yet, but today he had banished all thoughts of jumping into the frigid water from her head. She no longer wanted to die. She wanted to live, and make his life hell.

Tom couldn't understand why he kept thinking about the woman in the cramped quarters below. He had never been bothered by much of a conscience. It had been the only way of surviving the war without going completely mad. Yet battling his way through the fire, and then taking Deborah Sinclair hostage, had left a bad taste in his mouth. Something inside him had awakened. Something dark and disturbing, out of control.

The sound of the flare going off, and the arc of light overhead, had brought forth remembrances he'd thought long buried. For a brief, horrifying moment he was back on the battlefield at Kenaha Falls, racing hell-for-leather on the back of a sweating mare while Reb missiles streaked past him and bullets plowed up the turf and ripped the leaves from the trees.

It was a day he had not thought of in years. Yet Deborah Sinclair's act of desperation had reminded him. He wasn't sure why. Perhaps it was that flare against the bright sky. But more likely, a deeper spark was ignited by her unpredictability combined with her will to live, to survive. She made him remember the impulsive youth he'd been when he had first enlisted. Having been raised by Lightning Jack in the north woods, Tom had known nothing of soldiering. But he was young enough, bored enough and ignorant enough to plunge himself into danger. Impatient with the endless drills of the enlisted men, he had eagerly volunteered to ride courier for General Thaddeus Whitcomb. The old man had rubbed his sidewhiskers thoughtfully while studying the skinny sixteen-year-old. Then he'd said, "If you're stupid enough to volunteer, then I'm smart enough to use you where I need you."

His missions became one reckless dash after another, galloping underfed army issue mares into the ground, riding across unknown terrain in the dark of night or in the smoke of battle, never knowing when a shell or bullet would strike. He sensed that same unpredictability and volatility in Deborah Sinclair. Now, a distance of ten years from his own youth, he understood that recklessness was not the same as courage.

He steered clear of his hostage after the Milwaukee incident, sending Lightning Jack down to release her from her bindings as soon as they were well away from the city. The next leg of the voyage, to the narrow Straits of Mackinac and through the locks at Sault Sainte Marie, promised to be long and uneventful. He planned to avail himself of the telegraph station there, but he had little hope of a response from Arthur Sinclair. According to the accounts he had read in the Milwaukee *Sentinel,* the city of Chicago was in chaos. He would simply have to stick with his plans to drag the woman to Isle Royale and wait for Sinclair to come. Let him claim his daughter on the same bloody ground where his negligence had claimed seven lives.

Yet none of these thoughts brought Tom the heat of vindication. He craved the clean feeling of justice done, but each time he thought of the woman, guilt nagged at him. True, she was treacherous. She was her father's daughter. She would as soon stab him in the back as knee him in the groin.

But when he had held her in his arms, something swift and intense had passed between them. It was more than an embrace and a kiss designed to keep her from shrieking bloody murder to passing ships. He had dreamed afterward of her taste and the softness of her body pressed to his. Try as he might, he could not deny the elemental pleasure of holding her in his arms. Her delicacy. The scent of her. The pressure of her small hands pushing at him, her soft mouth protesting his kiss. She made him feel both excited and brutal at the same time.

She had not reacted as an ordinary woman should have.

She had neither surrendered helplessly nor drawn back and slapped him in righteous outrage. Instead, she had gone into a panic, beating at him, her fists raining blows at his chest. Her frantic response confused him. He knew damned well he was a man of few refinements, but he'd always thought kissing a woman to be one of his particular skills.

Of course, before today, he had never attempted to kiss the likes of Miss Deborah Sinclair.

Ten

No amount of threatening, weeping and pleading moved Tom Silver to set Deborah ashore at any point during the long, frightening voyage, though she tried her best. Once they had left Milwaukee harbor, he had given her the run of the ship, knowing full well that escape was impossible. And guessing—correctly—that she was too cowardly for suicide. Surrounded by nothing but water and fog, the *Suzette* steamed into a wilderness so thick and mysterious that they encountered no other boat for days.

The incident in Milwaukee had changed things between them—for the worse. Deborah didn't regret for a moment setting off the distress flare, but she should have been prepared for Tom Silver's immovable wrath, and for the cold fury he awakened in her.

It was strange, though. Even the most egregious captive state, bound and gagged upon her damp bunk, felt eerily familiar to her. With nothing to do but lie there and think of things, she had reflected that captivity took many different forms. A woman under the domination of her father or husband was as much a prisoner as a hostage on a boat. She had merely traded one form of servitude for another.

Lucy Hathaway, her best friend, would have applauded the radical thoughts that passed through Deborah's mind. She would have urged Deborah to act on them, proclaiming her independence from all forms of bondage. Ordinarily, Deborah did not trouble herself with social justice, having been taught at an early age that her opinion didn't matter. But being trapped on this steamship liberated her mind and unleashed a vibrant anger. Or maybe it was having to live in close quarters with an aggravating, bullheaded clod like Silver.

She neatened the tiny quarters, creating a space for herself, and spent the days reading—Silver and Lightning Jack kept a surprisingly extensive library aboard—and staring out at the fog, plotting escape attempts. Lightning Jack had bought her a sewing basket, a comb and some hairpins in Milwaukee. Sometimes she would sit and comb idly through her hair, thinking how foolish it was to have a maid perform such a simple task. And yet all her life, someone else had washed her hair and combed it. Someone else had mended the hems and tears in her gowns. She wondered what Kathleen O'Leary, her maid, thought about as she did Deborah's hair. Did she think Deborah was as mindless as a dressmaker's dummy? Did she resent spending her time fixing someone else's hair?

Silver ignored Deborah, even when she stared directly at him. This was something she caught herself doing far too often. She'd watch his big, rough, hardworking hands and remember what his embrace had felt like. She'd study his mouth, think about the way he had tasted and relive the explosion of panic his kiss had ignited. When it came to his touch, she felt a nearly insane desire to fight back.

On a leaden gray morning, the *Suzette* churned past a series of channel markers, and the blast of foghorns filled the air. Deborah went out on deck to see what was happening, and she encountered an unsmiling Tom Silver.

"We're coming up on the Sault Sainte Marie," he said. "Go below and wait until we get through."

"I prefer to stay on deck and watch." She walked to the forward rail and craned her neck to look ahead as the ghostly images through the fog resolved themselves into a churning waterway. The rapids between Lake Huron and Lake Superior formed a strange, watery hill marking the difference in depth between the two lakes. The current boiled and surged, tossing the steamer up and down like a cork. The sudden violent motion hurled Deborah forward against the gunwale.

She heard herself cry out. A fragmented whirl of hissing water, leaden sky and thick forest sped past. The small dog exploded into a barking frenzy. Her arms flailed and she grabbed a stay wire. Unable to support her weight, the wire gave way, strand by slender strand. She screamed, dangling helplessly over the icy water. Then she felt a jerk and heard a tearing sound. Something broke her fall before she went into the rapids.

"Woman, you just can't stay out of the water, can you?" Tom Silver said through gritted teeth. "I ought to let you drown."

"Reel her in, *mon gars,*" called Lightning Jack in an amused voice. "That is the best catch you've had in days."

In mere seconds, Tom Silver had dragged her back over the side. She slammed against him as her feet hit the deck, and at first she was too shocked to be alarmed. But then the warmth of him, his sheer size and his smell of lake wind and wood smoke overwhelmed her. She inched away. "Thank you—" She bit off the rest. The oaf had only rescued her because he wanted the ransom.

"I ordered you to go below," he snapped.

"I want to watch," she insisted.

"I can't stand around playing nursemaid to you when there's work to do." He grabbed her arm, and she immediately grabbed it back.

"Tom, I need your help here," Lightning Jack called from the pilothouse. "The rapids, they begin just ahead."

Deborah frowned dubiously at the marbled swirls of water below the bar. "You mean we aren't in the rapids yet?"

"Hardly."

A thrill shivered through her. "I'm staying on deck," she said.

Something in her expression made him stare at her keenly for a moment. Perhaps a twitch of amusement lifted his mouth. "Stay away from the side and hang on, because you're in for a hell of a ride," he said gruffly. He grabbed her hand and clamped it around the wheelhouse ladder. "If you go over again, I won't be around to save you."

She forgot to be alarmed by his touch. "Fine," she said. "I'll look after myself."

"You can stay above until we get to the canal," he said and went off to work the trawler with Lightning Jack. Deborah turned her attention to the scene that lay before her. Every once in a while Jack would call out, explaining the sights as if she were a guest on a pleasure cruise.

Peering through a long brass spyglass, she watched two-man canoes navigating the shoals, one man steering with a pique-de-fond and another dipping netfuls of fish out of the lake. A few skeletal drying frames, draped with cedar strips and whitefish, lined the shore. The Indians and settlers tending smoldering fires paid little heed to passing canoes and ship traffic. Larger vessels used seines and gill nets to lay in huge quantities of whitefish. "My stock in trade," Lightning Jack sang out expansively, weighing out coins to pay the toll at the locks. "The fish, they are more precious to me than gold."

Before the canal had been dug, he told her between Gallic curses as he wrestled with the wheel, everything had to be portaged from one side of the Sault to the other in order to avoid being caught in the dangerous cascades, spilling like a wall of glass between the two giant lakes. Through the spyglass, she made out the stately Stone House Hotel on the Canadian side in the distance.

She wrapped one arm around the ladder and gazed with yearning at the lovely, civilized-looking place. She dreamed of a luxurious long bath and fresh clothes, a spacious bed for the night. And more importantly, freedom from the brute who held her captive. But it might as well be as distant as the clouds, with the savage waters stretching endlessly to shore. She saw docks and storehouses, blockhouses and friendly dwellings with smoke puffing from their chimneys. The sight of civilization and humanity filled her with hope. She tried feverishly to think of a way to escape. They had hidden the remaining flares from her, and the torrent of water was too loud for anyone to hear her cry out.

''You've seen what there is to see,'' Silver said as if he had read her mind. ''Get below. Or do you want me to drag you?''

She shot him a poisonous look. But she knew she was defeated—for the time being. With as much dignity as she could muster, she went to her bunk. She heard it latch from the outside. Using the side of her fist, she cleared the fog from the small portal and looked out at the busy waterway. It took all day to navigate the crowded, log-lined canal. She heard the shouts and whistles of the drover to the team of oxen, and felt a dizzying lurch when the water level changed through the locks.

It occurred to her that she was having an adventure. Deborah had never had an adventure before unless she counted meeting President Grant on her eighteenth birthday. This was a true, honest to goodness adventure, complete with unscrupulous villains, physical danger, wild places. If it wasn't all so hideously frightening it might be fun. Something to tell her friends when she got home. But the way things were going, home grew more distant with each passing moment.

Finally they moored somewhere above the rapids, in a secluded spot a good mile offshore.

In the early evening Tom Silver came into her tiny chamber, Smokey the dog tucked under one arm. He always carried the dog as if it were a heap of dirty laundry.

He set it down, and it scrambled up on the bunk with her. Then he turned to leave.

"Where are you going?" Deborah asked. But she wasn't surprised when he didn't explain himself.

"I'm locking the door from the outside again."

She rushed for the exit. "No. Please, I swear I won't—"

The *thunk* of the bolt made her flinch. The bunk was too cramped to allow for pacing, so she sat on the narrow boxlike bed, drew her knees to her chest and idly stroked the dog's scruffy head. She had no candle or lamp, so she couldn't set the room on fire to attract attention. Besides, she might burn to death before help arrived. She could find nothing to use as a weapon to attack Tom Silver with when he returned. She tried calling out to Lightning Jack, who seemed a bit more softhearted than Silver, but he merely took out his harmonica and played a tune to drown out her yelling.

Frustrated, Deborah lay down on the bunk. It was too dark to read, so she stared at the wall and hated Tom Silver with every bit of her heart.

From the ruined black gash of Huron Avenue, Arthur Sinclair surveyed the blackened rubble that had been his home. The grounds, scorched and scarred, still exuded an acrid warmth, a deadly echo of the fire. The heat traveled up his legs, past his heart and through the top of his head. The trout pond had boiled away; the carriage house and all the outbuildings had disintegrated to blackened pits. Yellow-gray wisps of smoke rose from the charred skeleton of the house. But it wasn't a house anymore. It was a dead thing, empty, its insides seared away to nothing.

Since late Monday night, when a timely light rain had signaled the end of the great fire, his hired agents had fanned across the ruined city in search of his daughter.

Arthur had told them to begin with a search of the house and grounds. He had not allowed himself to think, to feel, as he made this request, for he knew what he was asking. The last he had seen of Deborah, she had raced out of the house while the burning roof collapsed over her head.

But no remains had been found. No sign of her. The assumption was that she had escaped the fire. But to where?

He picked his way through the broken remnants of the once-grand mansion. Hell of a thing, he thought, unable to decide how he felt about the loss. All the art and antiques, the fine things with which he had surrounded himself, had turned to ashes and embers.

Somewhere down the block, a woman began to keen with a thin, chilling wail of loss. Her grief sliced like a sword through the layers of fog that shrouded the avenue. He couldn't see her, but the sound she made cut into him, and his heart hurt with a cold fire.

The clop of hooves caught his attention, and he turned. Two men in long black coats approached him. The elder wore a full salt-and-pepper beard, the younger an eyepatch. Arthur had known Allan Pinkerton for years, ever since Pinkerton had made his name exposing counterfeiters for the sheriff of Cook County. Nowadays his detective agency guarded against train robberies, labor uprisings, bank jobs and any private matter that promised a reward. Arthur admired the way Allan worked. He was swift and sure—even when he was wrong.

"My operative, Price Foster," Pinkerton said in his rolling Scottish brogue. His gaze swept over the devastation. "You were hit hard, Mr. Sinclair. I'm sorry to see it. Right sorry indeed."

"It's my daughter, Deborah," he blurted out. "She is…gone."

Gone. He had turned the moment over and over in his mind until he could see it like a stereogram. The gunman bursting in. Deborah sweeping down, an unlikely aveng-

ing angel, crashing into the intruder. The thunder of gunshot.

It should have been so simple. The phaeton was waiting. He and Deborah should have driven away, leaving
the madman to burn with the Chippendale furniture.

Instead, something had gone wrong. She had lagged
behind, somehow got separated from him. The next thing
he knew, the whole of the alley had gone up in flames
and the horses had bolted. The carriage had clattered several blocks along Chicago Avenue before he'd brought
the horses under control. By then, the neighborhood was
a sea of flame, the way back to his house impassable.

He reported all this to Pinkerton in a flat, dispassionate
tone.

"So you last saw her in the alley. And the only other
witness was the looter."

Again that icy burn in his heart. He stared down at his
shoes. A fine gray dust powdered them, and the cuffs of
his trousers, settling in the creases. "He wasn't—" Sinclair stopped. How much to reveal? "He claimed he was
from up north. Isle Royale, in Lake Superior. I tried to
open a mine there last summer, but it ended in a mishap."

"A mishap."

"There was an explosion, ruled an accident. I think the
gunman—"

"He had a gun?"

"Seemed to be on a mission of revenge. There really
wasn't time—" He stopped again, appalled to hear a qua-
ver in his voice. "I want her found," he concluded. "Today."

"Sir, I'd like to make a note of her appearance," Price
Foster said, taking out a folded paper and the stub of a
pencil.

"I brought this down from the lake house." Arthur
handed him a small photograph of Deborah on a draped
stool, posing with an absurd porcelain pug dog. The
painter who had later rendered the image in oils had made

both the girl and the dog look real and natural. It struck Arthur that, in the photograph, Deborah looked as stiff and lifeless as the statue.

But there was no denying her beauty; he could see that by Foster's reaction to the picture. Everyone had that reaction to Deborah—a moment of intense, startled admiration, such as one might feel seeing the first rose of summer.

Arthur glossed over his last conversation with his daughter. There was no need to hash out their quarrel for this stranger. Despite the eyepatch, Price Foster had a keen way about him, as if he knew thoughts that weren't spoken. "Sometimes people who disappear," he said matter-of-factly, "don't want to be found."

"That's not the case this time," Arthur snapped. Yet still he was haunted by Deborah's unhappiness that night as she had begged him to let her break her engagement to Philip.

As Foster questioned him further, making notes, a coach lurched crookedly to a halt in front of the iron gates. Philip Ascot approached with long loose strides. He was impeccably dressed, not a fair hair out of place. It was as if the fire could not affect a person like him.

Arthur looked at this man and saw everything he wanted for his daughter—an aristocrat. An Old Settler gentleman to whom misfortune simply did not happen. Ascot had never known a day of want. Not the cramping hunger of an orphan picking through kitchen middens outside a rich man's house or the shriveling cold of a January night spent huddled in a woodshed. He didn't have that darkness, that blight on his soul that shadowed Arthur no matter how much money he spent gilding the past. With a man like Ascot, Deborah's days would be filled with light and frivolity, something Arthur could never give her. God Almighty. What was he going to say to Ascot?

"I saw her," Philip said. "I saw what happened."

As he explained the incident in Lincoln Park, the icy fire in Arthur's chest flared and burned with a forceful, steady ache.

Eleven

~~~~~~~~~~~~~~~~~~~~~~~~

The ancient timbers of the old fort rose in a picket line against the deepening amber sky. Hurrying along the plank boardwalk, Tom raised a hand now and then when he spied a familiar face. Since founding the trading post on Isle Royale, he had done a good bit of business at Sault Sainte Marie. It was a polyglot border town, bracketed by the red ensign of Canada, and the stars and stripes flying over Fort Brady. A traveler was likely to hear English, French, Chippewa or a patois of all three. The voyageurs and coureurs de bois were probably little different from the trappers who had founded the portage two centuries before. Clad in hide and fur, they sat in the dim, cramped tavern drinking toasts with big city businessmen from Milwaukee, Detroit, Duluth and Cleveland.

The whores were as friendly as ever, and Tom was no stranger to their plump, accommodating arms. This time, however, he passed them by with a wink and a wave. He paused to hand a few coppers to an old Indian holding out a trembling hand. The Chippewas had adjusted less readily to the rush of miners, lumbermen and fishermen through the Sault. Seining for fish in the rapids, gathering wild rice from the marshes and portaging furs around the rapids had suited them fine for untold centuries. Copious amounts of cheap whiskey did them far less good.

Martin Eagle had always preferred trading to drinking. Proprietor of the busy company store, he drove a hard bargain and had little truck with the men reeling and puking on the boardwalk outside. He greeted Tom with a cordial nod. "Headed back up to the island?" he asked.

Tom nodded. "I need a few things."

"Won't be long until ice-up," Eagle said as Tom set a large crate on the scarred wooden counter.

"That's a fact." He rattled off the usual list of provisions—flour, salt, coffee, beans and oil. Tom filled the crate with some fresh apples and a round of cheese. "I'll need some soap," he said to Martin Eagle. "And a razor and strop," he added, absently rubbing his rough cheek.

Eagle handed him a cake of oily lye soap wrapped in parchment. Tom hesitated, then handed it back. "Uh, do you have something that smells a little better?"

Eagle shrugged and tossed him a round cake that reeked of lilacs. "Nice Canadian lady makes that."

"These bed linens?" Tom asked, indicating a stack of folded fabric on a shelf.

"Yeah." The proprietor handed him a set. "Comes with a featherbed, too."

"A featherbed?"

"You know, like a mattress."

"An actual mattress," Tom muttered under his breath.

"What?"

"Nothing. I'll take the linens and the feather mattress."

While Eagle rolled out a length of newsprint for wrapping, Tom browsed the shop. "What's this?" he asked, handling a thin garment between his thumb and forefinger.

"Ladies' unmentionables," Eagle said. "Real batiste and lace."

"I'll take that, too."

Martin Eagle sent him a wink and a grin. "You laying in for a bride, Tom Silver?"

"Christ, no." Tom felt his neck and ears turn red. "Got

a passenger aboard the *Suzette*. Female passenger," he added. "Reckon I need some ready-to-wears."

Eagle's grin widened, showing teeth in varying degrees of decay. "Why the hell didn't you say so?" The diminutive man took a step back, crossing his arms and tucking his hands under them. "You have no idea how to provision for a woman, do you?"

Tom gestured at the crate. "Soap, linens, unmentionables. What else do I need?"

Eagle guffawed, then bolted into action, selecting gloves and a bonnet, ready-made plain dresses and fluffy white objects Tom could fathom no purpose for. "I don't need all that gear," he said. "It's only temporary."

"Perhaps so. But a woman's pride is forever." Martin Eagle took delight in provisioning Tom with dozens of ladylike objects.

Tom had no idea what most of the things were. Where he came from, the women made their own underthings and soap and such, and the men didn't hear a word about it. But Deborah Sinclair was different. High-strung, headstrong, skittish—qualities he couldn't stand in a woman.

At dawn the day after passing through the locks, the steamer set a course for the west. Deborah felt the engines churn to a high speed. Through a narrow louvered vent, she could sense a subtle difference in the wind and the current. The water, curiously enough, smelled different. Fresher, perhaps, with the green scent of the great pine forests riding the breeze. She had never been north of the locks, and she realized that this would be the strangest and wildest part of the voyage for her. Farther from home.

Thoughts of the strange and the wild seemed to summon Tom Silver. The dog growled malevolently at the intruder, then went scampering out of the room. She heard the tread of giant feet. She tensed up, feeling hideously vulnerable. Ignoring him, she stayed abed and kept her back turned. Her heart felt numb from the effort of hating him. She could hear him banging around, and curiosity burned inside her, but she refused to give him the satis-faction of turning to look. She made a game of trying to figure out what he was doing based on the noises he was making.

The metallic bump. The loud slosh of pouring water. The crackle of paper, as if a parcel were being unwrapped. More pouring water and, amazingly, the warm smell of steam. Was he making tea?

His harsh, impersonal hand poked at her shoulder. She forced herself not to flinch. "We're under way," was all he would tell her. Then he left the cabin, pulling the small door shut behind him.

Slowly, cautiously, Deborah rolled over. On the floor sat an oval-shaped hip bath of steaming water. Next to that lay a sea sponge, a square cake of surprisingly fra-grant soap and a towel. Amazed, she lifted a folded gar-ment to discover it was a set of fresh bed linens. Under that lay a huge, puffy featherbed. In another parcel she discovered a shift, a chemise and a blue wool dress. She also found thick woolen stockings, a nightgown and woolen underclothes. Things to wear in winter. Dear God. Was it possible she could be a prisoner that long?

A cold shudder seized her. She wondered if he was tidying her up for a reason. Maybe he intended to sell her, perhaps trade her to lake pirates or backwoodsmen. Her imagination ran wild, and she nearly resolved to stay un-kempt and dirty just to defy him.

Almost.

The hot bath beckoned her with wispy fingers of steam. Uttering a soft cry of gratitude, she stripped off her clothes and sank into the bath. The tub didn't allow for move-ment, but by crouching and ducking this way and that, she managed to clean her hair and every inch of her skin. A bath had never, ever felt so good. Not even in the huge marble tub in her father's mansion. Not even when she was attended by three maids. Here, all alone in this cramped shipboard bunk, she put her head back and felt the water trickle like silk over her throat. All the ash and grime of the fire flowed away, and she nearly laughed aloud with the sheer relief of being clean once again.

She stayed in the bath until the water grew tepid and Smokey scratched impatiently at the door. Wrapping herself in a towel, she picked up the clothes, turning each garment this way and that. The ready-made clothes were shapeless and lacking in any discernible style, but crisply clean. They were made of cotton or wool rather than silk or satin, but seemed serviceable enough. She put on each piece, grateful to discover that the fastenings of the chemise and shift were located in the front. Garments like this, she reflected, were designed for women who did not have maids to do them up in the back.

The wool dress, of a quaint print of small blue cornflowers, fit like a loose sack. She pushed back the sleeves, tugged the sash snugly around her and felt as fine as a princess. She did her hair as best she could, combing through the damp locks and pinning them back with the few celluloid pins Lightning Jack had given her.

When she stepped out of the chamber, Smokey yapped and pawed at her hem. She scooped up the little dog and brought him up on deck with her. "I imagine you don't even recognize me," she said with a chuckle. "I no longer smell like a burning city."

She found Lightning Jack in the galley stirring a pot of something bubbling and insanely fragrant.

"Ah. Luncheon is served," he said, ladling stew onto a tin plate.

Her eyes widened at the sight of fresh carrots, turnips and peas in the rich sauce. Her mouth watered when Jack sliced into a crusty golden brown loaf of bread.

"Oh, Mr. duBois, it's wonderful." She took a seat and gratefully sampled the stew.

"You seem much happier, mademoiselle."

"I'm not," she insisted. "Just more comfortable.

And...surprised.'' *I need a proper bath and a change of clothing and an actual mattress to sleep on....* Her own words echoed back at her. "I had no idea Tom Silver gave a fig for my comfort."

"It's to keep you from whining," Tom said, stepping into the galley. He sat down across from her and she did her best to ignore him, lending her full attention to the excellent chicken stew Jack had made.

But Tom Silver wasn't the sort of man she could ignore. It wasn't simply his large physical size but his presence that intruded into the very heart of the moment. And since he had grabbed her and kissed her, she had even more to think about. Like the shape of his lips and the disquieting feel of his arms around her. She set down her spoon. "I suppose you expect me to thank you."

"I expect you to shut up and eat," he said reasonably.

"Very well, then." She started eating again. It made her vaguely uncomfortable to feel beholden to this man. The situation demanded that she be at odds with him every moment. He was, after all, her captor.

He leaned back on the bench, stretching out his buckskin-clad arms in both directions. He moved, she observed, like a man who was entirely comfortable in his body. Not like the gentlemen she had known, who were always so stiff and starched in their bearing.

Not like Philip.

Her appetite suddenly gone, she pushed the dish away and automatically looked around for a napkin. There was none, of course, but a stack of folded papers.

Her eyes widened. "You have news of Chicago?" Without asking permission, she grabbed the paper and spread out the wrinkled pages.

"FIRE! Destruction of Chicago!" screamed the headline. It was the *Tribune,* emblazoned with shouters, illustrated by lithographs of fleeing victims and views of the city. The whole front section was devoted to the fire. Nearly a hundred thousand people had been burned out, and more than a hundred bodies had been pulled from the rubble. Reports of vigilante hangings littered the page.

Deborah was surprised to feel a lurch of fear in her chest. Vivid images of the fire burst to life in her mind, and she felt a delayed jolt of terror. She didn't remember being this fearful during the fire itself, but the news stories before her brought the impending danger back to life.

She moved on to the next paper and started reading an article by a Mr. Edgar of the *Chicago Evening Post.* He claimed the fire started in the slums— "'if those miserable alleys shall be dignified by being denominated streets,'" she read aloud. "'That neighborhood had always been a *terra incognita* to respectable Chicagoans—'" She stopped reading and looked up. "What an insufferable snob."

"Have *you* ever been to that neighborhood?" Lightning Jack asked.

"Certainly not. I— That's different," she insisted, taking up another newspaper. Amazingly enough, *The Evening-Journal Extra* had appeared only days after the fire. "'...caused by a cow kicking over a lamp in a stable in which a woman was milking,'" she read, her mouth twitching slightly with amusement. "Is this plausible?"

"You're the expert on the working classes," Silver commented sarcastically. He picked up the most recent *Times.* "They're all saying it. 'On the morning of the fire Mrs. O'Leary was found by a reporter for the *Times* sitting on the front steps of her own house. At first she refused to speak one word about the fire, but only screamed that her cow was gone and she had nothing left in the world.'" He chuckled. "I'm amazed she had front steps left, since her property was the first to burn."

Deborah felt a flicker of concern. "You say her name is Mrs. O'Leary?"

He scanned the column. "That's right. The *Extra* identifies her as Catherine O'Leary, wife of Patrick O'Leary, of 137 De Koven Street."

It couldn't be. But Deborah did not forget certain things. Like the fact that each Christmas, she ordered a generous basket to be delivered to Mr. and Mrs. O'Leary in De Koven Street. "Sweet heaven," she whispered.

He lifted an eyebrow. "Don't tell me they were friends of yours."

She disregarded his insulting skepticism. "Their daughter Kathleen is in my employ as a personal maid." She nervously curled the edge of the newspaper. "The whole city will be against them."

"I reckon so." He folded his large arms on the table. "Folks like to lay blame."

"The O'Learys are decent, hardworking people. Mrs. O'Leary goes out with her milk wagon to make deliveries before most people are awake. And Kathleen is much more to me than a maid. She is my friend." She fixed Tom Silver with a determined stare. "I absolutely have to get back to Chicago."

He laughed humorlessly. "Lady, you're in no position to be giving orders."

She tried to keep her anger in check. "The O'Learys could be dragged into public hearings or official inquiries. Possibly legal action. Kathleen will need me."

"She'll have to do without you."

Deborah wanted to scream in frustration. There was power behind her desire to get to Kathleen, and it was far stronger than her desire to return to her father. Being needed was a strong force, something she had rarely felt in her life. She believed with all her heart that her appearance at any sort of public hearing on the matter of the fire would help the O'Learys. It was one of the few benefits of being the daughter of the wealthiest man in Chicago.

She remembered the first day she had seen Kathleen O'Leary. They had both been ten years old, and Kathleen had been pulling a cartload of cream and butter along the boardwalk in Canal Street. Deborah had been in her carriage, forbidden to go out into the roadway where, her nanny insisted, the riffraff gathered. While Deborah stared idly out the window, a gang of boys had descended upon Kathleen, upsetting her handcart, stealing the butter and drenching the little girl with cream. They left her sitting on the sidewalk, as forlorn a creature as Deborah had ever seen.

She had managed to cajole her driver and nanny into allowing the Irish girl to come home with her, and there she had given Kathleen a bath and a clean set of clothes. The stern British nanny had protested all the while, but for once, Deborah stood firm. It was so much easier to stand firm on behalf of someone other than herself.

Rather than ducking her head in humble gratitude, Kathleen O'Leary had accepted the kindness matter-of-factly. Rather than weeping over her lost butter and cream, she convinced the Sinclairs' cook to take dairy deliveries from her mother.

Deborah's father believed French maids were the best—the most lively, intelligent and de rigeur for a young lady of the highest class. But Deborah would have none of it. She wanted Kathleen. "If you wish for her to speak French," she informed her father, "she can come to tutoring with me."

A week later, while Deborah paced her room in nervousness, her father had sent someone to convince Mr. and Mrs. O'Leary to let Kathleen hire on as Deborah's personal maid. Right from the start, a special friendship formed between the girls. With no mother to share the secrets of her heart, Deborah shared them with Kathleen. Having never known what it was like to have a bed all to herself, Kathleen learned a new way of life. And so it went, year after year, their girlhood intimacies tightening into the mature bonds of womanhood.

Ah, Kathleen. So feisty, so proud, so diabolically clever. These histrionic reports in the press would be devastating to her.

"Did you never have a true friend, Mr. Silver?" Deborah asked softly. "Did you never have a friend who meant all the world to you, someone you would do anything for?"

She heard him take in a sharp breath.

"Well?" she prompted, certain he had no understanding of the depth of her devotion and concern. He said nothing, just sat like a rock.

"Read this bit, here." Jack stabbed a finger at the middle of a newspaper column, clearly trying to divert her attention.

She had no intention of being distracted, but the words snared her attention. "'Chicago's leading industrialist and mining baron, Arthur Sinclair, is engaged in a search for his only daughter, Miss Deborah Beaton Sinclair, who was set to leave Miss Boylan's School in order to marry Mr. Philip Ascot IV. Mr. Sinclair is offering a handsome reward for information about the whereabouts of his daughter....'"

Deborah pressed her hands together, closed her eyes and offered up a brief prayer of thanks. The fact that her father had placed the notice meant he had lived through the fire. *Oh Father,* she thought. *You survived. Thank God you survived.*

"'Miss Sinclair was seen in the alley behind the Sinclair mansion in Huron Avenue. In the small hours of the morning, Miss Sinclair was found near Lincoln Park by Mr. Ascot. She was being most egregiously beleaguered by a stranger who assaulted Mr. Ascot, who described the assailant as a "great brute, better than six and a half feet tall, with wild eyes, long untidy hair, no whiskers." Mr. Ascot reported that the savage might be of Indian extraction....'"

"That's my favorite part," Silver cut in.

"Did it ever occur to you," she asked, folding the paper, "that you are performing an illegal act?"

"I went to Chicago to commit murder." He narrowed his eyes at her. "You saved me from myself, Princess."

"Your bickering bores me," Lightning Jack said with a long-suffering sigh. "I am going out to have a smoke."

Both Deborah and Tom ignored him.

"You're an outlaw. A wanted man. I can help you," she offered, leaning across the table, "but only if you let me go."

"I don't need your help."

"Once you're caught, you will be thrown in prison."

"I won't be thrown in prison," he stated.

"What makes you so sure?"

"That's not something that happens to folks like me and Lightning Jack."

"You presume to know a lot about kidnaping. Tell me, have you done this before?"

"Can't say as I have," he conceded. "Never had the call to."

"But your feud with my father gives you call," she said.

His face turned stony. "This is no feud. He can end this by coming for you." He glanced down at the densely printed papers on the table. "If he comes."

"Your heart is made of stone. You have no idea what love and friendship and family are."

Tom stood up from the table, and his broad shoulders blotted out the daylight. The expression on his face was pure thunder, and for the first time since he had seized her on that terrible Sunday night, she looked directly into his eyes. They were a deep rich brown. Dark, with lashes that would have looked girlish on a less imposing, rugged man.

And in that moment, she saw in those brown eyes a pain so keen that it made her flinch and look away. She didn't want to know the source of his hurt, didn't want to think of Tom Silver as a man who could feel pain.

Twelve

Lake Superior was so deep, its color did not even reflect the blue of the sky. When Deborah leaned over the side of the *Suzette* to look at it, the wide, flat water was some dark, impenetrable steely hue that made her uncomfortable. The vast and empty wilderness gave her the sensation that she had crossed through the rapids to another planet far removed from anything she had ever known.

She took to sitting out on deck, even though the wind from the north carried the icy promise of the coming winter. She wore the woolen clothes Tom Silver had provided, though she had not yet thanked him and didn't intend to. She finished reading *Gulliver's Travels* and delved into a preposterous and powerful adventure novel, something called *Journey to the Center of the Earth* by Jules Verne, which required her to sit on her hands to keep from biting her fingernails to the quick. Silver had a new copy of *Ragged Dick* by Horatio Alger, but after reading only a few pages, Deborah put it aside. She had no need to read a book about achieving the Great American Dream. She had only to consider her father, and she knew the entire story.

More and more, she knew the dream had its dark side as well as its light.

Silver and Lightning Jack believed her father's mining

company had caused a terrible tragedy. Whether they were right or wrong was debatable. But one thing Deborah knew for certain was that her father's company was hugely successful, though she had only a vague notion of its day-to-day operation. Sinclair Mining maintained locations all over the northern Great Lakes. From time to time her father went on inspection tours, but she had never been invited. If she thought at all of the industry that had made her father one of the richest men in America, she thought of it in only the most abstract of terms—faceless workers tearing ore from the earth, taking it away to be smelted and then shipped all over the country.

They passed Copper Harbor on the tip of the Michigan peninsula. Deborah recalled hearing the place mentioned in her father's business dealings, but that was all. She was vaguely ashamed of her ignorance.

With the best of intentions, her father had shielded her from knowing the nature of his business. In his view, women had no need to clutter their minds with vulgar matters of industry and commerce. She was not so naive as to believe her father was saintly in all his business transactions, but at his core, he was a decent man, and Tom Silver was obviously mistaken about his role in causing a disaster at one of his mines.

It was no use trying to convince him of her father's innocence. Her hope now was that she would survive this ordeal long enough for her father to come for her and the authorities to deal with Tom Silver.

Dark-winged cormorants swooped overhead, diving for fish. Deborah put aside her book and watched for a while, feeling the chill wind pluck at her bonnet strings.

Something flickered on the horizon. Shading her eyes, she looked more closely and discerned a long, thin strip of deep gray-green. A sense of mystery shrouded the sight, yet Deborah instinctively knew it was land.

She got up and patted her thigh, inviting Smokey to

follow her down to the stern deck. "Have you the spy-glass?" she asked Lightning Jack.

He nodded and passed her the glass. "Do you see it already?"

"Yes. Don't you?"

"Not yet, not with these old eyes," he said, passing a hand through the white streak in his hair.

She stood up on a crate and put the glass to her eye. "It's so indistinct."

"It is Isle Royale," Jack said, giving "isle" the French pronunciation of "eel." A hush of reverence softened his voice. "She will reveal herself to us slowly, in her own time."

She could tell from the way Jack spoke that the remote island was special to him. Often during the voyage, she'd had the urge to ask him—and even Tom Silver—about how they had come to settle on the wild island, and what it was they had found there. But she didn't want to know these men any better than she already did. Instinctively she understood that she must keep distance between herself and her captors. The moment she started seeing them as human and individual, she was in danger of coming even deeper under their power.

"It is not just one island," Jack explained as the dark shape dead ahead widened. "There are many small islands surrounding the main one. Many harbors."

Bit by bit, the jagged shoreline of the island materialized through the pervasive mist. Flocks of ducks and herring gulls swarmed around the steamer. Smokey yapped wildly at the birds, running from deck to deck on the trawler. In the wheelhouse, Tom Silver kept his eye on the burgeoning sight of the huge island.

No longer needing the spyglass, Deborah put it aside. The island reminded her of a fortress, mist-shrouded and impenetrable, surrounded by a chevaux-de-frise of jagged rock outcroppings. Fir trees formed slender spires against the pale afternoon sky, and the breeze now carried on it the unmistakable fresh scent of pine. The birch trees gave off a blaze of gold from groves and clusters on the slopes and high ridges of the island. Bright orange lichen banded the rock above the waterline.

As the steamer moved into a deep, sheltered cove where the restless water pounded at the rocky edge, Deborah felt a clutch of alarm. This *was* a fortress, surrounded by sharp rock and icy water, and once she went ashore, she would be as much a prisoner as Rapunzel in her tower.

This place was so remote that perhaps no one would ever find her. How odd, she thought, her whole being filling up with fear and desolation. How terribly odd. The night of the fire, that very thought had occurred to her. She remembered thinking that a disaster of such proportions could divide families forever, separate husbands and wives, parents and children. Friends might lose track of friends, never to find each other again.

No. She didn't believe she would be staying here long. First of all, she'd heard Silver and Lightning Jack talking about "ice-up," an event that came in late November, forcing the islanders to take refuge on the mainland. Second of all, Tom Silver despised her. Not just because he blamed her father for a mining accident, but because he resented who and what she was. He called her "Princess" as if she considered herself some sort of royalty. He made no attempt to hide his scorn for the fact that she had been raised in the traditions and conventions of the very wealthy. He looked at her and saw something he had no use for—except as a hostage.

She had spent hours debating with herself whether or not to reveal the truth to Tom Silver. He believed he had kidnaped an innocent bride-to-be from the protection of her powerful father. In truth she was something else entirely.

She shut her eyes against the mystical, lovely scene of the long, deep bay, and her thoughts dissolved into blackened memories. With cold deliberation, she turned her

mind to other matters. Now was not the time for thoughts
of the past. She was arriving at her new prison. She had
to concentrate on survival, perhaps escape. Tom Silver
had seized her, snatched her from the flames at the most
dreadful moment of her life, and he didn't even seem to
know that. Or care.

A man like Silver could never care about anyone, she
decided resentfully. He was too gruff, too mean, too savage. He held nothing but greed in his heart, and he viewed
Deborah as a means to feed his hunger for riches and
revenge.

During the voyage, he had done nothing to make her
change her mind. Even providing better food, clothes and
a bath was an act not of kindness, but of control.

The two men tied up at a long, rickety wooden dock
that projected out over a tumble of ridged rocks covered
in lichen. A weather-beaten building that reeked of fish
projected out over the water. Lightning Jack put the dog
ashore, and Smokey raced along the dock to dry land,
ecstatically marking territory everywhere he went. Deborah followed, showing considerably less exuberance. Her
legs felt wobbly and weak on the unmoving planks. The
pervasive mist muted all sound.

When she stepped off the dock and onto the island, a
peculiar sense of anticipation gripped her. For the first
time since the fire, she understood in the most concrete
way that she had left her former life behind. A new ex-
ploration lay ahead. She knew little of expeditions and
adventure, only that they were dangerous and inappropri-
ate activities for a young woman.

She didn't think Tom Silver would care whether or not
he thrust her into danger and adventure. But perhaps here
she would find someone who might help her. In fact, she
got the feeling he would take great delight in subjecting
her to unknown discomforts and terrors. If the voyage
from Chicago gave any indication, that was exactly what
he intended.

Hearing a tread behind her, she spoke without turning. "There's no one here."

"There is now," Tom Silver replied.

Deborah watched Smokey scampering to and fro, sniffing out the lay of the land. Then he disappeared into the underbrush.

She turned to glare at her captor. "He'll get lost. You'll have to go after him."

"Shut up. I'm not one of your servants."

"You're too offensive to be anyone's servant."

Laughing, he turned away to help Lightning Jack load a hand truck with supplies. When the hand truck was piled high, the men steered it along a path leading around a broad marsh and into a wooded area. Deborah followed, because she didn't know what else to do.

She had the feeling she had tumbled down a hole to a place where nothing was as it seemed. She walked through an emerald kingdom of towering evergreens. Paper birch trees formed stands of white columns. Sugar maples, aflame with deep pink and amber leaves, painted the rise of the ridge ahead. Huge ferns unfurled beneath the trees. Secret scuttlings went on in the underbrush, and Smokey reappeared. The forest floor, damp and fecund with fallen needles and leaves, muffled their tread.

The pathway formed a long green tunnel, and at the end, a misty light glimmered. Deborah trudged toward that light. The path ended at a ridgetop, and from there she found herself looking down at a... She wasn't certain what to call it. Too small to be called a town or even a village, the cluster of buildings stood around a rough roadway formed of split logs. It was a settlement of some sort.

She glanced over her shoulder at Tom Silver. "Now what?"

"We're here," he said. "We're home."

"*You* might be home." To Deborah, it resembled a desolate, foreign land. She scanned the log houses and clapboard buildings, pleased to see that smoke curled from nearly every chimney or stovepipe. She intended to form alliances with these people. Engage their sympathy. She would find someone here to aid her escape.

Leaving the men to struggle with the overloaded cart, she hurried along. The cabins and cottages were, for the most part, small and neatly if crudely built. In addition to the dwellings, there was one long, low building and another with a tall, flat front. Yet a curious sense of impermanence pervaded the settlement, as if the inhabitants of the houses might pick up and move at any given moment.

Smokey reached the settlement first, and was immediately set upon by a large shepherd dog. Deborah cried out in alarm, but she needn't have. The scruffy little mongrel held his own against the bigger dog, intimidating it into submission with a snap of his jaws. Within a few minutes, both dogs loped off together.

The barking shepherd had alerted some of the people of the settlement. Doors opened, curtains parted in windows and a herd of children tumbled out of one of the larger houses.

"It's Lightning Jack!" a boy called. "Lightning Jack!"

They swarmed past Deborah, most of them barely acknowledging her. She discerned immediately that Lightning Jack was well-beloved here in the heart of nowhere. The children badgered him with questions, wanting to know what he had brought from the big city, how long he was staying and whose house would he eat at tonight.

Lightning Jack laughed with an ease and pleasure Deborah had not seen in him during the voyage. *"Tenez, les enfants,"* he said. "All in good time. First, I need some help with the load."

By the time they reached the middle of the settlement, he had a group of enthusiastic helpers in tow. Smokey was already basking in the attention of the children. They gathered in front of the trading post, with its tall flat facade and a picket log fence in the front. A carefully lettered shingle blew in the breeze, identifying the building as the Windigo Trading Post. In small letters, it said "Thomas Silver, prop."

Deborah eyed him in surprise. "This is your trading post?"

"Yeah."

A dozen other questions crowded into her mind, but with all the activity going on, she knew she'd get no answers. The children who were so eager to welcome Jack were less forward with Tom Silver. They weren't afraid of him, exactly, but they kept their distance. Perhaps it was his size, but more likely it was the solemn and distant look on his face, a look she did not understand and did not want to question.

She became aware that a number of other people had come out of their houses to see what the commotion was about. They were mostly women, though an old man with his hair plaited in long white braids raised his hand in greeting from a place across the way. The other man wore one sleeve pinned up where he was missing an arm. The women wore bib aprons over sturdy, fading dresses of calico or dimity. Deep-brimmed bonnets shadowed their faces, though thick braids fell down their backs. Bit by bit, Deborah sensed the collective attention shifting to her. Unspoken questions hung like the lake mist in the air. They wanted to know who she was, what she was doing here.

Lightning Jack, his nature growing sweeter by the minute, gestured at her with a Gallic flourish. "Please say hello to Mademoiselle Deborah S—" He broke off. "You must call her Miss Deborah. She has come to stay for a while."

"Is she Mr. Silver's bride?" asked a small, loud child.

Deborah felt her cheeks redden. "Certainly not," she said, but no one heard her answer. The children all started peppering Jack and Silver with questions without waiting for answers.

"My mama said he better get him a woman soon," another child commented.

"*My* mama said he's already got too many," another countered.

"Where?" his companion challenged him. "We never seen one." He palmed his tow-colored hair out of his eyes and peered at Deborah. "Until now."

"I most certainly am not—"

"He keeps 'em in the wilderness somewheres," another boy suggested. "Or maybe at the Soo Locks."

"Enough," Deborah said, embarrassed and exasperated. "I am not Mr. Silver's or anyone's woman, for heaven's sake."

"Then what are you?" the blond boy asked.

"A visitor," Tom Silver broke in. He touched his hand to Deborah's waist and steered her along the plank road. "And with any luck, she won't be staying long."

She resented his implication that she was here by choice and shied away from him.

"Nels," Tom said to the tow-headed boy, "take that carpet bag to my quarters."

Deborah's gaze went to the small, snug cabin in the yard behind the trading post. The door was closed and the windows shuttered. She stood frozen, feeling a scream build in her throat, and only by swallowing hard could she stop herself from letting it out. "I can't stay there with you," she said faintly.

"Why the hell not?"

"It's not proper."

An insolent laugh burst from him. "Why the hell would I worry about that?" He sobered. "Look, even if I trusted you not to do something stupid, you wouldn't find a welcome with anyone else in town."

She bridled, her pride stung. "I beg your pardon."

"You're a Sinclair, Princess. Just wait 'til folks find out."

Part Two

The real voyage of discovery consists not in seeking new landscapes, but in having new eyes.

—Marcel Proust

Thirteen

Until this moment, Tom Silver had not been the sort of man who struck Deborah as having an actual home. The Tom Silver she knew was too wild, too angry, too implacable to possess mundane things like cookware and blankets and furniture, books and hearth plaques and kerosene lamps.

Yet when he led the way through the back of the trading post and across the yard, she found herself face to face with the place he called home. Violating all opinions she had formed of him, the place was not crude or makeshift. It had a porch with two rough-hewn chairs, a woodshed and a fieldstone chimney. It resembled the home of a decent, settled person, someone who cared about the way he lived.

Did Tom Silver care? She had not seen that in his behavior so far. Simply barging and bullying his way through each day seemed to be enough for him.

She stole a furtive glance over her shoulder at him, feeling the presence of his bulk as they crossed the yard. Perhaps she was wrong about him after all. It wouldn't be the first time her judgment had been wrong about a man.

The surface of the porch was made of split puncheons worn smooth by the years. The front door was not locked.

At Silver's nod, she stepped inside while he went along the porch, opening the window shutters.

Plain muslin curtains made of flour sacks tacked over the windows filtered the sunlight. A musty, smoky smell of spent firewood and disuse hung in the air. Deborah set down the parcel she had been carrying and let her eyes adjust to the dimness. Black iron stove and a ladder leading to a loft. A long plank counter of scrubbed wood with a pump sink. Wooden settle in front of the fireplace. Table and chairs, enameled plates and bowls stacked on a shelf above the sink.

Two of everything.

"You're to bed down in here," Silver said, opening the door with his foot. "I'll take the loft."

She followed him into a tiny, low-ceilinged room with a washstand and a bedstead covered by a drab woolen blanket. He jerked a thumb to a small exterior door. "Privy's out there, and you can get water from the kitchen." He set down the wicker trunk he had been carrying, then turned and left the room.

Deborah stood unmoving, trying to collect her bearings. He meant for her to stay in this house—alone—with him. Day in and day out, until her father came for her. The idea of being alone with any man, particularly a savage giant of a man, should properly terrify her. Instead, it made her angry.

"What am I to *do?*" she asked loudly.

His footsteps in the next room stopped for a moment, then started again as he came to the doorway. "Do?"

"With my time. What do you expect me to do?"

"I don't know." It was too dim to see if he was laughing at her. "Whatever you…debutantes do."

She sniffed. "I wish you wouldn't keep calling me that. You have no idea what a debutante is."

With one step he came close, looming over her, his form blotting out the daylight. With uncaring insolence he skimmed a big rough finger over the crest of her cheekbone. His rude stare swept her from head to foot. "I reckon I do now, Princess," he said with soft menace in his voice.

Her heart hammered out of control, a painful reminder of her cowardice. When would the fear end? Never, if he kept treating her like the enemy. Pretending disdain and disgust, she tossed her head and stepped back. "Does it make you feel bigger, more manly, when you bully me?" she demanded. She wondered where this streak of aggression had come from. Despite her anger, it pleased her to know she was capable of showing a little backbone every once in a while. "Is that why you do it?" she persisted.

He laughed. "Nope. I do it because you're a hell of a lot more interesting when you're mad." He left the room again, this time going to the kitchen door to bring in supplies.

Deborah felt herself dangling just inches from complete despair. She was in the oddest of places, among strangers, with no inkling how to get out of her dilemma. Going to the window, she swept aside the curtain, which was brittle with age and dust. A large brown spider scuttled across the sill. She gave a small shriek and jumped back.

Pressing her fist to her mouth, she staggered to the bed and sank down. She thought she might weep, but knew weeping would not help, so she buried her head in her hands. The ropes strung beneath the mattress creaked with her weight, and when she shifted, she felt a decided *something* pressing at her. With a frown, she knelt beside the bed and looked underneath.

There, she found a long, flat box with leather hinges nailed on one side. Extra blankets, she supposed. Since they had left the Soo Locks and crossed the waters of Lake Superior, the weather had grown steadily colder. The winter nights were probably brutal here.

She pulled out the box, bringing with it a roll of dust motes and cobwebs. Lifting the lid, she peered inside and found a collection of boy's clothing—dungarees and knickers, checked shirts and a thick flannel nightshirt—a tin cigar box containing a dead butterfly, a buckskin bag filled with glass marbles and a slingshot and a copybook filled with penmanship practice.

Deborah felt a mixture of wonder and confusion. These were probably things from Tom Silver's boyhood. It was hard to think of him as a boy who'd had a mother who loved him.

At that moment, he returned, bringing a cloth-wrapped parcel. "What the hell do you think you're doing?"

She flinched at the bite of rage in his voice. "What is all this?"

In two strides he had crossed the room. With a flick of his wrist, he slammed the box shut. "That's private."

"So is my *life*," she shot back, "but that didn't stop you from abducting me." Forcing herself to brave his temper, she opened the box again, filling the air with a cedary smell. "These are a child's things," she said. "A boy's clothes and books and...keepsakes." She held up a jar that contained a collection of fossils. "What a lot of pressure a delicate leaf exerts to imprint itself into the very flesh of the rock," she said, studying the ancient patterns. "Who would have thought something so fragile could cut so deeply into a rock?"

"Never thought about it," he muttered.

"Were these yours?"

"No," he snapped.

"Then...do these belong to your child, Mr. Silver?" she asked. "Where has he gone?"

For the second time, Silver slammed the box shut, then shoved it under the bed with his foot. Striding toward the door, he said, "Your father killed him."

Tom figured he'd given the woman something to think about while he took care of business. Ernie Sivertsen, maimed and disfigured in the accident, had minded the post in Tom's absence, but there were plenty of chores waiting for him. Business was always slow this time of year, toward the close of the season. Folks were packing up, getting ready to go to the mainland for the winter. Some of them moved house completely, taking everything that wasn't nailed down, even their big iron stoves. Tom had to pack and store the things he'd be leaving behind, tally up accounts for the season and do an inventory.

Thanks to Arthur Sinclair, some would not be back. Their menfolk—husbands, brothers, fathers—had died, and the women and old folks left behind couldn't carry on the fishing or logging.

He was stacking canning jars when Ilsa Ibbotsen stopped in, a sleeping baby cradled against her bosom. The minister's wife, she was the closest thing the island children had to a teacher, and on foul weather days, she gathered them in her kitchen to read the Good Book and do sums.

"Welcome back, Tom," she said. "Wasn't the same without you."

"Thanks, ma'am." He liked Ilsa. She had the large-boned, Nordic good looks of a woman suited to north woods living, with a nature as generous as her physique. "What can I do for you?"

"I need some clove oil," she said. "Baby's teething. And can you send over some kerosene? The days are getting short."

He nodded and found the oil on a small, high shelf of apothecary goods. "Has fishing been good for the pastor?" Tom asked, to fill the silence.

She nodded. The baby fussed a little, then settled again on her shoulder. Tom didn't usually pay much mind to babies, but he found himself studying the child's chubby hand, trustingly clutched into Ilsa's shawl, and the pink lips pursed in sleep. "Hope this'll fix what hurts," he said, setting the clear bottle of oil on the counter.

She nodded her thanks, then hesitated before speaking again. "Folks are wondering about your visitor, Tom."

"I guess they would be." He and Lightning Jack had told no one they had gone to Chicago. The *Suzette*'s normal run was to the Soo Locks, no further. He took a deep breath. Ilsa and the others in the settlement weren't going to like what they learned about Tom's captive, not one bit. He'd have to explain himself sooner rather than later, and he might as well start with the pastor's wife. Though she had lost a brother-in-law in the disaster, her sturdy Lutheran principles seemed to help her bear the grief.

"Lightning Jack and I went down to Chicago to settle the score with Arthur Sinclair," Tom said.

"Is that so?" Ilsa dropped her voice to a shocked whisper. "Tom, you shouldn't have done that."

He didn't look up, but concentrated on calibrating the oil in its container. "I didn't. The whole city was on fire when we got there."

"The mail boat brought news of the fires," Ilsa said.

He finished pouring the oil and made himself look at her. But in his mind, he was seeing Arthur Sinclair in the foyer of his mansion, blank-faced as Tom took aim. Why had he hesitated? The man's careless greed had taken seven lives, yet Tom had paused a mere second too long, and Sinclair had escaped.

"It was chaos in the city," he explained. "He got away, but I figured out a way to make him pay for what he did." He jerked his thumb in the direction of the cabin. "The woman's name is Deborah Sinclair," he said. "She's Arthur Sinclair's daughter."

"Oh, Tom—"

"Wait, hear me out. We sent word that Sinclair is to come fetch her here." Tom took a dark satisfaction in envisioning the moment. Sinclair kept his hands clean by paying others to do his work for him. This once, he would be forced to see what he had caused.

"Supposing he does come. Rich man like that—he'll

bring armed guards, wouldn't you think? Enough blood's been spilled on this island.''

"We'll settle with him then, gain restitution for the families of the victims.''

"You mean, pay us.'' Ilsa's pale face turned implacable and she pressed her lips together. "There's no payment can make up for a loss like that.''

"I know, Ilsa. But the insurance hearing declared it an act of God so there's to be no settlement. Folks have to eat, have to live day to day. That's what the money'll do.''

"Have you considered what the money *won't* do?'' she asked, a quiet challenge sharpening her voice.

Tom felt the brutal ache of Asa's absence. "Of course I have.'' Ever since abandoning the plan to murder Arthur Sinclair, he had been searching for another way to find justice. He wanted to see Sinclair face to face. He wanted him to see where people had died. That could only be accomplished by forcing him to come to Isle Royale.

"After the accident, my sister had to move off island to Duluth.'' Ilsa's voice trembled. "She's a saloon girl there, Tom. She...sells her body at the Immigrant House and drinks herself senseless every night.''

The news drove an icy wind through him. "I'm sorry, Ilsa. Maybe the restitution will help. If she doesn't have to work for a—'' he wasn't sure what to call it "—a wage, then she might settle down in a...quieter manner.''

Ilsa leaned back against a stack of feed grain. "Maybe,'' she said softly. "Maybe. But folks aren't going to like it. They aren't going to like knowing his daughter's here.''

"With luck, it'll be a week or less. She's his only child. He'll come for her.''

With one arm cradling the sleeping infant, she reached around and signed the credit chit on the counter. "You know,'' she said quietly, "it would be a fine tribute to the

Lord if we were to get a proper church on the island. Our little parlor's getting crowded.''

"Are you sure this is the way he went?'' Deborah asked, eyeing the steep serrated ridge of the hillside.

The boy named Nels nodded vigorously. "Cross my heart and hope to die. He comes here a lot.'' He shaded his eyes against the late afternoon sun and pointed. "If you stay to the right, the going's not too hard.''

"Thank you,'' she said. "It's lucky you happened by.'' She had encountered the boy walking home from a nearby pond with a bait bucket and a creel of fish. Nels swore he knew where she'd find Tom Silver.

She never thought she would find herself in search of her abductor, yet here she was. After stunning her with the news that he had a boy who'd died, he'd left her to speculate all afternoon. Determined to find answers, she had gone to his trading post. Through the back door she had seen him talking with a woman holding a baby. She suspected they were discussing her, and she had lost her nerve.

Nels stared at her openly.

"What?'' she asked. Surely a boy wouldn't notice her unfashionable dress.

"They said you were the devil's daughter.''

"Who said that?''

"Folks in town,'' he replied vaguely. "So…are you?''

"Do you believe that?''

The tips of his ears turned red as he grinned. "You don't look it.''

She smiled back to hide her distress. Her father was a hated man here. Everyone would assume she was cut from the same cloth. She had no idea how to face that hatred.

In the distance, a bell clanged, and Nels looked over his shoulder at the settlement. "I have to go,'' he said. "I got chores to do before supper.''

"I'll find Mr. Silver on my own," she assured him, though she was not at all sure of herself.

The boy slipped away to a clapboard house at the end of the rutted street. Deborah took a deep, determined breath and started to climb. It was a struggle to hold her long dress out of the way. Stumps and brambles caught at her skirts. No wonder frontierswomen wore such sturdy clothes. The moss and lichen covering the jagged rocks made for slippery going. She grasped at underbrush and tree trunks, pulling until her legs and shoulders ached.

She couldn't believe she was actually climbing a mountain on a wild island in the middle of nowhere. But since the night of the fire, everything that had befallen her was unbelievable, so this was no different.

A low bush came up by the roots and she tumbled backward. Bumping violently against a huge rock, she decided she would rather read about adventures than have them. At least you knew an adventure in a book was going to end well.

Except that there was something to be said for striking out like this, off into the unknown. True, she was scratched, sweating and terrified most of the time, but each time she took a step, each time she put one foot in front of the other, she felt a sense of accomplishment that was almost heady in its intensity.

When she cleared the top of the rocky ridge, she nearly shouted with her victory. But what she saw there struck her mute.

It was beautiful. Beyond beautiful. A sense of wonder broke over her. She found herself standing atop the very world, or so it seemed. From her vantage point, she could see the island's untracked wilderness stretching out in a carpet of evergreen and changing leaves. Here and there, inland lakes glittered like mirrors. Superior, its surface on fire with the colors of sunset, embraced the island, invaded its coves and inlets. The broken shore surrounded a wilderness so enchanting that her heart caught at the sight of it.

A feeling of complete solitude invaded her. She had never felt this way before, because she had never known a place like this existed. It was a pervasive enchantment, seeping through her; the sight of the water and the trees, the sounds of the wind and the wild birds, all drugging her with their seductiveness.

The colors alone took her breath away. Sunset sky, blue lake, rock in every shade of black and gray, cloaked in rich orange lichen. This was a place of magic, she thought. An island so far removed from the rest of the world that she was half convinced the rest of the world did not exist.

For some reason, it cheered her to think that way.

"What are you doing here?" demanded a rough, angry voice.

She nearly stumbled and fell. "Don't startle me like that."

"Then don't follow me around," Tom Silver said.

"Then don't tell me terrible things and walk away without explaining them," she shot back.

He stood in a slant of sunlight from the west, glaring at her. Behind him lay a broad clearing, overgrown with bramble. He wore Levi's, a plain broadcloth shirt and no hat. The wind toyed with his hair, and she could see the small wrapped lock with the eagle feather. Deborah had the same strange sensation looking at him as she'd had looking at the majestic island. Like the island, he was not threatening, but...imposing. And seductively wild.

"I want you to tell me about your child," she said. Then, aching for him, she added, "Please."

"Why?"

"Because I want to understand."

He pivoted on a booted heel. "Follow me."

As usual, he didn't look to see if she followed or if she was keeping up. When she stumbled and cried out, he didn't turn. She didn't resent him, though. The fact that he had lost a child explained so much about his anger and his bullying.

Thorns and scrubby fir trees tore at her as she followed him to the center of the clearing. Before her lay a deep, rockbound pit. Blackened timbers littered the ground around it. A little beyond the scarred earth, a row of roses grew.

"Isle Royale copper," Tom Silver said, staring into the hole. "It's not ore, but pure metal. Folks've been after it since before time was counted. There hadn't been a working mine here since before the war. Your father wanted to be the first to make some fast money."

She caught her breath, beginning to understand what was coming next. "So he sent in his mining company."

"He wouldn't have been the first, and he's not going to be the last, but he got greedy. He sent in his team last spring as the claim was being surveyed."

"Then my father was not directly responsible."

"So that's how he lives with himself? By paying other men to do his work for him, make his mistakes for him? Take the blame for him?"

Her shoulders slumped. Silver was right. Her father was responsible no matter how far he was from the incident.

"The islanders welcomed a new enterprise—at first," Tom Silver continued. "They're poor folks, loggers and fishermen. When the mining company came here with your father's grand plan, they found a ready audience. He made promises to desperate men. They'd get rich overnight. They'd never have to work again after finding the big vein." He shook his head. "Most had the sense not to believe him, but fifteen men and boys had their heads turned by all his talk. The team left a no-account supervisor in charge and promised bonuses if operations got under way ahead of schedule. Prizes for the first metal. They didn't care about safety or caution or taking the time to do things right. They just cared about mining that vein.''

A chill touched the base of her spine. Sinclair Mining had ceased operations in Lake Superior over the summer. She recalled reading a notice to that effect in the *Tribune*. Now she knew why. Yet her father had never spoken of any sort of disaster or tragedy. He had simply turned his attention to Sinclair Grain Futures or Sinclair Shipping or Sinclair Railways. He opened and closed enterprises like a fashionable woman trying on and discarding frocks.

It was no way to find the permanence he sought, she reflected. He craved the ''old money'' way of life, yet he wanted to use new money in order to buy it. She wished he could understand that it didn't work that way. Families that had founded themselves in the style her father craved did so by building something lasting and true.

She had no idea when she might see her father again. She had no idea what she would say to him after this ordeal. She had no idea, she bleakly admitted to herself, how her father would react to seeing this dead place, where his enterprise had ripped a wound in the earth and ended seven lives.

She surveyed the roses, a few of them bravely blooming despite the late season, but most barren to bald rosehips. There were seven struggling rosebushes in all. These had been planted in honor of the victims; she knew that without asking.

''Tell me about the accident,'' she said.

''Fifteen men came forward to work. They were lured by the promise of handsome wages, bonuses, perhaps a cut of the profits. But there were no profits. Seven died in the explosion. One of the dead was Asa. He was fourteen years old.''

Asa. A Biblical name, a name for kings. The sickness that had been pushing at the back of her throat grew more sour and urgent. She was barely able to swallow. ''Mr. Silver,'' she whispered, ''I'm sorry about your son.''

"He was mine, and I was his, but he was my foster son."

She felt herself being drawn to this man, learning to look past the hard shell of his exterior and into his heart. She had accused him of being heartless, but now she knew that wasn't true. She had probably known it since the moment he had given up his chance to shoot her father in order to save her from the flames.

"How did he come to be your foster son?"

"I knew a man in the war named Kane." Tom gazed off into the misty distance as he spoke. "He was an adjutant colonel from Michigan. Told me to visit him after the war, and I did. He had a little farm on Battle Creek, fresh graves in the side yard. He'd lost his wife and daughter to the influenza, and he was pretty sick himself. He and Asa didn't have any living relatives. When it became clear Kane wasn't going to make it, I promised him I'd look after his boy."

A long silence spun out, punctuated by secretive flutterings in the bushes, and the occasional chittering of a bird. Deborah's throat hurt with sorrow. Tom Silver's face said everything. The depths of his eyes held all the things he would not tell her. He'd suffered a loss she couldn't understand, yet she could feel it, a soft ache in her heart, where her mother was supposed to be.

Silver paced restlessly to the top of the ridge where the wind caught at his too-long hair and rippled through the sleeves of his shirt. "I can't abide broken promises," he said.

She didn't have to ask him what he meant. She knew. He felt that he had failed his friend, failed to keep Asa safe.

"You said the boy was fourteen years old. A boy of fourteen is apt to get his head turned by the prospect of fast money," she said, knowing there was no comfort in it. "I can't imagine what you could have said to stop him. Some people are simply driven by the lure of possibility."

Her father almost never spoke of the past, but she knew he had been on his own from a very young age. He had once remarked to her that by the age of six he was selling apples and newspapers in the streets of New York City. "I'm just sorry he was lured to the mine by my father's company."

"Asa thought it sounded like one big adventure," Tom said. His voice was eerily without inflection. "Sinclair addressed him personally, told him how he'd be the boy at the top of the shaft, working the air bellows so the miners below would have fresh air. It sounded like a picnic to a boy who had just spent the entire spring doing shore work."

He picked up a loose rock and flung it so far she couldn't see where it landed. "They never even took one ounce of copper," he said. "Sinclair's foreman didn't bother reinforcing the shaft, so the minute they blasted, the thing blew like a bomb in a trench." He turned back to face the blackened, narrow pit. "I was minding the post that day, but I heard it. We all heard the explosion and went running." His shoulders were stiff as if readying for a blow that would never come. "They said Asa was the first to die because he was at the top of the shaft." He hesitated. "I found part of his shirt in a tree."

Scalding tears poured from Deborah's eyes, running unchecked down her cheeks until, finally, her vision was too blurred and she wiped them away with her sleeve. "I don't know what to say to you." She'd never expected to feel sympathy for the man who had kidnaped her. She pressed her fists to her heart as if it were breaking. "You have been in hell, and I can't help you."

"I never asked for your help."

"It's not helping you to hold me captive, either," she pointed out.

He ignored the suggestion. "Your father ceased doing business as Sinclair Mining. His solicitors and claims adjustors fixed things so that no one accepted liability for the accident. No restitution was paid. Those who died were buried in paupers' graves, and if they left families behind, their wives and kids had to fend for themselves.''

''So that is why you wanted to kill my father.''

''It was never a question of wanting.'' He subjected her to a lengthy, narrow-eyed scrutiny that made her want to hide. ''Your ransom is going to force him into bankruptcy.''

The wind dried the tears on her cheeks. ''You don't understand my father,'' she said, and it occurred to her that she didn't understand him either. It was as if they were discussing a stranger. When she thought of her father, she pictured a handsome man with a lame leg, a parent who indulged her every whim, an ambitious social climber who wanted the world for her and would stop at nothing to get it. Now, new knowledge was transforming him into a stranger. Yes, she had always known he was an ambitious businessman, but had he truly lied and cheated just to be the first to get his mine started?

''Do you understand him?'' Tom Silver demanded.

Deborah flinched. ''Well enough to know you can't force him into bankruptcy. He is too diversified. I can't begin to tell you the enterprises he's involved in. Besides, even if you took every last cent from him, he would find a way to rebuild his fortune. He is that sort of man. A survivor.'' She said this without any pride. She could no longer take pride in her father's accomplishments. ''Still, he is wealthy enough to make a full restitution to every family involved in the mining disaster. Including yourself.''

''I lost Asa, not a lifetime of income. That loss can't be repaid in silver and gold.''

She wondered if he knew he had already done the one thing sure to wound her father. By taking her, he had accomplished everything he had set out to do. She was her father's hope for the future, for redemption, for respectability.

But only if she married Philip Ascot.

She shivered, and the evening wind skirled up from the lake, tearing pink and amber leaves from the sugar maples and rippling through the brambles.

"Best be getting back before dark," Tom said.

She turned to descend the way she had come up. The dry dirt path, littered with pebbles, was slippery underfoot, and she had to catch herself on branches and rock projections as she made her way back to the settlement. The whole way down, she felt Tom Silver's presence behind her. He never touched her, never spoke, and when they reached the bottom, it was full dark on Isle Royale.

Fourteen

Deborah Sinclair reminded Tom of a soldier in the aftermath of battle. He had been observing her furtively for days, and unlikely as it seemed, she exhibited a moody wariness that evoked memories of the war.

She was like a battle-weary, disheartened warrior. By the light of the fire in the grate that night, her face appeared drawn, her eyes overly bright and watchful. She put him in mind of—he couldn't believe he was thinking this—of himself, when he had been so beaten down after the battle of Kenaha Falls that he almost could not make himself take the next breath. Why did Deborah's eyes reflect the same shock and despair?

Of course, even the most stouthearted soldier would be stunned by the violence and devastation that had swept through Chicago that Sunday night. The holocaust had felt like the wrath of God, and Deborah, like everyone else, had witnessed horrors beyond imagining.

A burning log fell in the grate, sending a column of sparks up the chimney. Deborah didn't flinch. Perhaps she blinked, but that was all. She had not gone into hysterics during the fire as he had seen so many do that night. In fact, she had kept a level head about her, even rescuing a dog and keeping it safe. Tom began to wonder if her nervousness stemmed from another matter.

Maybe, he conceded, getting up to put another log on the fire, he might be misreading her altogether. Perhaps it was normal for a young woman like Deborah Sinclair to act so damned jittery. He had never met an heiress before. It was peculiar being alone without Lightning Jack around to act as a buffer. He had loaded his trawler with barrels of salt fish and gone off on the Duluth run.

"What are you looking at?" she asked suddenly.

He hadn't realized she'd noticed his pensive stare. "Just wondering if all your kind are as jumpy as you seem to be."

"And what, pray, is 'my kind'?"

"High-strung, overbred heiresses."

"Is that what you think I am?"

"If the shoe fits."

She didn't say anything at first. Then she said, "So you think I'm jumpy. High-strung."

"Yep."

"And you have no idea why?"

"I was thinking it might be the fire, but you kept your head about you that night."

She looked incredulous. "I've been kidnaped and dragged to the middle of nowhere. I have no idea what has become of my friends, my family, my home, my entire world. Do you wonder that I might seem a bit nervous?"

"I thought that was the explanation," he conceded. "But I was wrong."

"What do you mean?"

"Something else is bothering you. It's just a feeling I have."

She patted her lap, inviting the dog to jump up. "Your feelings are wrong, then. I'm sure my nerves will be just fine once you return me to...where I belong."

He frowned at the slight hesitation in her voice. "And where do you reckon you belong? That fancy house on Huron Avenue? That finishing school on the lake?"

"How did you know about Miss Boylan's?"

"I heard you telling Lightning Jack. So where do you belong, Princess?"

"Why do you ask? Are you planning on taking me there?"

"If your father knows what's good for you, he'll come soon and take you there himself."

A strange, humorless laugh escaped her.

"What's funny?" he asked.

"It's just an odd coincidence. My father and I were discussing what is good for me the very night you…burst upon our lives so dramatically."

He could tell from her inflection that she and her father had not been in agreement. "Did you and Sinclair have some petty spat about the proper fish knife to use or what to wear to the latest musicale?"

She went stiff and hard with indignation. "You can't imagine that a person like me might actually have concerns of importance, can you?" she asked softly, her hand stroking the dog's head.

"Woman, you can't even answer a simple question."

"And you can't even have a civil conversation." She put down the dog, shot up from the wooden settle and paced back and forth on the hearth rug. "Mr. Silver, there is nothing, absolutely nothing, that I can say to begin to comfort you for your loss. What happened in the mine pit was a tragedy no words could ever address. But I will promise you this. Treating me with cruelty will not assuage the hurt of losing Asa."

"Cruelty?" Amazed, he spread his hands in innocence. "All I did was ask you a few questions. It's not my fault you refuse to answer them."

"I'm not refusing to answer them."

"Then why don't you answer?"

"Answer what?"

"My questions. I can't believe this is difficult for you.

Or did they forget to teach you simple question and answer techniques at Miss Boiler—''

''Miss Boylan's, and I have no idea why it matters to you whether I answer your questions or not.''

''It doesn't matter,'' he barked. But in a small way, it did. In spite of who she was and why he had taken her, there were things he wanted to know about her. ''But only a daft woman could fail to answer such a simple thing as where she belongs in the world. That's all I asked.''

It *was* all he asked, but it wasn't all he wanted to know. He wanted to know what she thought about when she gazed into the heart of the fire. He wanted to know what it felt like to run a hand through her silky blond hair. He wanted to know what her laughter sounded like. He wanted to know why she'd balked at going with Philip Ascot the night of the fire.

''I simply don't see the point of this conversation,'' she said.

''Conversation,'' he shot back. ''We're not in Chicago anymore, Princess. There's no theater, no restaurants, no ballroom on Isle Royale.''

''Then what on earth do you do for entertainment?''

''We talk. To each other.''

''I see. And this is supposed to entertain me?''

''It's not a night at the opera, but—'' He broke off and stared at her. She had turned white as a sheet. ''Are you ill?'' he asked.

She said nothing. Even from across the room he could see a sheen of sweat on her upper lip and forehead. She swayed a little. He went to her and took hold of her elbow to steady her, because she looked as if she was about to fall.

The instant he touched her, she jerked violently away. The hem of her skirt wafted dangerously close to the fire.

Tom took a step back, holding his hands palm out. He reminded himself that she was a weak and delicate lady.

"Don't get your bloomers in a twist. You suddenly looked peaked."

She blinked with the disoriented look of an awakening dreamer. "I beg your pardon?" she asked vaguely.

Tom took another step back. He had never seen cabin fever strike a person so fast. Or maybe this was another symptom of her battle fatigue. "I thought you might be getting sick all of a sudden."

"I'm...fine." She edged over to the settle and sank down.

He went to the kitchen and took out a jug of cider, freshly pressed by the Kreidbergs up island at Rock Harbor. He poured some into a glass jar and brought it to her. "You'd better drink something."

She hesitated, then reached for the glass and sipped at the cider. "It's delicious. I meant to tell you that at supper. Mr. Silver?"

He was always disconcerted when she addressed him so formally. "Yeah?"

"What will my staying under the same roof as you do to my reputation among the settlers?"

He shook his head. She simply didn't get it. Arthur Sinclair's daughter was a pariah—*that* was what she should worry about. But he didn't want to bring that up again, so he said, "Folks here are down-to-earth and practical. Someone needs a bed for the night, people don't pay much mind where that bed is."

She had picked at her meal, eating no more than she had on shipboard. Tom didn't want to admit it to himself, but he was starting to worry about her. What if Sinclair came for his daughter only to find she was ill or worse— insane?

Deborah stood watching out the window. The town was stirring to life in the morning. A child toddled out onto the stoop of the house across the way. A woman in a nightgown and kerchief grabbed him and took him inside.

At the end of the street, a girl carried a milking pail into a house. The man with the long white hair walked along the roadway, his breath making frozen clouds in the morning air.

She had dressed this morning without a mirror, washing her face in the chilly water at the washstand and brushing her hair in the dark. She emerged from the room to find a lively fire in the grate and Tom Silver fixing breakfast. Today, after their first night in the house behind the shop, he looked...different. He had bathed for a very long time the night before. She'd lain in bed and listened to him filling the big zinc tub in the next room, trying not to picture him. But she had anyway, and in her mind's eye that big body didn't in any way resemble the smooth marble nude sculptures she had viewed in Florence last summer.

He looked alarmingly real, not a statue at all. His hair, though still savagely long, shone with bluish glints and the small braid with the eagle feather flashed in and out of the dark locks. He wore Levi's trousers, boots and a clean broadcloth shirt. As he boiled the morning coffee, he seemed entirely at ease.

There was an intimate domesticity to the situation that discomfited her. She had never been terribly interested in the way other people started their day, had never given the matter much thought. It was unbearably strange, this settled state of affairs.

He glanced up. "Coffee's almost ready."

"Um, thank you." She sat down at the table, and seeing no napkin, wasn't sure what to do with her hands. So she simply folded them in her lap.

Tom poured himself a mug and sat down to eat a piece of cornbread. She chafed beneath his gaze. "Shall I help myself?"

"I reckon the breakfast isn't going to walk over here on its own."

"You needn't be sarcastic." She took down the other

mug from a peg. "Forgive me if I'm unclear on the protocol of being a prisoner."

He laughed briefly. "Very dramatic. Did you learn that by going to the theater?"

She sniffed and reached for the black enamel coffeepot. Tom spoke sharply, but her yelp of surprise and pain drowned him out. She leaped back, holding her burned hand. At the same moment, Tom jumped up. Grabbing her wrist, he pulled her over to the sink and pumped a cascade of water over her burned hand. The icy water soothed and then numbed her hand.

"Didn't you know that was hot?" he asked, pumping the water with one hand and holding her with the other.

She didn't answer. Surely he knew full well she had never poured coffee from a stove pot. More astonishing to her was the fact that he was holding her and she didn't feel like screaming or fainting.

He lifted her hand from the stream of water and inspected it. An angry red welt cut across her palm. "You'll probably get a blister," he said. He grabbed a frayed cloth from a peg and carefully blotted at her hand.

"Wait here," he said. "I've got some ointment for this." He fetched a tin of something that smelled faintly of maple. "Hold out your hand." She turned it palm up and he used his large, blunt finger to smooth on the ointment. Then he wound the cloth and loosely tied it.

"You must think me such a bungler," she said. Her hand stung, but that wasn't what hurt.

Instead of releasing her, he steered her toward the table and bench. "No," he said. "Just never met a woman who didn't know how to tie her own shoes or pour coffee."

He set a full mug in front of her, then a small tin plate with a square of cornbread on it. She briefly considered another hunger strike, but she already knew that mutiny did not work with this man. He had no heart, no sympathy when it came to her.

With her uninjured hand she picked up the bread and

took a bite. As she ate, she felt sheepishness creep like a
rash over her. What a foolish thing to do, grabbing a pot
from a hot stove with her bare hand. And Tom Silver, of
all people, had been there to see her do it.

All her life she had been surrounded by men who had
made her feel inadequate. Her father did not deem it necessary or proper for a woman to study and learn matters
of business and commerce. Philip's sophisticated knowledge of vintage wines and fine arts had been impressive,
and he had made a point of correcting her ignorance in
such matters—and many others. Now Tom Silver, taking
her against her will to this strange new world, had dealt
her another blow. She was a useless ornament. Not
needed. Not wanted. Barely tolerated.

"It must amuse you to see me helpless," she said at
last.

"You're a lot of things, lady, but you're not funny,"
he said.

"I wonder how you would fare in my world," she challenged. "You would be as out of place there as I am
here."

"Which is why we're here," he said simply. "Believe
me, if this was a permanent arrangement, I'd shoot myself. Or you."

"Then end it now," she said, leaning forward. "Take
me back to Chicago. If it's money you want from my
father, I'll see that you get it. I saw the scene of the tragedy. And if it happened as you say—"

"It did."

"—then he was wrong, very wrong, and must be made
to pay. I shall make my father listen to me. You needn't
break the law."

He laughed. "You think that's important to me?"

"I suppose nothing is important to you—nothing but
revenge."

"Give me a reason to feel otherwise," he snapped.

His angry grief touched her in unexpected ways. She

carefully unwrapped the cloth from her hand. The red welts were becoming more defined. "I've never experienced a loss like yours. I can't begin to know how you feel." She held his gaze. "What I do know is that nothing you've done so far is helping."

He broke the stare and shoved back from the table. "And you think going begging to your father will help."

"I wasn't suggesting begging. I never beg." She flushed scarlet, knowing it was a lie. She was lost then, locked in painful remembrances. It was the strangest sensation. She was aware of Tom Silver in the room with her, aware of the smell of coffee and the sound of the wind off the lake, yet she felt detached, unconnected to the rest of the world. She felt like a small boat unmoored, adrift in fog-shrouded waters.

She was going mad, she truly was.

"...hear what I said?" Tom Silver's voice interrupted her dark thoughts.

"I'm sorry?"

"I'll be in the shop." He pushed away from the table.

"What shall I do?" she demanded, looking around wildly. "You haven't answered my question. Why won't you let me go to my father, convince him to make a settlement to these families?"

He stopped in the doorway. "You're on an island in the north woods. No one's going to take you to see your father."

"Very well. Take me to the mainland and I'll go by stagecoach or train." She had never taken the train alone. Her father had his own salon car, lavishly made by George Pullman's company, but when she traveled, she was never alone. "I shall see to it that justice is served. You have my word of honor."

"Forgive me for being skeptical of a Sinclair's word of honor."

"He doesn't realize what happened here," she insisted. "He was obviously misled by his subordinates."

"He knew what he was doing. He knew what was at risk. He just didn't care."

"No." She refused to believe it. Her father was ambitious, yes. Of course. But not ruthless or heartless. "Hundreds of men work for my father. He does his best to employ men of skill and principle. Most are upstanding men of affairs, but perhaps this mining supervisor was unscrupulous. I shall simply tell my father exactly what you have told me. I'll explain what happened. He will dismiss the man responsible and make restitution to the families." She glared at him. "You would have executed him in cold blood with no regard for the law, without hearing his side of the story. Providence alone stopped you."

"As I recall, a crazy woman sliding down the banister stopped me."

She was still amazed at herself for actually having done something resourceful.

"The answer to your question is no," he concluded. "You'll stay here until he comes for you."

"What if he doesn't get your messages?" she demanded.

"He will," said Tom Silver. "He needs you, remember?"

"To marry Philip Ascot," she said, feeling a thump of panic in her chest.

"So his grandkids can join the Porcellian Club."

She gaped at him. "How on earth would you know about that?" It was the most exclusive private club at Harvard, open only to indisputably old-money students.

"Even a troglodyte can read Judge Lowell's memoirs," he said. "I once won a copy in a card game. If your father's not here by ice-up, you'll have to go to Fraser. That's where most islanders spend the winter."

"What is ice-up?"

"Just what it sounds like. When the lake freezes over and you can't navigate it, the island's cut off for the win-

ter. Some folks've been known to dogsled across the ice,
but it's dangerous. The islanders come back in March or
April when the ice breakers can get through.''

"And when does this ice-up happen?''

"November, December.''

"And the island is evacuated.''

"Yep. Being left behind's a death sentence, so folks
generally leave by December.''

"That's five weeks away.''

He dismantled the coffeepot in the sink. "I have work
to do.''

"What of me?''

"Princess,'' he said, "I don't much care.''

She felt herself spiraling away as she sometimes did,
down into that shadowy place where fearsome memories
lived. Trying to avoid such thoughts, she went to the window and studied the rutted track that comprised the main
street. "Do they all know who I am?'' she asked, regarding two women who stood in a yard, talking as they
pegged out laundry.

"Reckon so, by now,'' he said.

"They'll all hate me.''

He didn't deny it. "Just don't wander away anywhere.
It's easy to get lost on the island. Hard to be found.'' He
walked out of the house leaving a curious emptiness
heavy in the air. She stared at the space where he had
stood, and a shiver blew through her. Winter was coming
on.

On the same day, Arthur Sinclair received a social snub
and a mysterious package. His social secretary, Mr. Milford Plunkett, sat with him in the study of the Lake View
house, his impeccably clean, pale face drawn into lines of
sympathy. "So it's true, then,'' Plunkett said with quiet
resignation. "The brute Mr. Ascot encountered in Lincoln
Park did indeed abduct her.''

Arthur felt an uncomfortable heat in his chest. He stared

at the torn-open parcel containing a flaxen curl, and had a strange urge to touch it. But he didn't. Instead, he picked up the lavaliere and laid it on the table. Many years ago, he had spent a month's wages on the bauble, and not once had he regretted it. He remembered the way the pendant used to look on his wife when she would wear it to Sunday services. The facets of the blue topaz had seemed dim compared to the sparkle in her eyes. May used to laugh when Deborah, as a baby, would play with the jewel. "You'll have this when you're older, my precious," May used to say, "but only if you are very, very good."

May would have loved this room, he thought. It was painted her favorite color of blue, with a white marble fireplace, the flames dancing cheerily in the grate, chasing off the autumn chill. But back when May was alive, the only way she'd have seen a room like this would have been with a feather duster in her hand.

"The kidnapers could be bluffing," Plunkett suggested, though not with much conviction.

Arthur held his silence. The man called Tom Silver wanted money, but he wanted something more. He wanted Arthur himself to go to Isle Royale. He could not imagine that, could not imagine seeing the hole ripped into the earth by men who had died doing his bidding. He would never sleep another night if he let himself dwell on his mistakes. He survived by painting away the past, much like a painter brushes over a bad stroke.

Though he knew it wasn't reasonable, he aimed his anger at Deborah. Her childish refusal to marry Philip had precipitated all this. If she had gone where she was supposed to go that night, none of this would have happened. *And Silver would have shot me dead,* he reminded himself.

"Mr. Pinkerton has advised me not to negotiate with them," he said at last.

"You should probably trust his experience in these

matters, sir.'' Plunkett cleared his throat. ''About the supper you're hosting tonight—''

Sinclair detected a rare hesitation in his secretary's tone. ''Yes?'' He had been looking forward to the exclusive, elegant supper planned for that evening. It was a time to forget the horror of the fire, to look ahead to the future with the most important people in the city.

''Sir, perhaps you should postpone it. There have been several cancellations.'' He indicated the letters and cards in his hand.

''Several?''

''Er, all, sir. Everyone has sent their regrets.''

For a few seconds, Arthur couldn't breathe. Then he made himself say, ''The Ascots as well?''

''Yes, sir.''

The city, even in ruins, was a gossip mill. The disaster had hardly slowed down the wagging tongues and scandalized whispers. People were drawing their own conclusions about the disappearance of Deborah Sinclair.

''You're my social advisor,'' he said to Plunkett. ''I pay you handsomely to deal with things like this.''

''Begging your pardon, sir, but I've never encountered anything like this.''

''Then be blunt. Tell me what people are saying.''

''Sir, I really—''

''Just tell me, damn it.''

''They seem to dwell upon the fact that a savage abducted her. People's imaginations run wild at this sort of thing. There's speculation...''

''About what?''

''She's unmarriageable.'' For the first time, color flooded his smooth face. ''Who would have her now? She might give birth to a savage infant.'' He stared down at the cards in his hands. ''I'm sorry, sir.''

Arthur Sinclair knew of only one way to handle the situation. It was a matter of business, nothing more. He took a sheet of paper and a lead pencil, wrote a brief message in his heavy scrawl and shoved it across the table. "There's my reply." He severed the air with a sharp gesture of his hand.

Milford Plunkett didn't bother to conceal his relief as he hurried out. Arthur took the old lavaliere and put it in his pocket. Then he picked up the parcel with the lock of hair, tossed it into the fire and left the room.

Deborah stayed in the house for as long as she could stand. She inspected the dwelling where Tom Silver lived, finding it spare and utilitarian. Other than a shelf filled with all sorts of books there was nothing but plain wooden furniture, bare plank floors and unadorned walls. The only colorful object was the braided oval hearth rug.

She wondered what Asa had been like, then wondered what Tom Silver had been like before the boy had been killed. Had he smiled and laughed? Had he relaxed in front of the fire, playing checkers with the boy, telling him stories? She could almost imagine him doing such a thing. Almost.

Going into the other room, she pulled the blanket up over the bed and stood back, considering. The coverlet didn't look quite right. How did a maid do it? Deborah had seen a nicely made bed every day of her life yet she had never wondered how it was done. So she just smoothed out the drab blanket as best she could.

"What am I doing here?" she muttered under her breath. Feeling frustrated, she went outside. Smokey lay on the porch in a patch of weak sunlight. The dog thumped his tail in a cheerful greeting and she reached down to pet him. The fact that the only welcome she'd received came from a dog filled her with bleakness.

Yet at the same time, it occurred to her that she did not miss her old life. Her typical day started late, with a light breakfast served to her on bone china and sterling silver. Then came a French lesson, though her French was quite different from the colorful patois of Lightning Jack. She would organize her social engagements with the assistance of a social secretary who had a fine hand and an unerring nose for gossip. In the afternoon, she might have a dress fitting or perhaps one of those all-important engagements. A luncheon or tea, perhaps a philanthropic event. Without fail, there would be a supper engagement possibly followed by some sort of entertainment—the theater, dancing, the opera.

She shuddered, hearing echoes of Mozart's *Don Giovanni* in her head, but like someone touching a hot stove, she drew back quickly, stung. Who *was* that girl who had drifted from hour to hour, day to day? She was like a boat directed by the wind and water. Her will was not her own. And yet she had been content. As a caged bird is content, she reflected. The canary sings despite its captivity. Does it even know it's a prisoner?

She had gone from one sort of prison to another. From the gilded cage of a Chicago heiress to a rockbound island in the far north, she was as much a captive in one place as another. All that had changed was the identity of her jailer. And the worst of it was, she had no idea how to escape.

Loneliness finally drove her to seek company even though she suspected she would encounter hostility. She walked across the yard and out to the main road. There were a few people around, mostly women and children. The women who had been doing laundry were still there, pegging clothes on a cord stretched between two fenceposts. When they saw Deborah they fell immediately silent. The open hostility of their stares assaulted her, and she fought the urge to flee back into the house.

It was unlike her to be bold with strangers, but her recent adventures had been so unlike her own life that the rules of etiquette no longer applied.

''My name is Miss Deborah Beaton Sinclair,'' she said formally, stepping close to the fence. She looked from the pale, fair-haired woman to the dark one. "I would guess that you already know that."

"Then I would guess you already know why we're not welcoming you with open arms," said the dark-haired woman.

Deborah kept a pleasant look on her face, though she wanted to run and hide. All her life, everyone had always fawned on her. Open hostility was new and unwelcome. "I don't want to be on this island any more than you want me here," she said. "But since I've been forced to stay here, I feel compelled to address the tragedy blamed on my father."

The woman's gaze flicked to Deborah's silver combs and snapped downward to her manicured hands. "So you're the reason a man like Sinclair is so greedy. So he can keep buying pretty things for you and your mother."

"I have no mother," Deborah said. "She died when I was very small. And yes, my father indulges me by buying pretty things. He always has. But to suggest that I am the sole reason for the mining disaster is as wrong as Tom Silver was to kidnap me."

They looked reluctantly interested. She realized that the fire and her capture made for an intriguing tale, and that for all its improbabilities, it was true. It had happened to her.

"I am so sorry for the families of the men who were killed. I have already vowed to Mr. Silver that my father will accept responsibility. I know it's horribly inadequate but—" Seeing their flat stares, she changed tack.

"I *am* guilty," she said starkly, "but not in the way you believe. I'm guilty of willful ignorance. I never gave a thought to my father's business affairs. I didn't think they concerned me. I was taught that it was unseemly for a woman to take an interest in business and so I shut my eyes and ears to his mining deals, to all his many other enterprises." She folded her hands in front of her.

"We have a different way of living up here," said the

big blond woman. She spoke with a clear, simple dignity. "Families work together. You know what your sons, daughter, neighbors are doing."

Deborah was unprepared for the intense yearning those words evoked. Families living and working together toward a common goal was an alien notion to her. In her world, families embraced ostentation and posturing for the sake of raising their status. None of that seemed to matter to these people.

"We have work to do." The dark woman indicated the basket piled high with wet clothes. A subtle pride shaded her words. In that moment, Deborah knew for the first time in her life what it felt like to be excluded, set apart. The feeling sat like a rock in her stomach. She pressed herself against the fence, determined to stay. "I hope one day you'll tell me your names and the names of your loved ones who died. And I hope, too, that you'll believe me when I say I am determined to help. Now that I understand the nature of my father's involvement, I must return to Chicago to tell him what occurred here and see that he does the right thing."

"There's no making this right," the dark-haired woman said coldly. Both of them kept working, their hands deft and mechanical.

"I can't argue with that." Deborah swallowed past a lump in her throat. She looked from one woman to the other. Their faces might have been carved of granite. "I would really like to know your names," she said softly, then turned to head...she didn't know where. Down to the landing, perhaps, to look out at the vast and endless water.

"Ilsa Ibbotsen," said a quiet voice behind her.

Deborah turned slowly to face the pale woman.

"My name is Ilsa," she repeated, "and it was my brother-in-law who died in your father's mine. He was buried, and we never recovered the body."

"Thank you for telling me that. I do wish to God you still had him with you," Deborah said.

"I am Celia Wilson," the dark-haired woman said. She seemed more reluctant than Ilsa, her overture less genuine. But it was a start, Deborah thought.

"We could use some help." Ilsa indicated the shallow wicker basket piled high with just-washed clothes.

"Of course." Deborah stepped through the gate into the yard. On the beaten-earth surface, two children played with a hoop and a stick. Even she could do laundry, she reasoned. Emulating the others, she picked up an item— a nightshirt, or so it appeared—and shook it out. Celia held the pegs in her teeth. Deborah couldn't quite bring herself to do that. She pegged the shirt to the line and immediately the garment dropped into the dirt.

Ilsa said nothing. She picked it up and gave the fabric a shake, inspecting it. "Not too soiled," she said. "Use at least two pegs."

Embarrassed, Deborah tried again. She worked more slowly than the others, but managed to do her share. She felt slightly chagrined, realizing that all her life she had taken this for granted. When she carelessly soiled a cuff and left it in a heap on the floor, it never occurred to her that someone had to come along behind her, pick it up and restore it to pristine condition. She had heard women refer to the drudgery of chores, and now she was experiencing it first hand. Except that, in the company of other women, it was certainly no less boring and toilsome than doing petit point in her father's cavernous summer parlor. The mound of clothes quickly shrank to the last item—a large quilt. It was made of small hexagonal pieces that ranged from deep blue to pale cerulean, arranged so the light ones appeared to reflect the dark.

"This is simply beautiful," Deborah said.

"My mother made it for me as a Christmas gift," Celia said. "That pattern is called sky river."

Deborah pictured a small woman with small hands, like Celia, working by lamplight. How many stitches had it taken to join these hundreds of bits of fabric together? "A true labor of love," Deborah said, folding a corner over the line. "I envy you."

"Me? What could a rich girl from Chicago find to envy in me? I bet your blankets come from London or...or Persia."

"I'd rather sleep under a quilt made by my mother." She pinned the corner, marveling at the tininess of the stitches. "I never knew her."

"Ah, that's hard indeed," Ilsa said.

"Yes, it is," Deborah replied. "In ways I am only beginning to understand."

"Do you know how to quilt?" Ilsa asked.

"No, but I'd like to learn. I know petit point and a lot of fancy work." Deborah gave a self-deprecating smile. "Hat making used to be a pastime of mine."

"Quilting's not that different." She picked up the basket. "Come on in for a spell. I'll show you."

Celia flashed her a look but went into the house with them. Deborah was struck by the brightness of the big main room. The walls and floor had a light, scrubbed look, and a large plank table dominated the room. Rows of benches lined the periphery.

"We hold Sunday services here," Ilsa explained, catching Deborah's inquisitive look. "My husband is the pastor." As she crossed the room, she touched the back of the large chair in the parlor—a man's chair. Pride and affection softened her plain, pale face.

She pulled a wooden rack from the corner. "My quilting hoop."

It resembled a large embroidery hoop. Stretched across it was a pieced-together quilt of faded bits of fabric. "I'm doing a vine," she said. She bent and lifted the lid of a wicker hamper to reveal colorful bits of fabric. "I've collected far too much," she said. "This is all extra." She picked out a square of warn red flannel. "My son Nels's fishing shirt. He swore he'd never catch another fish if I put this in the rag bag. But he simply got too big." She sifted through more scraps, relating a story to go with many of them.

For the rest of the morning, Celia and Ilsa showed Deborah how a design was imagined, the components cut and pieced together to make the design. Deborah felt drawn to the craft. There was something slightly mystical about the idea of transforming old and useless scraps into a quilt to warm someone on a cold winter night.

"Would you like to take the scrap box and try something for yourself? You could start with something small, just for practice."

"Thank you, yes," Deborah said. "Lord knows I shall need something to occupy me while I'm here. Tom Silver has deemed me—let me see if I can remember his charming phrase—useless as tits on a fish."

Celia ducked her head, but Ilsa laughed outright. "Sounds like our Tom."

"Does it?"

"You've crossed two lakes in his company," Celia pointed out. "Surely by now you know what he's like."

"As you can imagine, we are not on the best of terms." She looked from Celia to Ilsa, falling easily into the rhythm of their conversation. In some ways they were not so different from Lucy and Phoebe back in Chicago. "Did he tell you how he kidnaped me?"

Suddenly they were rapt with attention. Deborah related the story of the fire, from the moment Tom Silver burst into her father's house.

"You slid down a banister and hit him?" Celia gave a low whistle.

Deborah hadn't thought she'd done anything extraordinary at the time, but she could see they were impressed. She described the mayhem of the collapse of the alley, being separated from her father, seeing Tom rescue a lost child and using the chance to elude him. She told them of the trapped dog and how she had nearly lost herself in the crowd, only to be recaptured at Lincoln Park. She did not speak of Philip, but still wondered if she should have gone with him. Tom Silver had taken the decision away from her.

"And so here I am," she concluded, "with a strange man who has some crazy revenge scheme." She shuddered. "Has he always been...odd? Or is it just since the accident?"

Ilsa began sorting the scraps. "He has lived at Isle Royale since he was a boy. Grew up helping Lightning Jack duBois on his trawler. He was always a wild, restless boy, given to running off into the woods and getting into mischief. Years ago when they were mustering troops for the war, he ran off and signed up."

"Lied about his age and joined a Michigan regiment," Celia added.

It was hard to picture him as a soldier. She couldn't imagine him marching in a drill, following orders. Although, all too easily, she could imagine him rushing into battle. He had that reckless, deadly look about him sometimes. She'd noticed it the moment he'd first burst upon her father in Chicago. Tom Silver had the look of a man who didn't care about the risk to himself.

During the war years, it was considered a young man's duty to fight for the Union. Most came back thin and sad and unnaturally quiet, but some never returned. Philip had not gone off to fight. In addition to being the sole son and heir to his family line, he suffered from nearsightedness and could not take to soldiering, or so he said. Deborah pulled her mind back to the matter at hand—Tom Silver.

"Tom was a courier," Celia supplied. "Ran messages between regiments."

"He's not one to talk about what went on," Ilsa said. "He came back after a few years with a little boy. Said it was his friend's son, that the friend died after the war."

"He never said a word, but Asa once showed me a box of medals and decorations Tom earned," Celia continued.

"One is the Congressional Medal of Honor. His citation was for conspicuous bravery and heroism."

Deborah heard a warmth in the young woman's voice that had not been there before. Could it be that Celia had set her cap for Tom Silver? It wasn't so far-fetched, she supposed. Some women might favor a brutish man like him. He was certainly strong. She had seen him lift a dinghy one-handed out of the water. Protective, too. He definitely had that tendency.

"What sort of bravery and heroism?" she asked Celia.

"No one knows. He won't talk about it."

"Have you asked him?"

"Of course." Her mouth softened, though she didn't smile. "Doesn't mean I got an answer."

"Lightning Jack was told he braved an intense fire that mowed down his unit at Kenaha Falls," Ilsa stated. "He climbed the breastworks so close to an enemy gun that the blast hurled him into a ditch, and somehow he managed to enter the gun pit. When the gun crew saw him, they all fled."

"That," said Deborah, recalling his aggressive presence, "does not surprise me."

"Lightning says he used the last shot in his pistol to capture a Confederate flag bearer and guard."

His past was a vast wilderness to Deborah, as hers was to him. Best they keep it that way. "You know this man well," Deborah said, hope rising within her. "You could speak to him on my behalf. Convince him that what he is doing is a mistake."

"Is it?" Ilsa asked.

"No good can come of keeping me here against my will. If he lets me go, I can persuade my father to help the mining families. I can convince him not to prosecute Mr. Silver for his reckless act."

"Seems to me Tom's not the reckless one."

"But holding me prisoner won't solve a thing. It'll only create more trouble." She shivered, imagining what her

father would do. The revelations she'd had about him over
the past few days had left her shaken. Almost reluctantly,
she recalled an incident that had occurred when she was
very small. Unbeknownst to her father, she used to hide
in the kneehole of the massive desk in his study, creating
a tiny dark cocoon just out of reach of his feet. He had
not known she was there when a man had come to his
office.

"Please, Mr. Sinclair," the man had said, "I'll have
the money in a week—"

"You're three months in arrears already," her father
had said in an angry voice. "I've no room in the lumber
mill for a worker who doesn't earn his keep."

"It's the wife," the man had persisted. "She's been
sick since the baby came—"

"Get out before I have you thrown out."

Even now, years later, she remembered the harshness
in her father's voice. It had made her stomach feel all
hard and cold. After that day, she had stopped playing in
his study.

"My father often hires the Pinkerton agents to look
after matters of security," she told the women. "Tom
could be thrown into prison. Hanged from the nearest
tree."

"Really?" Celia asked.

"I'm afraid so." To her surprise, Deborah didn't want
that to happen to Tom Silver. She simply wanted to go
home. "I have to be given the opportunity to settle this,"
she said. She ran her hand over the mounds of scraps. "I
might be useless when it comes to practical matters, but
I do know my father. I can make him listen to me."

Ilsa and Celia exchanged a glance.

"Please." Deborah sensed an advantage and she
pressed at it. "Help me to convince Mr. Silver to send
me back to Chicago."

"That's what you want, then," Celia said. "To go back
to Chicago."

Deborah bit her lip. Her mind flashed on the sort of life she had there. "I don't have anywhere else to go," she said quietly. Philip, a New Yorker, wanted to move back east once they were wed. She hadn't given the prospect much thought, but now she realized she had no interest in living in New York City.

She picked up a few faded floral fabric scraps and set them against the muslin. Birds, she thought suddenly, her mind forming an image of the waterbirds rising from the mist on the lake. If she ever learned to make a quilt, she would want it to depict birds in flight.

"How do we know you're not just saying that?" Celia asked. "You'll probably get back to your father and ignore all the promises you made. People like you don't care about poor folks."

"That's not true," Deborah objected. "I saw the mining pit. I see what the loss did to the families around here. For pity's sake, I sleep in the bed of a boy who was killed. Do you honestly think I would ever forget? Or fail to keep my promise?"

Celia's handsome, square face sharpened with suspicion. "We don't know anything about you."

"She grew up without a mother," Ilsa pointed out. "She survived the burning of Chicago."

Deborah sensed an ally in the pastor's wife. "I will take up this matter with my father," she said. "But I can't do a thing unless I get back to Chicago."

"Tom Silver is a man of his own mind," Ilsa said. "I don't know that there's anything you can do or say to make him release you."

"Couldn't you talk to him? Convince him that releasing me is the right thing to do?"

"You don't 'release' a person up here. It's not as if you can simply swim away like an undersized fish."

A terrible, closed-in feeling squeezed at her. "Surely there are boats coming and going."

"Occasionally," Celia admitted. "Mail boat's due in today or tomorrow."

"And where does it go from here?"

"Stops at the other settlements, then goes on down to Copper Harbor."

She looked from one woman to the other. "Will you help me? Will you speak to Tom Silver on my behalf?"

"It won't do any good," Celia said. "No one tells Tom Silver what to do."

Ilsa placed the scraps in a drawstring bag. "Take these with you. It'll help to pass the time."

"I'd best run along." Celia went to the door. "I promised Mr. Sivertsen a game of checkers, poor old thing." As she left, a large man with a ruddy, wind-burned face strode into the kitchen. "Where is my beautiful wife?" he bellowed, then snatched Ilsa into his arms and planted a loud kiss on her mouth.

"Peter," Ilsa said, suppressing a giggle, "we have a guest."

The pastor greeted Deborah with a reserved warmth, but clearly he had come to see his wife. "We filled the nets by ten o'clock," he said. "I told the Wicks I would help them in the fish house, since they're shorthanded."

Deborah knew without asking that the shortage of workers had something to do with the mining accident. Pastor Ibbotsen helped himself to a big piece of pie and another kiss from his wife and then he was gone.

Deborah had the feeling a tornado had blown through. The air seemed to hum in his wake. A smile of quiet joy lingered on Ilsa's mouth. "For a churchman," she said, "he is a very informal man," she said.

Deborah knew she meant the kiss. It appeared that Ilsa deeply loved her husband, that she enjoyed being married. Deborah could not imagine such a thing.

"Do you have a sweetheart back in Chicago?" Ilsa asked.

Caught off guard, Deborah nodded. "I was supposed

to marry a man named Philip Ascot,'' she said. ''But I
don't think I shall now. Do you know, when he first asked
for my hand in marriage, I thought it was because he
loved me.''

''An understandable notion,'' Ilsa said. ''Some folks
do, you know.''

''Do what?''

''Marry for love.''

Deborah had never seen it. All the marriages between
her friends and acquaintances had the flavor of dynastic
mergers. It was the way of the world. Two families
merged by marriage and often—often enough for her to
dream it could happen to her—the love happened afterward, forged by years of living together, raising a family.
She was certain it was supposed to happen that way. If it
didn't, what was the point of anything?

But she knew there was a darker side to marriage,
something women never spoke of. Or perhaps, she conceded, there was simply something wrong with her. She
lacked some fundamental quality that would make her the
sort of happy wife Ilsa appeared to be. Maybe it was because she had grown up without a mother. Maybe it was
because her father was so hard to please. She was no
longer certain what happiness was, or how to find it.

''I might never marry at all,'' Deborah said. ''I think I
would like that.'' A while later, a distant whistle sounded.
She felt a clutch of hope in her chest. ''The mail boat?''

Ilsa nodded. Deborah rushed outside and headed down
to the landing. Finally, a way out of her dilemma.

Fifteen

The first person Deborah encountered on her way to the landing was Tom Silver. In his jeans, broadcloth shirt and tall boots, with the breeze in his hair, he looked more like Paul Bunyan than ever. Her chest caught at the sight of him, and she had a strange, unexpected reaction—a warmth, a tightening inside her. When he saw her, he lifted one eyebrow inquiringly. She thought about what Celia and Ilsa had warned her about—that Tom Silver didn't take orders from anyone.

She sniffed and stuck her nose in the air. She was not about to explain herself to him.

She would have carried on with her dignified progress if she hadn't stepped in the puddle. Her right foot struck chilly water and sticky mud. With a cry of dismay, she brushed back her skirts and extracted her foot from the puddle.

Tom Silver kept walking as if nothing had happened. Her foot sloshed as she walked, and she wished in that moment that she knew an oath or two, for surely if ever there was a time for oaths, this was it.

"So much for mincing around with your nose in the air, eh, Princess?" Tom Silver asked at last.

She felt the now-familiar sting of interest in him. No.

She could not have—could not abide—an interest in *any* man. "You needn't gloat."

He glanced at her bandaged hand. "I'm not gloating. So who told you about the mail packet?"

She saw no harm in revealing to him that she had made the acquaintance of Ilsa and Celia. And she took a certain satisfaction in the expression of surprise on his face. "You were certain they would blame me for the sins of my father," she said.

"I don't claim to know any woman's mind," he said carefully. There seemed to be something he was holding back from her, but she wasn't certain what it was.

"Not everyone believes that revenge is the way to redemption," she said.

He narrowed his eyes. "Who said I was looking for redemption?"

She gave a little laugh of disbelief. "Mr. Silver, if ever there was a man in need of redemption, then you are the one."

"How's that?"

She aimed her gaze at the roadway ahead. "Never mind. I've said too much. Your immortal soul is none of my affair." She couldn't believe she had said as much as she had. Perhaps this was part of being a captive. She was developing an unhealthy attachment to her captor. She was better off concentrating on figuring out a way to escape him.

The mail packet turned out to be a little tug, its steam engines seething as it angled for the dock. By the time she and Tom reached the landing, a bearded man with close-set, light eyes was setting crates out on the dock. Tom Silver greeted him. The man peered at Deborah, openly curious, his odd, flat gaze lingering a shade too long for comfort.

Tom didn't address the unasked questions hanging in the air, but busied himself putting the three crates on a two-wheeled cart. "Can you stay a spell, Silas?" he asked.

"Not today. I'd best get around to Rock Harbor before the weather kicks up."

Deborah had seen Rock Harbor on one of Lightning Jack's charts. The settlement lay at the other end of the island, perhaps forty miles away.

"Wait," she said. "Take me with you."

The man rubbed his beard. "You want to go to Rock Harbor?"

"No. I want to go back to the mainland with you." She didn't dare look at Tom Silver, though she could feel the bruising intensity of his glare. "I can pay you."

"Can you then, miss?" The pale man called Silas looked intrigued. He held a cheroot between his fingers, and the smoke and tobacco had stained his hand amber.

"Please." Deborah clasped her hands together in supplication. "I don't belong here. Tom Silver forced me to come here against my will. Anyone of honor and decency would help me. There is a reward out for my safe return, I'm sure of it."

The light eyes drifted over her, lingering too long again. "That a fact?"

Something about the way he was staring chilled her to the bone. She felt a frisson of unease at the prospect of getting on the mail boat with him. The breath locked in her throat, but she swallowed hard, fighting past the fear. "All I want is to get back to the mainland so I can make my way to Chicago."

"I suppose that could be arranged." Within the pale hair of the beard, his lips were red and wet. "For a price."

Deborah told herself to walk out on the dock. She told herself to defy Tom Silver and simply get in the boat with the skipper. But there was something about him that put her off. The twist of fear in her gut reminded her that some men were a danger to women like her. She felt hopelessly torn. Here was someone who could offer a way off the island, and she was too afraid to take the chance.

Frustrated, disgusted with her indecision, she admonished herself not to get weepy. "I...I believe I've changed my mind," she said. Then she turned and marched up the road toward the trading post. By the time she reached the porch of Tom Silver's house, she wanted to howl with disappointment. She didn't know what to do, whom she could trust. She sank to the bottom step and looped her arms around her drawn-up knees.

When he arrived in the yard, parking the cart at the side entrance of the shop, she sent a dagger look at him.

"You made the right choice, staying here instead of going with him," Tom said.

"How would you know what is the right choice for me?"

"He's a good skipper," Tom explained. "But he has a reputation for being a little rough when it comes to women."

Rough. The term conjured images she didn't want to see.

Tom Silver opened the supply doors at the rear of the post. "I thought you might like to know. A wire came from your father," he said.

She sat up straight, as if he had poked her in the back. Silver picked up the handles of the cart and steered it around back. Unwilling to shout after him like a fishwife, she hurried to follow him. Thank God, she thought. Thank God, her father now knew where she was. Arthur Sinclair was a problem solver. Let him tackle a situation and he would resolve it. She had seen him do so in everything from settling disputes among the household help to mediating strikes at the Union Stockyards.

Surely he would find a way to rescue his only daughter from this vast wilderness.

"What does he say?" she asked, unable to stay quiet a moment longer. "When will he be here?"

''I reckon we'll find out.''

''Where did the wire come from?'' She tried not to grind her teeth in impatience.

He didn't look at her but walked up the supply ramp. ''Nearest telegraph office is in Copper Harbor.''

As she followed him into the shop, she was already working out in her head how soon she could be back home with her father. True, they had not parted on the best of terms. He had refused to hear her out in the matter of Philip Ascot, but she felt certain that, in time, he would understand that she could not have such a man as her husband regardless of his position and importance in society.

She glanced at Silver, who lifted the hinged counter and moved behind it. With great deliberation, he unfolded the amber-colored piece of paper and spread it out on the counter. He stared down at it, then looked up at Deborah.

He uttered a word she had never heard before, and his tone of voice suggested she did not ever want to learn its meaning. Then he strode out of the room. She could hear him at the back of the building, stacking crates with angry energy.

A chill coursed over her as she took a step toward the plank counter. The message from her father lay there, tantalizing with possibilities.

Her hand shook as she picked it up, turned it toward her.

She had to read the body of the message twice before its meaning registered.

The sound that escaped her was strange, unfamiliar, the cry of a cornered animal. She clutched the telegram in her fist and pressed her hand to her breastbone. She could feel her heart beating hard against her chest, could hear the rhythm of her breathing, but she felt like a stranger to herself. All her life she had been the daughter of Arthur Sinclair. Now, in the space of a moment, she was not. She was no one.

She recalled her fantasy of disappearing in the midst of the fire. Now her wish had come true. She didn't have to obey her father because she had no father. She had been set adrift by the man who had been her protector. Like a piece of bad business, she had been put aside.

"Oh, Father," she whispered. "Father, how could you?"

Tom Silver could not have heard her agonized whisper, but he stalked in from the back and inspected her with some concern. But he said nothing. He had said nothing since the oath that had come out of him a few moments ago.

There was only one thing she could do when she saw the expression on his face, and that was laugh. She had to, or else she would melt into a puddle of tears. So she threw back her head and laughed with all that she was, with everything that was in her. She laughed until the tears came, and kept laughing until they dried. Laughing until her chest nearly burst with hurt. Through it all, Tom Silver stood watching her with the sort of wary suspicion of someone observing an inmate in an insane asylum.

Finally, after a very long time, he crossed the room to her and held her by the upper arms. She forgot to fight him, forgot to recoil from his touch, forgot to be afraid when he put his face very close to hers.

"You'll have to explain the joke, Princess," he said. "Because I don't get it."

The hysteria of her laughter finally subsided. In its wake came a sense of hurt and abandonment so sharp that she flinched. "The joke is on you, Mr. Silver." She stared at his hand on her arm. Why wasn't she fighting him? Why didn't he make her afraid anymore?

She shook back her hair. "You thought you had managed to kidnap the most valuable hostage in Chicago," she said. "Yet it turns out I'm worthless." She chuckled, the sound weak, for she had nearly spent herself laughing. "Completely, absolutely worthless."

Saying the words aloud confirmed it. She realized that she would never, ever be forgiven for refusing to marry Philip Ascot. The planned alliance with the venerated Ascot family had meant everything to her father. She had never quite understood, until this moment, just how much store he had set by the upcoming nuptials.

Arthur Sinclair was a mystery to her—she had only just realized that. When had her father stopped seeing her as a daughter and begun to regard her as a chess piece in his game to capture a foothold in society? Perhaps he had never seen her as a daughter. She was only now realizing her place in the world he had made.

She had no place in his heart. Only in his plans.

While Tom Silver held on to her—she still had no idea why his touch didn't create panic in her—she forced herself to unfold her hand and reread the telegram.

The words struck into her like hurled rocks. They sounded so like her father, so like Arthur Sinclair.

You took her, you keep her. An unmarriageable daughter is worth nothing to me.

She wondered what Tom Silver was thinking. His face betrayed nothing. At first. Then he let go of her abruptly. She stepped back, waiting. He said that word again, the one whose meaning she didn't know.

Yet on some level, she did know.

"What the hell does he mean, 'unmarriageable'?"

She had trouble breathing. "Why, exactly what you think it means. I cannot be married."

His dark eyes narrowed. "Why not? Do you have any idea why he'd respond like this?"

Shame flashed through her, searing hot. "Yes."

"You mind explaining?"

"Yes," she said again. Her stomach churned. She clutched at herself, trying to stave off the sickness. She went outside for air, heading away from the settlement. She stopped at a small crystal stream that tumbled down from the rocky heights above the shoreline. Tom Silver came up behind her.

"I'm still waiting for an answer," he said.

She knew what her father's message meant. At her center, she managed to find an oasis of numbness and she spoke from that place.

"I—" She could not, would not, explain the secrets of her heart to this cruel stranger. She held her hands low, wringing them together in desperation.

"You sick or something?"

"No, I'm not sick, damn your eyes. I am ruined!" The words burst out of her and hung there, between them, echoing through the silence of the empty day. She wished she could take them back, swallow them, hide them. She had not meant to reveal so much of herself to this man. She walked away, taking a path down to the edge of the lake.

He stared for a long moment at her wringing hands, then at her face. "Ruined," he said at length. "If you were a horse, I'd reckon it means you'd been ridden rough, bit-spoiled." He scowled, then raised his eyebrows with dawning comprehension. "Ah, I see what he means. He thinks his perfect, sweet daughter has lost her virginity."

She buried her face in her hands. It was a word she had never before heard uttered aloud, and in the majestic wilderness, it was a profanity. Whispering through her hands, she said, "I'm quite certain he thinks so."

Tom Silver threw back his head and roared with laughter. His reaction caught her by surprise, and she lowered her hands to watch him. His voice rang across the flat water and bounced off the sides of the rock cove. Mirth transformed him from a brooding, angry woodsman into someone quite human. Human and attractive, with remarkably straight, strong teeth and lively character etched in the lines of his face. Except, she reminded herself, that he was laughing at her.

"You're amused by this?" she asked coldly.

"You were too, a minute ago." He was still chuckling. "Lady, I'm the one losing out here. I've got nothing. No justice, no ransom, nothing but your father's assumption that I took your virginity. And here I never even got the pleasure of taking it."

She gasped, her fist flying to her mouth. She hadn't considered that. Yet now that she thought about it, her father's assumption was perfectly logical. He believed she had been compromised by her captor. Of course he would. He had seen Tom Silver at his wild-eyed worst. A hun, or a Nordic chief, bent on raping and pillaging like the Viking hordes of legend.

"What?" he asked through his laughter. "You're looking at me funny. What are you thinking about?"

"Viking hordes."

"*What?*"

"Never mind." She thought fast. "Now you have more reason than ever to let me go. I must tell my father that you weren't—you never—" She broke off, turned away.

"Now, why would you defend my honor?" He looked genuinely amused.

She heard him take a step closer, could feel the aggressive heat of his nearness. "It wouldn't matter if I did," she conceded. "I am unfit to marry."

"What, because he thinks I—" Silver broke off and chuckled. "Guess I've heard of men who prize an untried wife."

"All men do," she whispered. "It is a factual certainty."

He laughed again, briefly. "That something they taught you at that fancy-ass ladies' school?"

She put her hands down. "Believe me, if it were up to the ladies, it would not be the case." She took a gulp of air. "I cannot believe we are having this conversation."

"Then you should know," he said, "it's not the case."

"But—"

"Maybe with that Ascot fellow," Silver said with a grimace. "But I don't know of a man with a lick of sense who would judge a woman by that standard."

"I don't know a man with a lick of sense, period," she said, surprising herself with the insight. She stared pointedly at him.

"It's a bluff." He indicated the printed paper. "Sinclair's a fool, but he's bluffing."

"No, he's not," Deborah said. "My father always says exactly what he means." She stared out at the long blue horizon of the lake, the hard line where water and sky met looking so close and clear she thought she could touch it.

You took her, you keep her. Like a stray cat, she thought, and a wave rolled through her, gathering momentum. She knew she was about to burst, to break, and she could do nothing to stop it. Her father had been her anchor. Without him, what did she have to hold her? Why did she need anyone? She would have to make her own way in the world but did she want to? The only thing she knew for certain was that she did not belong in this wild, haunted place.

"There is no point in keeping me here further," she said to Silver. "I am only an extra mouth to feed. And now you have no hope of recovering what you've spent to kidnap me. The only possible solution is for you to send me back to Chicago at once."

"Doesn't sound like you'd find much of a welcome there."

She clung to an image of Kathleen, the sister of her heart. Kathleen and Lucy and even Phoebe would shield her, support her, perhaps one day restore her faith in herself. "I have other options besides my father," she insisted. "That should not concern you."

"Believe me, it doesn't."

She studied his face. He was looking at her with hard, assessing eyes, but the singular thing was, he seemed to see *her.* Not a commodity to be traded. Not a possession to be used and discarded. Not a brood mare to be bred. But simply herself. Which was more than she saw when she looked in a mirror.

"Please," she said. "Let's declare this entire thing over. I won't hold you responsible for dragging me to this island and you won't hold me responsible for the tragedy caused by my father's mining company. We shall both put this behind us."

"It's not that simple. There's not a boat on the way to Chicago every day of the week."

"There's the mail boat. I'll take that to the mainland and then take a stage or a train." She forced herself to hold his gaze even though she wanted to look away. "It's over, Mr. Silver. Can't you see that it's over?"

Saying the words aloud broke her. The wave rolling through her grew too strong to resist. Shock gave way to the acute perception that her own father had rejected her. She felt her soul shrivel up, and nothing stood between calm and hysteria. At first, her sobs were silent, as voiceless as her pain, but when she drew in her breath, it came out on a moan of anguish so searing that Tom Silver actually flinched and glanced around as if he wanted to run from her.

But he didn't. Instead, he put his hand on her shoulder in an awkward attempt to console her. "Don't cry," he said. "Don't cry."

Deborah fought for calm. She took the red bandana he offered her and crushed it against her burning eyes. *Don't cry.* And at length, she drew composure from a well of strength she had never tapped before. "All right," she said unsteadily. "All right. I shall not cry anymore."

He made no attempt to hide his relief as he shook the telegram, then crumpled it into a ball. "You claim he's not bluffing. That must mean he's serious about this 'unmarriageable' horseshit."

"What do you care? You just said you didn't." In spite

of herself, she felt a welling of relief. Being unable to marry anyone was exactly what she wanted...wasn't it?

"You think your Philip Ascot had something to do with this?" Silver stuffed the paper in his shirt pocket.

"I have no idea what Philip thinks. Please," she said, feeling desperate. "You must let me go."

"Back to Chicago," he said flatly. "Back to your father."

"Yes."

"For God's sake, why?" His earlier mirth took a dark turn. "Do you understand what he means by this?" He yanked out the telegram, thrust it into her hand. "Do you know what he's saying?"

"Yes, but—"

"And you want to go back to this son of a bitch? You want to be his daughter again?"

"I can't simply stop being his daughter just because you hauled me to this godforsaken island."

"He thinks you can."

She felt tears crowding her throat again, pushing behind her eyes, but with Tom Silver, tears didn't mean a thing. "I need to see him, to explain—"

"You've probably been doing that all your life. Justifying yourself to a man not worth the effort."

"You can't stand the idea that I might forgive him."

"He doesn't deserve forgiveness."

"From me, he does. You've hardly given me an attractive alternative," she snapped. "Why would I want to stay here with a person who hates me, holds me in contempt, thinks I'm barely competent?" She glanced at her burned hand.

"I don't hate you," he said. "I don't hold you in contempt." He didn't address the competency issue.

"Hah. You've given me no reason to want to stay."

"You're not supposed to want to, damn it. You're a hostage."

"Rendered worthless. And I'm asking you to release me."

She longed for the genteel quiet of Miss Boylan's staid halls and tasteful parlors. She longed for a life in which her biggest dilemma of the day had been whether to wear the blue serge or the cream silk to the afternoon musicale. Yet she wasn't that person anymore. She knew now that she couldn't find fulfillment in such things ever again. But she had to find...something. A new purpose, a new direction in life. Simply hiding away in the north woods wouldn't accomplish that. "I want to know what became of my friends."

"They could be dead," he speculated. "Judging by what the papers said, half the city was left homeless."

"How did you get to be so callous?"

"I'm just stating the obvious."

"Then you understand that I am frantic to see them," she replied. "It is the height of cruelty to hold me here, where I can do nothing but worry."

"Worrying. That's something." And with those final words, he turned and left her standing by the lake.

Sixteen

Deborah resigned herself to waiting out the rest of the season on Isle Royale. It was only a few weeks, she told herself, trying to stave off desperation. Just a few weeks, and then she would evacuate the island with the rest of the people. Once on the mainland, she would find a way back to Chicago. She refused to speculate on what might happen after that.

Judging by Tom Silver's contempt, it should not be too difficult to persuade him to send her on her way.

She would not let herself think too long or too hard about her father. She would not let herself believe she meant nothing to him. His judgment had been addled by the fire, that had to be the answer. Surely he valued her for more than her worth on the marriage market. He loved her…didn't he?

She remembered the way he used to sit at her bedside when she was small, tending the lamp himself because she was afraid of the dark. When Nanny MacGregor had warned him against spoiling her, he'd laughed and said, "She's only a child." And Deborah would secretly smile and snuggle down under the covers and fall asleep with his scent of aged leather and ink in her nostrils.

To keep from going mad, she decided to move beyond the confines of the cabin and explore the unique com-

munity of fisherfolk and loggers. Ilsa Ibbotsen and Celia
Wilson had accepted her. They taught her the craft of
quilting, and she showed them how to make absurd, elaborate hats. The news that her father had abandoned her
actually worked to Deborah's advantage. Now she had
people's sympathy, for she had been forsaken by the man
who was their common enemy.

Except Arthur Sinclair was not her enemy; he was her
father.

Desperate to stop herself from thinking about his refusal to come for her, she observed the people of the settlement, wondering with increasing interest about their
way of life. In a shake house across the way lived the
Lindvig sisters, who corked nets by day and in the evenings sat by their stove, knitting big colorful sweaters.
They spoke in Norwegian, but always managed a smile
and a charmingly formal bob of the head when Deborah
passed.

Mabel Smith and Jenny Nagel were two young mothers, both widowed by the explosion. As their children
raced around the settlement, the mothers looked on with
a quiet desperation that tore at Deborah's heart. She
adored children, though she had never actually known any
personally—another lack she had barely noticed in her
busy Chicago world. She had always assumed that children were none of her affair, even though she expected
to become a mother one day. Among her set, youngsters
occupied the private, shadowy realm of nursery and
boarding school, appearing only when commanded by
their parents, spit-shined and as well-behaved as trained
spaniels. The small boy and girl standing in the clearing
at the end of the roadway were most definitely not spit-
shined.

Neither am I, thought Deborah, and she was perfectly
comfortable being that way.

"Hello," she said, smiling down at them. Ilsa had told

her their names were Paul and Betsy Smith. "What are you doing?"

The girl held up a battered kite and pulled a long face. "We can't make it fly."

"Papa could make it fly," Paul said.

"Papa's gone," his older sister pointed out. "He won't be back."

With those words, Deborah felt a tremendous flash of anger against her own father, but concealed it behind a smile. "Then we must make it fly on our own." She held up the kite and eyed it critically. "I know just what this needs."

"You do?"

"Of course. When I was your age, I used to fly my kite in a great green park far away from here." She did not tell them how closely supervised those outings had been, how she had only been allowed to hold the string for a few minutes before Nanny MacGregor had hustled her home. "It needs a lot more string and a long, beautiful tail," she declared, pleased with herself for remembering the mechanics of kite flying.

"A tail?" Paul lifted his eyebrows comically, and she laughed, knowing he was picturing the wrong thing.

"Come," she said. "We'll need to go to the trading post."

It was a strange and wonderful feeling to be walking across a field of knee-deep meadow grass, two eager children in her wake. Inside the dim shop, she looked Tom Silver right in the eye and said, "We need some string for this kite."

He didn't smile, his expression didn't even change, but she thought she saw a twinkle in his eye as he gave her the string and a horehound candy for each of the children. They fashioned a tail from quilting scraps and went to the field again. Deborah instructed Betsy to hold the kite up to the wind while she and Paul ran, paying out the string.

"Now," Deborah called, and Betsy launched the kite.

It dipped, then caught the breeze and started to climb. The children cheered, their faces lifted to the sky, and the blue heavens were reflected in their shining eyes.

Deborah left them tending their kite, her spirits lighter as she walked back to the settlement. No one, she reflected, should have a life without children. They seemed so resilient, so exuberant, as wild and natural as the terns flying over the lake. Deborah wondered if she had ever been like that, and realized with a twinge of regret that, other than sliding down the banister of the Huron Avenue mansion, she had not. An army of nannies, governesses and tutors had channeled whatever natural joy she possessed into dignified reserve. Sometimes she wondered what it would have been like if her mother had lived. Would they have flown a kite or picked flowers together? Would her mother have made a difference?

She looked up at the autumn sky over Isle Royale, and just for a moment, she managed to recapture the faint, ineffable feeling from her childhood that proved to her, beyond doubt, that she'd had a mother who'd loved her. The memory of that one vivid precious moment, that voice from her past, reminded her of something she had always known in the depths of her heart—if her mother lived, it *would* have made all the difference in the world.

Dear heaven, she wished her mother were alive. She needed someone with the experience to know the way of things, someone who loved her enough to be honest with her about the matters that occupied a young woman's thoughts. Was a woman required to lie in tight-lipped submission while her husband pushed at her, poked, thrust and panted? Was a woman required to endure that, night after night, for all the nights of her marriage?

No wonder no one ever talked about it. No wonder youngsters were swiftly hushed when they asked questions about men and women and the ways of married people.

But what of the yearning that sometimes swept over

her unexpectedly? There was something in her makeup, something weak and needy, that made her want to be cherished and held, not fawned over but loved. She couldn't help herself. She wanted that. And she sometimes thought she would like to be someone's mother. For no particular reason, she thought she might be good at it.

The old, old ache of loss had a new sharp edge, because now she felt she had lost her father, too. But wallowing in self-pity would not solve a thing. Glancing at the field, she saw the Smith children with their kite, and she couldn't help smiling. She wanted to meet the people of this new, strange world rather than brood about her past.

Henry Wick, who had fished the waters of Isle Royale for three decades, was one of the few who had not been seduced by the glittering promises of mining. He was having a legendary season, owned his own boat and had no need to embark on a new enterprise. The tragedy had touched the Wick family, of course, but had not wounded them as deeply as it had the grieving parents, widows and orphans created by her father's company. Wick's wife and daughter kept busy cleaning and salting the catch. The two women seemed friendly enough, so Deborah decided to approach them. Her father had set her adrift, but in a way it was liberating. Perhaps she should learn a new occupation, learn how other people made their way in the world.

As she walked down the rough main road, she tied on a smock apron from the shop. The day was bright and cold, the colors in the maple grove high on the bluff so vivid that it almost hurt to look at them. The lake mirrored a deep blue late-autumn sky. Even in the short time she had been here, she could see the changes sweeping across the landscape. The leaves turned color, thinning as the wind whisked them away. The afternoon sky lowered, deepened, as the days grew shorter. The birds arrowed purposefully to their winter homes, wherever that might be. The lake itself had a peculiar character—shifting in the morning, flat and placid in the late afternoon, quiet in the evening as it lapped at the shores. With the coming winter, the general restlessness of nature was more pronounced. On the north shore of the island, ice-up had begun. The shallower waters would eventually form a thick bridge of ice across to the mainland.

The fish processing plant was a long building of weathered wooden planks, built directly on the landing. That way, she supposed, the fishermen didn't have to go far when they unloaded their catch.

She reached the landing just as the Wicks' skipjack was tying up at the dock. His wife, Anna, and daughter, Alice, were out readying the cart to bring in the catch.

"Hello, miss," said Anna, noticing Deborah's approach. "You'll forgive me if I don't stop. We've a catch to haul." Henry must have had another good day on the lake. The fisherman and his brother had brought their boat in early, and their nets appeared to be bulging.

"I know," Deborah said, eyeing the straining nets, the flopping, gasping bodies of the fish. "That's why I've come."

Alice turned, her thick strong arms forming wings as she set her hands on her hips. "What do you mean?"

"I want to help you with the work. I'd not expect any pay," she added hastily. "I simply wish to do something useful around here."

Henry gawked at her. "This ain't no work for a lady," he pointed out.

"Your wife does it every day," said Deborah.

"Aye, but she's no—" With belated diplomacy, he broke off before he got his ears boxed.

"I'd be grateful if you'd show me how to do that," she said.

Anna and Alice motioned her over. "Here's a barrow full of fish. You wheel it into the plant and dump it into the processing trough. When everything's in, we'll show you how to dress the fish for transport."

Deborah was certain that "dressing the fish" didn't mean what it sounded like. She gripped the handles of the barrow and took it inside. Already the work was harder than she had imagined. Who would have thought a barrow with one wheel would be so unstable? She wobbled and wove as she staggered along the dock. At one point she strayed almost fatally close to the edge, nearly dumping her load back into the lake. In the nick of time, she managed to angle away from the edge and made it inside the warehouse.

Then the wheel of the barrow caught on something, and before Deborah could stop it, the load twisted to one side and then sank inevitably to the floor. Silver trout squirmed across the knotty planks. "Eek," she cried, jumping back in horror of the half-dead, flopping fish.

Anna stepped into the doorway and muttered something in Norwegian. She picked up a large, scoop-shaped shovel and scraped the fish into a pile. Then she handed the shovel to Deborah. "Accidents happen," she said, not unkindly. "Here you go. Scoop them back into the barrow and get them over there." She pointed at a long plank table.

Deborah gritted her teeth and took up the shovel. How hard could it be? she asked herself. How hard could it be to dress, weigh and pack the trout in boxes?

The fishermen and the women got down to work. Alice stood next to Deborah and the heap of long silvery trout. "So here is the way of it," Alice said. She grasped a fish in one hand and a slender-bladed fillet knife in the other and slit the trout along the belly. Deborah forced herself to watch, study, to imagine against all odds that she herself could do this.

Alice showed her how to gut the fish, taking care to toss the trout heart to the corner of the table. "The little ones," she said with a smile, "they like to fish for sculpins under the dock."

A small girl with a shy smile and a missing tooth grabbed the slimy heart and ran outside to bait her hook.

Deborah swallowed hard. A cold, clammy sweat broke out on her forehead. Alice sent her a knowing grin. "That's the way Mama looks when she's expecting." She rinsed the fish and tossed it lengthwise into a wooden crate on the scale. "Hundred pounds to the box," she said. "Then we chop the ice and put it over the fish, nail the box shut. This'll go to the fish companies in Duluth."

Deborah perked up. "How does the catch get to Duluth?"

"Steamer out of Grace Harbor, usually. Grace is up island a ways."

A week ago, Deborah would have been desperate to find the place called Grace Harbor, to beg transport to Duluth. But now she had no reason for haste. Now her father didn't want her back.

Alice held out a knife, handle first. "Ready to try cleaning your first fish?"

Deborah gulped back her revulsion and took the fillet knife. "I might need some help," she admitted.

"I'll help you."

Deborah eyed the pile of fish and gingerly picked one up by the tail, holding it delicately between thumb and forefinger. The thing was a lot heavier than it looked.

"Lay it on its side and take a good grip on it," Alice advised. "Like so." She grasped a fish and demonstrated.

Deborah forced herself to do the same, pressing her splayed hand on the fish. Its flesh felt cold and slick, and she could not tell whether it was still alive. Dead, she told herself firmly. The fish was dead, as dead as the *truite au bleu* she ordered at Sheppard's Restaurant on Michigan Avenue.

To her horror, the fish moved beneath her hand. With a yelp, Deborah jumped back.

Alice calmly picked up a wooden mallet and whacked its head. "There," she said. "It'll hold still now."

Deborah would not let herself look the trout in the eye as she followed Alice's instructions. She laid the fish down on the plank and pressed her palm upon its side, then used the knife to make the incision.

Except that it wouldn't cut into the fish. Alice's blade had sliced smoothly and cleanly along the fish belly, but Deborah's slid uselessly along, removing nothing but a couple of scales.

"You have to cut in," Alice advised. "Cut deep. When you think it's deep enough, you're probably halfway there."

Deborah felt runnels of sweat course down her neck. Here it was November, and she was sweating in a cold fish house. "Deeper," she said under her breath, and tried again. And again. The third or fourth time, she managed to make a slit in the fish belly.

"Try not to be timid," Alice said. "Try not to hesitate, there you are."

As Alice spoke, Deborah's knife made a deep, long cut, and she found what she sought: fish guts. She gave a little scream as the innards spilled. Without saying a word, Alice handed her the scraper.

I can do this, Deborah told herself between gritted teeth. I *must* do this. She wasn't sure why, but it was something she needed to do.

"None of us knew a thing about working the fish house before the summer," Alice said, seeming to read Deborah's thoughts. "We left it all to the menfolk."

"You had to learn to work here after the mine started up, didn't you?" asked Deborah. It helped to talk as she worked, though she knew the conversation was headed to a place of discomfort.

Alice nodded, tossing a cleaned fish into the box. "The hired men took off. Mining company promised them better wages. Never did get it, on account of the explosion." She worked in silence for a while. Deborah did better on her second fish, yet the guts made her nearly faint with revulsion.

"Made us all sick, too," Alice said, giving her a sideways glance. "Worse than dressing a chicken, you know?"

Deborah didn't know, so she said nothing.

"When the hired men left, there was nothing else for it but for us to pitch in. So here we are. Not the best shorework I can think of, but we'll get along 'til the season ends."

Deborah rinsed a fish and added it to the box. "You must be looking forward to winter."

"Not really."

"Why not?"

The big woman shrugged. "Here on the island, I know my place. Know where I fit in. Off island, I always feel a bit lost."

"Then you know how I feel *on* the island."

Tom was sure the afternoon in the fish house would defeat Deborah entirely. He worked on building a new set of shelves for the trading post, but kept one eye out for his hostage. He expected her to come running back, horrified by doing actual work for the first time in her life.

An hour passed, then two, then three. And still he saw no sign of her. He found himself wandering, with elaborate casualness, out along the boardwalk, trying to catch a glimpse of her. Down at the dock, the scene at the fish house appeared as it did every single day the boats went out. Men washing down the docks, cleaning seines. Others moving the iced-down fish to the small warehouse for transport. A few children running here and there, lying belly-down on the dock as they gigged for suckers and specs.

After a while, curiosity got the better of him. He walked down to the fish house. Jens Eckel, a fisherman who planned to retire at season's end, sat on a barrel smoking his pipe and asking the usual questions—How was the wind? How many fathoms deep were the fish?—as the women worked at the long plank tables.

For a moment, Tom didn't recognize Deborah. She wore a big oilskin apron and tall rubber boots, a kerchief over her hair. Her arms were red to the elbows with fish guts and her face was paper white.

Against his will, Tom felt a flash of emotion for her. Pity, he told himself. That was it. Pity, maybe tinged with reluctant admiration. He had dragged her from a millionaire's mansion to an Isle Royale fish house. A lesser woman would have curled up into a ball and given way to despair. Instead she seemed determined to prove that Arthur Sinclair's daughter could meet any challenge. Sinclair didn't deserve her.

"Hey, Tom, how is it with you?" asked Jens in his subtle Nordic accent.

Deborah turned sharply from the plank table. She said nothing but went back to work as if she hadn't seen him.

"Thought I'd buy a fish for the table tonight," he said. "Looks as though you can spare one."

"That's a fact," Jens agreed, taking Tom's coin. "Help yourself."

He deliberately selected the fish Deborah had just cleaned. "Hope you didn't make friends with this one."

"Why do you say that?"

"Because it'd give new meaning to having a friend for supper."

"I will never let a bite of fish pass my mouth," she vowed.

"Everyone says that at first. You'll get over it."

"I won't. I swear I won't." She turned away and pulled another trout off the pile.

Chuckling, Tom went back up the hill to the post.

There was an expression Deborah had heard often enough in her life, but never had she pondered its meaning. Bone-weary. Laborers often claimed the affliction. The occasional traveler, delayed on a long train trip, might make use of it. Anyone who worked long and hard was qualified to make the declaration. "Sure and I'm bone-weary entirely," Kathleen O'Leary used to say. "Thought I'd never see the end of the ironing."

Now, at this late stage in her life, Deborah finally understood. Bone-weary meant you had worked so hard that the hurt and fatigue of all the hours of labor had worked into the very center of your shoulders, neck, back, legs and feet—into your deepest marrow. It meant a dull ringing in your head, because your head was weary too. There was no pain, not particularly, although she had cut and scratched herself repeatedly throughout the day. This went beyond pain. This went into the realm of numb shock, not so very different from the way she had felt in the aftermath of the great fire.

Somewhere along the way she had come to think of the laboring classes as mental dullards who were capable only of menial work. Now she knew how foolish she had been. Menial work had its own challenges and she was woefully unprepared for them.

Yet at her very center, she felt quietly triumphant as she trudged up the hill from the fish house. No one had thought she could do it. No one had believed Arthur Sinclair's pampered daughter capable of doing anything but sitting around fanning herself, making a fancy hat for a lady to wear to Sunday meeting. She had proved them wrong, all of them.

And so, her boots slick with fish refuse, her curls springing wildly from the edges of her kerchief and a defiant look on her face, she stepped into the house behind the shop. Smokey greeted her with whimpers of ecstasy.

"I'll thank you to leave those boots outside," Tom Silver said without even looking up from his ledger books. "They stink."

Deborah said nothing, but turned to the door.

"Be sure you hang them from the line," he called. "Otherwise the critters might get to them."

She ground her teeth together as she pulled off the work boots. They weren't so horrible, really, for Jens had thrown a bucket of water on them before she'd left the fish house. As she strung the boots up on the line, she scowled through the screen mesh door at Tom Silver. She had not expected an open-armed welcome tonight, but a little civility might not come amiss.

While he worked at his bookkeeping, he wore delicate gold wire-rimmed spectacles. Fascinating.

She went back inside to find him still absorbed in his work. She kept sneaking glances at him, drawn to his unexpectedly scholarly look. Her father's assumption that Silver had compromised her was absurd. He had never liked her; he thought she was a blond runt, and now she wasn't even worth a ransom to him.

In a soft, distracted voice he asked, "When's supper?"

"Pardon me?" she asked, certain she had heard him wrong.

"When's supper?" he repeated.

She was too incredulous to be angry. With excessive calm and patience, she said, "I'm afraid I don't understand. You seem to think I'm going to fix supper tonight."

"You claim you can fit in on this island, live and work like other folks."

She spread her arms. "I believe my labors today prove my capability."

He pushed back his sleeves. His forearms looked aggressively muscular as he rested them on the writing table. "I don't deny you worked damned hard at that fish house today," he conceded. "But what makes you think your work ends when the last crate is iced down?"

"Because we finished, that's why."

"Do you really think Alice and Anna are home sipping sherry and eating bonbons right now? This might be a game to you, but it's not to them."

"Ah," she said. "I understand now. My friend Lucy tried to warn me about men like you. I should have listened."

"Men like me."

"Those who believe they are superior by virtue of their se—gender. Who would make slaves of women and force them to do their bidding."

"Lady, I don't need to force you to do anything. You do a good enough job of that on your own."

"What is that supposed to mean?"

"You drive yourself like a fool. No one said you had to prove a thing to me or to the people of this island. And believe me, no one's going to forget or forgive who your father is just because you turn out to be a good woman."

She stared at him, then sniffed disdainfully to cover her confusion. "I simply wanted to do something more in this godforsaken place besides sit on the porch and pray for deliverance." She pondered his words for a moment. "So you think I turned out to be a good woman."

"Did I say that?"

"It sounded as though you did."

He shrugged, turned up his lamp and went on with his work. The contrast of the thin gold rims of the spectacles against his rough-hewn face struck her with a secret warmth she didn't quite understand. Glaring at him resentfully, she felt unbearably smelly and crusty. She longed to peel off her clothes, to dive into the icy cold lake and never come up for breath. Perhaps deep beneath the surface of the water lay another world, a secret world where people behaved in a caring way, where—

"You're swaying on your feet, Princess," Tom Silver pointed out helpfully.

Her eyes snapped open. "I'm fine," she retorted. "I must change into a clean frock."

"I can hardly wait."

She narrowed her eyes at him but said no more. Then she went into her bedroom—and nearly bumped into the tall-sided zinc tub by the small stove. Wisps of steam rose from the tub and she shut her eyes for a moment, inhaling the moist, clean aroma of hot water. A little cry broke from her as she peeled off her soiled clothes and settled into the tub. It was a tiny one, no more than a hip bath like the one on the *Suzette,* but the steaming water felt heavenly as she sank into it, took up a cake of soap and began scrubbing, humming a little. She washed herself clean of the vestiges of guts and scales and other unmentionables. Only when she was half finished with the bath did she pause to think about the fact that a hot bath was waiting for her at the end of a hard day.

Tom Silver had drawn her a bath. Again. Drat. That meant she would have to thank him. Again.

She finished washing, and after a while the stench was gone even from her hair. She wrapped herself in towels and an old blanket she'd found in the box at the end of the bed, then used the bath water to wash out her clothing. She wrung out the garments and strung them up to dry. Her bone weariness had become something else entirely. It was now a fatigue so all-pervasive and deep that it pounded through every part of her, moving like warm syrup through her veins.

When's supper?

Indeed, she thought, her stomach growling with hunger. The nerve of him, demanding supper from a woman who was half-dead of overwork. She'd show him where supper was.

Tom tried not to notice how quiet it had grown in the next room. At first he had contented himself with listening to the slosh and swish of water as she bathed in the tub he had readied for her. More than any thanks she might— or might not—tender, her indulgence in the bath and the sound of her humming told him she appreciated his efforts. Lord knew, having a hot bath waiting was more than most women at the fish houses of Isle Royale came home to.

But long moments after the sloshing and humming had ended, it had grown unnaturally quiet. "You didn't go and drown on me, did you?" he asked, calling out across the room.

No response.

"Princess?"

Silence.

"Miss Sinclair?" He took off his spectacles and got up. "Deborah?" It was the first time he had used her name. It tasted of the forbidden, of something he must not say. So he said it again. "Deborah?"

When the silence drew out, he went to the door of her room and tapped. He hesitated a beat, then pushed the door open. In the dim twilight, shadows hung throughout the room, and at first he couldn't find her. Then he realized the untidy mound that lay upon the bed was her— wrapped in linen towels, sound asleep.

The sight of her shook him. She was always on her guard, always keeping her distance, and he preferred it that way. But fast asleep, with her damp hair swirling across the pillow and her hand turned palm up and defenseless beside her face, she no longer resembled the snippy, annoying heiress he had dragged kicking and screaming into his life.

Simple murder would have been so much easier.

But here she was, living in his house, sleeping in Asa's bed, and he had no idea what to make of her. She seemed to belong to another species, and according to his reading of Charles Darwin, it would be against her very nature to survive in this remote wilderness. Yet she was determined to make the best of it. Maybe she was bored or needed to forget what her bastard of a father had done to her. As soon as the novelty of the island wore off, though, she'd be more than ready to go back to Arthur Sinclair. If the old son of a bitch knew what was good for him, he'd welcome her back, no questions asked.

A log fell in the woodstove, and through the mica doors, a fountain of sparks flared up. The light grew for a moment, long enough for him to see that she had laundered her clothes in the bathwater and hung them up to dry. She sighed in her sleep and drew up her knees.

Tom told himself not to look, but of course he did. Beneath the heap of bedding, she was naked. Her movement caused the covers to slip down, baring a pale rounded shoulder. Her skin looked softer than silk, softer than a cloud, maybe. A small, dainty foot poked out of the other end, and though he had never before given much thought to a woman's foot, the sight of Deborah's made him wonder why he had gone through life ignoring that particular appendage. Her foot was a beautiful thing, with a pretty arch, a smooth heel and toenails that bore—he leaned closer to make sure he wasn't seeing things—a coat of pink enamel paint. Fancy that. A woman who painted her toenails.

He grinned cynically. Not Deborah. She probably hired someone else to do it.

Yet the cynicism he employed to hold her at bay was failing him as he watched her sleep. It was the damnedest thing. She was the daughter of Arthur Sinclair. She had been raised like a hothouse rose—beautiful, fragile, untouchable, ultimately good for nothing but show, with a gloss that would fade like dropping petals. Yet he was drawn to her. He'd been feeling it for a while now, but he kept telling himself it was nothing, just his normal male desires kicking in. If the need became too great he could always take a boat over to Thunder Bay where a friendly widow woman didn't mind company for a night or two.

Now he had to admit, though only to himself, that for some strange reason, the widow woman wouldn't do. Nor would the saloon girls of Fraser, who had always been mighty friendly in the winter time. No, his current desires all centered on this one annoying, useless excuse for a female—Deborah Sinclair.

She kept surprising him. Every time he expected her to give up, to turn into a sniveling mass of womanly whining, she squared her shoulders and did something like volunteer to work at the fish house or to mind Jenny Nagel's baby.

It had been easier to dislike her before she had made up her mind to be an asset to the community. And it was a lot easier before he had seen her naked, fast asleep, exhausted by a day of hard labor which she had endured without complaining.

Tom's thoughts weighed heavy as he emptied the bathwater and went to fix himself some supper. This was bad. He couldn't start wanting her in that way. In *any* way.

Seventeen

The strangest thing happened. Deborah actually started to make herself useful to the small, busy community. She was more amazed than anyone that she had learned to clean and ice down a box of trout, to rock a baby to sleep or knead bread dough. She excelled at filling out bills of lading and interpreting invoices for the fishermen or the logging foreman.

She had been raised to believe she would never do a day of work in all her life. That had not struck her as odd, not in the least. It was simply the way things were. No one, not her father, her tutors, her dancing master, her social secretary, nor the faculty at Miss Boylan's, had ever told her any differently. But being on Isle Royale challenged everything she had thought about her former life. Here, a woman worked, as hard or harder than a man. She thought for herself, made her own decisions and ultimately found value and fulfillment in what she was doing.

Deborah found solace in work and discovered within herself a hunger to deepen the bonds with these isolated island people. From Mabel Smith she learned to knit and crochet, and in exchange created fashionable bonnets for Mabel and her daughter, Betsy. Anna showed her innumerable ways to prepare fish, smoking it over a fire or roasting it on a birch plank. The village children taught her games that made her silly with laughter.

She was growing accustomed to the rhythm of the community. She awakened each day to the cock crow that brought out the men in the still dark dawn. She adapted to the smell of wood smoke and baking bread as fires were stoked and breakfast made. She learned to listen for the sound of small children playing. Some of the men whistled as they went down to the boats to start their day on the water. Some of the women sang as they busied themselves with shore work, mending gill nets and oiling cork bobbers. Into this mix, Deborah became an unlikely component.

Island children took her greenstoning and hiking during the day, and on the night Lightning Jack returned from the mainland, there was a sangerfest around a bonfire. He sat like a king before his subjects, smoking a pipe and dispensing gossip with great relish. He spoke of a near-drowning in Rock Harbor and a pack of marauding bears spotted at one of the inland lakes.

Deborah watched him from her seat on a log, her hands draped around her drawn-up knees. The children's faces glowed with the colors of the fire, and their eyes shone like stars. How magical it must be to grow up here, she thought, natural and free, hardworking, surrounded by people who cared about each other, watched out for one another.

Before the singing started, the children begged for another story, and Lightning Jack waved his hand in mock weariness. "I have no more talking in me tonight," he swore. "None at all."

"How about the tale of Charlie and Angelique Mott, eh?" Jens suggested remorselessly.

"Charlie Mott," the children yelled, though clearly they had heard it before, for even Deborah was familiar with it. "Charlie Mott!"

Thirty years before, the young Mott couple was sent to

look after a copper mine over the winter. Their employer failed to send the supplies he'd promised, and Charlie and Angelique found themselves abandoned to the brutal cold and isolation of winter. Charlie starved to death, shrinking away to skin and bones even though Angelique tried to sustain him with bark tea and shoe leather. Unable to bury him in the frozen ground, his grieving wife couldn't bear to throw him out into the snow for the carrion birds to get at. So she left him in their cabin where she could see him from time to time, and took her little campfire to a new hut she had built. Huddled alone over the fire, she slowly starved, all the while battling the terrible temptation to make a soup of her husband.

Come spring, the miners found her half out of her mind, but alive. The story left even the noisiest child silent with horror and awe, until Lightning Jack clapped his hands and roared "boo!" to startle them out of their spellbound state. Relieved laughter rang across the water.

To break the tension of the dark tale, the singing began. Deborah taught them "Camptown Races," and the islanders led a round of "Skoal, Skoal, Skoal."

From the corner of her eye, Deborah saw Pastor Ibbotsen come up behind Ilsa and steal a kiss. Ilsa laughed and cupped his cheek in her hand, a gesture of honest, uncomplicated affection. Love was so easy for some people, Deborah reflected. She wanted to talk about it, but there was no one to tell.

Though she lived in indecently close quarters with Tom Silver, he was as distant from her as the stars. He was living proof that some hurts could never be forgotten. The way he had lost Asa had made a wound of anger too deep to heal. His condemning gaze stalked her through each day, darkening each time someone acknowledged her, thanked her, laughed with her. His disapproval made her more determined than ever to prove that she was not the spoiled, overprivileged article he thought she was, that she was a person of substance deep in her core.

She excused herself from the gathering, walking to the edge of the marsh at the end of the road. The evening air held a sharp chill. The winter season was coming on strong and cold, etching the edges of the marsh with frost.

One evening, when the wind off the lake lashed at the windows and roared through the trees on the ridges above the settlement, Deborah decided to fix supper to show Tom Silver that she was no longer a woman who didn't even know enough not to touch a hot coffeepot. Donning an old carpenter's apron, she stoked the stove to what she thought to be a proper cooking temperature. Then she put two potatoes in a pot of water to boil and heated the frying pan for the fish.

That wasn't so difficult, she thought, watching the potatoes simmer. She stepped back and tapped her foot, wondering what to do next. Ah. She must lay the table. At home this was done by a servant, perhaps more than one, who decked the formal table with Limoges china, Irish crystal goblets and Florentine flatware. Tom Silver had nothing of the sort, of course, but she made do with the speckled enamel plates and pewter forks and spoons. She hurried outside and plucked some dried Queen Anne's lace from the hedge by the garden fence and stuck the wispy sprigs in a jar on the table. He had never been much for napkins, so she improvised with a pair of faded clean cloths with ragged edges. Perhaps later tonight she would hem them.

She shook her head at her own foolishness. It wasn't as if these things mattered. In a short while, she would leave Isle Royale, never to return.

Making certain a thick towel was at hand for the hot pan, she laid a cleaned trout in the skillet. The browned fat sizzled and spat at her, and she jumped back with a yelp.

The pan on the stove caught fire at the precise instant that Tom Silver came into the house. He looked tired, his face and hands chapped by the wind, but he moved swiftly toward the blaze. Deborah was quicker, dumping some of the hot water from the potatoes onto the fire even as Tom shouted, "Don't do that!"

In a split second, she understood why. Some alchemy between water and burning fat made the flames flare even higher, licking black tongues of soot onto the ceiling.

Swearing, Tom grabbed the frying pan and rushed outside with it. She heard more cursing, then silence. He returned, holding the pan with the charred fish in it.

"I take it supper's ready," he said.

She poked her nose in the air. *"Truite flambé,"* she said. "It's a new recipe."

She could tell he was trying to scowl, but as he set the pan on the side of the stove, his mouth was tight, the corners upturned as he fought a smile. She acted equally disdainful as she dipped out the boiled potatoes and put them on the plates. He boned the trout and peeled away the blackened skin. The cooked fish within was surprisingly edible.

They ate in silence, yet it was oddly companionable. He didn't thank her, but he ate every bite of fish and potatoes, and she found herself strangely gratified by that.

"What're you staring at?" he asked, noticing her gaze.

"I was just thinking."

"About what?"

"Feeding someone. I've never done it before."

"So I guessed."

"It wasn't such a horrible chore. There is something very elemental about it, about…nourishing another person." Embarrassed by her own words, she blushed and looked away.

He leaned back with great ease into a long-bodied position, ankles crossed, arms folded over his chest. "You can nourish me anytime you want, Princess."

She drew away, growing even hotter and redder with her blush. "I must clean the dishes," she said, hastily

getting up from the table. She felt his stare boring into
her as she poured hot water from the kettle into the dry
sink and began scrubbing the dishes.

"Is there anything that *doesn't* make you nervous as a
cat?" he asked.

"I am not nervous."

"Right."

She continued working in silence. She heard him walk
over to the hearth, give the embers a stir and add a log.

"Winter evacuation'll start in two days," he said.
"Some of the harbors are already iced in."

It took a moment for the words to sink in. Winter evacuation. The residents of Isle Royale would leave the island
to freeze up. They would all return in the spring to light
fires in their little houses, bringing the village to life again.
But not Deborah. She would go back to civilization at
last, back to—

She didn't finish the thought. Didn't know how, didn't
want to. Since the moment Tom Silver had kidnaped her,
she had thought of nothing but escape, nothing but going
back to her former life. Now she was worried. She didn't
know if she even *had* a life there. Chicago had burned.
Her father's house had burned. The conflagration might
have traveled as far as Miss Boylan's, or Avalon in Lake
View. Besides that, her father had declared her to be without value to him.

She could only assume Philip did not want her either.
That thought, at least, provided her with some comfort.

"You hear what I said?" Tom's voice broke in on her
thoughts. "Folks'll be leaving the island for the winter
pretty soon."

"I heard you."

"You don't seem too interested in the news."

"I've known this was coming. It snowed yesterday.
Everyone's been busy packing for days." She finished
washing the dishes and used a towel to dry them, piece
by piece.

"I reckon Lightning Jack will want to weigh anchor as soon as the weather quiets."

"Is that how the evacuation is done? On Jack's boat?" she asked.

"Yeah. His steamer, a couple of the skipjacks and a schooner. When the weather lets up, the fleet will head for Fraser or Duluth."

Finally she turned to face him. "And then what?" she asked. "What happens on the mainland?"

"Most families have winter quarters with relatives and friends. The bachelors might take rooms in town, hire on at the shipyards or at Decker's brewery for day labor."

She pressed her lips together. He was going to make her ask, she realized. "I mean, what do you intend for me to do? I certainly don't see how you can hold me hostage on the mainland, for heaven's sake."

He pushed back his shirtsleeves, leaning his bulky, muscular forearms on the table. "I can hold you any way I damn well please."

She ground her teeth in fury. "Your scheme failed because my father doesn't want me back. Meanwhile, I have done my utmost to cooperate with you. I understand the depth of your loss. My heart breaks with it. I've offered to exact restitution from my father. I've promised not to press charges against you, and to convince my father not to, either. I've worked until blisters formed on my hands." She turned them palms-out to show him. "What more do you expect of me?"

A quick lightness flickered in his eyes, but the look was so fleeting she thought she had imagined it. "Just be ready to sail when the weather calms," he said.

"I deserve to know what's in store for me."

"You'll know when we get there," he shot back.

"You are a poor excuse for a kidnaper, then," she retorted. Aggravated, she made short work of the after-supper washing up, scrubbing the table with extra vigor and putting up the pans and dishes with a satisfying clatter. He sat impassively, watching her, and she pretended not to notice. When she finished, she took out the mulberry hat she had been working on, holding it out at arm's length and regarding it with a critical eye.

"Do you think the brim is too wide?" she asked, somehow having spent her irritation in the washing-up.

"Will anyone care?" he asked with a shrug.

She sniffed. The oaf would never understand. "If I am going on a voyage, I should have a new hat."

Eighteen

The day of the evacuation dawned bright, clear and cold, the water as flat and glossy as a polished mirror. An invisible sense of urgency sharpened the air, for ice-up was coming on faster than anyone had predicted. Snow dusted the ground. Already the island wore a brittle lace collar of white frost, the lake frozen at the edges and around the pilings of the docks. The cliffs were hung with ice that sparkled like crystal in the sunlight. Beyond the sharp blue sky, an ominous low brow of clouds weighted the atmosphere in the west. Jens Eckel swore he tasted a blizzard in the air, and the skippers decided to head for the rough encampment at Fraser rather than risk the longer voyage to Duluth.

Deborah took out the smooth velvet bonnet she had recently finished and put it on, tying an artful bow to one side of her chin. The brim *was* too deep, shadowing her face and hair, but it was too late to change it now. She pulled on her only pair of gloves and took Smokey out into the yard. Tom was coming out of the shop as she wrestled with the impossibly tiny glove buttons while the dog leaped impatiently around her feet.

"We sail in an hour," he said. His breath made frozen puffs in the air. "Don't wander far from the landing."

"I won't even get out of this yard if I don't get these gloves buttoned."

He hesitated for half a second, then said, "Hold out your hand."

It would be foolish, childish to refuse him. Swallowing past a surge of nervousness, she offered her hand. His big, blunt fingers fumbled with the dainty mother-of-pearl buttons.

"No idea why you have to button on a pair of gloves, anyway," he grumbled. "It's not like they'll fall off if you don't do up all these buttons."

"It's a matter of fashion," she said. "You wouldn't understand."

"Wouldn't want to," he replied, finishing with the first glove and grabbing her other hand.

When he was near, when he touched her, her heart sped up.

"Your hand's shaking," he said. "Hold still."

"It's not shaking."

"Is so." He took her elbow and held out her hand. "Look."

She scowled. "It's the cold," she said, ducking her head. The bill of her bonnet caught him on the chin.

"Jesus, woman, you're a menace," he said with laughter in his voice. "I reckon that purple hat's a matter of fashion, too."

"It's mulberry, not purple, and it's a bonnet. And yes, it happens to be very fashionable." She snatched her hand away. "I'll get Ilsa to finish buttoning me. She'll do it without any impudent remarks."

"Good for Ilsa."

She clapped her hands to get Smokey's attention and they walked outside the gate. The dog scampered along the frozen roadway with his nose to the ground.

"Hey, Princess," Tom Silver called from the yard.

"Yes?" She conveyed with her tone that she didn't want to be delayed any longer.

''Don't be late boarding the *Suzette*. You miss the evacuation, you spend the winter on the island. You don't want
to wind up like Charlie Mott's wife.''

She shuddered. ''Better than ending up like Charlie
Mott.''

As she walked along the main roadway of the nameless
little settlement, Deborah felt an unexpected twist of emotion. She would never see this place again. Would never
hear the wind in the tall trees or see the sun rise over the
vast lake or listen to the hiss and howl of the waves beating against the rocky shore. She wouldn't find the likes
of Jens Eckel again, nor do anything so odd and disgust-
ing as cleaning fish for a living. She wouldn't see the
island children chasing a kite, nor collect agates in the
streams with them, nor cradle Jenny's baby in her arms
and have a cup of tea with the young mother.

Never again.

Watching the flurry of activity down at the landing, she
wondered what Jens was feeling now. He, too, was leaving Isle Royale forever, only his departure was far more
bittersweet than her own. Two nights earlier, at the town
supper, he had stood up and announced that he was retir-
ing. After fifty years of fishing the waters around the island, he was going to stay in his snug little bungalow on
the mainland, where he could sit by the fire smoking his
pipe. He'd finally have a chance to read all those books
he had been saving up for years.

He had fought tears as he made his announcement, because he loved this island. Others had cried, too, for Jens
Eckel was a fixture here, the quiet strong center around
which the entire community seemed to revolve. Yesterday
he had gone for a walk with Deborah, and had shown her
a rapid, sunlit creek with a bed of the most marvelous
agate she had ever seen. Now she wished she had taken
some of the brilliant tumbled stones as a memento.

When she went down to the landing, she realized Tom
Silver had not been exaggerating the fact that space was

at a premium. The boats were laden to the gunwales with goods to be transported to the mainland for the winter. It was hard to imagine people so poor they had to travel with their iron stoves rather than buy two, but that seemed to be the case. The knowledge only firmed her decision to secure restitution for them.

No matter what her father thought of her, she would stand up to him. It took an adventure like Isle Royale to teach her to stand up to him. She had been a leaf in the wind of his ambition, fluttering helplessly. Now she understood that she had a will of her own, if only she dared to obey her own heart rather than try to please him.

A brisk wind blew in from the east, and she walked along the dock, Smokey trotting at her side. She said good morning to the Wicks and the Nagels, and held Jenny's baby one last time. With the child in her arms, she turned to face the small settlement, hugged into the side of the towering rock ridges, where these people built their homes and raised their families and made a life for themselves. There was a simplicity in their ways that appealed to her, yet at the same time she understood that there was nothing so challenging as building a life in a close-knit community, with its infinitely impassioned relationships, rivalries and cooperation. The richness in their lives came, not from things they bought with money, but from the splendor around them and the fruits of their own hard work.

She handed back the baby, then walked down the length of the *Suzette,* encountering a grinning Lightning Jack duBois at the stern.

"Eh, ma'm'selle," he said, inclining his head. "I almost didn't recognize you."

She smiled, unaccountably gratified. "Am I that different?"

"Oh, yeah." He lashed a hogshead to the side. "You're not whining."

In spite of the insult, she laughed. "Was I that bad?"

"No," Lightning Jack said.

"Yes," Tom Silver said at the same time, coming through a hatch to take on more firewood to stoke the boilers. "But we kept you because of your yellow hair."

"Very funny," she muttered, shading her eyes to admire the ice-hung cliffs one last time. A few anemic strands of sunlight managed to filter through the clouds, touching the ice with fire. Dazzled by the sight, she stood and absorbed the magnificence of the island, a place like no other she would ever see again.

Smokey leaped into the boat, scrabbling around the deck with excitement. Lightning Jack grabbed another keg from the dock. When he dragged it down into the hull, the lid came off, rolling across the deck. Deborah jumped back instinctively with a little cry of alarm.

A stream of Gallic oaths spewed from Lightning Jack as the entire contents of the barrel spread across the deck. The mongrel retreated with a whimper into the pilothouse. A terrible stench filled the air.

"Oh, dear," Deborah said, wondering how on earth she could help. "Is that…?"

"Fish liver oil," Tom Silver spat in disgust, hoisting himself up through the hatch.

"C'est dégueulasse." Lightning Jack watched the fetid liquid pooling around his moccasins. "Who is the jackass responsible for sealing that barrel?"

When Deborah took a step toward the boat, Tom waved her off. "We'll clean it up on our own. No sense in all of us getting covered in this stuff." He pointed at the *Koenig,* docked at the other side of the harbor. "You'll have to sail to the mainland with the Wicks and the Ibbotsens."

The prospect of traveling without Tom Silver should have held enormous appeal for her. She reminded herself that her goal should always be to escape him. He was her captor, she was his hostage. Yet to think of the situation in those terms seemed absurd to her now. "All right," she said.

Tom nodded distractedly and waved her off. He was already swabbing the reeking deck with an old, gray mop. Deborah went to the *Koenig* to tell them of the change in arrangements. While the men laughed about the spilled oil, Ilsa beamed at her. "Last day on the island, eh?" she asked.

"So it appears. For me and Jens both."

"We been trying to get rid of the old coot for years," Henry Wick said, speaking over his shoulder as he worked. "Should have left him here to freeze to death."

Jens chuckled. "Then you'd have no one left to tease, Henry. There's ways to keep from freezing, you know," he said to Deborah.

"Another one of his whoppers," Henry warned.

"I heard tell of two men stuck in a blizzard. They were half-froze when they managed to kill a moose. They gutted the body and sheltered inside the carcass."

"See? A whopper." Henry cranked in a shore anchor.

"Maybe it was a caribou."

"Maybe it never happened."

"Way *I* heard it," Ilsa said, joining the silliness, "is the two men got naked under a moose hide and stayed warm skin to skin."

Jens and Henry made gagging sounds and spat over the side. "I'd rather die, eh?" Jens said.

Deborah blushed, but she was laughing.

"You're such a lady," Ilsa said admiringly, eyeing her bonnet. "I wish I could be so fashionable."

Deborah was amazed that simple, contented Ilsa could wish to be anything like her. Ilsa had a husband and son who adored her and needed nothing else. But one thing a woman always possessed, Deborah reflected, was a bit of vanity. On impulse, she said, "I have something for you."

When she reached to untie the bonnet, Ilsa stood in the boat. "Ah no. I can't let you—"

"You must. I'll be insulted if you don't." Deborah heard the firmness in her own voice. Now, where had that come from? She sounded like a different person. Sure of herself. Bossy, even. She took off the mulberry velvet bonnet and made Ilsa take off her plain gray wool one. ''We'll trade. I'll be warm, and you'll be fashionable.''

''That would be a first for me.''

The truth was, the deep purplish fabric and black trim were enormously becoming on Ilsa, a perfect foil for her blond hair and Nordic coloring. She preened for old Jens, who sat quietly astern, his pipe clamped between his teeth, his weather-beaten hand nervously toying with his bear claw necklace.

''You're too damned pretty for me, Ilsa,'' he said, but he seemed distracted as he spoke. His blue eyes had the soft, washed-out look of decades of wind and weather, and his way of life was etched in every line of his face. He was a fisherman of the island. Now that he was moving to the mainland, what would he be?

It was a bold move, embarking on a new life, but a necessary step, thought Deborah, both for Jens and for herself. Yet her heart went out to him, because he looked so lost, so desperate, already lonely as he contemplated the winter maples in the high hills, stripped bare by the icy wind, the blanket of new snow across the land and the gleaming surface of the lake spreading out before him.

''What will you do on the mainland with all your time?'' she asked, hoping to distract him.

His hands worked over his necklace as if it were a seine. ''Same's I've always done every winter of my life. Sit by the fire, smoke my pipe, read some. Maybe have a game of cribbage with another old fisherman, and we can tell each other lies about our glory days.''

''That doesn't sound so bad.''

''Yeah. It'll be like winter, but a winter with no end.''

''But—''

Jens stood up in agitation. At the same moment, the bear claw necklace fell from his grasp and hit the water with a soft ping. Deborah gasped as it sank out of sight.

"Oh, Jens," she said. "Your necklace."

He looked bleak. "Not mine anymore. It belongs to the lake." His voice sounded thin and fearful. "Eventually, the lake takes back its own."

She didn't like seeing this hopeless attitude in a man she admired.

Henry Wick heaved a long-suffering sigh. "God forbid that you should leave without a keepsake, Jens," he said, then took out a fingerling net and leaned over the side. The water was thick and slushy with ice. "Another night like the last one," he said over his shoulder, "and the harbor'll be frozen up solid." After several minutes of fishing around, he managed to snag the necklace and handed it, dripping and cold, to the old man.

Jens grinned from ear to ear. "You earned a bottle of schnapps," he declared.

"What about you, Deborah?" asked Alice Wick. "What keepsake will you take back with you?"

"I hadn't really thought about one." Deborah was surprised at herself. She had always been a sentimental sort. Always one to want a memento. Unconsciously her hand went to her throat, and she wished Tom Silver had not sent her mother's lavaliere to her father.

A keepsake. Perhaps she should take something of the island with her. Otherwise, years from now, it might be as if this adventure had not happened at all. Some memories she wanted to keep. Isle Royale, surprisingly, was one of them.

She knew what she wanted. She had seen it just the other day, walking with Jens. "You're right," she said to Alice. "I should bring something back with me. I'll only be a few minutes."

"We're about to cast off," Henry Wick objected, one rubber-booted foot on the dock, the other on the boat.

"I'll go on the *Suzette*," she said, resigning herself to a rough voyage on a deck slippery with fish oil. Even so, she admitted to herself that she wanted to make the crossing with Tom and Lightning Jack. "It's fine. My dog is probably insane without me, anyway."

"See you on the mainland, then," said Henry.

She picked up her skirts, straightened Ilsa's scratchy gray wool bonnet on her head and climbed up on the dock. Then, running, she headed for the streambed she had found the other day.

As she ran, she felt unaccountably wild and free. Ah, she would miss this place in all its splendor and isolation. Perhaps one day she would return, not as a hostage but as a visitor. Yes, that's what she would do. Secure the financial reparation from her father, even if she had to battle him in the courts to do it and deliver the money in person come spring.

What a perfect idea, she thought, disappearing into the woods and cutting through the tall, clacking reeds for a shortcut to the rapids. She heard the rush of the stream before she parted the reeds and saw it. A skin of ice coated the rocks at the edge of the water. In the middle of the shallows lay a gleaming treasure of agates.

Deborah unfastened the buttons of one glove and peeled it off. Then, holding back her skirts, she bent to gather the small, smooth stones. The water was terrifically cold, the rocks coated with ice, and her fingers went numb by the time she had fished out the tenth stone. She knew she should work faster, but she might never again get this chance. The trail of gemlike stones led halfway across the stream. Holding out her arms for balance, she attempted to step from rock to rock in order to get to the middle.

She fell, of course. Her skinny-soled shoes, the ones Tom Silver so delighted in making fun of, slipped on an icy rock and she went down hard in the middle of the stream. The shock of the cold water drove everything— breath, thought, feeling—out of her and she couldn't even cry out. She was that cold.

It took all of her energy to drag herself out of the stream and slog her way to shore. She sat in a frozen daze, her mind moving sluggishly. Had she hit her head on something? What a clumsy oaf she was. She knew she would endure extra scorn from Tom and Lightning Jack during the voyage.

Just then a boat whistle pierced the air. Deborah looked down to see that the hem of her skirt was already frozen. Her teeth chattered out of control as she put the stones into her pocket and struggled to put her glove on over her stiff, nerveless fingers. She started back through the woods toward the landing, knowing she'd better hurry. She had wasted enough time already.

Nineteen

"This damned boat reeks," Tom grumbled as they hauled out past Rock Harbor. He had to raise his voice above the insane yapping of Deborah's dog.

"Wasn't my idea to take on those kegs of fish oil," Lightning Jack said defensively. "You were the one. *Parbleu*, I'll be swabbing my deck with it for the next three seasons."

"I'll work on it." Tom swirled an ancient mop in the oil.

"You might not have to worry about working in the future," Lightning Jack pointed out. "If *la jolie demoiselle* gets her father to come through like she promised, we'll all be rich as kings."

"Sinclair wouldn't ransom her. Hell, the old bastard didn't even send a boat for her. What makes you think she'll get a copper cent out of him?"

"He will come to see reason. Even now, he has probably realized none of this is his daughter's fault."

"He's had plenty of time to realize that I'm to blame, and I'll be the first to claim it." The whole matter left a bad taste in Tom's mouth. He had taken Deborah without a single thought of what it would do to her, how it would affect her future. "So where the hell is he?"

Lightning Jack kept his eyes on the deep gray horizon.

"He needs time. Some men, you know, have a head like a rock. It takes them a long time to see what is right before their eyes." He cleared his throat. "You can tell me, *mon gars.* You have been sleeping with her, haven't you?"

For a moment, Tom couldn't speak. "Why the hell would you say a thing like that, you old bugger?"

"I see the way you look at her when she doesn't know you're looking. I see the way she looks at you."

"You're dead wrong," Tom said, his heart knocking in alarm at the very idea.

A troubled skepticism shadowed the older man's face. "But those other symptoms of hers..."

"What other symptoms?"

"She gets tired, you know. And sick. I just assumed...she was *enceinte.*"

Deborah? Tom thought incredulously. Pregnant? The very mention of the word would make her swoon with embarrassment. "You're way off, Lightning. She has a delicate constitution, is all. She's not cut out for what we put her through."

"Then maybe that fiancé she mentioned," Lightning Jack ventured. "Perhaps he—"

"*Not Deborah.*" Tom scowled into the icy, harsh wind, discomfited by Lightning Jack's wild assumption. It was preposterous to imagine himself with a woman like that. And yet he did imagine it—far too often. He'd best put it out of his mind and concentrate on bringing this to an end. The trouble was, he didn't know how to end it. Neither did Deborah, he suspected.

She was simply fragile, just didn't know the way of the world. What did she think she was going back to, anyway? What did a man like Sinclair do to a ruined daughter returned? He hoped Lightning Jack was right, that Sinclair would get over his anger. The son of a bitch didn't deserve her, but she loved him. And he was her father. Tom recalled a time or two he'd been mad enough at Asa to tan his hide, like when the boy had sailed a leaky little skiff all the way up to Rock Harbor and stayed gone for two days, or the time he had drunk half a pint of corn whiskey and puked all over the floor. Tom had always been furious...and he had always forgiven the boy. It was what a father *did.*

Until that last quarrel. Tom had forbidden Asa to work at the mine. Asa's beautiful, sullen face had darkened to an angry red and he'd stormed out, determined to choose his own path. He had been offered a position as bellows boy at double the pay he earned fishing. He and Tom had parted in anger that day, and there had been no chance for forgiveness.

Arthur Sinclair had damned well better learn to forgive his daughter.

Preoccupied, Tom watched the foolish mongrel racing up and down the decks from stem to stern, facing the fast-disappearing island and barking his head off. He and Smokey barely tolerated each other, but coexisted under an unspoken truce due to Deborah's presence. The dog was never far from her side. That was probably why he was so upset, stuck aboard the *Suzette* while Deborah sailed on the *Koenig.* Taking care not to slip on the oily decks, he picked up Lightning Jack's spyglass and climbed to the high bridge of the boat. The *Koenig,* the *Queen* and the *Little Winyah* were well ahead of them, puffed-out sails bearing them along more briskly than the engine of the trawler. The wind was almost *too* brisk, blowing just shy of a gale.

A winter gale, he thought uncomfortably, facing the brooding steel-gray sky to the west. The clouds had rolled in, bringing the dense, weighty look of heavy snow. By nightfall, Isle Royale could well be blanketed, the harbors impassable. Ice crackled as the bow broke through the thin sheets. Within a few days, ice-up would be complete, and the island would slumber, undisturbed, until spring.

He put the glass to his eye and recognized Deborah by the funny purple hat she had insisted on finishing the night before. Aboard the *Koenig,* she sat astern in the shelter of a canvas tarp, but a moment later she went below, disappearing from view.

Tom swung back to scan the shoreline of the island. How desolate it looked from this distance, the crust of ice a white, jagged necklace around its rugged periphery. It had been his home since time out of mind, but in winter it looked as forbidding as an enemy fortress.

Just for a moment, he thought he detected a flicker of movement at the edge of the settlement. Then the boat hit a roller. He lurched back and nearly lost his footing. When he looked again toward the island, he saw only emptiness. Bare rock, bare trees, bare earth.

Bye, Asa.

He knew it wasn't logical, but he felt disloyal leaving like this. For the past six years he and Asa had left the winter island together. Now Asa was left behind in a cold grave where Tom could never reach him again. Never touch him, never ruffle his hair, never hear the sound of his laughter.

Tom gritted his teeth. He tried to make himself think of anything besides the boy and the fact that Asa would never again see the springtime. He forced himself to scan the lake through the spyglass as if there were something for him to see.

Having Deborah around had kept him from brooding about Asa as much as he had before going to Chicago. She was no substitute for the boy he loved, the boy who gave shape and meaning to his life, but her presence had given Tom something to think about besides the powerful hurt of knowing Asa was gone.

Watching her discover the island for the first time had been like seeing Isle Royale all over again, through the eyes of a child. Her sense of breath-held wonder at the grandeur of the wilderness reminded him of something he hadn't thought about since before losing Asa. The world was a beautiful place. Life was worth living. Ironic that it took a spoiled debutante, the daughter of his enemy, to remind him of that.

The fact that nothing in Tom's scheme for revenge had gone as planned didn't seem to bother him so much these days. Truth be told, the need to kill Arthur Sinclair had cooled considerably even as the city burned. Deborah had reminded Tom of something he had shut his mind to in his crazed grief and thirst for revenge: Arthur Sinclair was somebody's father.

Apparently Sinclair had been planning to send her like a sacrificial lamb into the keeping of the prominent Ascot family, and she was reluctant to go. Tom could only imagine the way events would unfold once they reached the mainland. He figured he would take Deborah overland to Duluth, the terminus of the St. Paul and Pacific Railroad. She could take the train to Chicago—assuming all the depots in the city had not burned—and that would be the end of it.

It didn't matter the way things turned out, Tom told himself. After she left for Chicago, he would have no reason to see her again. Ever.

Another swell hit, and a fine, needlelike spray of half-frozen lake water smacked him in the face. The air had grown so cold that by the time the wind swept the mist off the wave tops, the spray froze in midair.

It was a good wind, though it froze his bones to the marrow and brought with it the promise of a terrific blizzard. If it held steady, they'd make the mainland well before nightfall.

Panic didn't set in right away.

Deborah was too naive to understand, the moment she reached the landing, the implications of missing the boat. When she'd finished gathering her agates, she had been filled with dismay at her wet feet and cold, drenched backside. The people on the mainland would think she looked a fright. Her mind was occupied with this thought as she picked her way gingerly down to the landing by the Wicks' fish house.

Odd, she thought. All the boats had gone.

Even seeing this, she didn't quite panic. Perhaps some of the fleet had departed while others had only... disappeared for a while. The *Suzette* had probably steamed around to Checker Point to take advantage of the big spray there in order to cleanse her decks of the spoiled fish oil. That was probably the case, and the others had not wanted to wait.

When she thought about the absurdity of that idea, her mind took another tack, turning to the inevitable thought she had been avoiding. They had somehow managed to leave her by mistake. It was an outrageous idea. Never in her life had she been overlooked by mistake or even on purpose for that matter. Yet somehow, in the frenzy of loading and leaving and people rushing from boat to boat, she had been forgotten. She was prepared to shoulder her share of the blame for that, switching between boats. It had been foolish of her to run off in search of a souvenir of her days on the island. But it was easier to look back than to plan ahead. It was an honest mistake, and if truth be told, entirely her fault.

Yet still she did not panic. It was only a matter of time before the oversight was detected. Then a boat would come back for her.

"Yes, that is exactly what will happen," she said aloud. "Someone will come back to fetch me."

There was no one to hear her. What a singularly odd notion. Deborah could not think of another time in her life when she had been completely and utterly alone. From the day of her birth, she had been surrounded by nurses, servants, maids and every manner of person imaginable. Yet here she was, alone on an island in the heart of a wilderness so vast and isolated that it boggled the mind.

"Well," she said. "Well, there is no point in staying

here freezing to death.'' She picked up her stiff skirts and walked away from the landing. She went halfway up the hill toward town, then turned to have one last look at the horizon to the west. A northerly wind had stirred violent swells in the lake. There was no sign of a ship.

But something did catch her eye. Far in the west, the sky darkened like a wall of smoke. Until this moment, she had never actually seen a winter storm forming. The drama and violence of it amazed her; wind and darkness and snow came down from the atmosphere as if hurled from the hand of God himself. She walked backward up the hill, moving slowly, mesmerized by the sight. Blackness stalked the surface of the water, forming a vast, angular shadow on the lake. Then the whitecaps kicked up. It was a magical sight—seeing cold water boil. The thick, broken-edged ice that surrounded the island cracked with the motion, but did not break up. The majesty of the coming maelstrom took her breath away—until she understood that she would have to endure it alone.

That was when she finally panicked. A small sound came from her throat. It wasn't a sob or a cry for help, but a strange, succinct expression of fear. Deborah knew she was not a brave person. She had never been brave, had never been required to show courage.

Now she was. And she was so miserably unprepared for the necessity of bravery that she could walk no further. She sat down on the path, hugged her knees up to her chest and shivered, gritting her teeth to stop them from chattering. Her breath came in quick gasps, making a sound like a rare breed of bird. The shivering convulsed through her in waves.

Think, she told herself. Then she said it aloud. ''Think, Deborah. You're all alone on this island and a storm is coming. What must you do in order to survive?''

She hadn't the first idea. But she determined that sitting out in the cold, on the frozen ground, with the wind plucking at her bonnet strings, would not serve her needs. She got up and trudged the rest of the way to the settlement. The abandoned village was a frighteningly empty ghost town, all the inhabitants fled before some unnamed menace.

Deborah knew the name of the menace now. She dared to look back at the lake just once, hoping against hope that she had exaggerated the storm in her mind. It was worse, closer and more violent than it had been just a few moments ago.

She hunched her shoulders up against the wind and hurried for shelter.

"*Parbleu,* but that was ugly." At Commercial Landing in Fraser, Lightning Jack tied up and counted coins from a pouch. "Storm was too close for comfort. We should have left last week."

Tom nodded distractedly. He respected the power of the weather on the lake, but for some reason he had never feared being out in it. "Did you see where the *Koenig* is docked?"

Lightning Jack sent him a knowing glance. "Eager to see your little guest, eh?"

"I just want to make sure she doesn't get in trouble or try something stupid."

"Ah, but those are her specialties."

"I know. I'd best find her." With a pathetic whimper, Smokey leaped out of the boat and trotted at his heels. The critter had been miserable without Deborah on the crossing.

Lightning Jack tied the coin pouch to his belt. "I am going to find a woman and get roaring drunk."

"Women love that."

They paid the harbormaster and Tom inquired about the *Koenig.* It was full dark, and the dog started in on his annoying and ceaseless barking. What was wrong with the fool critter? Its voice was hoarse, almost weak. The gale force winds blowing off the lake nearly drowned its pathetic howling.

Bending into the storm, Jens Eckel lifted a lantern and motioned them to the dock. "How was your voyage?" He scowled at the dog. "Can't you shut that thing up?"

"Nope."

"I say we use the little yapper for bait."

"Deborah's the only one he minds."

Jens craned his neck, peering through the lashing snow flurries. "Where is the girl? Did she weather the storm well aboard the *Suzette?*"

At first Tom felt only mild confusion. "She's not with me. We just made port."

"Oh." Jens raised his voice over the rising wind. "I must have misunderstood. I thought she said she would make the crossing with you."

"We told her to go on the *Koenig,*" Lightning Jack said, scratching his head.

"Yeah." Jens chuckled. "Too bad about the oil spill." His mirth faded and the scowl returned. "But she said she would sail with you."

Maybe the old man was confused. "I *saw* her," Tom pointed out. "She was sitting under *Koenig*'s spray hood—" He broke off as Ilsa appeared on the dock, a worried expression on her face...and a fancy bonnet on her head. "That's Deborah's hat," Tom said. He prayed the lantern light distorted the color of the hat, but there was no denying it. Ilsa's bonnet was purple. He felt a slow, cold crawl of apprehension starting up his spine. "Isn't it?"

"She gave it to me as a gift." Ilsa touched the brim. "Only this morning. She is a nice woman, Tom Silver. One of these days you will learn that for yourself."

Lightning Jack managed to hush the dog by giving it a bit of dried fish to gnaw on. "Let us sort this out, eh? Deborah did not sail aboard the *Suzette*. And you're saying she wasn't on the *Koenig*."

"She wanted to fetch something—she didn't say what." Jens scratched his head. "Told us to go ahead, that she would sail with you."

All three men swore at once. Ilsa flinched and grabbed the pastor's hand. "We must figure out where Deborah is."

"I'm afraid everyone thought she was with someone else," Pastor Ibbotsen pointed out.

"She is back on the island," Jens said mournfully. "Where else could she be?"

Ilsa touched the brim of her hat. "What will we do? We can't leave her out there."

The mongrel dog finished scarfing down the fish and paced up and down the dock, its restless movements unnerving.

"We must check the other boats," Henry said.

"She won't know the first thing to do in order to survive. She doesn't even know how to get to the lumber camp. She'll die," Ilsa said.

Tom said nothing. He walked away from the squabbling group of islanders at the waterfront. There were lights aglow in the town. The howl of the wind mingled with the faint jangle of piano music drifting from the boardinghouse. Ordinarily this was a night a man might savor, when the season's work was over and it was time to hunker down for the winter. Ordinarily Tom would join Lightning Jack on the quest for strong drink and a willing woman, and they'd stay warm by the fire, replete and content long into the night.

The storm wind slashed sideways across the lake. Waves exploded on the dock and along the water's edge, bearding the rocky shoreline with ice. The snow came on fast and thick. By morning, it would be thigh deep.

Tom couldn't think about that. He already knew what he had to do.

Part Three

When is man strong until he feels alone?

—Robert Browning

Twenty

"**Y**ou're not stupid," Deborah said. "Just inexperienced."

Several hours after realizing she had been stranded on the island, the snow had begun coming down in earnest and she was already getting used to talking to herself. "That might mean I've lost my mind," she said, balancing a stack of firewood in her arms as she staggered toward the house. "But then again, does it matter? If I'm all alone, then the standard for sanity is up to me entirely."

She laughed at herself, but the howling wind snatched at her laughter and stole it away. She ducked her head and pushed her way into the cabin. The shriek of the wind pursued her, even inside. She dropped the logs and one of them hit her foot, bruising deeply. She yelped in pain, hopping on one foot and clutching the other. The hem of her skirt caught in the door. She was forced to open it and free herself, and that let in more wind.

She had never felt a cold quite as piercing as the cold of the blizzard that blasted across the lake that day. She had never seen the snow come down quite so fast. Perhaps that had been what Charlie Mott's wife had seen, that terrible veil of white, promising icy suffocation.

Pushing the door shut behind her, Deborah dragged the

firewood piece by piece over to the stove. Only this morning—was it just this morning?—Tom had thrown the last
live embers into the yard to burn out. He had swept the
stale ashes from the stove and climbed onto the roof to
scour the pipe with a large wire brush. He hadn't expected
to use the stove again until springtime.

Vigorously Deborah rubbed her hands together. She
opened the door of the stove and sank down on her knees
in front of it. Now. How did one make a fire? She must
have seen it done thousands of times. She wished she had
been paying attention.

"All right, Miss Deborah, you spoiled young article,"
she said, emulating Kathleen O'Leary's brogue and bor-
rowing one of her favorite expressions, "let's see if this
dog will hunt."

Deborah opened the tin of matches, and they scattered
all over the floor. As she gritted her teeth and leaned forward to pick them up, she felt a wave of longing for
Kathleen and for Lucy, and even for Phoebe.

Life at Miss Boylan's had been a long chain of mean-
ingless delights. She and her friends had been willing par-
ticipants in social engagements and contrived, self-
important meetings of philanthropical societies, wardrobe
fittings and shopping expeditions. Leisurely, chatty con-
versations that went nowhere. Pointless lectures and en-
tertainments. It was no wonder, she thought, scooping up
the last of the spilled matches, young women pursued the
empty pleasures of society so avidly.

The alternative was painful. She knew that now. It was
difficult to examine one's own life and one's place in the
world, difficult to realize one's worth was calculated in
terms of dollars and cents, difficult to have to make one's
own way in the world. She wondered, if she had simply
resigned herself to marrying Philip, how long she would
have gone on in an easy, numb state of false contentment,
never knowing there might be another path for her.

With her breath making cold puffs in the air, she set

aside the matches and laid the fire. She wished she had paid closer attention when Tom Silver had performed this task. She had a vague notion of tinder and kindling but not what to do with them.

A fire was a simple matter, she decided. You laid the wood in the hearth, and you set it on fire.

"Fine," she said. "I can do that."

She pushed a log into the round-bellied stove and, for good measure, put one on top of it. Then she struck a match, taking several tries before it caught. She turned her face away from the sulfurous flare and smell and touched the match to one of the logs. But the match burned down to a black curl of nothingness. Deborah dropped it just as she felt the sting of heat on her fingers. She lit another match with the same result, and then another.

"Drat," she said, sitting back on her knees. "What am I doing wrong?"

She persisted, lighting match after match until she had only a few left in the tin. The matches were too feeble and didn't stay lit long enough for the logs to take. The burned sticks lay in a useless heap in the stove, and the whistling wind rattled mercilessly at the windows. Deborah felt humiliatingly close to tears. This should be child's play, yet she could not seem to start a fire.

That was the patent absurdity of her existence, she reflected bleakly. She could perform complicated Latin declensions. She could play the pianoforte, memorize lengthy epic poems and recite the peerage of England, but she was unable to build a fire to keep herself from freezing to death.

"Oh, Lucy, you were right," she said, her teeth starting to chatter. "Women are slaves kept in the darkness of ignorance."

Darkness. Over the past few weeks the sun had been setting earlier and earlier in the day, but with the blizzard raging outside, she couldn't even begin to guess at the

time. She found a lamp and a bottle of lamp oil. Tom
Silver had been thorough in closing up the house for the
winter, but he had left a few bare necessities for use when
he returned in the spring.

Dear God, it was months until spring. She would not
let herself dwell on that, would not let herself dwell on
the fact that she had no fire and no food. She used one of
the remaining matches to light the lamp. Just the sight of
the glow within the glass warmed her. She stared at the
flame, mesmerized, thinking what an exhausting day it
had been. She was hungry and cold and thirsty, but above
all, she was tired. She could just crawl under the covers,
fully dressed, and sleep forever. Hibernate like a winter
creature, and when she awakened, it would be spring. The
notion tantalized her. It would be so incredibly easy just
to slip off to bed.

"No," she said through gritted teeth. "If you sleep
now, you'll never wake up. Get that fire started."

The lamp oil sloshed a little as she brought her light
back to the stove, and the flame spat and flared momentarily. At first she thought nothing of it, but then she carefully set the lamp down and fetched the rectangular can
of oil.

If this fuel could keep the lamp wick burning, then it
logically followed that it could keep the logs burning in
the grate. She tipped the can and sprinkled the logs. This
time when she touched a match to the wood, the fire took
with a loud *whoosh* that made her stagger backward, away
from the leaping tongues of flame. Those flames shrank
with disappointing quickness. Deborah fed a few smaller
sticks to the fire and breathed a sigh of relief when they
caught and burned steadily.

Making fires was a dangerous business, Deborah
thought, touching her eyebrows to see if she had singed
them. Yet she felt such a thrill of triumph upon seeing the
big logs burn that she laughed aloud…and nearly choked
on the smoke.

For some reason, the smoke wasn't going up the pipe, but was pouring into the cabin. Deborah knew she would choke to death within minutes if she didn't do something. The flue, she remembered suddenly. Open the flue, close the flue. She had heard servants mention this. What on earth was a flue? It might be the iron lever protruding from the side of the stovepipe, she decided. She lifted it and waited.

The billows of smoke changed direction as if the big stove suddenly decided to inhale. Success. The pipe started to work immediately, drawing the smoke and the flames upward.

Deborah sat on the bare floor, her knees pulled up to her chin and stared at the rising flames. "I am warm," she said to the flickering fire. "Finally, I am warm. Who would have thought getting warm was such an ordeal?"

She was tempted to simply make a nest of her cloak, lie down and sleep in front of the stove. But she was fast learning that survival was a matter of planning, not indulging the momentary urge. First she needed to lay in enough fuel for the night and find something—anything—to eat, or she'd be too weak to get up in the morning.

She forced herself to go outside for more wood. The lash of the wind and cold took her breath away. The storm was made of thin steel blades, all of them slashing at her with a cold so intense it hurt her very bones. As quickly as she could, she brought a stack of logs from the wood bin at the side of the house. She had no idea if the logs would last the night, but it looked like enough. The howling wind chased her inside, and she imagined that it was a great monster, pursuing her, bellowing at her door, shrieking through the chinks in the walls and roaring up through the floorboards.

Enough of being fanciful, she told herself sternly. She had work to do.

She stacked the wood in the bin beside the stove. Surprisingly, after all that activity, she felt slightly flushed and more hungry than ever. The pantry offered virtually nothing. Tom Silver had either taken the excess supplies to the mainland or sealed them away in barrels in the cellar under the trading post. Leaving food out, he had explained, only invited marauding bears or the occasional squatter or trapper.

She found a small jar of salt and a tin of cornmeal. Supper consisted of three spoons of cornmeal cooked in melted snow. The bland and thick-textured meal stuck in her throat, but she forced herself to swallow. Tomorrow she would get into the trading post and find something a little more appetizing.

With something akin to relief, she set about making a bed for the night. Since there was no need for privacy, she dragged the mattress over near the stove and piled it with rough wool blankets. Her damp skirt, stockings and shoes steamed when she hung them on the back of a chair to dry. How remarkable to think only a day had passed since she had fallen into the stream.

Deborah Beaton Sinclair used to have one, sometimes two skilled maids to help her with her nightly toilette. They used to remove her clothes with reverence, exclaiming over the perfection of the French fashions. They would put her in a gown of white cotton lawn so finely woven that it felt like soft water against her skin. They brushed out her hair until it glowed, gave her a cup of chamomile tea sweetened with honey and asked if she had any other needs before she retired for the night.

She laughed when she thought of the Deborah who had so thoughtlessly accepted such treatment as her due. That shallow, uncomplicated girl existed no more. Now her "needs" had narrowed to the need to fill her belly and keep from freezing to death. And astoundingly, there was only one person present who was capable of fulfilling that requirement. Even more astoundingly, she had managed to do it and not die.

As she made a crude pallet and snuggled under the

mound of covers in front of the fire, it struck her again
how truly alone she was. Truly alone, for the first time in
her life.

She stared at the louvered iron door of the stove,
watched the flames dancing and prayed she would awaken
in time to add fuel to the fire. And then, as the roar of
the blizzard outside crescendoed, she squeezed her eyes
shut and felt herself hurtling into restless sleep.

She dreamed of a bear, a great brown one like the one
Nels had shown her at Gull Lake. The huge creature had
tiny black eyes and a red, hungry mouth. Rearing up on
two legs, it came at her and opened its mouth to roar. But
instead of an animal bellow, a horrible tenor voice came
out, singing Mozart.

The beast drew close, and she could feel the rank heat
of its body, red pulsations surrounding her, thawing her,
forcing her to feel again, licking at her.

Gunshot.

Deborah sat straight up, her heart pounding wildly, her
body drenched in sweat.

Disoriented, the sound of the exploding gun ringing in
her head, she clutched the blankets to her chest and cow-
ered on the bed. Only it wasn't a bed, but the pallet she
had made for herself. And it wasn't a gunshot, but a log
popping in the fire.

Slowly, inexorably, reality broke over her. She was in
the middle of nowhere. She was frozen in some eerie
realm separate from the rest of the world, a floating ice-
bound kingdom where nothing and no one could come
near her. Sitting in front of the only fire she had ever
made, Deborah pulled her knees up to her chest and stared
into the blue heart of the flames. It was a dream. And now
she was awake, and it was over.

Over.

She gave a short, sharp laugh that was filled with irony.
She must be the only woman in the world who would
awaken to the white nothingness of a blizzard and feel

relief rather than alarm. Odd. She didn't even remember falling asleep. She must have been more tired than she'd thought.

Just as a precaution, she took down the old buckshot gun from its pegs in the loft. Her hands shook a little as she loaded in the shot, remembering the shooting lessons at her father's lakeside estate. Leaning the gun in a corner, she pushed a heavy trunk against the door and stared out the window. The nightmare gradually dissolved in a blaze of winter white, and she forced her attention to the matters at hand. First, the fire. Her intuition about it had improved, for she now knew how to lay the smaller sticks loosely on the coals, under the logs. She fiddled with the bellows until she figured out how to use them. She generated puffs of air to fan the flames, and saw with inordinate pride that the technique worked quickly and well. Once she had a nice blaze going, she heated water in the only pot she could find. She suspected that the well would freeze, and then she would have to melt snow for water. Yesterday the notion would have panicked her. Today she felt rather matter-of-fact about it.

But first she should eat. The cornmeal did not tempt her and the thought of trying to make it into a pasty mush turned her stomach. She decided to go to the trading post and raid the stores. Tom and Lightning Jack had left very little behind, but surely she would find something edible.

When she opened the door, the wind practically snatched it out of her hand and smacked it against the side of the house. The cold bit at her with teeth of steel. She hauled the door shut again and pressed herself against it, breathing hard as if she had escaped the talons of a monster.

"All right, Deborah," she said to herself. It was strange to hear her voice for the first time this morning. "For once in your life, think things through. Be prepared."

She went about the room, shaking out the clothing she had hung to dry by the fire. For some reason, the nightmare still clung in her mind, hanging about like cobwebs in the corners of her thoughts.

As her mind wandered, she dressed in every article of clothing she could find, including an old soft flannel shirt she found hanging on a peg behind the door. When she put the shirt on, something unexpected happened. She was hit by a wave of scent that she recognized. The smell of the lake winds and the north woods and...Tom Silver.

She gasped, her heart knocking in her chest, and clawed at the garment, intent on getting it off. But as images of Tom penetrated her panic, she slowed down. She saw him in all his guises—the wild man bursting into her father's house, the big protector saving a little girl from the flames, the mariner, the businessman, the trader. The man grieving for a boy he had loved as his own son. She had seen many facets of Tom Silver, but never once had she seen a man to be feared. And it was so odd that she had never feared him, for hadn't he come blazing into her life for the purpose of shooting her father?

Yet even then, some subtle instinct had whispered in her ear that this man was not a killer.

Slowly, letting out her breath, she buttoned the shirt down the front. She put on her gray wool hat, pulled on her gloves...and was struck by the memory of Tom's big, blunt fingers struggling with her glove buttons. He was everywhere, haunting every corner of this house, haunting every corner of her heart and mind. She couldn't seem to escape thoughts of him, though she wished she could. She needn't worry about him now, at any rate. He had gone to the mainland without her. She was all alone.

The coarse woolen blanket made a serviceable outer cloak. She was only going across the yard to the trading post, but the trouble was, when she looked out the window, she could not even see the end of the porch. The snow was coming down that thick.

Lowering her head into the wind, she went outside. The storm swept her footprints away as soon as she lifted her foot, and within a few moments, she realized she could not see the house. Blind with cold and panic, she groped her way back, praying she had not lost her bearings. When her shin bumped the stoop, she nearly wept with relief.

But instead of weeping, she fought her way back inside and paced up and down, trying to think of a way to go out without getting lost. She found a ball of twine and tied one end to the door handle. By keeping hold of the twine, she wouldn't get lost even if the snow blinded her.

She took a deep breath, like a diver about to plunge in, and opened the door again. The icy wind sliced into her like razor blades, cutting her breath. The slinging snow threatened to drive her back inside. It was tempting to retreat, to simply curl into a ball by the fire and pray the storm would pass before she starved, but something extraordinary happened to Deborah Beaton Sinclair in those frozen moments. She became determined to survive.

She pulled in a deep, painful breath of the arctic air and then fought the storm, lowering her head and leaning into the howling wind. By the time she had gone ten steps, she could no longer feel her feet. Ten more steps and her fingers, chin and nose seemed to be gone. Frustrated, frightened sobs gusted from her and the cold seared her lungs.

Her shin bumped against something and she realized she had reached the steps to the back of the trading post. Stumbling with haste, she found the door.

It was locked with an iron hasp.

"No," she screamed, pounding her fists against the stout wooden planks. "For the love of heaven, no!"

Hysteria would serve nothing, she told herself.

The ax. Get the ax. Back across the yard to the woodshed adjacent to the house, paying out the twine as she went. She found the long-handled ax suspended on the wall and took it down. It felt heavier than it looked. She had no idea how to use it, but was learning to turn terror into grim determination. Wading through the snow—it was waist deep now—she nearly lost her way, but found the door again and hit it with the ax.

The blow reverberated down her arms, but otherwise had no effect on the weathered wood of the door. With the next blow, the blade stuck into the wood, though not deeply enough to do any damage.

Deborah gritted her teeth and struck again. This time the blade sank into the wood, but when she wrenched it out, only a splinter of wood came with it.

"I'll die if I stay out here much longer," she said through her chattering teeth. The thought made her more angry than frightened. She pulled back and swung with all her might—at the lock, not the door itself. The frozen, brittle iron broke away, and the lock hung askew.

Tears of relief flooded Deborah's eyes. She pushed her way into the dim, ice-cold shop and scavenged all the food she could find, filling a burlap sack with jars of maple syrup and applesauce, bottled berries, tinned meats, coffee beans. Then she slung the sack over her shoulder and started toward the cabin.

The day had gone white. Pure, stinging white. She couldn't see a blessed thing. If she took one wrong step, she could get lost and freeze to death just a few feet from the house. She gave a tentative tug on the twine in her apron pocket. The end still seemed to be tied to the doorknob. She staggered across the yard, hand over hand, stumbling and awkward with the sack of supplies on her back.

At long last she made it back to the warm cabin and nearly wept with relief. No time for tears, she admonished herself and peeled off the outer layers of clothing. Her face, hands and feet prickled and burned as they thawed, but she welcomed the sensation as proof that she had survived the ordeal. She built up the fire, then broke open a jar of applesauce and wolfed it all down right out of the jar, with a shocking lack of table manners. When she finished, she stared into the fire until she felt herself relax,

her eyelids grow heavy and her breathing finally catch up
with itself. Sleep beckoned, and she began sinking into a
well-deserved nap.

Survival—it was an exhausting business.

Twenty-One

The horse gave out at sunset the second day, keeling over like a felled oak. Tom leaped out of the saddle as the big-boned shire gelding collapsed, narrowly escaping being pinned beneath the huge carcass.

A steady stream of obscenities erupted from him as he fought to extract the saddlebags from the saddle. Fifteen hundred pounds of dead horse made for a considerable struggle, and Tom had to retrieve his belongings by cutting a perfectly good saddle to pieces.

While he worked, Deborah's dog huddled against his chest, pressed between his layered woolen shirts. Tom hadn't wanted to bring the critter along, but a mile from the settlement, he'd heard a muffled yapping sound and turned to see the dog leaping through the snow after him. The fool thing had followed him. He'd sworn, scooped the thing up and thrust it inside his coat.

He cursed again as he looked down at the shire. The liveryman at the lakeshore settlement had declared the big workhorse a "sound" animal and had sworn he'd make it to Thunder Bay even in the midst of the storm. Thunder Bay was the closest spot on the mainland to Isle Royale. Assuming the lake had frozen hard enough, Tom could cross the ice to the island, a distance of just ten miles. It was the fastest way he knew to get there.

But he hadn't counted on losing the hired horse.

Hell, he hadn't counted on anything that had happened since the great Chicago fire, now that he thought about it. Each event seemed to lean on others, and when one situation changed, everything else did too.

His first impulse, after realizing he had to return to Isle Royale for Deborah, had been to go by boat. By that evening, the first blizzard of the year walloped the lake, and it was impossible even to launch, much less navigate. Even so, Lightning Jack practically had to tie Tom up to keep him from going out on the lake after her. "*Tiens,* you will do the girl no good if you die," the old voyageur had railed at him. Lightning Jack and the others had begged him to wait for the storm to pass before he set out to find her. He had waited for as long as he could stand—perhaps a whole hour before worry gnawed a huge hole in his patience. Lightning Jack had forced him to wait for first light and provision himself properly.

Jack had even tried to come along, but Tom had argued him out of it. There was no sense in both of them going. In the end, he had gone off without saying a word, because he was sick of hearing about the dangers of traveling through a storm along the lakeshore, with the jagged tops of the Sawtooth Mountains hemming him in from the west.

Tom had scoured the area for a team of dogs, but there was none to be had. He'd settled for the draft horse and left at dawn. The horse had been balky and slow through the day and had coughed the night through in the shelter Tom made inside a snow-draped cedar tree the first night. Now the damned thing was dead and stiffening fast in the arctic weather.

After struggling for about an hour, Tom managed to collect the most necessary items—a thick blanket, matches, dried fish, a knife and a pistol. He tied everything together and fashioned a knapsack out of the blanket, fitting it on his back the best he could.

He had to get to Deborah.

Since the first, gut-squeezing moment when he had realized she'd been left behind, that one thought had pounded in his head, his chest, and telegraphed itself along every limb. She'd been left behind in a blizzard. He could not—would not—rest until he went back for her.

He had never experienced a feeling quite like the worry that had been gnawing at him since that sick moment of realization. He had worried about Asa, that was true. But he'd always known where the boy was and how he would fare, up until that last day.

That day, the sound of the rumbling explosion had frozen Tom's heart. Blasting was a part of mining. He understood that. But somehow when the roar of the dynamite reached him that day, he knew.

He had raced up to the mine with his heart in his throat, but along with the rage and the panic had been ice-cold knowledge. The certainty had not comforted him, but at least he knew.

In Deborah's case, the wondering made him crazy. The wondering and the self-disgust. He was not a stupid or incautious man. He had his moments of lunacy, such as believing he could shoot Arthur Sinclair in cold blood, such as taking a helpless debutante hostage, but in general he was a calm and considered man. He was not one to leave the island for the winter without checking, double-checking and triple-checking everything down to the last detail.

And yet where Deborah was concerned, he had done the unthinkable. He had let himself be persuaded she was safe aboard the *Koenig* without checking for himself. He had trusted his assumptions rather than test them.

Now his stupidity might have cost Deborah Sinclair her life.

And he was entirely to blame. A hostage taker had to obey the unwritten code. You didn't let a hostage die while in your custody.

By the time he set off on foot, the cold was aiming straight for his bones and the wind slashed horizontally across the horizon. Yet never once did it occur to him to hesitate, turn back, give up. How could he, when Deborah had been left behind? She would starve. She would freeze to death.

The island was not entirely uninhabited, he reminded himself, shoving down a rise of panic. A logging company had left a skeleton crew on the south end to guard its claim over the winter. A fisherman or two in Rock Harbor might have decided to winter over. But that was miles from Deborah. She wouldn't know how to seek help. The island was too big, too wild, to find another settlement even in the best of conditions. In a blizzard, an overland trek was impossible. And, truth be told, they might not be the sort of men to give her protection without exacting a payment Tom refused to contemplate.

The wind dragged at him, ripped at his clothes. He was grateful for his fur coat, mittens and leggings, even grateful for the small, ill-tempered dog huddled against him. Lightning Jack had been insistent on the matter of the coat in particular. He had given Tom a full-length hooded coat made from the hide of an entire grizzly bear. Tom hoped the garments would keep him from freezing to death before he reached Deborah.

He had no idea how much farther it was to the bay, but he recognized the curve of the natural harbor and knew Isle Royale lay just across the lake. He stood at the shore, his numb feet sunk deep in new snow. The lake had iced up, to be sure, but how deep was the freeze, and did it reach all the way to the island?

The wind made rivers of snow flow across the ice. Snakelike, they slithered over the frozen surface, beckoning, mocking him. He knew that once he went out on the ice, he would be at the mercy of the lake. He took out a flask and fortified himself with a swig of schnapps, then started walking.

Time passed. There was no sun and no dark, just the vast and endless white of the winter storm. He squinted his eyes, hoping to avoid the snow blindness. The bone-aching cold made him slow and stupid. It was all he could do to consult his compass and set his feet on a course across the ice. For some reason it helped to keep Deborah Sinclair's face in his mind's eye.

He found that strange, since he didn't even like the woman. Yet not even he could deny that she was as beautiful as the winter moon, pale and perfect and distant. An ice princess. Her image glowed like a beacon, summoning him ever closer, one step and then another. He played a game in his mind, trying to remember every facet of Deborah Sinclair, beginning with the human missile sliding down the banister and crashing into him. He had seen her furious, frightened, stubborn, proud and vulnerable. He had watched her struggle to fit in with the people of the island, trying to learn their ways even if it meant dealing with fish guts and backbreaking physical labor. She had pursued the work as some sort of atonement, he supposed, because the islanders had proved him right about Arthur Sinclair.

Her disillusionment with her own father had been unexpected. As far as Tom knew, the rich usually stuck together and denied that any of their own could possibly do wrong. Yet Deborah had listened. She had believed. She had cared.

As he struggled through the driving wind, Tom thought of all the ways he knew her...and in the end concluded that he did not know her at all. She was as much a mystery to him now as she had been that first night. He knew she hid things deep inside her, and he wanted to know what those things were. Thoughts, fears, secrets—he wanted them all. He had no idea what to do with them, yet that didn't stop him from wanting to know her. He felt like a fool for not realizing this sooner. She was a woman he wanted to know. He had started out her captor, but in a way, she had captured him. And he had been too stupid to see it happening.

As he battled the storm, his thoughts were the thoughts of a madman. The slow violence of freezing to death made it hard to reason. Did madmen pray? he wondered. Maybe he wasn't so mad after all, because he found himself praying desperately for deliverance. Just get me to the island. Just get me to the island and to Deborah.

He refused to give up until he found her.

Almost there. But the force of the storm slapped down his intentions. He had been walking on the ice for hours. Surely he would see Isle Royale any moment now. He paused to squint through the needles of snow at his compass, to make certain he was on course for the island. The dog stirred and whimpered inside his coat. It really was hard to concentrate. Something was nagging at him. A feeling, a strange noise, perhaps.

Deep within the shriek of the wind he detected a new sound, a low, gradual click and rumble.

His gut knew what it was before his mind caught on, and he started to run. He ran for his life, seeing nothing but white, and hearing nothing but the sound he had learned to dread—the unmistakable snap of cracking ice.

The section of ice came away, the fissure crawling along like a black snake. He was at the mercy of the storm. Wind and lake currents bore him away from the mainland, and he could only hope he'd be pushed toward more solid ice, or miraculously, to the rock bound north shore of Isle Royale. The chances, he conceded with a sick feeling in his gut, were damned slim. Only time would tell.

Tom hunkered down, tucking his face into the hood of his coat, trying to hide from the wind. He had lost his bearings, and everything seemed to float in a sea of white toward a dreamlike place. Maybe he'd get through this, he thought. Or maybe the storm had set him adrift in the endless vast lake, never to be seen again.

* * *

Deborah stared dully at the shallow notches she had dug in the wall by the stove. Four days had passed since she had been left all alone on the island. She wasn't sure why she felt it necessary to make a record of her days in the cabin, to mark them off, but some compulsion for order and history urged her to do so. The storm had abated, leaving great heaps and drifts of snow blanketing the wilderness. The strange empty beauty of the snow-covered land took her breath away even as it frightened her. The snow blotted out everything—the roadways and the shape of the land, the rocks and cliffs, even some of the smaller buildings like the Wicks' weir house and Ilsa's gardening shed.

How tempting it was to picture herself as a small part of the landscape, cloaked by a perfect covering of pure white. In her more eccentric moments she was tempted to walk out and let the snowfall take her, cover all her flaws and scars. But she always talked herself out of it, because she knew that the rough, jagged landscape inside her could never be fully hidden. It was something that had happened to her, something she had to learn to live with.

But it was hard. So hard.

She was weakening. She could feel it in her chest, in her bones. The constant work of keeping the fire burning sapped her strength. A steady, bland diet of cornmeal cakes with syrup proved to be inadequate. Most of all, the complete nothingness of her isolation beat her down.

She didn't know what to do with herself. If she wasn't careful, her thoughts wandered to the deep, dark places inside herself, places she did not want to go for fear of what she would discover there. And if she somehow found herself in that dark place, she felt she would never find her way back into the light.

"I need an occupation," she said aloud to the empty room. "I'll go mad if I don't find one."

She searched the cabin, but found no paper, nothing to

write with and reading failed to hold her attention for long. Tom Silver had been annoyingly thorough in clearing out the place for the winter.

It was a terrible blow to realize that she knew of no way to entertain herself. She had no inner resources for passing the time. All her life, entertainment and pastime had been provided for her, just like the tea that magically appeared each afternoon on a silver tray. She didn't have to do anything but show up.

How pale and empty her life had been, she reflected. How shameful that she had not noticed. She'd existed as someone half-alive, letting the other half slumber in bland ignorance. Here in the terrible winter woods, she was coming to know herself in a way that used to be obscured by the dizzying social whirl of Chicago.

Her gaze fell upon the rickety box of quilting scraps under the bedstead. She remembered the images of birds in flight she had thought of during her first quilting lesson.

For the first time in days, she felt a hint of warmth; a pressure, a little surge, a thing so rarely felt that it took her some moments to recognize it. It was a clutch of inspiration. She realized the magnificent quilts made by Ilsa and the others came from years of practice. If she could create something half so fine, she would be satisfied. A project, then. There was a certain comfort in having a project.

As she laid out scissors and muslin, Deborah was amazed to hear herself humming. At last, a project to give shape and color to her days. No longer a prisoner of the white silence of winter, she had actually found something to do.

She began by strewing the colorful scraps across the muslin sheet. Most of the fabric came from torn child-sized shirts and nightgowns she knew had once belonged to Asa. How much nicer, she thought, to turn the scraps into a quilt than consigning them to rags. She had almost no memory of her mother. She couldn't stand for that to happen to Tom. Perhaps this would help him remember the things he'd shared with the boy she'd never known.

Working by both instinct and the remembered instructions from Ilsa and Celia, she grouped the colors in patches. She stood on a stool above the work area, peering down at it with the concentration of a master painter. Unlike the dry, mechanical lessons she'd endured in her art classes, taught by starving artists who were bored and resentful of their overprivileged, uninspired pupils, this excited her. All on its own, an idea began to emerge, and suddenly she could see the finished quilt as if it actually existed. She pictured the goldeneyes and mergansers soaring over the lake or swimming along the shore. Creating the design was a new and curiously exhilarating experience.

She had no idea if it was good or bad. She only knew that it pleased her to snip the soft bits of cloth into shapes and to lay them out in a pattern. The deep blues and greens reminded her of woods and water, with faded denim for the color of the sky. Recalling the way Ilsa and Celia had worked, she separated the quilt into large sections. First came the cutting and piecing, then the application of the colored pieces to the muslin, making certain the pattern had logic and balance.

She fell to her task with a smile on her face, and the flash of the needle took on a rhythm all its own. She savored every moment of the sewing, wondering if it was the novelty of making her own quilt that appealed to her, or if she actually loved the work itself. It didn't matter, she decided. She had found an occupation, and she would pursue it for as long as it took. Somehow, it made the idea of facing a long winter alone much more bearable.

The labor of her hands calmed her mind. It was quite remarkable, she realized, how the work of quilting seemed to quiet her thoughts. Even the posture of sitting with the blanket spread over her lap promoted warmth and serenity. The worries of the past slid away. By the time she sought her bed next to the fire, she felt calm and sleepy rather than nervous or jumpy. She knew she was growing weak from the poor diet and winter conditions, but even so, she was learning to rely on herself, to know what to expect from herself.

That night she dreamed about the bear again.

The nightmare came on tiptoe as it always did, whispering threats that spread like poisoned wine through her body. The rearing bear advanced on her, and she stumbled back, her feet pounding, pounding on the floor of the red-draped opera salon as she gritted her teeth and tried to run from him....

The pounding dragged her out of the dream.

She came awake with a start, sitting up straight and breathing hard.

"A dream," she said between panted breaths. "It was only a dream."

The glow from the banked coals in the stove cast a faint orange light across the planked floor, but everything else lay shrouded in darkness. Outside, the wind howled at the windows with the voice of a mezzo soprano. But within the black shriek of the storm, she heard a thumping sound.

Perhaps the door to the woodshed had flown loose, she reasoned. Perhaps a shutter or awning was banging against a building. But even as she rationalized her fear, she began to move, stumbling through the darkness. Groping along the wall, she found the buckshot gun where she had left it after the first nightmare.

The mysterious thud sounded closer than ever. She envisioned a man-eating bear trying to paw its way into the cabin. Her hands shook as she checked the chamber and cocked the gun. At least a bear made a big target, she thought, trying to still the trembling of her hands.

Shooting was one of those genteel pastimes her father approved of. It was considered the sport of the rich to destroy clay pigeons. At her father's lakeside home she and her friends had laughed their way through shooting matches. She never dreamed she would have to shoot to save her life.

Now she was glad for those lazy afternoons, glad Phoebe's brother had taken it upon himself to teach her to shoot along with his giggling younger sisters. She was even glad Phoebe Palmer had such a competitive nature, for she had goaded Deborah to practice.

She seated the gun against her shoulder.

The cabin door flew open. Wind and snow blew in with the force of slung blades. And with them came the bear.

The giant intruder stood at full height, filling the door-way, bigger and hairier than the one in her nightmare. She jerked the trigger with her finger, and the gun exploded.

The creature gave a strange moan of pain, then keeled over.

Twenty-Two

Pain from the recoil of the shotgun reared up Deborah's arm and slammed into her shoulder. She dropped the gun with a *thunk.* The acrid burn of gunpowder filled the room as wind and snow poured in through the open door.

And on the floor lay the man she had just killed.

In that last instant, as her terrified finger had tightened on the trigger, she had seen that the intruder was no hungry marauding bear, but a man covered in bearskins for warmth. Yet the realization had come too late. Had she swung the barrel away in time? Had the old, unreliable gun misfired? No, for once her aim had been true and the weapon had worked.

Bright flames from the logs flickered over her victim. Merciful heavens, had she committed murder?

She sank to her knees beside the hulking, fur-clad form. Even now, fear buzzed through her. She'd rendered him helpless, but she was still afraid. He lay facedown, immobile, silent. In the dimness she could not see the gunshot wound. Gingerly she touched his shoulder.

"Are you...?" She didn't know what she wanted to ask. She pushed a little harder, but the man didn't move. "Dear God, are you dead?" she whispered, pressing frantically at his shoulder.

The body rolled to one side. She pulled off the fur hood

and firelight from the stove illuminated an unshaven, very familiar face.

"Oh my God," she said, her voice rising in a sob. "I've shot Tom Silver!" Her teeth chattered uncontrollably. *Please don't be dead. Please God please please please....*

The disjointed prayer shrieked in her mind as she opened the stove to light the room. At the same moment, Smokey scampered inside, his paws caked with snow and ice. He leaped around in a frenzy, but Deborah spared no time for him.

The slicing north wind intruded through the open door, chilling the tears on her face. Pushing the door shut, she turned her attention to Tom. Then, from a place she didn't know she had inside her, Deborah found an eerie, focused calm. He was frozen, shot, maybe dead. Getting hysterical would not help him.

She took his face between her hands, wincing when she felt the hard chill on his skin. She supposed she had always known he had a wonderful face, stamped with strength and character, but she had never let herself see that until this moment. Now she might be too late. The coolness of his skin struck her like a blow. "I'm not losing you," she said between gritted teeth. "I won't let you go."

She bent over him and put her ear very close to his nose and mouth, but couldn't tell if he was breathing or not. Knowing she had to find out where he was wounded, she pulled at the leather buckles of the thick bearskin coat and parted it. He wore layers of clothing—a knitted shirt and two flannel chemises under his buckskins—and she had to pull these aside to see if she could detect a pulse in his neck. The smell of snow and pine emanated from him as she worked, and she wondered how he had come to be here.

At last she revealed his neck and put her hand there.

It never occurred to her that she should not be touching

him. All she knew was that he was helpless, he needed her.

Perhaps it was only wishful thinking, but his throat felt warm compared to his face. She rested her fingers lightly at the side of his neck, closed her eyes and willed him to let her feel the pulse of blood there.

Nothing.

Maybe her hand was shaking too badly. Maybe she wasn't touching him in the right place.

"There must be a pulse," she whispered fiercely. "There must be. There has to be."

Try as she might to avoid morbid thoughts, she could not help remembering the sad tale of Charlie Mott and his wife, and how after he died the poor woman was stuck with a frozen corpse the entire winter.

Deborah pushed back her sleeves and tried again. Unable to keep her hands from trembling, she could not find a pulse. She could not detect the faintest breath, could not find any evidence whatsoever that he was alive.

But he *had* to be. He had come from Lord-knew-where, obviously enduring incredible hardships in order to come back to her. He had sounded like a small army tramping across the porch. A man like that didn't simply die of a gunshot wound.

The dog shivered by the fire. She added a log to it and lit a lamp, setting it close by so she could see him better. She had to get his clothes off in order to find out where she had wounded him. The bearskin coat was impossible; she could not get his arms out of the sleeves, so she concentrated on removing his mittens and boots, then unbuttoning the various shirts, chemises and trousers. She didn't balk at the task. When a man's life hung in the balance, one could not afford to be bashful.

Small flickers of hope kept cropping up. With each passing moment, each bit of him that she revealed, she began to suspect that there was no bullet wound.

She pulled aside the clothing as best she could, revealing his chest. It was stunningly broad. Hairy. Amazingly unlike anything she had ever imagined. She placed her hand there, unexpectedly moved by the act of touching him, wondering if it was his heartbeat she felt, or her own.

Live, she thought. *Please live. You must live.*

No response. The burning logs popped and spat resin, and outside, the wind raged. But in the cabin, the stillness had the pall of death.

A sense of helpless loss crept through Deborah. He was her abductor, her captor, and yet if she could have exchanged her own life for his at this moment, she would have. Her devastation was so intense that she surged to her feet, too filled with terror and grief to think straight.

Then she saw the buckshot.

A pellet was embedded in the wall of the cabin, easily three feet from the doorway. Others lay scattered on the floor.

"I only fired once," she said, hope burning in her chest. "I only fired once, and I missed. Thank God I missed."

But it was buckshot, not a single bullet. She had shot him with a deadly spray of lead pellets. She dropped to her knees beside him and renewed her efforts to warm him, to wake him. All the time, she spoke to him, babbling but afraid to stop. "You're not dead. You've just caught a chill. You'll be all right as soon as you're warm...."

It took every ounce of strength she possessed, and then some, to push and pull and drag him over to the pallet where she made her bed by the fire. By the time she wrestled him so that he lay half on and half off the heap of blankets, she was sweating.

She dared to touch his face, her hand steady now.

Warmer. He felt warmer to the touch.

"Dear heaven," she said, "it's working. You're going to get warm, and you're going to be fine." His hands and feet were still icy cold, so she built up the fire as high as she dared. Once the flames were roaring, she went to work. His clothes, especially the outer ones, were damp. She had to get him out of them.

Rolling him one way and then the other, she managed to extract him from the thick fur coat. To her horror, the movement exposed a deep, bleeding wound in his head. Fresh blood smeared the inside of the hood.

"I didn't mean to shoot you," she whispered over and over again. She used a long scrap of muslin from the quilting basket for a bandage, winding it around his head. Later she would clean the wound, stitch it closed if need be. But at the moment, she had to follow her instincts. *Get him warm first.* Laboriously she peeled away his buckskins and shirts down to the last flannel chemise. She removed this as well, for it was damp and clammy.

His denim trousers began to steam with the thawing. She set herself to removing them, thinking that trousers were an enormous bother. She had to inch the fabric down one leg, then the other, alternating between the two in a process that was excruciatingly slow. Beneath the Kentucky jeans, he wore long woolen leggings, also damp and chilled. She gritted her teeth and willed herself not to think of anything but warming him up so he wouldn't die on her.

She managed to wrestle the jeans off him, and then the woolens. Beneath that she discovered flannel trews cut thigh length.

"You're keeping those on," she said through her teeth. She covered him with every blanket she had and propped his head on a pillow. Then she checked the water in the kettle to make certain there was plenty to make him tea if he awakened.

But the way he was lying there, so still and pale, she feared he would never wake up. He had frozen to death right at her door. Somehow he'd had the strength to come back through a storm for her, but now the storm was winning the battle.

"No," she said defiantly. "You will survive this, do you hear me, Tom Silver?"

He didn't, of course. He was cold to the bone, and the woodstove's warmth wasn't enough. The mound of blankets wasn't enough.

She sat beside him on the floor, absently stroking the dog. She suspected Tom Silver had carried him inside his coat, keeping him warm. The stove filled the room with heat, yet she shivered.

Because she knew what she must do next.

She had to warm him with her body heat. Like the two men under the moose hide in the campfire story. The men who had warmed each other with their body heat. Skin to skin contact.

Everything inside her recoiled, quailed at the idea. She battled her way to logic. This was a matter of life and death. This had nothing to do with the way a man and a woman touched, she told herself. This was a survival procedure.

She didn't dare think any more. She just acted. Peeling off her clothes, she lifted the covers and slid beneath them, hesitantly at first but then with growing conviction. The man was freezing. Next to her, he felt like a giant icicle. She had to impart the warmth of her body to him. If she didn't, he would die.

Inside her, a furnace raged, and she wondered how on earth he could possibly be cold. Setting her jaw with determination, she wrapped her arms around him. He was so big, she couldn't find a way to hold him in her embrace. She put out one trembling hand, resting it on his shoulder, then felt a jolt and drew back her hand as if she had touched a hot stove. It hurt to breathe. Blinding bolts of apprehension attacked her. A man's body, pressed to hers. The smells and textures of him surrounding her, filling her.

She reared back in horror, and for a dizzying moment lost herself, going away for a while to a far place. Then, very slowly, the world came into focus, to winter stillness and firelight and the wounded man lying half-dead on the floor.

Touch him, she told herself. *Touch him.*

She tried again, reaching out with her hand, and as she did, she felt such a seething frustration that she nearly wept with it. She must force herself to put aside the fear. She must use her body warmth to warm Tom Silver.

This time her hand stayed where she put it—on his chest. He needed for her to be closer still. She could sense that. Spasms of fear jerked through her, and she shut her eyes, thinking of things that were benign and far away from this place and this moment. The trill of a lark outside her window. A conversation with her friends on a sun-drenched verandah. A carriage ride in Lincoln Park.

Touch him. The longer she delayed, the more she put Tom Silver at risk. The cynical part of her wondered why he had come. To save her life or to reclaim his hostage?

Or had he come back because he was afraid for her, all alone on a frozen island in winter?

The thought pushed down her terror. Drawing a deep breath, she laid her head on his shoulder, then moved it to cover his chest. She could hear the sound of his heart beating, the shallow breaths rising and falling. She pressed her foot to his long, hard leg, then her thigh to his thigh, her belly to his belly.

Her breast to his chest.

The fear reared up but she forced it back. She wrapped her arm around his middle and pressed her legs against his. It helped to avoid thinking. Instead she let images drift through her head. The sun on the lake. Joking Norwegian voices from the fish house. Tom Silver walking with a hundred-pound sack of flour on each shoulder. Quilt patterns. Tunes from Lightning Jack's harmonica.

These were the musings of a woman who was, quite possibly, losing her mind, but she clung to random notions because they held the fear at bay. It was there, lurking, waiting for her to give it a chance to leap up again, but she wouldn't let it. Instead she concentrated on those inane thoughts that had nothing to do with anything except that they kept her from screaming.

And in the middle of thinking about nothing and laying her hands and arms and legs on Tom Silver, putting her cheek against his chest, something strange happened. Or more precisely, *nothing* happened. He didn't move, didn't reach out for her, didn't close his big hand around her wrist, didn't attack her. Didn't hurt or frighten her.

"Of course not, you goose," she said under her breath. "He's unconscious."

A man could be so agreeable when he was unconscious.

The dog settled right in the covers with him. She gave herself wholly to the job of warming him, moving slowly with instinct as her guide, rubbing his cold limbs and touching his face. The stones she had warmed earlier cooled, and she put them under the stove to warm again, and then she stayed close to Tom Silver and even said a broken little prayer for this big, strange, wounded man who had come across the ice for her.

Twenty-Three

The fire was all around him, lethal tongues of flame devouring hands and feet, a torture beyond endurance. When he tried to cry out, his throat locked up. He saw only the red haze of the deadly fire and heard only the dull roar of its inevitable progress. The inferno that had destroyed a city was upon him, and he was stuck, unable to move, to breathe or even to make a sound.

"Oh good," said a voice through the thunder of the fire. "You're awake."

Shrill reality cleaved into the dream. Tom Silver's eyes flew open. For a few seconds, he saw nothing but blinding white. Then an image took shape. Blond and anxious, with eyes the color of the lake in summer. Miss Deborah Sinclair.

"Hey, Princess," he said. His voice sounded appallingly weak. The rasp of a rusty hinge, no more.

"Are you all right?" she asked.

He blinked, squinted at a light too bright to endure. The blinding white resolved into an image of the cabin window, snow outside, white against a white sky. "I'm alive," he said. His words slurred together as if he were drunk. He didn't recall drinking anything.

His feet and hands were on fire, and he was shivering

violently. He lifted his hands and stared at them. The tips were blistered, an angry purple in color.

"I think your hands and feet are frostbitten," Deborah said. "I have never actually seen a case of frostbite, but I believe that's what has happened. Does it hurt very much?"

Like holding a branding iron to his own flesh. But he didn't see the point of telling her that. He concentrated on trying to remember, for the ordeal on the ice had muddled his memory. He hadn't expected to survive. After the horse had collapsed, he'd had no choice but to press on through the driving storm, crossing the ice that had not yet frozen in the deepest parts of the water.

"How on earth did you manage to come back to me?" she asked.

After the ice floe had broken away, he'd lost track of the hours. But it could not have been long or he would have frozen to death. Instead, providence or pure blind luck had favored him.

When the detached ice had nudged up against the whiter, thicker ice of the shore, he had been hovering at the edge of unconsciousness. He didn't know whether he'd reached the island or the mainland. Not until he'd gone ashore and picked out, through the drifts and roaring wind, the distinctive jagged peak of Sugar Mountain, had he been certain he'd reached Isle Royale. Even then, he could not be sure of success. The island was big. Long and wild, filled with inhospitable rock ridges and impenetrable forests.

He barely remembered his staggering trek up the ridge, consuming the last of his hard tack and dried fish while forcing himself to walk. All he recalled was the cold, and the wind shrieking through the trees, and the notion that he was the only thing alive for miles.

"I came on foot...over the ice," he said, too weary and in too much pain to explain further. How could he describe the agony of walking on feet that had frozen miles

ago? Or the dizzying relief that had spiraled through him
when he had sniffed the air like a wild animal and caught
a whiff of wood smoke? Or the rise of hope that had lifted
him out of his stupor when the cold winter moon had
given him a glimpse of smoke twisting from a chimney?

He groaned and moved his feet, unsure whether or not
they were still attached because at some point, he had lost
all feeling there. Sensation was coming back with a vengeance. His feet and hands screamed in fiery protest, and
he fought the searing pain, cursing between his gritted
teeth. His vision swam as if he were under water, looking
up.

Then she came back into focus. Deborah. The ice princess. Her image had floated in his mind, drawing him
along one step at a time, like the grail. She had been his
beacon, his quest as he struggled to survive. Perhaps she
had even kept him alive. But she looked...different. Gone
was the haughtiness, the disdain, the polished snobbery.
Now she looked simply weary and worried.

"Do you think you're going to be all right?" she asked.

He blinked, tried to swallow. "I guess I will."

The dog trotted forward and licked him.

He grimaced, but couldn't suppress a smile, even
though it caused his lip to crack. "So the rat survived."

"It was sweet of you to bring him."

Sweet. No one had ever called him sweet before. No
one had ever dared. "I didn't. The fool thing followed
me."

She held out a cup. "Tea with honey. I can't believe
you came back."

Neither could he. If she had merely been his hostage,
would he have crossed the ice to find her?

He reached for the speckled enamel cup, but his blistered hands were clumsy, bumping against the mug. She
pulled it away before the hot tea could spill. "Here," she
said. "Let me help."

Though he despised the weak feeling, he submitted as

she set aside the cup and propped a pillow behind him. Then she held the cup in her hands and put it to his lips. He sucked down the heavily sweetened, lukewarm liquid. By the time he finished drinking, he felt noticeably better. Stronger.

He propped himself up on his elbows and looked around. Morning. His cabin at the settlement.

"Where are my clothes?" he asked.

The color rose in her cheeks. "I hung them by the fire to dry."

He squinted at her, trying to picture her undressing him. The image wouldn't form, yet despite the battered state of his body, he had a deeply primal reaction. "Wish I'd been awake for that."

"I was afraid you'd die in those wet, frozen clothes."

"Reckon I was afraid of the same thing."

"I thought I'd—" She broke off and swiftly glanced away.

He followed her gaze to the shotgun lying on the floor. He would never leave a gun lying out like that. Gradually memory returned in small fragments. He remembered seeing the twist of smoke from the chimney. A faint glow— moonlight flickering on an iced pane of glass. The dog scampering across the snow. He had felt such hope in those moments. *I've found you at last.* He remembered thinking that.

Then he'd flung open the door to an explosive bang.

"You shot me," he said, sitting up straight. The wooziness caught at him, but he held himself steely and still until it passed.

She clutched her hands together in her lap. "I didn't mean to."

"You pointed the gun at me. Pulled the trigger. Should I read some other meaning into that?"

"What I mean is, I thought you were an intruder, a bear, actually."

"*A bear?*"

"It was dark. You were wearing a bear skin."

"*Shit.*"

She flinched. "I missed," she said, lifting her chin defensively. "Well, mostly," she added, ducking her head guiltily.

Time to get up, he decided. See for himself what damage had been done. He shoved aside the blankets, ignoring her gasp of outrage. When he stood, his feet felt as heavy and unresponsive as bags of sand. His head seemed to float from his body, and images melted into a smear of color. He felt himself sway and stagger, and he grabbed for the first thing he could—Deborah.

She wobbled beneath him, fragile as a spindly stick of furniture. She made a weird little squeaking sound.

"Quit whining," he said. "Give me a second." The world slowly swam back into focus. A stinging pain thudded in his head. Reaching up, he felt a crude bandage on his forehead. The fabric felt as if it were caked with drying blood. He inspected his fingers. Sure enough, blood. He let go of Deborah. "How'd this happen?"

"I missed. I swear, I missed. See?" She hurried over to the door, pointing out fresh gouges in the wooden frame. "A stray shot must have caught you."

"Shit," he said again.

"You shouldn't swear."

"Fine. What should I do, Princess? Pray?"

She stared at his bare chest while a flaming blush lit her cheeks. "You should get dressed. And then you should eat something. And then you should sleep some more."

Grumbling under his breath, he yanked on his dry, stiff trousers, stuffed his feet into socks, then put on his boots and went outside to relieve himself. When he returned, she was setting out bowls on the table.

"There's warm water in the basin," she said without looking up.

He washed at the creaky old washstand, then sat down

at the table, suddenly ravenous. She served him some sort of pasty corn porridge drenched in maple syrup. The dish would have turned the stomach of the stoutest of lumberjacks, yet to Tom it was pure ambrosia, and he ate every bit without saying a word.

When he finished, he had his first good look around the place. Her things were everywhere. Female things. Not very many of them, for most had been transported to the mainland, but Deborah Sinclair was the sort of woman who managed to strew bits and pieces of herself in her wake. Like a boat dragging a herring net and drawing a flock of gulls, she left things behind—a stocking, a hair comb, a bit of ribbon or lace, a bottle of some enticing and mysterious fragrant liquid.

Wood was stacked haphazardly by the stove. Foodstuffs from the shop littered the counter—a sack of meal, a jar of syrup, tins of potted meat, smoked fish.

She followed his gaze along the plank sideboard. "I broke into the store," she said with a sheepish shrug of her shoulders. "I used an ax." She waited, watching him like a rabbit poised to flee.

"I'm not going to yell at you," he said. In fact, he was somewhat amazed. Not so very long ago she couldn't even button her own shoes. She had survived a blizzard alone out here. Some men wouldn't have been able to manage that.

"So what happened?" he asked into the frozen silence. "How'd you manage to get left behind?"

"How did you manage to leave me behind?"

"You were supposed to be aboard the *Koenig*."

"I had to go back for something." Agitated, she stood up from the table and started cleaning up.

"Back for something. What'd you forget?"

"It was silly, really," she said without looking at him. "I wanted to collect a bag of agates from the stream. A memento of Isle Royale. I thought I'd never see this place again.'' With quick, nervous movements she began putting things up on the pantry shelf.

What an odd bird she was. She had been forced to come here against her will, yet she wanted a memento of her time here. Had she developed a certain fondness for the place?

''You should have told me. We would have waited.''

''Truly, I thought I'd be only a moment, and I didn't want to keep people waiting. I had a mishap. The night of the fire, I went back for a jewel that once belonged to my mother. That was the moment you broke into my father's house.'' She shook her head in self-disgust. ''You would think I'd learn to leave things behind rather than risk keeping them.'' As she spoke, she dropped a jar of hazelnut oil, and it shattered on the floor, splattering its contents every which way. ''My whole life is a mishap,'' she muttered, stooping to pick up the pieces. The dog came to sniff, and she shooed it away from the broken glass.

''That's a damn fool thing to say.'' He pushed back from the table and hunkered down to help. ''What the hell do you mean by that?''

''I don't know. I—I don't need any help.'' Their hands brushed and she snatched hers away. ''Truly,'' she said.

Irritated by her skittishness, Tom scooped up the dog.

''Poor Smokey,'' she said. ''The sooner we get out of this fix, the better for all of us.''

''Listen, Princess, there's no getting out of this fix.''

''Whatever do you mean by that?''

''I mean we're iced up for the winter. Snowed in. Stranded. We're not going anywhere until the first thaw.''

She turned pale. ''And that would be...?''

''April, I reckon. Maybe March if the thaw comes early.''

Her color changed from chalk to green. ''But that...that's more than three months from now.''

''I can count.''

Her mouth worked soundlessly for a moment; then she got up and staggered outside. He heard a retching sound, followed by a long silence, then the dirgelike rhythm of her footsteps as she trudged back inside.

Twenty-Four

Over the next week, Deborah tried to come to terms with the fact that she and Tom Silver were snowed in for the winter. In the forbidden adventure novels she used to read on the sly at Miss Boylan's, being snowed in meant thrills and excitement, the crystal wonder of a world gone white. The reality was quite different. Being snowed in meant a biting arctic wind hissing through chinks in the walls, endless dark nights of a silence so deep that it pierced her heart, blinding white snow covering everything and dreaded, painfully cold trips to the woodshed or privy.

She regarded the winter as a long and torturous trail that lay before her. Most days, she could not even imagine reaching the end of it.

One afternoon, she stood staring out the window at the dull gray view of the marshlands leading down to the lake. A thick blanket of white covered everything, obliterating the hummocks of spiky grass, the upended dinghies and fishing gear, the midden pile out beyond the settlement. She propped her elbows on the windowsill, studying the pattern of frost etched around the edges of the glass. Two tiny chickadees landed on the windowsill to peck at the cornbread crumbs she had placed there. They seemed aware of her presence, wary of her, yet they came each day and stayed as long as they dared.

Tom Silver entered the cabin in a swirl of snow and blustering wind, his arms laden with the day's supply of firewood. Even now that she was accustomed to the sight of him in his full-length coat, he still looked like a bear. No wonder she had shot him.

He was still recovering from his ordeal on the ice. The head wound from the gunshot seemed to be healing well, and he had insisted on removing the bandage to expose the three-inch gash that streaked back from his hairline. His hands and feet had blistered and peeled. Anxiously they watched for signs of gangrene, but none appeared.

The signs of his recovery made her want to sing, but she held her tongue.

By the second day, he had been well enough to remark, teasingly, that she had helped herself to the bed in the loft.

"I wasn't expecting company," she'd said.

"Neither was Goldilocks."

His grin had made her blush. She hadn't known what else to do. With Tom Silver lying wounded by the stove, she'd simply taken the loft bed for herself. Then a thought had struck her. "With the whole town empty, perhaps we should take separate quarters."

"Why?" he'd demanded. "Think we'll offend the snow geese and the marmots?" He had laughed and called her absurd, declaring, "You don't cling to propriety when your life's on the line. Keep the bed. I'll take the loft."

And so he had, climbing uncomplaining to the loft while she had dragged the mattress back onto the bedstead in the adjacent room. As they had since arriving on the island, they lived at close quarters, yet they seemed miles apart.

She almost smiled now, filled with admiration for his recovery and possibly—just possibly—a sense of accomplishment for her part in it.

"Morning," he said.

"Good morning." She turned her gaze back out the

window. "You know, I think I've figured out why animals hibernate in winter."

"Yeah?"

"So they don't have to face this every single day."

He gave a short, dry laugh and began stacking the wood by the stove with a series of hollow-sounding thunks.

"Although," Deborah mused aloud, gazing out at the bleak, quiet white day, "the snow does have one virtue. It covers up all the flaws and imperfections and ugliness of the landscape."

"Never really thought about it."

That didn't surprise her. He was such a...literal man.

She turned to see him adding a log to the fire. The bellows wheezed and cinders pinged inside the chimney as he fanned the flames. As captives under the same roof, they had found, if not true friendship, then at least a calm accord. They set up housekeeping, developed a routine, learned the rhythms of each other's lives. With no one else around, the atmosphere felt different, and they were coming to know one another in different ways.

He rose early, seeming to have some sixth sense about when the gray thread of first light would appear on the eastern horizon. In the mornings, she would hear the creak of the loft ladder as he lowered himself to the ground floor, followed by splashing sounds at the washstand. Then she would hear the clack of the coffee grinder, and before long, the aroma of brewing coffee would reach her. Always a man of few words, Tom Silver was particularly quiet until he had consumed at least one mug of coffee.

"What're you staring at?" He wiped his brow with the back of one gloved hand.

"You," she blurted out.

"Why?"

"I've never really observed a man's daily routines at such close range before." Realizing what she'd just said, she blushed deeply. "I mean, of course my father and…well, I never really watched the way a man goes through his day.''

"Believe me, I've had better days than this." He closed the stove doors and adjusted the vents. "If every day was like this, I'd go hang myself."

"Well," she said, flustered by his pessimism. "Well, I certainly don't understand you at all. You seem like the sort who would not be in the least troubled by the idea of spending all winter in a cabin."

"Only if I can choose the company."

"Ha," she said triumphantly. "You did choose me. Back in Chicago, you chose to drag me here."

"That was before I knew what you were like. Damn it, you were reckless as hell, leaving the landing to collect stones, of all things—"

"I'm reckless?" She let out an incredulous laugh. "You're the one who is reckless. You *kidnaped* me."

"If you'd done what you were told, you'd be on your way home," he stated.

Home. Such a simple word to create such confusion in her. She looked at Tom Silver for a long time, then finally said, "The one thing that can make this situation worse is our being at each other's throats. If we can't be friends, we could at least try to be civil."

"We could try to be friends." He mumbled the words so quietly she thought she might have imagined them.

But she hadn't, and an unfamiliar warmth bloomed in her chest. It occurred to Deborah that she had never even had a male friend before. Her relationship with Philip, even before the opera, had not been so much a friendship as an alliance. An association brokered and sanctioned by her father—yet another male she knew only on the surface. It made her melancholy to realize that she didn't understand her father at all.

She knew more of this big, rough man of the north woods than she did her own father. She knew he could split a day's worth of wood in mere minutes, and that he whistled through his teeth as he worked. She knew he liked his coffee strong and black, and could eat three bowls of porridge without complaining that he was tired of it. She knew he could read a book swiftly and with deep absorption, and that he was, in his own crude way, a rather thoughtful man. Without being asked, he always made certain there was a kettle of hot water ready when she arose in the morning. When it was her turn to bathe, he managed to stay away a good hour or two, doing Lord knew what. On the nights that he bathed, he waited until she went to bed before dragging out the tub. Lying in the chill dark with the covers pulled up to her chin, she could hear him sloshing and scrubbing, and no matter how hard she tried not to, she kept picturing his large, muscled, hairy body. She had tried not to look when she'd taken off his clothes to warm him, but it had been impossible not to see the way his physique was sculptured by hard work. Impossible not to remember as she lay very still, listening to the scrape of the tub as he dragged it to the door to empty the water.

With each passing day, she grew more used to his presence, the sound of his tread on the porch, the rustle of pages as he read a book in the evening, the way the lamplight glinted off his spectacles, the appreciation on his face when her cornbread turned out delicious. Something was happening between them, something she didn't quite trust. But like the chickadees that came to peck at the windowsill, she couldn't resist the danger.

Twenty-Five

Simple survival filled their days, but in the evenings, there was little to do but sit by the stove and read a book or sew. Deborah became more and more interested in her quilt, in the intricate tesselations of the patterns emerging as she pieced the bits of fabric. Tom had decided to go fishing through the ice, and he sat at the table making lures. Hooks, bits of wire and tiny feathers lay on a chamois cloth on the table before him, along with scissors and pliers that looked too small for his big, blunt hands. As he worked, he talked of the book he had recently finished reading—*Origin of Species* by Charles Darwin.

"Did you know my pastor called that book 'balderdash' and banned the congregation from reading it?" asked Deborah.

Tom was enormously amused by this. "He thinks by forbidding people to read, he can make the ideas go away?"

"I suppose he does." She had not thought of Dr. Moody or her life in Chicago in many weeks. The night of the fire, she was supposed to have attended his lecture with Philip. She frowned, wondering how things would have turned out if she had gone with her friends that night.

"You think a man's got any business telling folks what to read?" Tom persisted. "How to think?"

"I never really thought about it at all. My father always said action was more important than philosophy." She caught the look on his face. "It disturbs you," she observed, "to think of my father as a man, not a monster."

His hand tightened into a fist. "How else can I think of him, knowing the suffering he caused?"

"But you've bested him, don't you see?" She sat down on the bench at the hearth and picked up her needle and hoop again. For all that her father was a mystery to her, she did understand certain things about him—very clearly. "I don't think you realize how important it was for me to marry Philip Ascot. That would have given my father the one thing his millions could never buy—respectability and acceptance into the highest social circles in the country. The Ascots are acknowledged even by English royalty. My marrying into that family would have been my father's crowning achievement. He would have seen all his dreams realized. You stole his dream from him. Can't you be satisfied with that?"

The mention of Philip's name etched a look of contempt on Tom's face. "One punch, maybe two as I recall, and I didn't even break the skin of my knuckles. If you were my betrothed, I would have worked a hell of a lot harder to save you the night of the fire."

His words created a moment of headiness, which she quickly quelled. "I should have saved myself and escaped you both," she said. She stopped, catching herself. She had no business discussing private matters with Tom Silver.

He fell silent and she thought he would leave the subject alone. But after a while, he said, "What about you, Princess? What's your dream? Do women like you live for social conquests as well?"

"I won't lie to you. Women like me live and die for status."

"What's that supposed to mean?"

"My position in society and the way I appear to the people who matter are supposed to be the most important things in the world to me." Her needle flashed in and out of the fabric.

"Yeah? Are they?"

"They were—until the fire. What's left, after everything burns away, is all that matters. It was something of a shock to realize that I was living like a figure on a stage, going through the motions and reciting things that were deemed proper. It was never really me."

He scowled. She wondered if he did that to hide his surprise at her frankness. "So who was it?" he asked.

She ducked her head to hide a tiny smile. He was the most literal person she had ever met. "What I mean is, I did not act true to myself. I always carried out someone else's expectations. My father's. Those ingrained in me at finishing school. Those of Philip Ascot and his family. I never thought for myself. I let others dictate who I was and how I acted."

"And now?" He took a pair of needle nose pliers and clamped a tiny hook, holding it in place while he threaded fishing line through the eye.

"Now I'm in the middle of nowhere. My father doesn't want me back because I'm no longer of value to him." The words burned her throat. The pain of her father's rejection was as deep and sharp now as it had been the day the telegraph had come through. In a small, hidden place inside her, she had cherished the fantasy that he would have second thoughts, that at any moment she might look up and see the *Triumph* nosing into the harbor. But it had never happened. She had to swallow several times in order to find her voice again. "I'm of no value to you, either, which means you went to a great deal of trouble all for nothing."

He took off his eyeglasses and studied her for a long, slow-moving moment. "I wouldn't say it was all for nothing."

Something about the way he stared at her made her blush. She went on babbling and sewing. "Everything I was taught simply doesn't apply to my current circumstances. So perhaps that means I am a *tabula rasa*. That is the Latin for—"

"Clean slate," he said, laughing at her surprise. He put his spectacles back on. "Another bit of troglodyte erudition."

"You will never let me live that down, will you?" She was slightly ashamed of herself for assuming he was ignorant just because he'd had no formal education. The days stuck in the cabin had been a strong lesson in looking beneath the surface. She'd discovered a man who loved reading and learning as much as he loved the mystical beauty of the island. During the long northern winters, Tom had gained as broad and thorough an education as any college man. But with a deeper center, put there by living close to nature as God made it, she suspected.

"Never is a long time," he said.

"So is forever."

"And what do you want to do with your forever, Miss Tabula Rasa? Will you rewrite history, become someone new?"

"I think I would like that." She ran her hands over the quilt in her lap. Given a choice, who would she become? "I was always Arthur Sinclair's daughter, and then Philip Ascot's fiancée. But never actually my own person."

"Maybe you'd best figure out who she is."

"I am," she said softly, the pattern of the quilt slipping beneath her fingers. "I am figuring that out."

It was an hour past dawn, and Tom had already caught a whitefish through a hole he had chopped in the ice. His fingers and toes still bothered him, lingering effects of the frostbite. He stood warming himself by the fire, waiting for Deborah, who had gone outside to the privy. When she came back in and took a seat at the table, she looked paler than ever, as if she were fading into the winter whiteness. He guessed, from the way she dabbed at her lips with a

corner of her apron, that she'd taken ill. He wanted to say
something, but felt awkward asking after her health. She
probably wouldn't tell him if she was ill anyway.

But this was not the first time she'd been sick after
breakfast. He couldn't stop thinking about his disturbing
conversation with Lightning Jack the day of the evacuation.
Lightning was rarely wrong about people, and he had noticed her habit of going green around the gills.

A pointed icicle touched the base of Tom's spine. Pregnant. Not Deborah. How could that be? She was so sheltered, so innocent. Ignorant, even. And skittish as hell. She
could barely tolerate even a casual touch. She couldn't possibly be...

But she had been engaged to be married and it clearly
wasn't a love match. When Sinclair's wire had accused her
of being unmarriageable, she had readily called herself "ruined." Could this be what she'd meant?

Those symptoms were so telling. He wracked his brain,
trying to recall if he'd noticed her tending to her monthly
laundry. For the life of him, he could not remember.

Damn it. If Deborah Sinclair was pregnant, the prospect
of spending the winter with her on the island would be a
nightmare. He rubbed his hands together, pretending to be
totally preoccupied with the fire. In reality, he didn't even
see the fire. Deborah? he kept asking himself. *Pregnant?*

"I need to ask you something," he blurted out, swinging
around to face her.

She glanced up, her brow puckering at his gruff tone.
Already he felt stupid for bringing up such an absurd matter. He regarded her gentle doe eyes, the mouth he had
dared to kiss just once, in pretense. There had been no
experience in her kiss. Just shock, anger, fear. And a softness and sweetness he had never forgotten.

"Yes?" she prompted.

There was nothing to do but simply come right out with
it. "Are you in the family way?" he demanded bluntly.

Deborah gasped, clutching the edge of the table with

white-knuckled hands. Then she stood up from the table. She looked as if she had swallowed a live toad. Her eyes opened wide and her jaw dropped, and the sickness that had claimed her earlier seemed as if it might erupt again. Then her color changed once more, to a vivid purplish red, as if she were choking on that toad.

"What?" There was no voice behind the agonized query. It was an empty rasp shaped by her too-pretty, disbelieving mouth.

"It's no idle question, so don't go all prim and proper on me. I have to know. Are you pregnant?"

Her hands dropped to her middle and trembled against her apron. She moved toward the door as if she might flee like a wild thing. "P...preg...?" Again, no voice behind the word, just a horrified breath.

"I know it's probably against your religion to say the word aloud, but we're stuck here, so I need to know what I'm dealing with. Are you?"

Like a blind person, she groped her way to the door and clutched at the handle. She stood as still as a statue of ice.

Say no. Tom willed her to set his mind at ease on the matter. But she stayed mute, her face blank and battle-shocked.

"Well?" he prodded. "It's a simple question."

Say no. He waited, holding his breath.

"I...I don't know," she said at last.

Grim amazement gripped him. He clenched his jaw to keep from swearing. She hated it when he swore. Then he forced himself to speak softly, gently. He realized the implication—the accusation—of what he was about to say but he said it anyway. "So it's a possibility."

She exploded. He had never seen anything like it. One moment she was a stone icon, standing by the door like a trading post Indian, the next she was a sobbing mass of misery. She wept with the force of a hurricane. Great, gusting sobs shook her entire frame and bent her like a wind-torn tree.

Tom Silver had raced across fields in the heat of battle. He had fled from angry mother bears, battled storms on the lake, survived a deadly blizzard, walked across miles of unstable ice. But as he confronted Deborah Sinclair, it occurred to him that he had discovered the most dangerous and frightening thing in the world—a weeping woman.

He stood watching her, feeling completely helpless. He had no idea what to do, so he crossed the room to her and awkwardly patted her on the shoulder. She lurched away in alarm, nearly stumbling to the floor. He drew back and cast about for something to say. The feeling of helplessness engulfed him until he was awash in it. She cried as if her heart would break, and there wasn't a damned thing he could do about it.

"Stop," he said, too quietly. Her tears drowned out his command, so he raised his voice. "Stop. Please, for the love of Christ, quit bawling."

The harsh command seemed to penetrate her misery. She sucked in a deep breath and said, "I can't."

"You just did," he pointed out.

That made her weep again, but not as explosively as before. Not with that terrible violence she had shown earlier. Now she simply hung her head and stared at the floor as her body convulsed with gusty sobs.

He found a towel and held it out to her. "Mop your face," he said.

She took the towel and wept into it. But after a while, she blotted at her cheeks and nose, and the sobs subsided to soft hiccups, small echoes in the aftermath of a storm.

Tom wished he were somewhere far away. Instead, he got a chair and held it for her until she inched forward, then gingerly sat down. He took the other chair and turned it around, straddling the back and crossing his arms over the top.

"Stop staring at me as if I were some sort of sideshow freak," she said.

"I'm not," he said.

"But you're staring."

"Not at a freak, at someone who is going to explain a few things."

Her chin trembled.

"Without bawling her face off," he added. When he spoke kindly and tenderly, she wept. For some reason, she seemed stronger when he was harsh with her.

She sucked in a broken breath of air. "How did you know?"

He heard such shame and anguish in her voice, he was almost sorry he'd asked. But having opened that door, he now had to hear the rest. "You haven't been well, especially in the morning. Happens to most women when they get in the family way."

"It does?"

He figured it wasn't one of the things they'd taught her at finishing school. "Lightning Jack noticed, too, and he thought you and I were—that we'd—" He broke off, wondering how it had suddenly turned so hot and stuffy in the cabin. "I told him we hadn't," he added quickly. "But then I got to thinking, you were about to be married, so maybe you'd been...like married folks." He tried to state things as delicately as possible, but it wasn't working. She looked more horrified than ever.

"Why must I speak of...this?" she asked weakly.

"Because it's eating at you like a poison, damn it."

"I have no idea how to explain—"

He laughed rudely, determined to goad her into an explanation. "Talking is the one thing you do better than anyone else I've ever met. So talk. No harm ever came of talking."

That raised her dander a little, and he didn't regret angering her. Anything was better than her shattering grief. "This is private," she said. "You must never—"

"Not a problem," he assured her. "Trust me on this. Be plain about it. Just start talking."

Twenty-Six

Didn't he realize she could not speak? Didn't he know there weren't any words to tell him what she had hidden from him all these weeks? She felt as though Tom Silver was pushing her through a long dark tunnel, and everything in her resisted going to that murky place. Until now, she had not allowed herself to dwell on it. Each time the memories had assaulted her, she had fled from them. But that had not made the shame and the pain go away.

The dam had been broken open by one simple question. *Are you in the family way?*

She couldn't hide from the past because it was a part of her. She had to go back. Back to that night, to that moment, to the incident that had changed the entire landscape of her life. She knew she must speak of it, and soon, but she waved her hand to beg for time to gather her thoughts. Tom Silver simply waited, undemanding, yet clearly unwilling to back down.

She shut her eyes and forced herself to relive the night before the fire. Philip had taken her to the opera, though she had not seen much of the production. She had certainly heard the music, but she'd heard it from the flower-decked salon behind the private Sinclair box. She would never forget watching Don Giovanni sweep Zerlina away to seduce her, but Zerlina had screamed and was rescued.

Deborah had not screamed.

Perhaps she *should* have called for help, yet all her life she had been taught to be quiet, polite. Submissive. Even when terror and panic ripped through her. This was Philip, after all. The man she had promised to marry. She had no call to fear him.

He took her hand and, ignoring her hissed protests, brought her to the lavish salon behind the box. Among the well-born of Chicago, decorating one's salon was a competitive art form, and Arthur Sinclair had made certain no one would outdo him. He had hired a French designer to create a miniature evocation of the Hall of Mirrors in Versailles.

Gaslight burned low in brass and crystal wall sconces. Gilt-edged mirrors lined the walls, and Deborah could see the endlessly repeating reflections of herself and Philip. They resembled any embracing couple, except that she wasn't embracing him, but trying to push him away.

He claimed he wanted to show her exactly what her duties as a wife would be. He wanted to give her a taste of the secret delights of marriage.

Leave me alone. She had said it playfully at first. Truth be told, she'd been a little intrigued. Like all brides-to-be, she had been wondering about the wedding night. But she hadn't thought he was serious about sampling the pleasures prematurely. She had been certain he would pull back, laugh with her and return to watching the opera on stage.

Ah, my darling. You will never be alone, not ever. He had whispered the words in her ear, and she supposed he meant to sound grandly romantic. But his promise disturbed her, as did the insistent press of his hands on her. She looked into Philip's face, his handsome face, the one in the daguerreotype that had stared at her from a gilt frame upon her dressing table. She felt his touch, closing around her wrist, heard his voice rasping harshly in her ear and smelled his scent of bay rum and macassar oil, filling her with sickness, making her gag.

He had mocked her apprehension, and then he'd grown impatient with her. High-handed. Insistent. If he had been crude, she could have protested, stood up for her dignity and honor. But he had simply been himself, a man entitled by virtue of his social standing to help himself to whatever he wanted. The sort of man she had been taught all her life to honor and admire.

That's enough, Philip. Please. That had been a mistake. She should not have said please. She had begged, begged him to stop. Instead he had pressed hard on her shoulders and forced her to her knees.

"You plead so prettily, my darling girl," he had said in a very soft, deadly whisper. "I like it when you beg." He pressed harder, there in that dark velvet-shrouded private room. He laughed and kissed her, then thrust her into a corner. "You like this, don't you?" he'd persisted. "I'll bet you're going to want to move up the wedding date." The edge of the gilt chaise, padded by tufted brocade in a fleur-de-lis pattern, cut painfully into her back. She felt something—his hand—up her skirts.

Shock froze her. She could not move, blink, breathe.

This is what you were made for. He accompanied the words with a brusque, harsh tug on her undergarments, tearing them away and putting himself there. *This is the whole duty of a woman.*

As if it were only yesterday, she could hear the leading man's clear voice filling her mind. *Don Giovanni* had been a fitting accompaniment to her deflowering, although why the event was called—in awed whispers at Miss Boylan's—deflowering was beyond her.

This is what a wife does. This is the whole duty of a woman.

He had chuckled, low and intimately, and she was ashamed to think that there had been a time when she found his laughter attractive, had found his mild features endearing, his personality engaging. Only at that moment, with Mozart's opera trumpeting in her ears and Philip's breath hot upon her face, did Deborah realize that she had been party to a huge lie, the lie that kept a woman ignorant of the true cost of becoming a married lady.

It's not amusing anymore, Philip. Stop. I want you to stop.

That night, she had discovered the lie, but it had been too late for her. The man she had pledged her future to had wooed her into a smug sense of complacence. She had been all too pleased with his courtship, all too happy with her father's wholehearted promotion of the match. Many of her friends had been promised to men who were old, had nasty grown children or bore obscure European titles. Not so Deborah. She had landed an Ascot, from one of New York City's first families. While other American heiresses had been sent kicking and screaming across the Atlantic to live in gloomy castles with impoverished noblemen, Deborah had eagerly embraced a future with a young, handsome, vital man who laughed often, flattered with sincerity and pursued pleasure with charming abandon.

The trouble was, his idea of pleasure had somehow changed.

The reaching hands groped relentlessly, tirelessly. Covering her horrified mouth with his, he pressed and pushed. Even when she managed to twist her head away and free her mouth from his kiss, his slender, elegant body, which she had so often admired on the dancefloor, pushed deeper into her.

And she was struck mute. Not out of shock, although she felt shocked, and not out of outrage, although a deep anger flashed through her. No, what held her as silent as a tongueless slave was politeness, a sense that calling out for help would bring more shame on her than enduring whatever Philip had in store for her.

That, perhaps, was most shameful of all. She was too

polite to stop him. Life had trained her to be quiet and compliant. She'd had no idea that this was what she was in training for. This was the big secret, the big lie.

His voice whispered into her ear. *You like this you want this you've waited for this.*

She had no idea what to say to him, what to do.

And so she did nothing. Maybe that was why she was so ashamed. She had allowed herself to trust—to *esteem*—a man who would do this.

Shrouded by the sounds of a haunting Mozart duet, with the smell of carnations and Philip's brandy breath thick in the air, she could not move, could not speak. And when she finally did struggle and scream, she discovered that it was only in her head. On the outside, she lay on the settee, doing exactly what Philip forced her to do, and all the while, the opera trumpeted in her ears.

The welling of the music, the soaring voices, cleaved through her like a knife. She felt disembodied, for she knew she was gone, finished, murdered, and the strangest thing was, she could still see and feel and hear everything. In the draped privacy of the salon, she had discovered that there was something wrong with her, that unlike normal women, she could not perform those duties without going half mad with terror.

Only when Philip was finished with her had she broken down, curling herself into a ball on the brocade chaise and sobbing uncontrollably. Her weeping had infuriated him, but when he had taken her back to Miss Boylan's that night, he had seemed quite proud of himself.

"I saved you the discomfort of the wedding night, dear heart," he had boasted. "Hereafter, you will find only enjoyment in being my wife."

She had sat across from him in the phaeton, as unfeeling and unmoving as a pillar of salt. He had taken her utterly by surprise, rendering her completely unable to act. Had she always been that useless when disaster struck?

Philip, of course, had exhibited his own brand of…she

wasn't sure what it was. Arrogance, maybe. But perhaps he would beg her forgiveness and lift her hand to his lips, and all would be right with the world again. Surely that would happen.

But he showed no remorse, and Deborah had never been able to make sense of what had just happened to her. There *was* no sense in an act of violation. But there was shame and humiliation and flashes of impotent rage. She didn't know if those feelings would ever go away.

She used to adore opera, used to love everything about it. Now the very thought of listening to one single note of an aria or chorus made her squirm with fear. All because of Philip. He had made her afraid to touch any man, even an unconscious man, dying of cold. Philip had damaged her in ways she was only beginning to understand.

The realization made her skin crawl. Sweat trickled down between her breasts. *No.*

She forced herself to regain control. It was over. She had come, albeit against her will, to a place where Philip Ascot would never pursue her, even if he wanted to.

But dear God, how on earth would she explain all this to Tom Silver?

Pregnant. Sweet Heaven, what if she was?

Her mind swimming with poisoned memories, she faced Tom Silver. His presence gave an unexpected boost to her confidence. He sat there like a rock, not in judgment, though he looked supremely uncomfortable in the role of counselor or confessor. Instinctively she knew it was safe to tell him the truth. He had told her to just start talking. She wished it were that easy.

So, she took a deep breath and began.

Twenty-Seven

Tom waited patiently. He didn't allow himself to move, for he sensed she would bolt like a hare if he pushed her any more.

And then, very slowly, moving like a wounded soldier, Deborah turned her head and stared out the window. The words came reluctantly, from the hidden places inside her. "The night before the fire," she said, "I attended the opera with my fi—with Philip Ascot. We watched from Father's private box at the opera house." Her fingers knit together with nervousness.

Tom didn't know much about opera—some stage act with a lot of singing and hollering. Fancy costumes and fake sword fights, the sort of thing city folks liked to pay money to watch and dress up to attend. He could easily picture Deborah Sinclair, done up like a fairy-tale princess, escorted by a swell in a fancy suit.

As these thoughts went through his mind, he stayed silent, waiting. She would get the confession out in her own time, in her own way. Instinct, and the storm of sobs that had preceded the conversation, convinced him not to push her.

"It was a Mozart opera, *Don Giovanni,* the story of an immoral man who uses his charm and handsomeness to seduce women."

She was skirting the issue, setting the scene for what she probably considered an unspeakable act. He wanted to interrupt, to reassure her that it was a wholly natural thing for a man and a woman to be eager for the delights that would seal their commitment to one another. But he held silent, trying to fill in the gaps in what she was saying.

"Our wedding had been all planned out, down to the last detail," she said, not looking at him as she spoke. She stared out the window, but he knew she wasn't seeing the raw, white field of snow. "I suppose that was why I...we..." She bit her lip and stopped.

He waited some more, wondering how it had played out. Had she looked at her pretty man and been overwhelmed by carnal desire? Had he plied her with champagne and compliments?

Tom gritted his teeth, hating the fact that he could never be that sort of man for her. Hell, she was probably ashamed that she could want any man in a passionate way. Or maybe what she wanted and what she'd experienced had turned out to be two different things.

"During the course of the opera...Zerlina rushed off stage to escape Don Giovanni. That was when Philip asked me to...retire to the salon with him. Each private box, you see, has an adjacent private salon where the men go to smoke or the women to socialize. That night it was just Philip and me. His sister was supposed to accompany us as chaperon, but she fell sick at the last moment. Now I realize he probably asked her to beg off so that we could be alone. He was amorous that night. I...I have no idea why."

Tom held in a snort of disbelief. *Why?* To begin with, she had a face and body that made a man want to rediscover original sin. Yet she was also favored by a fragile melancholy in her big eyes that made a fellow want to take her in his arms. Or maybe it was the shiny waterfall of pale blond hair that made her look like a Christmas angel. Or the quiet, gentle quality of her presence he found more compelling than the lively, lusty women of the outposts and towns he passed through in his travels. Or the combination of disdain and vulnerability that made him wonder what lay in her heart. Or— Tom stopped himself. He was developing a bad habit of thinking about Deborah Sinclair in ways that he shouldn't.

"He's male," he said, choosing the simplest answer to her quandary. "Even the weak ones tend to get... amorous, especially with a woman like you."

She paled, and he had the sense that he'd said the wrong thing, and he had no idea why.

"So I reckon," he said, trying to help her out, "you were feeling amorous, too."

Her white throat worked as she swallowed. "I believe, looking back, that Philip thought so. And like you, he was wrong."

Tom felt the subtle sting of her censure. He didn't like the idea that he had anything in common with this Ascot character. He didn't like the idea that, for all he had been in the company of this woman for weeks, she was still a puzzle to him. Deborah was like the mysterious ice floes that blew across the lake in the teeth of the wind. She had a bright white surface he could see and touch, but he had no idea what lay beneath.

"So he was feeling amorous, and you weren't," he prompted quietly. Now the picture sharpened at the edges and began to make sense. When that was the case, as it often was between lovers, the man generally got his way. At least, in Tom's experience, he did. A man knew of any number of ways to persuade a reluctant woman that he would bring her joy if she would simply let go and obey the urges of her body. He wasn't proud of using insincere speeches and clever caresses to get his way, but he, like most men, was not above such methods.

"That is correct," she said, and he felt her slipping away from him, back into the shadowy remembrances of the night that had so clearly become a dark obsession with her. "He, um, held me and kissed me. Through the drapes of the salon I heard the soprano's voice soar, and there was a long high note so piercing I thought it might be me, screaming." She took her gaze from the window and looked down at her white-knuckled hands. "But I wasn't screaming, of course. That would be too absurd. Rude, even. I have never been a rude person, and that night was no exception. So I simply...lay there. While he...Philip...shoved and pressed and made me—" She broke off, her face burning with color. "There is probably a word for this, but I don't know what it is."

Suddenly Tom's understanding of the situation changed. With a lurch of his gut, he realized that Ascot hadn't merely seduced his bride-to-be. He had forced himself on her. Tom had heard of cowards who resorted to force but he had never heard it described by the victim, particularly a victim who seemed to have no idea she had been violated. Tom pictured Deborah in a fancy dress, on a cushioned chaise with the opera music wailing through the building. Ascot grabbing her, maybe cupping his hand over her breast and tasting those soft, silent lips, his hand pushing up under those frilly skirts. Tom clenched his jaw to keep from swearing in helpless anger.

He could tell it was beyond her to give voice to precisely what the son of a bitch had done. His mind filled in the parts she would not speak of. This woman was painfully naive, sheltered. She had been raised without a mother, by an army of caretakers bowing and scraping to her every whim, but never giving her the one thing she needed—a sense of herself. A knowledge of what she would and would not tolerate.

Ascot probably understood that. And like most men, he probably used it to his advantage. She was young, beautiful and unimaginably wealthy, and she was about to become his bride. He saw no wrong in helping himself to something he regarded as his due. Tom had known men like Ascot in the Union army. West Pointers who thought they owned the world. They made him sick.

"You say he shoved you," Tom said. "Pressed you. Was it in a…rough way?" He had no idea how to do this. All he knew was that he had to pull the truth out of her. He had to draw the words from her like extracting venom from a snake bite.

She cleared her throat. "He was…fast," she managed to say. "I really didn't have time to think. My mind went blank, and I simply didn't know what to say. And so I did nothing, said nothing, and finally…it was over."

Tom let her words hang unanswered. In some strange way he understood that she had described to him an abomination, but she had done it with such delicacy and control that it simply underscored the horror.

A dark fury welled up in him. He didn't question why it was his task to delve into her secrets. He was responsible for getting her into this fix, but not for what Philip Ascot had done. Concern for her had awakened in him, and he couldn't steel himself against her now. Suddenly all her strange behavior over the weeks began to make sense. She acted like a battle-scarred soldier because she was one. She had not been wounded on the field but by a man she trusted.

"One thing I've asked myself ever since that night is why, afterward, I simply sat through the rest of the opera with him. I did that, you know. I simply…tried to put my hair to rights and then took my seat beside him for the last act."

The image of her, primly seated in the gilt opera box beside the man who had raped her, ripped across Tom's mind. Maybe that was the worst of all, that after Ascot had forced himself on her, she had gone on as if nothing had happened. They didn't teach a girl such things in finishing school, he reckoned. Didn't teach her what to do when a man she trusts violates her.

"My memories are a bit confused after that," she ad-

mitted. "I went home and went to bed, and the next day
I slept a great deal, and stayed in my bed. There was an
important function to go to. An evangelical reading. My
friends at Miss Boylan's had been anticipating it for
weeks. Philip was to meet me there. But when the time
came to get ready, I realized I could not go. That was
when I drove into the city to see my father."

"You were going to tell him what happened."

She looked appalled. "No. How could I..." She
cleared her throat. "I told him only that I had changed
my mind and wasn't going to marry Philip. My father
didn't take me seriously, of course. This marriage meant
the world to him, and the fact that I was absolutely terrified of Philip didn't matter." For the first time, she
looked Tom in the eye. The stark misery on her face made
him want to turn away, but he wouldn't let himself. He
had brought her to this moment with his questions and his
prying, and he owed it to her to stay with her.

"So there is the answer to your question," she concluded. "*Yes.* It is possible that I am with child because
I was too polite to stop Philip from—to stop him."

A leaden foreboding haunted him. "Ever since...that
night," he began hesitantly, venturing into unknown territory, "there's been no—ah, you haven't had your
monthly..." At a loss, he let his voice trail off. He had
no idea how to talk to a woman about such things, especially a woman like Deborah.

Her cheeks reddened. "I have never been reliable in
that respect, so until you asked your question, I didn't
think a thing of it." She stood and turned away. "Excuse
me. I feel tired all of a sudden." She went into the bedroom and lay down, facing the wall.

The knowledge of what she had suffered smoldered inside Tom. He felt a dark, violent clamor of outrage and
fury, and it had no outlet. Surging to his feet, he went
outside, not even bothering with coat and gloves. He lit
into the firewood, splitting log after log with the long-

handled ax, but the rage wouldn't go away. Here was a woman who had trusted a man, who did not realize immediately what was happening and who failed to speak up for herself because society would condemn her for it.

The fact that Philip Ascot had raped her explained so much. Her long, tense silences. Her nervous response to being touched. Her lack of self-confidence stemmed from being forced to service a man like a two-bit whore.

It was one thing to understand, and another matter entirely to help her. Trying to force the fury to abate, he ceased his chopping and stared down at his big, sore, peeling hands. His breath came in loud, white puffs. The damage done to her was not the sort of wound that would mend with liniment and bandages. It was a wound to the self, to the soul, and he had no business poking around in Deborah Sinclair's soul.

Yet he wanted to. He wanted her to stop hurting. She didn't deserve what had happened to her.

He wondered if he would have taken her prisoner in Chicago if he'd known what she had endured. If he would have forced that kiss on her aboard the boat. Probably, he conceded. His anger and hatred for Sinclair had left no room for compassion. Now, though, she was more than simply a bargaining chip to him. She had become a person with hopes and dreams and fears, just like anyone else. Except in the case of Deborah Sinclair, he cared what happened to her. He cared far more than he should.

Twenty-Eight

Deborah pressed both hands to her middle and tried to imagine that a baby grew there, under her heart. No matter how hard she tried, she could not picture it, nor feel it, nor imagine it. Just as well, she told herself. Perhaps if she didn't dwell on the matter, it would not be true.

But true or not, she was certain of one thing—the night at the opera was real. After so many weeks of hiding from the truth, she had been forced to face it. She was surprised at how deep the hurt had gone. She knew with unerring instinct that Tom Silver would never look at her the same way again.

The day after her unforgivable breakdown and confession, she recalled the conversation with shame and a touch of horror. How could she have spoken aloud of what occurred between her and Philip Ascot? It was the most private of matters, that intimate act, and she had no business confessing the secrets of her soul to a stranger.

But Tom Silver was no stranger, she conceded as she drew a brush through her hair. Tom was…Tom. Her captor. Her protector. The only living soul she would see until spring.

She could not think of him as a stranger because she was coming to know him in a way that she had never known another.

Still, did that give her the right to speak to him of the most private of moments between a man and a woman? Right or wrong, she had confessed. The words had flowed from her in a torrent, in a cataract. Once she'd started speaking, she hadn't been able to stop. And amazingly, she felt better for it.

What must he think of her? He knew her secret now. He knew she could never be like other women, knew she could never enjoy the act of intimacy between a man and a woman.

She finished brushing her hair and didn't bother braiding it. She impatiently tied it with a scrap from her quilting basket, making a tail at the nape of her neck.

Finally, she knew she could put off seeing him no longer. Brushing her hands over her skirt, she longed for a new dress as armor. A heavily corseted ballgown to protect her from his scorn.

She found him sitting at the table, tying a fishing fly. Smokey yapped a greeting. She had a sudden memory of her father, who pursued fly fishing with a vengeance. Each summer he would take the steamer yacht up to Three Rivers to go fishing with the Palmers and Higginsons. As a tiny child, Deborah had amused them all when she had stood watching the fishing from the riverbank and upon seeing the small object at the end of her father's line had clapped her hands and shrieked, "You've caught one! You've caught a fly!"

That was the last time he'd allowed her to accompany him. He didn't even particularly enjoy the sport, but practiced it with the grim relentlessness with which he conducted his business affairs. He went fly fishing because the people he yearned to befriend went fly fishing. She understood this now.

Deborah was not certain when she had first noticed this about her father. He did not enjoy life so much as pursue it. House parties, gala events, art shows, pleasure tours.

He attended such things because it was expected, not because he wanted to.

The happiest she had ever seen him was when he'd taken her out on the lake in a little cat boat one summer. They'd flown along in a warm wind and had not encountered a soul he wanted to impress. She still remembered the spray on his face and the happiness in his eyes, reflecting the fluffy white clouds of summer. Sometimes when she closed her eyes, she could still hear his laughter on the wind. But as she grew older he did things less and less for the pleasure, concentrating instead on what was expected. That was exactly what she had been brought up for, she realized, and she had conformed unquestioningly. Now for some reason, she wanted to know the point of all the posturing.

She mentioned none of this to Tom Silver. She feared the fury she saw in his eyes at the very whisper of her father's name.

"There's coffee," he said without looking up.

She couldn't tell if it was contempt or the usual gruffness she heard in his voice. With slow, deliberate movements she helped herself to the coffee. The silence drew out unbearably, until she flushed with shame and forced herself to voice the matter that had been troubling her. "If it turns out that I am..." She searched her mind for some delicate way of putting it. "That I am in the family way, what will you do?"

He didn't stop working, but wound a delicate thread around a wispy feather, his brow knit with concentration. "I reckon I lay awake all night thinking about that."

The admission that she had caused him to lose sleep had a curious effect on Deborah. She didn't think she had ever caused anyone to lose sleep before.

"And?" She closed her eyes and waited. As she did, she tried again to imagine what it would be like to be with child. She had no idea, none whatsoever. She had never even seen a visibly pregnant woman before. From what she could glean from the servants' backstairs whispers, unmarried women who found themselves expecting were dismissed before their condition was apparent.

This is what you were made for. Philip's voice came out of the shadows of memory. *This is the whole duty of a woman.*

She shuddered and opened her eyes. "I'm not sure there is anything one *does,* particularly."

He looked as uncomfortable as she felt. "If you need help with...your condition, I suppose I could try to get up to the camp at Rock Harbor, see if there's a woman who would come."

She shuddered, assailed by a vision of a shadowy midwife from the north woods. "I don't want you to leave me," she said before she could stop herself. "We should wait and see if...if it's true."

He took in a sharp breath, then grimaced as the barb of a hook stuck his finger. "Then we can't do anything but wait for spring to come." He extracted the hook and wrapped a bandana around his finger.

She forced herself to drink a cup of cider, although she had no appetite for anything. As the moments passed, a strange feeling overtook her. She could sense the old Deborah flowing away to nothingness, spilled out of herself by something new and different.

Her life had changed so much; she was a stranger to herself. She could scarcely believe she was the same person as the carefree girl who had spent summers at the lake, attending dances and musicales, going into the city for the theater or opera, laughing with her friends late at night and planning a grand tour of Europe so that Phoebe could meet the duke or earl she swore she was destined to marry.

Deborah's spiral had been nothing short of dramatic. She had begun the month of October at the pinnacle of Chicago's social whirl, scheduled to marry a prince of society and give her father entree into the innermost circle of the elite. Now she was stranded for the winter, possibly with child.

"You all right?" Tom asked.

She studied the floor, pushing the toe of her shoe at a knot in one of the planks. "I was just wondering how my father would react to all this."

"You reckon a child from Philip Ascot would have made the old bastard happy?" Tom Silver asked.

She hesitated. "I'm not certain my father is the sort to concern himself with happiness. He is a man of goals and accomplishments. When he reaches a goal, he is satisfied. I believe that's what is important to him." She refilled her cider cup. "So you, too, should be satisfied, because you have thwarted his most cherished goal. He has only one daughter, and circumstances have rendered me entirely ruined and unmarriageable."

"You don't seem to regret that too much."

"I don't." A lightness rose in her chest. "I feel... liberated, in a strange way. I don't have to marry Philip. I don't have to move to New York and attend stuffy society events. I can become a pioneer in the west, or a missionary in exotic lands."

"Is that what you want?"

"I'm not sure. But until the fire...and...what happened after, I had no choice. Heaven knows, I was not suited to be a wife." She spoke in a breezy fashion, hiding the devastation and disappointment she felt inside. It was not so easy to give up on a dream or to accept her own limitations. True, she had experienced a stifled feeling each time she considered a future as *the* Mrs. Philip Ascot of Tarleton House, New York. The thought of using her father's millions to rebuild Philip's fortune had filled her with distaste. Yet at the core of it all, she had wanted to be married. She had wanted a husband to hold her close, to cherish her and share her deepest thoughts, to raise a family and finally to grow old and mellow side by side.

What a stupid, ignorant dream that had been. She should have known better. From what she could see of marriages within her circle, the husband and wife went their own separate ways. But of course, like any naive girl, she used to feel certain that *she* would be different. Hers would be a love match.

"What's that supposed to mean, you're not suited to be a wife?" Tom asked.

She ground her teeth in frustration. "I told you things last night that I should have kept to myself. Am I to believe you weren't listening?"

"I heard every word you said."

"Then you must have heard me say that my...experience with my fiancé, a man I have known and trusted for years, made me aware of a fundamental flaw in my character."

"Wait a minute. In your character?"

"The very act that makes a man and woman married is repugnant to me. The only explanation I can think of for my failure is that I had no mother to—"

"Goddamn it, you don't get it, do you?"

She jumped at his sharp tone. He had abandoned all pretense of working and his full, fierce attention was fixed on her.

"I beg your pardon?" she said faintly.

"The night you told me about—"

"Please, I don't wish to discuss it anymore."

"We're going to discuss it until you understand, damn it."

"What is there to understand? Perhaps I should count myself lucky to have discovered my inadequacy before Philip was trapped into marriage with me."

"I don't believe you." He pressed the palms of his

hands to the table and stood up. "You're blaming yourself because the son of a bitch raped you."

Rape.

She knew the word. It was a curt, ugly little word spoken in whispers, even by her Sunday school master when they had studied the Bible stories of Amnon and Tamar, Shechem and Dinah. She had read history and the classics—Visigoths and barbarians committed rape, along with pillaging and burning. In each case, the rape had been an act of hatred or violence that had left the victim either dead or hopelessly maimed. In Ovid's classical tales, women committed suicide as a result of being raped. The attackers were always deranged strangers lurking in the shadows. And of course, in the forbidden novels she and her friends had read at boarding school, the women who were raped were those of the lowest moral character anyway.

"No," she said slowly. "You don't understand. Philip was my fiancé. There was no r—" She couldn't bring herself to say it. "He didn't do what you say he did."

"He didn't force you, push you down, interfere with you?"

"Yes, but—"

"Did he lift your skirts, tear at your underclothes, put himself inside you—against your will?" Tom Silver's words struck her with the bluntness of physical blows.

A painful pulse beat at her temples. "I will not speak of it again."

"Then just answer me this, Deborah."

That caught her attention. He almost never called her Deborah. "Yes?"

"Did you tell him to stop?"

"In a whisper," she admitted. "But—"

"The fact is, he forced you to do something you didn't want to do. It was an act of violence. It was rape, goddamn it, and you keep on blaming yourself."

"Philip has never been violent with me. He never struck me in anger, or hurt me—"

"Not even that night?" Tom persisted. "Can you swear you weren't hurt that night? Just because he left no bruises doesn't mean he didn't hurt you."

Philip had left no mark on her. If he had, she could have called his behavior an act of violence that had wounded her. So in a way, what he did that night was worse. He had left his mark upon her soul, upon the most invisible part of her, the part that could hurt and bleed and no one but she would ever know.

She wanted to run and hide, but Tom Silver held her riveted to the spot with his intense gaze and unrelenting questions. She fired back a question of her own. "Why are you asking me these things? Why is it so important to you?"

"Because I see you hating yourself for something that bastard did to you."

"All he did was show me a woman's duty to her husband. It's not his fault I felt—" She clamped her mouth shut and went to the door, wishing there was a place she could escape to.

"You felt what? Betrayed? Violated? Hell, woman, of course you did. He attacked you and acted without your consent. You hated the experience because he raped you, not because of some failing on your part." Tom stood up and paced the room like a restless wild animal. "Did you think I wouldn't notice your reaction to being touched?" he asked. "You can't stand it. The son of a bitch taught you to be afraid of a man's touch."

"So my fiancé is a brutal, violent man who would do me injury."

"Yes."

"And this is supposed to make me feel better?"

"The way I see it, you couldn't be feeling any worse."

She pressed her hands to her mortified face. "You don't understand," she said.

"Then explain to me. I'm listening."

She took a long, shaky breath. "If he is a rapist, then that means I am too stupid to know whom to trust. And if he is not, then that means I would be inadequate as a wife. Either way, I lose."

Twenty-Nine

Tom threw himself into work. There were a hundred things to be done in order to provision the cabin for the winter, and it was up to him to make sure nothing was overlooked. Besides, work gave him something to do. Chopping wood, clearing a path to the storeroom, making a snowmelt for fresh water, setting snares for rabbits and catching fish through the ice were demanding tasks, but they demanded things of him that he knew how to give.

Deborah Sinclair was a different problem altogether. He couldn't just fix her like a leak in the roof. He didn't know how.

A fortnight after he had shocked and infuriated her by informing her that her intended was a rapist, they behaved like wary strangers trapped under the same roof. She clearly regretted having told him what had happened to her. Although forced to take their meals together and to face the fact that they weren't going to see another living soul until spring, they managed to go for long periods of time without speaking or even looking one another in the eye.

It was better that way, he told himself. When they spoke, he said what was on his mind, and he always managed to offend her.

Which was an odd thing, because in spite of who she

was, he did not much care to give offense to a woman
like Deborah Sinclair. What an idiot he had been, trying
to convince her that her fancy man was not the debonair
gent she thought she was getting. And he could be wrong.
He hadn't been there. He knew only what Deborah had
told him. It was none of his business.

But his gut told him exactly what had happened. He
didn't know whether she had come to believe his explanation or not. He kept telling himself he shouldn't care,
but they had gone beyond that. An injustice had been done
and she was the victim. He wished he knew how to make
her see that. He had felt this same sick, boiling rage when
the mining accident occurred. If he wasn't careful, he
knew the fury would make him crazy—crazy enough to
do what he had almost done in Chicago.

He knew now that venting his rage wouldn't help. Only
one thing would, and that was to make Deborah understand what had happened so she wouldn't be haunted by
it. He wished he knew how to explain to her that the act
of sex, when done with mutual caring, was a fine thing
indeed, not something hurtful, not something to be feared.
It infuriated him that she believed the rape was her fault,
that there was some defect in her.

She had taken it dead wrong, of course. She generally
took everything he said wrong. He just didn't know how
to talk to a female like her.

He muttered under his breath as he shoveled the snow
away from the storeroom door of the shop. It had snowed
for the past four days, stopping only in the middle of the
night last night, when a high cold moon had suddenly
burst through the clouds and lay in milky blue splendor
over the ripples and hummocks of snow.

At night, the sight had been beautiful beyond words.
By day, it meant work to do, and Tom was damned grateful for the diversion. It took him a good two hours to dig
out the sloping cellar doors. The hinges had frozen, and
creaked when he opened the door. Clear winter sunlight

streamed over a few barrels of wild rice, flour, sugar, coffee beans and milk powder. There wasn't much, since he hadn't planned on needing winter provisions, but he hoped it would be enough. He took his time prying open the barrels and laying in stores. Then he resealed the kegs with care to guard against vermin and shut the doors behind him.

In the house, Deborah sat in her usual spot by the stove, working on her quilt while the dog slept on the hearth rug at her feet. Light from the window slanted over her. The quilt had grown to cover her lap and drape to the floor, and when she looked up at him, his breath caught for a second.

Damn. Somewhere, hidden in his heart, was a picture just like this. It was something he had wanted ever since losing his family when he was so young he almost couldn't remember them. It was a sharp yearning that swept over him at odd moments—like now.

"Brought some supplies from the cellar," he said, gruffness covering up what he was feeling. He set the cloth sacks down on the table. "Rice and such."

Her needle flashed in and out of the quilt. "That's good. Do you want your supper now?"

"No. I'd best check my snares while there's still light."

"All right." She glanced out the window. "It's pretty as can be outside when the weather's calm."

"That it is." Plain words. An unremarkable conversation. Yet, like the current under the ice, other meanings flowed beneath their words.

She sighed. "I wish—" She cut herself off and sighed again.

"What?"

"It's silly."

"Tell me anyway."

"Sometimes I wish I could take a walk," she confessed. "When the sun is out, and everything is so beautiful, I get the urge to go out into that white world." A wry smile tugged at her mouth. "But my hands and feet get cold when I step out to fetch firewood. I wouldn't last two minutes in the snow."

She didn't seem to desire an answer, so he added a log to the stove. Then he went to the door, turning up the collar of his big coat.

"Tom?" she asked softly, tentatively, from her chair.

He turned back, too quickly. "Yeah?"

Her gaze held his for a moment that drew out until it turned awkward. Her teeth worried her lower lip. "Nothing," she said, her cheeks turning pink as she looked down at her quilting. "I forgot what I was going to say."

"I'll be back before dark," he said, and left the house. His heart was beating hard, and he knew the reason why. For the first time ever, she had called him by his given name. She had called him Tom.

On Christmas day, Deborah spent two hours bent over a washboard, scrubbing clothes and bedding. Gritting her teeth, she wished she did not know what day it was, because the notion that she was spending Christmas as a washerwoman was simply too pathetic to be borne. But like a fool, she had kept track of the days she spent on Isle Royale, and this morning when she had awakened to an empty cabin, she had known it was Christmas.

Tom Silver was, as usual, nowhere in sight. She told herself she should be grateful that he was so strong and that he worked so hard to keep the place warm and comfortable, to keep food on the table for her. But every once in a while, she just wanted his company. Not a rabbit for the stewpot or a log for the fire, but a pleasant conversation.

She knew she should not be so curious about him, but she couldn't help herself. She would look at him and wonder so much. She wanted him to talk about Asa, and about the war, and what it had been like growing up here. But she never quite knew how to ask.

She scrubbed extra hard at her bloomers and petticoats, letting the tepid water run down her arms. The lye soap stung her hands, which bore small scratches from all the housekeeping and needlework she had been doing. But the small wounds were preferable to the alternative— boredom and idleness. She had discovered an agreeable calm in the soothing rhythm of sewing, stitch by stitch, and an unexpected satisfaction in the feeling of finishing a section of the quilt. At the rate she was working, the quilt would not be completed for ages, but it didn't matter. If she just kept stitching, eventually the job would be done.

Washing did not impart that quality of serene gratification, she noted sourly, but it had to be done. Particularly today, she noted with a small lift of nerves in her stomach.

She finished her clothes and bed linens, hanging them across the room to dry. Against her will, she remembered other Christmases. Stringing cranberries and popcorn had been the most daunting tasks she had faced. Servants always festooned her father's mansion with swags of pine boughs and holly wreaths. Bayberry candles glowed everywhere, and a great noble fir, hung with tinsel and glass stars, presided over the formal drawing room.

The season had consisted of one glittering party after another, and excitement mounted higher and higher as the holiday drew near. She loved the secrets, loved the sense of anticipation, the caroling and merrymaking. Her father's extravagance knew no bounds when it came to Christmas. Over the years he had given her a pony, a rare white canary in a gilded cage, a hand-painted troika imported from Russia, a diamond tiara, silver combs for her hair and other presents too numerous to recall. She had reciprocated with a walking cane studded with gemstones, a silver-riveted saddle from Morocco, dozens of silk cravats and a fine gold watch.

She looked back across the years and recognized a disturbing emptiness in the gestures. Receiving gifts from her father was not nearly as important as gaining his complete, undivided attention. For him, her enjoyment of the gifts was secondary to showing them off. Arthur Sinclair had a personal secretary whose sole job it was to make certain his name was put before the people who mattered. Thanks to Milford Plunkett's breathless letters to the newspapers in Chicago and New York, all the world knew what Arthur Sinclair had given his daughter for Christmas.

The year she turned ten, something—excitement, anticipation—had awakened her very late one Christmas eve. Tiptoeing through the house, she had spied her father in the winter parlor. He sat alone, a crystal snifter of brandy in one hand and a small oval framed photograph in the other. There was no light in the room except the glow of the fire. Deborah didn't make a sound. She recognized the photograph. It was usually kept on a highboy in her father's private dressing room, for his eyes only. He never knew how often she sneaked into that room to peer secretly at the picture of her mother, wearing the lavaliere and serenely smiling out from eternity. Deborah used to stare at it for hours, trying to will life into the unmoving, flat image, trying to recapture the scent of her mother, the sound of her voice, the essence of her smile.

Until this moment, Deborah had no idea her father had the same awful yearning. She wanted to go to him, to say something, but she couldn't. Because she could see her father was crying.

She had never seen him cry before, and she knew then that there was no gift she could give to fill the empty places inside him. Perhaps that was the night she had decided to obey her father in all things, to please him in any way she could.

Restless, Deborah willed her thoughts back to the present as she climbed to the loft. So long as she was doing the washing, she might as well do it all. She felt a forbidden tremor of intimacy as she handled his bedding and clothes. Then she chided herself for a goose, rolled up her sleeves and got to work.

She finished the wash and emptied the basin out the back. A thick slide of ice had formed on the spot where she threw bath and wash water and the sight of it reinforced her feeling of confinement.

Shivering from cold, she went over and over in her mind what Tom had said about her ordeal with Philip. A rape. Could it be? In Tom's well-worn Bible, she read and reread Deuteronomy, pouring over the accounts of rape she recalled from Bible study class. Slowly her mind came to accept the idea that Philip had indeed violated her, that it was more than possible. Amnon, who had raped his sister, was the son of King David. Horrible things happened in the best of families. But knowing that her betrothed had assaulted her was scant comfort.

Compelled by a burst of angry energy, Deborah worked the morning away. For the midday supper, she fixed a stew with tinned tomatoes, wild rice and a fish Tom had caught through the ice. Her skill at cooking improved every day, though the resources were limited. She surprised herself—and probably Tom as well—with her creations.

In the early afternoon, while she was busy folding clean clothes and making up the beds, Tom came in from the cold, bringing the scent of snow and pine with him. From her room, she could hear him stomping the snow off his boots. The dog scrabbled inside and headed for his bowl.

"Something smells good," Tom called out.

"Your dinner. It'll be ready in a few minutes." She tucked the corner of the blanket under the mattress and smoothed her hand over the surface. It was hard to believe there had been a time when she'd had no idea how to make a bed.

Bemused by the thought, she stepped into the main room and felt her jaw drop. In the middle of the room was a very small pine tree. Candles set in jar lids adorned the branches, the little flames casting a magical glow over the room.

"Merry Christmas," he said gruffly.

She was speechless for a moment. Then she felt a smile that started inside and spread like sunshine to her lips. "I didn't think you'd remember."

"I figured you wanted to forget, but wouldn't be able to."

How was it that this man knew her so well? She had a strange sense about him. He might be wild and unconventional, but he would not hurt her. He was a stranger, but he knew the secrets of her heart better than anyone she had ever met. He was a rough man of the woods, but his strength was something she could rely on. It was an odd thought to be having about a man who had held a gun pointed at her father's head.

"It's quite a surprise," she said self-consciously. "I'll get your dinner."

"Thanks," he said, hanging his coat on a peg.

She ladled up two plates of fish stew. "You must be hungry, being out in the cold all morning."

They had warm cider with their meal, eating in silence as had become their custom. If they spoke for any length of time, it so often degenerated into an argument. She wanted to tell him about Christmas in Chicago and ask him what the holiday had been like with Asa. But she was afraid of prying. It was his first Christmas without Asa, and she didn't want to cause him pain.

After they finished, Deborah took the dishes to the basin. When she turned back to the table, she saw a good-sized bundle at her place, wrapped in hopsacking secured with an awkward bow of baling rope.

She frowned, immediately suspicious. "What's this?"

"A Christmas present."

She stared at him. He looked as if he wanted the floor to swallow him.

"For me?" she asked stupidly.

"Reckon so. Go on, open it."

Her hands trembled as she tugged at the rope. "I didn't get you anything."

The corner of his mouth lifted in a half smile. She had grown accustomed to the unexpected boyishness of that rare smile, so incongruous in his rugged face. "I don't need any presents, Princess."

She removed the rope and hopsacking, and let out a soft, involuntary gasp. "Oh, my. These are beautiful." She felt a thrill of pleasure as she held up the most perfect white fur mittens and fur-lined boots she had ever seen. She plunged her hand into one of the mittens and shut her eyes, savoring the silky heat. The rabbit fur was softer and warmer than down, sewn in a double thickness with painstakingly small stitches.

She opened her eyes. "Where did these come from?"

"I made them," he said simply. "Do they fit all right?"

She unlaced her shoe and slipped her foot into the boot. It felt heavenly, soft and snug around her foot and ankle, the leather sole creating a sensation as shockingly pleasant as walking barefoot through warm sand. She put on the other boot and then the mittens. "They are perfect, Tom." She swallowed past a sudden swell of tears in her throat. "Simply perfect." How foolish, she thought, to get so sentimental about these simple gifts. She had received diamonds and pearls without flinching, and here she was getting all teary-eyed about a pair of rabbit boots. If she wore something like this in Chicago, she would be laughed out of town. But Chicago was very far away. And no one was laughing now.

"Good." He bent and took her foot between his hands, pressing it to his thigh.

Instinctively she stiffened.

"Easy, there. I'm just going to lace them up for you." With slow, deliberate movements he laced the boots moccasin style with long leather cords.

A heated fascination took hold of Deborah. It wasn't something she could control—or deny. The way he touched her made her wonder about touching him.

Oblivious to her thoughts, he held out her cloak and put on his own. "I want to show you something."

She hesitated before going outside. She had often wished to take a walk, but had always believed she'd freeze before she took ten steps. Now, with Tom, it seemed possible. Anything seemed possible.

Another surprise awaited her there. "Oh," she whispered, her breath misting the cold air. "You made a path."

He had cleared a long, narrow walkway from the bottom of the porch leading to the woods and the marsh and the lakeshore. Smokey raced outside, leading the way. Tom held out his big, mittened hand as she came down the stairs, and without thinking about it, she put her hand in his. Through his thick mittens and hers, she felt a pleasurable current of reaction. As soon as his fingers tightened around hers, she realized what she had done, and self-consciously took her hand away.

But she was smiling as they headed toward the woods. She could walk with ease along the path, her boots and mittens keeping her deliciously warm. She tilted her head to the cold sunshine and let her eyes be dazzled by the blue of the sky.

The woods resembled a crystal palace. Frozen branches formed an archway over the path he had cleared, and when Deborah stepped beneath the arch, she imagined a touch of magic. Though it was only late afternoon, the sun rode low in the sky, spreading pinkish fronds over the path. The carpet of snow glinted like diamonds. Icicles dripping from the trees refracted sunlight into rainbow hues that spilled across the pure white ground. The occasional chitter of a pine siskin or the clack of the birch branches in the wind only served to magnify the muffled hush of the winter world.

Caught up in a state of quiet wonder, Deborah walked along the newly cleared path with her face raised to the forest ceiling. A feeling of tranquil reverence filled her with awe. "I used to go to church on Christmas to see and be seen," she said, whispering for no reason she could name. "But this feels grander than any cathedral made by man."

"Can't say as I've ever been inside a cathedral."

"You *are* in one," she said, turning in a slow circle with her face lifted to the lacy canopy of the forest. "On a day like this I can believe a savior was born. I mean it," she said, trying not to laugh at the expression on his face. Her voice sounded loud in the hollow stillness. "Thank you," she said. "For all of this."

"You're welcome."

"But I feel guilty. I didn't get anything for you."

"Sure you did. A good meal, and it appears you did the washing."

Remembering the reason for the big wash, she bit her lip, feeling hideously awkward. "Perhaps there *is* a gift for you," she said. "Well, not that exactly. But something you might...want to know."

"Yeah?"

She couldn't bring herself to look at him. Her cheeks burned with a wildfire of mortification as she stared at her soft leather boots, the white lining so thick and abundant it showed at the tops. "This morning I...discovered that I cannot possibly be with child."

He stood silent for so long that she forced herself to look up at him. He wore a grin from ear to ear.

"I take it that's welcome news to you," she said.

"Oh, yeah." He threw back his head and laughed. "You're a pain in the ass, Princess, but the idea of you being pregnant was even worse."

She bristled, ready to feel insulted, but somehow couldn't summon any anger. Even his careless, blunt use of the word "pregnant" didn't offend her. He had made

Christmas special despite their hardships, and she had made him happy by settling a very large worry. For a few moments they simply stood grinning idiotically at each other. "So it appears," she said, "that I made my big confession for naught."

He sobered. "Not so. A bad thing happened to you. Telling someone can't undo what happened, but you're not carrying the burden alone."

His words struck her like a revelation. She felt a lightness of heart that had not been there in weeks. The deep wounds caused by Philip had created a frightening dark place inside her. Tom seemed determined to drag her back into the light. "Why are you doing this?" she asked.

"Doing what?"

"Making Christmas into a holiday for me. Helping me to sort out what happened with Philip. Why?"

He looked uncomfortable as he picked up a handful of snow and packed it into a ball. "Because forcing you to come here was a big mistake. I wanted revenge against your father, and I should have stuck with that. I never should have dragged you into it."

"So you're acting out of guilt."

"Appears that way."

"I see." She started walking again, moving slowly along the path so she didn't miss a thing. The shadows lay deeper here, colder. She caught him regarding her oddly. "You must not feel guilty on my account." And as she said it, she realized what she wanted. She wanted his kindness because he liked her, cared about her, not because he regretted the rash act that had saddled him with her for months. The distinction shouldn't matter but it did.

"What a complicated arrangement this has become," she commented. "Things were so much easier when I was just a simple hostage."

He tossed the snowball at the marsh, startling a flutter of crows. "Woman, you were *never* simple."

She went to the edge of the marsh and surveyed the scene. A gloss of thick ice covered the surface, and the wind had swept it nearly clean of snow. At the fringes, reeds poked up through the ice and ripples of blown snow, and tiny black birds flitted in and out of the brittle wheat-colored plants.

"Have you ever ice skated?" she asked.

"Yeah. There wasn't much else for kids to do in the winter. You?"

"Of course. There are skating parties in Lincoln Park every winter."

"Can't say as I've ever made a party of it." He glanced at the deepening sky. "We'd best get back."

They walked at an unhurried pace, surrounded by silence. The only sound came from the dry squeak of the packed snow beneath their feet. When they reached the house, Deborah was amazed to look down and see that she was holding Tom's hand. She didn't even remember taking it.

Discomfited, she let go. "Thank you again."

"Merry Christmas, Princess." He took her by the shoulders and brushed his lips over her brow. Warm breath. Soft lips. Not at all like that kiss on the boat. And then it was over. He stepped back, a grin tugging at his mouth. "Don't look at me like I'm the big bad wolf. It was just a kiss."

"But...but..."

"Here, I'll show you again." He rested his hands lightly on her arms and bent down, this time kissing her mouth. Warm breath. Soft lips. She shut her eyes and felt an unusual, pleasurable heat inside her, and she leaned forward to deepen the contact. No thinking, she told herself. Just feeling. The stubble of his cheeks. His cool lips, quickly warming themselves against hers. The firm, sure grip of his hands on her shoulders. And then there was a jolt of remembrance, and she reared back.

"Don't," she said, her voice low and rasping with panic. "Don't do that."

He regarded her calmly, but with implacable resolve. "I'm not him," he said. "I'm not the bastard who attacked you. You're not going to tar me with that brush."

"I know that, but...I just don't like it," she said, her voice quavering over the words. She walked briskly toward the house. "I don't like being held, kissed—"

"You don't just like it, honey," he said. "You *need* it. Maybe I'm not the one you need, or maybe I am, but you need to learn the pleasure of being close. You can't be afraid of all men just because one attacked you."

"Why? Why must I learn to like being...close?"

"Because...just because," he said impatiently. "Without that, what's the point of anything?"

She tried to disregard her yearning to trust what he said. She couldn't let herself believe him. She had believed Philip, and he had wounded her in the worst possible way. How could she ever trust in her own judgment again?

"I don't know what to say to you." She moved past him and went into the house, savoring the warmth of the stove and the sight of the little tree looking so cheery on the hearth. "I never know what to say."

He laughed, stamping the snow from his boots. "You're doing a damned good job in spite of yourself, because you talk plenty."

"That's not what I mean. You speak of things so casually and with such candor. It's disconcerting." She stroked the incredibly soft fur of her new mittens. "The thing I fear most is that I cannot judge things for myself. I was going to marry Philip. I was about to step blindly into the arms of a man who abused me, if your assessment is correct. Do you blame me for being cautious?"

"Look," he said, "it's not *your* judgment that's faulty. Remember the mail boat skipper? You were right to balk at going with him. He's no good. And you were all set to marry Ascot because everybody around you convinced you that it was the proper thing to do. All your life you've been told what to think and say. You never had to think for yourself.''

''What do you know of my life?'' she asked, both hurt and startled by his perception.

''I have eyes. I bet if you'd let yourself make up your own mind, you never would have agreed to marry him in the first place. Now you can think what you want,'' he said, holding a flame to the candles to relight the tree. ''Say what you want. You might surprise yourself.''

And whether she wanted to or not, Deborah thought about his kiss. She thought about the solidity and the softness and the taste of him. She thought about those first delicious, magical moments when she had forgotten to be afraid.

She took that notion to bed with her and held it close within the warmth of her body. Before drifting off, she caught herself smiling in wonder and picturing Tom Silver, lighting the candles on the tree, his big, rough face softened by the tiny flames. In the middle of the bleakest, coldest winter she could imagine, he had given her Christmas.

Thirty

꘎꘎꘎

Though the routine of their days settled into a predictable rhythm, Tom sensed an undercurrent that had not been there before. By taking her in his arms and kissing her, he had crossed an invisible barrier, and now there was no going back.

The fact was, he wanted to go forward. He wanted to touch her more, kiss her again. He wanted to make love to her, to feel her naked against him, to whisper the thoughts that slumbered in his heart. But that wasn't all. The worst thing was that making love to her wouldn't be enough. He wanted to be with her always. Wanted to see the years change her face and the color of her hair. He wanted the contentment he felt when he walked into the cabin and found her reading a book or sewing by the fire.

He was crazy in love with her. And it wasn't the kind of thing that was going to go away.

At first he thought he could ignore it, maybe hide the insanity behind the things that he did—shooting a pheasant for the supper table, getting up extra early to put hot water in the basin, keeping the path clear so she could take a walk each day, fixing a lamp to the wall behind her chair so that she could see better to sew or read. But the need to be closer to her ate at him, and he kept getting tantalizing signals from her that maybe she wanted the same thing. Sometimes he'd catch her watching him, and she'd smile briefly before looking away. It wasn't much, but it made him suffer with a lust more powerful than he'd ever felt before.

He knew he and Deborah could never have the lifelong love his heart craved, but that didn't mean they had to ignore each other until the thaw.

Coming in on a clear midmorning in January, he carried his latest project, which he set on the table with a cake of paraffin wax.

"What are you doing?" Deborah asked, picking up the wax. "What is all this?"

"Ice skates." He took the wax and started polishing one carved wooden blade. The skates were crude but sturdy, and once waxed, they would glide smoothly across the ice. Deborah watched in keen interest as he waxed them, then measured out a leather strap for each one.

"Ready?" he said.

She didn't have to be told twice. She hurried to put on her cloak and boots and mittens, and tied a muffler snugly under her chin. Tom grinned at her eagerness. She didn't complain much about the tedium of the short winter days and long nights, but her eagerness meant she was probably bored much of the time. She had a spring in her step as she went out the door. He banked the fire and followed her outside, the skates dangling from his shoulders.

"What a perfect day," she said, flinging out her arms to embrace the air. She hurried down to the marsh pond. The wind had swept most of the snow away, and the surface was as clear as glass. Tom had made it slicker by tossing several buckets of water across it earlier in the day.

"Sit here," he said, indicating the hump of a boulder at the edge of the pond. "I'll put the skates on you."

She obeyed without hesitation, which was new to Tom. Though not nearly as skittish as she had been, she still maintained a pronounced distance. Today she seemed easier with him. With each passing day, she relaxed a little more. He hoped he wasn't just imagining it.

He knelt in front of her, the packed snow freezing his knees, and took her booted foot in his lap. He worked matter-of-factly, sensing that if he made a big deal over the fact that he was touching her foot, she'd get nervous on him. Her bones felt tiny and delicate, and her face looked as fresh as a child's. Yet when he wrapped a tie around her ankle, she lowered her eyelids to half-mast for a moment, and she looked nothing at all like a child. Discomfited, he strapped on her skates, put on his own and held out his hand. "Ready?"

She stood, wobbling slightly and grabbing his hand. "Ready."

"Are you sure you know how to skate?"

"Of course."

They took a few clumsy steps to the pond. He had lain a plank across the thin, crusty ice at the edge, and he'd used a twig broom to sweep away all the snow. They walked across the plank, then stepped out, still holding hands. Tom started slowly, pushing with one foot and then the other, making sure she kept up. He needn't have worried. All those snooty skating parties in Chicago had taught her a thing or two. She glided along with the fluid grace of a swan, her cloak and the ends of her muffler sailing out behind her, her free arm swinging easily at her side.

"We're skating," she exclaimed with merriment in her eyes. "It's glorious!"

Hand in hand, they circled the pond, startling a snow-shoe hare from the reeds. Redpolls and a lone goldfinch flitted nervously in the trees. Though the sky was bruised by the low, brooding gray of winter, the day had a stark beauty. When he was with her like this, Tom thought, it was almost enough.

Almost.

* * *

Deborah had never enjoyed a day of skating more. Unlike the mannered, well-groomed pairs that circled the pond in the city park, she and Tom skated with the exuberance of children.

"Want to go faster?" he asked after they had explored the shape of the pond, finding where the bumps were and the smoothest places for gliding.

"Let's race," she said, dropping his hand. "That is, if you don't mind being humiliated by a woman."

"Sometimes I think that's why women were put on this earth." The lust that addled his brain each time he was with her made him mutter, "Partly why."

She pointed to the end of the pond. "Last one to that stump fixes supper tonight." Even as she spoke, she brushed back her skirts and glided forward, claiming the lead. She spread her arms and laughed aloud, listening to the silver echo of her own voice rushing through the empty winter wilderness. She felt alive as never before. Cold air seared her lungs until they tingled and her long gliding steps carried her forward.

Inevitably, Tom caught up with her, then passed her with powerful strides. As he swept by, Deborah grabbed hold of his thick coat and pulled herself forward, surging ahead with a shout of delight. Tom roared out a protest and tried to break free.

They both lost their footing at the same time and came down near the edge of the pond. In a tangle of flailing arms and legs, they skidded to a halt in a snowbank amid the crackly reeds and bare thornbushes. Deborah found herself entwined in Tom's arms as he lay flat on his back. On the shore, the dog launched into a fit of mad barking.

Breathless, she asked, "Did you hurt yourself?"

"I'm fine," he grumbled, "no thanks to you." But he wasn't fine. When he lifted one hand, she saw that a three-inch thorn had pierced clean through his mitten, the sharp point protruding on the other side.

Deborah gaped at it. "Please tell me that didn't go through your hand."

With his teeth, he removed the mitten from his good hand. Then he grasped the thorn and yanked it out. "Not anymore." He took off the other mitten, briefly inspected the puncture wound and put his hand in the snow.

"You're so brave," she said. "Doesn't anything scare you?"

He shook the snow from his hand and put his mitten back on, giving her that crooked smile she couldn't help but like. "You, Princess," he said simply. "You scare me."

Suddenly it occurred to her that she was lying practically on top of him. Their faces were so close, she could feel the warmth of his breath and smell the scent of pine and snow that clung to him. She found herself unable to move or look away. His eyes were a deep, moist brown, fringed by lashes of a startling length. And his mouth was such a delicious shape, she couldn't help remembering his Christmas kiss and how it had filled her with such unexpected pleasure.

"Do it," he said softly, holding her spellbound with a look.

"Do what?" she whispered, feeling an inner warmth that made a mockery of the weather.

"Kiss me," he said. "That's what you were thinking about."

"Yes, but—I mean, *no.*" Her face felt unbearably hot.

"Kiss me, Deborah, and tell me you didn't like it."

"I can't." But she wished she could. Oh, how she wished it.

"Liar," he said, his voice low and husky. "I won't lie to you. I think about kissing you all the time. I want to. Bad."

His words made her tremble—with fear or excitement, she wasn't sure which. The urge to run seized hold of her, but just as quickly, it subsided, replaced by a keen fascination with him.

"Are you afraid?" he asked.

"Yes."

"Don't be."

She had no idea how to put aside her fear. Yet the temptation was so compelling that she couldn't resist. She bent her head closer, a whisper away, a breath away, and then she touched her lips to his. The soft shock of contact reverberated through her. She pressed closer, wanting suddenly to know the deep intimacy of a kiss that did not make her afraid. She closed her eyes as her lips parted, and his tongue flickered almost playfully into her mouth. The sensation aroused a desperate heat inside her, and she made a quiet, involuntary sound of pleading and pleasure. Surrounded by the profound silence of the woods, they kissed long and deeply, and by the time she finally pulled back, she felt light-headed and amazed by her desire for him. Was this what a woman was supposed to feel for a man? This fierce pull of longing?

He stared into her eyes for a long time, and she tried to read the expression on his face. What she saw there was tenderness, a sentiment that should have seemed incongruous in a man so big and rough. And yet it didn't.

She spoke before she knew what she was going to say. "I want to do more than kiss you."

"I know," he said simply.

"How do you know?"

He chuckled. "Not everything has to be explained in words."

She grew very still for a moment, feeling a firm decision push up through her consciousness. It was a desire that had never once occurred to the Deborah of old, but now it came to her as naturally as the next breath. "Then...could we?"

The tenderness in his face disappeared, sharpened to

implacable denial. "You don't know what you're asking."

"Yes, I do."

He fell silent. His long body was so warm and vital
beneath hers. The yearning inside her flared to a fire as
she awaited his answer. She imagined his hands on her
body, his mouth on her mouth, and the fire burned higher,
hotter.

"Please," she heard herself whisper. "You're the one
who said I can't keep being afraid."

He surprised her by grinning a little incredulously. "All
right," he said.

Nervousness and excitement held Deborah in their grip
as they got up and took off their skates. She found herself
chattering inanely about nonsensical things: the fact that
a muskrat broke the ice in order to feed on water plants,
that the heavy brooding clouds held the promise of more
snow and that it would fall dark soon, and that if the snow
passed over, they might see the northern lights.

Tom bore her nervous monologue with measured patience. He held her hand during the walk home through
the woods, and when they reached the cabin, he stoked
the fire until it was warm and cozy inside. Deborah removed her wraps and hung them on pegs to dry. Her
hands moved slowly over the fabric as she thought about
what she was about to do. She wondered if the fear would
come later, or if it was truly gone.

Tom put aside the bellows and stood up. "Have you
changed your mind?"

"No." The answer, like the conviction, came swiftly.

He gently added another log to the fire. The room went
dim, and then with a hiss the flames flared in an embrace
around the wood. "I'll make it all right," he said. "With
me, you won't hate it."

A clutch of nervousness took hold, and for a moment

she couldn't speak. When she finally found her voice, what she said surprised her. "Truly?"

He smiled, and she realized with a start how much she had come to depend on that smile. "Oh, honey," he said softly. "It's one of the things I'm good at." He held out his large, rough hand, palm up. "Come here."

She hesitated, then put her hand into his and had no urge at all to snatch it back. Perhaps living in such close quarters with him for so long made her feel easier around him. Or perhaps it was the calm confidence of his stare as he brought her to the settle by the fire. He sat her down, knelt at her feet and took her heel in the palm of his hand. While he unbound her boots for her and slipped them off, his gaze never left hers.

"Here's why you don't have to be afraid," he explained. "I won't make you do anything. If you want me to stop, just say so, and I will. Word of honor." He set aside her boots, took her hand and brought her to the bed. The low bedstead looked inviting in the falling dark of early evening. She stood uncertainly in the doorway.

"I don't know what to do," she said, and nearly cringed when her voice broke.

"Oh, love." He unbuttoned her dress slowly. "I do."

"Why are you undressing me? Philip certainly didn't do that."

"What I'm doing is nothing like what he did. Nothing at all. It's different in every possible way," Tom said. "I want to make love to *all* of you."

She stood spellbound as his big fingers made surprisingly quick work of her buttons. He peeled the gown to her waist and over her hips, then untied the drawstring of her warm wool petticoats. She found the sensation of his gentle touch unbearably provocative, and she shivered.

"Cold?" he asked.

She stepped out of the pool of petticoats and skirts. "No."

"Still scared?"

"Maybe," she admitted. "A little." At the darkness that shadowed his face, she added, "But I still want this."

And oh, she did, more than ever as he brought her to sit on the bed and went down on one knee before her, drawing her stockings down and discarding them. He took one foot in his hand, his thumb caressing the delicate arch. His manner of touching her went against all that was proper and right. This was the black sin railed about in Sunday sermons, the forbidden secret that led straight to perdition, and she wanted to go there, wanted it with all her heart.

Then, shockingly, he kissed the arch of her foot, his tongue darting out to trace the tender instep. She didn't bother to stifle a gasp.

"So tiny," he said, picking up the other foot and kissing that one, too. "You are so impossibly tiny, my love." He looked up at her. "Will you take off your bloomers and shift?"

"Is that necessary?"

"No."

She thought for a moment while he caressed her feet. "Very well. I will." She stood and pulled the drawstring of her bloomers, then skimmed them down. Last came the shift, thin and nearly translucent from weeks of wear.

"Lie down," he said. "Lie back and wait for me."

She settled into the bed, feeling so unlike herself that this might be happening to someone else, someone wicked and sophisticated and dizzy in love. A heated lassitude enveloped her in a dreamlike state.

Tom undressed quickly, and she couldn't help watching, awestruck by his size and musculature. When he removed his trousers, she tried to force herself to look away, but she didn't. Instead, an involuntary whisper escaped her. "Dear sweet heaven."

He grinned and came down smoothly to take her in his arms. "I've been called worse," he said. Then he grew serious, taking her hand and gliding it down the length of his torso. "I won't hurt you," he said. "You can touch me any way you like. You can stop me whenever you want."

She did like touching him, Deborah discovered. She liked the feel of smooth flesh over hard muscle, the extraordinary differences in his body and hers. He kissed her in a new, slow manner, his tongue pushing in and out of her mouth in a way that made her hips rise involuntarily. His hand played over her breasts and then went lower, creating a terrible, beautiful ache. His kisses trailed down her throat and lower still, making her mindless and helpless, yet at the same time filling her with a powerful and dark knowledge that she was not the cold, unresponsive creature she thought she was, but someone who could catch fire and burn with the pleasure of it.

And the beauty of it was that her touch was as powerful as his. She discovered this by cupping her hand against his chest and then shocking herself by stroking downward, deliberate and bold. He groaned aloud, parting her legs with his knee.

"Ah, Deborah," he said in a broken whisper, "You are ready, aren't you?"

"For what?"

"For..." He kissed her again in that surprising new way, and at the same time he held himself above her, braced up on his arms so they were joined only by their kiss. Then, ever so slowly, he lowered himself.

And panic seared her from head to toe.

"Stop," she said in a thin, thready voice. She felt trapped, terrified.

"Now?" His big arms trembled as he held himself back.

"I can't do this," she whispered.

His jaw hardened with taxed patience. He dipped his head to lightly kiss her. "I'm not him, remember? I won't hurt you. I promise." He touched her gently and whispered, "You're beautiful, and every choice is up to you.

Including the choice to trust me. And you should, you know.''

"Should what?''

He feathered kisses along her hairline. "Trust me. I never got frostbite on account of a woman. Because you're not just any woman.'' Despite their intimate position, he smiled. "You're the princess.''

His sincerity, his humanity, touched her even as his humor charmed her. She noticed then that his brow glistened with sweat and his shoulders rippled with strain. Deep in his eyes, she saw a profound devotion. "Tom,'' she said, her confidence returning. She reached for him with both hands, curving them up over the knotted muscles in his shoulders and lifting her head to kiss him. She opened her legs to accommodate him while her arms twined around his neck. She felt him touch her, and then there was a subtle insistent pressure and he was inside her.

Remarkably, there was no pain, only a rush of anticipation and soon, a sting of pleasure that made her gasp. That was when she knew beyond doubt that Tom *was* different. He became part of her in a way that made her forget this was not the first time. Tom's gentleness and slow erotic pace made her feel safe and cherished, and she welcomed the rocking motion that fused their souls. The deep caress of his body against hers was like a match to a flint, igniting swiftly, inevitably.

Something strange and wonderful happened to Deborah in those moments. She felt herself rising to a peak where she hovered, a bird flying above the earth on wings of light, her breath held back in anticipation. Then suddenly she was swept into a maelstrom of sensation that made her cry out and cling to him. He quickened his motions, and she moved with him, close to him. He gave himself up with a single low-throated sound, and then settled softly over her, kissing her and saying her name between kisses.

Long moments passed. He moved to one side of her and drew the covers over them. Cradled against the bulky warmth of him, she tried to speak but couldn't. Instead, she burst into tears.

Tom swore softly. "What's wrong? Did I hurt you?"

"No." She wiped her face with a corner of the sheet.

"Then what's the matter?"

"I should have come to you clean and new. Not... sullied by what Philip did."

He swore again. "He didn't sully you. No one can. You are clean and new. That's why—" He broke off and swore again. "Get that damn fool idea out of your head." He pressed a kiss to her temple. "You should rest. I'll find something for supper."

"I don't want to rest and I don't want to eat. I want to talk."

He sighed. "So talk."

"I can't help but wonder if you would have made love to me if I was a virgin."

"What?"

"Maybe you figured I was already compromised, so you might as well—"

"Oh for chrissake—"

"Is it true?"

"No."

Early on, she had discovered one vital fact about Tom Silver. He told the truth. From the moment she'd met him, he had never lied to her, even when it would have been easier for him. So she had no choice but to believe him. "Thank you," she said.

She wondered if he knew what she was thanking him for. She wondered if he understood what he had given her. He had shown her that she was not a failure in the art of loving someone with her whole being. He had taught her not to be afraid. Yet she could not say such things to him, and so she remained silent while he rose from the bed, pausing to kiss her tenderly and then getting dressed to build up the fire and fix supper.

This, she thought, listening to the quiet, comfortable sounds of Tom moving about the cabin while a warm veil of contentment spread over her, this was the essence of life. She didn't need parties or social engagements or fine things. She needed the incredible feelings aroused in her today. She needed that forever.

But the trouble was, they had no forever. Spring would inevitably come.

Thirty-One

Tom spent the next several weeks trying not to think. Thinking was a dangerous thing, because it took him places he didn't want to go. He and Deborah lived in a fairy-tale realm of their own making, drifting through days comprised of small, domestic pursuits and nights of long, uninterrupted lovemaking. He showed her the melting colors of the aurora borealis and then made love to her. Each time, he was moved by the beauty of the experience. All her barriers of fear and confusion had faded away, and now she embraced him with a delight that filled him with love and tenderness so deep he ached inside.

When the sap ran in the maple trees, they tapped the liquid and boiled it over a fire outdoors. He dribbled some of the hot syrup onto the snow where it hardened instantly into candy. They took long walks in the woods, and when he stopped to kiss her cold mouth, she tasted sweeter than the candy. They went skating, and in the evenings he read aloud to her while she sewed on her quilt.

On the day that would have been Asa's fifteenth birthday, the sun showed its face and they dug a trail up to the old mine site to plant a marker he had carved for Asa. Amid a tangle of wild dead roses forming a hump in the snow, Deborah held the ornately carved marker while Tom nailed it to a tree. He stood for long, agonizing moments remembering, grieving. Her arms came around him from behind. Feeling her warm and vital presence, Tom felt alive again. He still missed Asa so much that he hurt in his bones, but sharing the moment with Deborah helped, somehow.

In March, she finished the quilt and spread it like a handmade blessing over the bed they now shared. He was touched by the way she had used bits and pieces of Asa's clothes in the design. It depicted birds in flight, their patchwork wings spread as they headed for a spray of stars.

When he lay beneath that quilt, he knew for certain that Deborah had done something he thought was impossible. She made him love again.

It was a hard thing, loving a woman and not being able to tell her. So he loved her in the wordless ways that had always suited him better anyway, and he would keep on doing so.

They were like the animals in winter that lived in the warm underground darkness, far from the bright, busy world. Nothing could disturb their peace and contentment, but inevitably, the spring would come. With the melting snow, they would have to face the world again, and the world would divide them. They were two different species, from two different worlds. Like a tropical orchid that could not survive outside its protected warm home, Deborah was too exotic and delicate to live in the frozen north.

They didn't speak of the future, nor did they speak of their tacit agreement not to discuss it. They both knew there was a risk of pregnancy but they never spoke of that, either. Made reckless with a fever of passion, Tom refused to think of it. His love for her was a quiet thing expressed in looks and gestures and in the deep long night when they made love and fell asleep together under the quilt she had made. He forced himself to be content with the arrangement because he didn't know what else to do. With each day it was harder and harder not to think.

His trouble, he knew, was that he had always gone seeking things beyond his reach, and it had always ended badly, proving to him that he should learn to be content with what he had. As an underage, oversized youth he had joined the Union Army only to learn that war was an ugliness that destroyed the soul. As a young man, he had taken in Asa, believing he could give the boy a safe home. He knew if he tried to keep Deborah as his own, his woman, his wife, no good would come of it, and he'd be a damned fool to think it would.

One morning Deborah was awakened by a new sound—the constant drip of water. She ignored it for a while, reluctant to leave the warm nest of their bed. With a smile on her lips, she indulged in the lazy contentment of holding her sleeping lover close. Each day was a wonder to her, and it was all because of what they had discovered together.

As he did each day, Tom somehow sensed her wakefulness and stirred gently against her. They didn't speak; theirs was a conspiracy of silence that added to the intensity of all Deborah felt. Each morning he knew without asking that she wanted him to make love to her.

On this particular day he matter-of-factly lifted her gown and slid it over her head, then skimmed his hands over her breasts, awakening in her an exquisite sensitivity that would stay with her all day. She had learned to be bold when it came to touching him and to take delight in his pleasure. She stroked him and felt his urgency, and when his big hands grasped her waist and positioned her atop him, she gasped. And then slowly, sweetly smiled as she took charge of the rhythm. His hands slid up and over her torso, moving lower, taking advantage of the freedom to roam and caress her. She shut her eyes, threw back her head and let the magic happen.

When she opened her eyes, she looked through a gap in the curtains and saw a veil of water dripping from the eaves. There was something odd about the sight. She bent and kissed Tom, then pulled back and drew on her shift. The planks of the floor chilled the soles of her feet as she went to the window. She heard Tom getting up behind her, knowing he would start the day by building up the fire and filling the basin with warm water for her to wash.

A curious apprehension seized her as she parted the curtains to look out at the day. Rather than the customary overcast skies and light snow flurries, she saw a mist rising off the lake, and snow and ice from the roof melted and dripped down. A flicker of movement caught her eye and she said, "Tom, look. Is that a warbler?"

"First sign of spring," he said, then bent to pull on his boots.

She dressed quickly and joined him outside. *First sign of spring.*

Traditionally those were hopeful words, but not now. There had been a time when she couldn't wait for spring to come. Now she dreaded it. But the sight before her was unmistakable. The ice was thawing. The air was dense with a certain heaviness and the temperature was noticeably warmer. Disturbed by the roving dog, a flurry of birds rose in agitation from the birch woods at the edge of the settlement. The snow felt wet and slushy beneath their feet as they walked along the roadway past the abandoned houses.

When they came into view of the harbor, she saw that the ice on the lake bore many more cracks than usual, like pieces in a great puzzle.

Later that morning, she asked him, "What happens when the thaw comes?"

"There's an ice cutter that will move into the harbor and break up the ice. After that, the fishing fleet returns. And things...start up again."

Her heart understood what he would not say aloud. Some things started up. Others ended.

Arthur Sinclair had never had any trouble holding his head up with pride, but as he walked into the newly refurbished Founders Club on a Wednesday afternoon, his heart was heavy. Who would have thought he would miss her so much, even after so much time had passed?

It was, he conceded wearily, because he had forgotten that he loved his daughter. He loved her as he had loved May—simply for the mere fact of her existence. Somehow, in his ambitious climb to success, he had lost sight of that. The very idea shamed him, and it had been a long time since he had felt shame.

After passing a lonely, empty Christmas, he had finally concluded that he'd made a horrible mistake in refusing to bring Deborah home. He'd sent the Pinkerton agent, Price Foster, up to find her in January, but the news was not good. An old voyageur in Northern Minnesota had revealed that she had stayed on Isle Royale over the winter. Foster had made inquiries about the man called Tom Silver, discovering that he was a decorated war veteran and a man known and respected in the region. Arthur could only pray that he hadn't harmed Deborah.

In February, with the rebuilding of the city in full swing, Arthur had been struck low with his heart ailment. After enforced bedrest, he had regained his strength. And, without even trying, he'd reclaimed his place in Chicago society. He wasn't quite sure how or why it had happened, but the invitations had begun to arrive again. The funny thing was, he didn't care anymore. He knew then that he would pay any price to get his daughter back.

Now it was March, and the most surprising invitation of all had brought him into the city for a meeting. He accepted a glass of whiskey and a cigar from a waiter, sat back in a leather wing chair and waited.

Philip Ascot arrived like the prodigal son, hand outstretched, a faintly sheepish grin on his face. "I can't thank you enough for coming, Arthur," he said.

Arthur knew then why the doors to society had opened for him once again. Philip must have arranged it. He wanted to be angry with Ascot for dismissing Deborah, but it was no less than Arthur himself had done. "You have something to discuss with me?"

Ascot ordered a drink with no more than a discreet nod; he was known in this club. "Your daughter," he said. "I won't mince words with you, sir. I cannot stop thinking about her."

Arthur pondered the rumors he'd heard over the holiday. "Seems to me you stopped long enough to get yourself engaged to Miss Bartell." Another heiress. Not as well-fixed as Deborah had been, but who was?

"A mistake." Philip sipped his bourbon, shaking his head in self-disgust. "She broke it off abruptly. Women just don't know their place anymore," he concluded. He lowered his voice. "I've been such a damned fool, Arthur. It's always been Deborah for me."

"Deborah, or her fortune?" Arthur asked bluntly.

Ascot winced. "You wound me, sir. If you choose not to give us your blessing, that won't change my mind. I don't care if she's been sullied, dragged through the muck. I wouldn't care if you disinherited her. I want her back."

A fine speech, Arthur thought, but despite his cynicism, his heart felt lighter. Philip Ascot knew damned well that Deborah would now come with an even bigger dowry.

"Then we are in accordance," he said. "I want her back, too."

In early April, lying in the delicious cocoon of Tom's arms, Deborah heard a noise. Without opening her eyes, she tried to guess what it was. Smokey gave a warning growl in his throat.

The spring thaw was coming on so fast that something

new happened every day. Only yesterday, a beaver dam she'd been watching over the winter had been swept away by a flooding creek. She and Tom had watched the lodge being broken up and she'd felt absurdly sad for the homeless creatures.

Feeling Tom stir, she snuggled in closer, wrapping her arms tight around him. He was always trying to get up at the crack of dawn. She was always trying to find ways to keep him in the warmth of their bed. It wasn't difficult. A few sleepy kisses, a suggestive caress, and he was more than willing to linger with her. They drifted off to sleep again, and she forgot to tell him about the noise she'd heard. A row of icicles falling from the eaves, perhaps.

But the second time she heard the noise, she knew it wasn't icicles.

She sat straight up in bed, pulling on her nightgown. The dog gave a sharp bark. Tom grabbed his jeans, yanked them on and went for the door.

But it was too late. Four men crowded into the cabin and three gun barrels pointed at Tom's chest. He backed into the room, shielding Deborah with his body.

For a moment no one moved, spoke, breathed.

After a shocked silence, Deborah swallowed a horrible dryness in her throat and scrambled to her knees on the bed. "Father!"

He had changed. In his long dark cloak, he looked smaller than she remembered, his usually florid face a shade paler. The thought swiftly came to her that he had not been well.

She kept moving, pushing herself in front of Tom. He grabbed her arms and shoved her out of the way, and immediately two of the gunmen moved in, aiming the muzzles of their long-barreled pistols at his chest and neck.

"No!" Deborah screamed, planting herself in front of Tom again. She didn't care that she was in a state of indecency, that her father and three strangers were seeing her barefoot, her hair loose and wild. "You wouldn't dare," she said. "You wouldn't dare start shooting."

"Take a good look, Princess," Tom said. "They can do whatever they want." He tried to pull away from her, reaching up to disengage her arms from his neck. "Let go. It's me they're after."

"Never." She held fast to him. "I won't let them gun you down." Even as the words came out of her, she looked at her father and saw the fury in his eyes. She knew, with an ugly shock of certainty, that her father was not above such things. Unarmed, Tom had no defense and her father would show no mercy.

"I figured I'd find you cowering behind a woman," her father said, addressing Tom with acid contempt.

Deborah refused to let herself be hurt by her father's failure to greet her. "Call off your…whoever these men are."

"What the hell are you doing here, Sinclair?" Tom demanded. She saw his tension in the tautness of the muscles that banded his chest, and in the rapid, shallow breaths he took.

"I came to collect what's mine."

"Why didn't you come before?" Deborah snapped, and her tone made her father look at her in a way he never had before. With something akin to respect.

"I don't negotiate with outlaws," he said.

"Not even on behalf of me?" She spoke softly, unable to keep the anguish from her voice. A menacing growl rolled from the dog's throat.

Her father stared at her as if regarding a stranger. "I can only imagine what you have suffered at the hands of this madman. Come home with me." His gaze dropped. "I was too rash, angry and confused by all that happened the night of the fire. Forgive me, Deborah. Forgive me and come home."

A flicker of yearning, fanned by the old obedience trained into her, came to life inside her. He sounded so

sincere. She let herself hope she and her father could forgive one another. But she'd had no self, not until she had
come to Isle Royale and discovered what truly mattered.
Until then, she had been a hollow shell—one of her father's creation.

"Call them off, Father," she repeated. "I will not
budge until you do."

She heard his breath catch at the steady command in
her voice. He hesitated, then thumped the tip of his cane
on the floor. The men lowered their weapons, but kept
them cocked. In the coming light of early morning, she
saw that they wore braid-edged hats and long coats with
sharp red piping along the seams, and each had a small
collar stud depicting a single open eye. Allan Pinkerton's
men. Hired detectives. Hired guns. How much had her
father paid them to come here?

"How did you find me?" she asked. "How could you
have known we were snowed in here?"

"I made inquiries."

The Pinkertons had done their work thoroughly. She
wondered if they had harassed and threatened Lightning
Jack or the island families wintering on the mainland.

"I'm not well," her father said. "I need you with me.
Come home, Deborah."

She studied the deep haggard lines in his cheeks, the
shadows of sleeplessness under his eyes. This was her
father, she told herself. Her *father*. He was a man whose
humanity was deeply buried, but it was there. It was
something that could be saved.

"Let's go," her father said, aiming his cane toward the
front door.

"Tom comes with me, and that's final."

"Don't worry about a thing," he said, a hint of his old
indulgent smile softening his face. "I have your things
aboard the *Triumph*."

"Do as he says," Tom whispered, bending to push his
feet into boots. "Then...we'll see."

They were barely given time to don coats and boots. Her father wore a cloak and beaver hat. In the sweeping garment he resembled the *condadori* in *Don Giovanni*, sent to tell the hero to redeem himself while he still could. The Pinkertons were as silent and impersonal as foreign servants, yet never once did they relax their vigilance over Tom. Deborah clung to his hand as they stepped outside.

A great steamship lay to in the harbor. In a channel between broken ice floes, two launches had made it in to the dock. "Stay close to me," Deborah said to Tom. Inside, she grew as cold as a stone. *I have your things....* But her father had said nothing about arrangements for Tom.

She didn't want to believe her father capable of the thing she feared, but the thought stopped her in her tracks. "I want you to see your mine," she said suddenly, turning to her father. "The one that was supposed to make this settlement so prosperous." Who was that, speaking with such acid authority? She caught his look of surprise. She had made the suggestion in order to stall for time, but also because the man responsible for seven deaths should be made to look upon his handiwork.

Prodding Tom in front of them, the men walked in almost military formation. Their footsteps made moist slapping sounds in the wet earth. Tom wasn't sure what Deborah had intended, insisting on bringing her father here, but he stayed on his guard. His instincts made him want to turn and fight, but he wouldn't risk it, not in front of Deborah. He didn't want her to see him shot.

The snow had melted considerably since they had put up Asa's marker on his birthday. The seven graves lay barren and forlorn in the winter chill. Moisture wept from the trees that fringed the clearing. The dog trotted restlessly back and forth, clearly confused by the intruders.

The inverted cavity of the mine formed a snow-filled wound in the frozen earth. Arthur Sinclair walked toward the broken hole in the ground, his feet crunching over the half-frozen terrain, his cane stabbing holes through the crusted snow. The old man walked slowly to the edge of the pit, motioning for his bodyguards to stay back. He stood there for a long time, looking more human than Tom had ever imagined him. Leaning on his cane, he went down on one knee to read the Bible verse Tom had carved on the new marker. *For the Lamb at the center of the throne will be their shepherd; he will lead them to springs of living water. And God will wipe away every tear from their eyes.*

When he arose, he gave one curt nod that told Tom there would be no good outcome to this.

"I won't say I'm sorry because that won't help," Sinclair said quietly. "But we'll pay whatever claims are made."

Tom looked into the face of the man who had destroyed so many lives, and he felt…nothing. The killing rage was gone. This man had also brought Deborah into the world. He was glad he hadn't killed him that night in Chicago. Sinclair was not worth the price of his soul.

"You can't buy your way out of this," Tom said. "You'll rot in hell. It doesn't matter who puts you there."

Sinclair didn't flinch, but his knuckles whitened around the head of the cane. "You ruined my daughter, you bastard. You're scum—"

"Father, stop." Deborah's voice cut like a knife. Though she was disheveled, she looked magnificent, as blond and strong as a Valkyrie. "Enough of this. Tom Silver *saved* me from ruin. I can't begin to tell you the ways. He has given me more honor and respect than any drawing room gentleman." She put out her hands, palms up. "I love him, Father."

Tom's jaw nearly dropped. He supposed he had known it, but this was the first time he'd heard the words. Yet even as his heart soared, he understood that her stark, honest declaration wouldn't change a thing.

Sinclair rounded on him. "You took advantage of a naive young woman, and for what? You're a man with no prospects, nothing to offer her." He lowered his voice to a hiss only Tom could hear. "You can make this hard, or you can make this easy. Let her cherish whatever memories you've made here, but don't break her heart. Let her go, damn it."

Two things became clear to Tom in that moment. Sinclair, in his cold-blooded fashion, cared for his daughter. And in that same cold-blooded fashion, he meant to march Tom out into the woods and shoot him like a dog.

He said nothing, but walked away from the pit. He heard Sinclair's uneven footsteps behind him. "Take my daughter aboard the *Triumph*," Sinclair called to the detectives.

Wide-eyed, her beautiful face nipped by the morning chill, Deborah moved toward Tom. "I'm not leaving him," she said. "He's coming with me."

The tallest detective, who wore a silk patch over one eye, stepped in front of her.

"Don't be difficult," Sinclair said, taking her arm. "If you go along peacefully, we'll leave him be. If you continue to defy me, it'll go ill for him."

"Go on," Tom said, infusing his voice with brusque command. "Winter's over. You can't stay here."

She stared at him as if he had slapped her. "Oh, yes I can."

"Your father's right," he forced himself to say, when what he really wanted to say was that he loved her. "You don't belong here. You never have." He took in the island with a sweep of his arm. "What happened here…is over."

She raised her face, wet with tears, eyes wild with panic, and stared at him in disbelief. He wanted to comfort her fears, to tell her not to be afraid, not to grieve for him. He knew of only one way to do that. And that was to lie.

For if he told her the truth, she would hurt for all the rest of her days, and he didn't want that.

He looked her square in the eye, hoping she would never guess at the ache of love that clutched at his heart. "Save your tears for someone else, Princess. You were just a means of revenge for me."

Her mouth froze in a shocked *O*. Her face drained of color.

He took one last look at her. She had the face of an angel. Hard to believe he had awakened this morning with her warm and loving in his arms. And with that thought, he forced himself to turn away.

Deborah wondered why two of the Pinkertons lingered on the island while she and her father got into one of the launches at the dock. Ever loyal, Smokey leaped into her lap. The third detective picked up the oars and rowed powerfully out to the steamer. She felt sick and dizzy from the events of the morning. In the back of her mind she had known that changes would come with the spring thaw, but she had never believed those changes would be forced on her by her father.

Once she was aboard the steamer, a steward and a maid scurried to settle her into her stateroom, but she lingered on the midships deck, grasping the cold iron rail. *You were just a means of revenge for me.* Tom, who had never, ever lied to her, had spoken the words with rock-hard conviction. They pounded at her, mocked her, and for a moment she hated him.

She hated him because she knew he lied. He loved her. Oh, he'd never said so, not in so many words, but in every thoughtful gesture and handmade gift. Every fleeting smile across a cozy, firelit room. Every caress of his hands and mouth, his body. He loved her, yet he was making her go away from him.

She heard her father approach and stared at him with dull eyes. "I will never forgive you for this," she said.

"My dear, it's for the best. You'll see. Now, go inside where it's warm, and—"

A loud *crack* split the air. The dog yelped in alarm.

"What was that?" Deborah asked.

Her father made the mistake of looking over his shoulder at the settlement. And then she knew.

In the split second afterward, her soul flashed white and burned to ashes.

"He was a menace, a madman," her father said, speaking quickly, almost nervously. "If we'd left him be, we would have no peace. We'd always be wondering if he would come hunting us again."

At first she could not react. Her hands seemed to freeze around the guard rail, to atrophy there like the hands of a corpse. The two remaining detectives strode quickly down to the dock, got in the launch and rowed for the steamer. A high, thin sound came from Deborah, a sound of insane rage that crescendoed into mindless screams. With no thought but getting to Tom, she threw her leg over the rail.

Instantly, strong hands grappled with her, hauling her back. She fought and scratched, kicking out, but someone grabbed her from behind. A hand holding a cloth closed over her mouth. She turned her head wildly, but the pungent, sweet vapors of chloroform assailed her, drawing a flood of tears from her eyes. The lake became a shimmering gray and white nothingness, and she thought it was odd to be drowning, for she hadn't even jumped in the water.

Part Four

The longest journey is the journey inward.

—Dag Hammarskjold

Thirty-Two

Deborah awakened in her opulent stateroom aboard her father's yacht. Heavy red draperies festooned the alcove berth, held back by thick gold tasseled cords. For a few moments she floated, unmoored and groggy. As a girl, she had whiled away many delightful hours aboard the steamer, on long lazy cruises over the lake while her father entertained guests.

Then she remembered. That life didn't belong to her anymore. Moving too fast, she sat up and had to hold the wall to keep from falling. Cobwebs of the surgical chloroform hung in her mind, sticky and sluggish. She fought her way free of them. Tom, she thought. *Tom.*

Only this morning she had thought she could see her future unfurling like a dream before her. Then her father had arrived, trapping her like a fly in a spider's web. She had been forced to trade her freedom for Tom's life. Like a fool, she had trusted her father to honor the terms of their agreement.

Instead, his hired assassins had shot the man she loved.

Had Tom died instantly? Or had he bled slowly and violently into the snow until the bitter cold took him?

Sick horror welled up in her, but she forced herself to go to the door. She pulled down on the lever. Locked. Of course it was locked. She was a prisoner again, bound away to the gilt cage of her father's world. Smokey trotted beside her, but she was too numb to pay him any mind.

She went to the narrow clerestory window, holding the edge and standing on tiptoe to see outside. The grim, striated lines of the island's ridges were still in close view, telling her she hadn't been unconscious for long. She could hear the stokers feeding fuel to the boilers. Soon she would be on her way.

"No," she whispered, and the hiss of the boilers drowned out her voice. Even if they took her away she would find a way to come back. But to what? Tom was gone. *Gone.*

She dropped to her knees before the basin and wretched. The veil of confusion lifted, letting in the truth. The horror and grief. The memories of hatred and violence that had occurred on Isle Royale.

She wanted to remember this as the place where she had been happy. Not a place of nightmares. Her father had taken that from her, too.

Yet she wanted the pain, she craved it. She wanted to remember, to feel. For that was what she had learned here. Life was not a matter of marrying the right person or residing at the right address or attending the right functions. It was knowing the beauty of nature, the warmth of a true friendship, the pain and joy of love. That was what she had found here. And that was what she had lost.

Pulling herself to her feet, she returned to the window to watch the jagged shore of Isle Royale and remember every moment with Tom. His long thoughtful silences and the sound of his laughter. His habit of listening to her as if her words were the most important ever spoken. The unexpected slow, gentle caress of his hands as he made love to her. The way he had whispered endearments in French patois into her ear as they lay together each night. The way he had sometimes seemed on the verge of telling her something, then changing his mind.

Her breath came in short, hurtful gasps, fogging the window. How would she go on without him?

Courage. She was brave now, far braver than the quailing, cringing creature dragged aboard the *Suzette*. The night of the fire seemed ages ago. She had learned so much from Tom Silver. He'd lost Asa but he had forced himself to go on, honoring the boy's memory by living. By not just surviving but learning to embrace life again, to love again. Regardless of his parting words, she knew he had loved her in a way no one ever had before.

She could do no less for Tom. She must do honor to the gifts he had given her. She must go on. She must find justice, not only for Tom but for all the islanders scarred by her father's careless quest for more wealth. She knew she would have to work quietly and carefully, but one day she would see her father and his cold-blooded hired guns punished.

But not now, while tears scalded her cheeks. For now it was all she could do to keep from going mad with grief. As she stood at the window, hearing the thump and grind of the steamer preparing to get under way, she heard a noise outside the door. She didn't move.

She heard a metallic click as a key turned in the lock. Smokey growled and scampered to her side. The door opened and shut. Finally she pushed away from the window.

Shock slammed into her like a physical blow as she stared at the man who stepped into the room. She felt as if she had plunged into icy water and was drowning.

Philip Ascot spread his arms with negligent grace. "Surprise, my darling," he said.

Echoes of remembered terror rang through her. This was the man who had raped her. He had reduced her to a timid creature filled with self-doubt. If not for Tom, she would still be that creature.

Had she ever thought Philip handsome, with his beautifully cut hair and even white teeth, his perfectly tailored clothes and manicured hands? She could not remember because she was no longer the superficial young woman who believed marrying well was her purpose in life.

"What are you doing here?" she asked in a voice that revealed nothing.

"I came to help your father fetch you home," he said reasonably. "If not for me, he wouldn't have come at all." Philip cut an elegant form as he quietly shut the door. "You see, my dear, your father had declared you a lost cause. He believed I would forsake you after your adventures with that savage from the north woods."

The telegram. The declaration that she was of no value. Her father must have underestimated Philip's need for her fortune.

"Yes," Philip went on, "he was going to leave you to rot with those savages. But I convinced him that I am a man of my word. I promised to wed you and I intend to make good on that promise. Just because you had the misfortune to fall into that barbarian's filthy hands is no reason for me to abandon my vow of honor."

"How selfless of you," she said. "Tell me, did you force Father to double or triple my dowry in order to keep your promise?"

He laughed with delight. "It's not as if anyone else of consequence would have you now. All Chicago knows the savage ruined you. But I am a man of great common sense—"

"And what was it, common sense or cowardice that made you stay hidden instead of coming ashore?" Even as she asked the question, Deborah knew the answer. Philip Ascot was a coward in every sense of the word.

"Since we quarreled when we were last together, I feared you might think I was still angry with you, so I thought it best to stay out of sight," he said in all sincerity. "I explained to your father—"

"We did not quarrel," she said. Anger nearly drove

out her grief. She leveled her gaze at him and refused to look away. "You attacked me, Philip. You raped me."

He threw back his head and laughed. "Is that what you believe? My darling, I gave you what every bride-to-be yearns for—a taste of the pleasures of the marriage bed. It's not my fault you were too immature to appreciate it." His gaze flicked over her, taking in her plain dress and unkempt hair. "Maybe Tom Silver did me a favor, turning you into his whore. Maybe now you'll appreciate a man of refinement."

"I would take more pride in being his lover than your wife."

A look flashed in Philip's eyes that she had seen many times over the years. But until now she had not recognized it for what it was. Rage. It had lived in him for a very long time.

He took a step toward her. The dog growled again.

Deborah felt a flicker of apprehension. Philip had shown himself to be a cold and violent man. But here? On her father's boat? She realized she couldn't depend on her father to help her. He was blinded by his desire for social acceptance.

"Get out," she said in a strong, loud voice. "I don't ever wish to see you again."

He kept walking toward her. She caught a glimpse of the pearl-handled pistol he had been carrying the night of the fire. Oh, how she wished she had snatched it up that night and kept it. But she had been too timid back then. Too indecisive.

"Go away, Philip," she said, taking a step back. But that was a mistake. The beautiful draped bed loomed behind her, an opulent cage of red velvet and gold braid.

"Don't be absurd, darling." He reached for her, grasped her by the shoulders, put his face very close to hers. "This is what you were made for," came the familiar whisper. "This is but a sample of the pleasures that await you once we're wed."

It was happening again, just as it had at the opera. His hands, grabbing, pushing. His mouth speaking vile lies. His body pressing her back. She was too shocked to respond.

"Lie down now," he said, pushing hard. The small mongrel latched onto the cuff of his pants, but Philip just kicked the dog aside. He tore her gown, splitting the seam at the shoulder. "Spread your legs for me. Play the whore for me like you did for that savage."

The memory of Tom stirred her spirit to life. "No!" she yelled in her loudest voice, a voice she had never heard before. Even as she screamed a protest, she brought her foot up swiftly and hard. Her knee connected with his groin, the most vulnerable part of a man.

Philip's lungs emptied. He doubled over, clutching himself. She seized the advantage to bring her other knee up, smashing it into his face. Hot blood spurted from both nostrils.

Deborah experienced a flash of amazement. What a weak, powerless creature he was, and always had been. It was she who had changed, finally able to see him as he was.

As he choked out a name she had never been called before, she grabbed the lapel of his coat, reached in and took his gun. It felt small and heavy in her hand. The panicked dog scampered under the bed. She had no idea if the gun was loaded, but when she pointed it at Philip and saw the expression on his bloodstained face, she knew.

With the snub nose of the gun leveled at her assailant, she knew the truth of what Tom had discovered, facing down her father. There was no redemption in killing a man.

She kept her gaze fixed on his, aimed the pistol toward the bank of pillows on the bed and fired once to summon help. The gun convulsed like a hot, live thing in her hand.

Philip jumped, then recovered and grabbed her wrist. He wrenched the gun from her as acrid smoke filled the air.

"You've lost your mind," he snapped, pale from her attack but fast gaining strength. "How dare you assault me—"

Suddenly the cabin door banged open. Arthur Sinclair swept the scene with a look of pure confusion. "What's going on here?" he demanded, coughing from the light layers of gunsmoke. "Philip? What's all this blood?"

"That," Deborah said stonily, "is my reply to his proposal." With icy dignity, she pulled together the pieces of her nightgown.

She felt her father's gaze fall on her bare shoulder and saw the moment his confusion turned to realization. "Dear God, I should have listened to you, Deborah," he said. "This was what you were trying to tell me that night. You son of a bitch," he said, wheeling around to face Philip. "My daughter was right about you after all—"

Philip's expression didn't change as he extended his arm and pulled the trigger twice.

Deborah's father kept his eyes on her as his hands came up to cover his chest. The blood that leaked between his fingers was the color of ink. He sank down, never once taking his gaze from her face.

She didn't feel herself move or hear herself scream. She suddenly found herself on the floor in a spreading pool of blood. With her father's head in her lap, she heard shouts and the thud of running feet on deck.

Her father's hand groped clumsily at his chest. She thought it was from pain, but in a moment she saw that he had extracted something from his pocket. It was her mother's lavaliere, stained with his own blood. His eyes were open, his mouth working. She bent to hear his whisper.

"...mistake. He loves you. He loves you."

Even now, she thought, her heart sinking. Even now,

as he lay dying, her father believed in Philip Ascot, not her.

"Please, Father, save your strength. Help is coming."

"Too late for me. You were right. You were right all along. I didn't do...what you think..." He pushed the lavaliere at her, and she closed her hand around the legacy from her mother. In a strange, terrible moment she remembered the day from her childhood when she had seen the happiness in his eyes, reflecting the fluffy white clouds of a summer sky. *That* was her father, not the bitter, dying creature in her arms.

"I didn't..." He tried again and coughed, spraying blood. "You...were right."

At last his words made sense. Her eyes flooded with tears. "About Tom," she whispered, understanding.

Arthur's chest jerked, and then he fell still. The flow of pooling blood slowed; perhaps it stopped.

Deborah didn't have time to absorb the moment of exquisite grief. She felt the caress of the gun barrel at her temple, brushing her hair out of the way with deceptive gentleness. The gunmetal still held the heat of the shots that had killed her father.

"Fancy that," said Philip in a whisper, "you're his sole heir. Your dowry is even bigger than I'd hoped, my darling."

Tom was gone. Her father was gone. The vicious suddenness of her losses made her careless. With a strength she didn't know she possessed, Deborah shot to her feet. But Philip was prepared this time. He pressed the gun to her neck.

"You learned the ways of a savage," he said through gritted teeth. "Shall I be rough with you, then? Shall I treat you like a savage's whore?" His free hand twisted into her hair, yanking her head back so that her throat went taut. He shoved her toward the bed. She reached for the gun but he held it away from her. She felt the edge of the bed against the backs of her legs.

The last time she had been with Philip, she had been too polite to object to his bullying. No more, she thought. *No more.*

"Murderer," she yelled, hurling her fists at his chest, kicking out, heedless of the gun. She knew he wouldn't dare kill her, for he needed her money.

He grunted in pain as she struck him.

Then a huge shadow darkened the doorway and an unearthly bellow, like the roar of a wounded bear, filled the stateroom.

Disbelief froze her for a split second. *"Tom!"* Deborah strained toward him.

Philip shoved her back at the same moment he started shooting. Earsplitting reports and yellow-gray smoke filled the air. She could see nothing as she picked herself up. Each second was an eternity of confusion. At last two hollow, frantic clicks signaled that Philip had run out of bullets.

"Your aim's no better than your timing," said a deep voice. Out of the smoke stepped Tom Silver, arms extended to gather Deborah against his chest. She felt his strong, vital warmth surrounding her. A moment later, the Pinkerton men rushed into the stateroom.

"Seize him," Philip said in a shrill, frantic voice. "I tried to save Mr. Sinclair but the devil shot him! Then he attacked me!"

She faced the detective with the eyepatch. "Philip Ascot killed my father," she said. "You know. *You know.*"

"The savage is making her say that," Philip insisted, edging toward the door. He seemed to have forgotten that he still held the gun in his hand. "He made a whore of her, drove her mad over the winter—"

The man with the eyepatch gave the slightest of nods. His companions backed Philip up against the wall, and one of them plucked the pistol from his hand like a toy from a child.

"Take him away," Tom said. "Get him out of her sight."

Coughing on the smoke, Deborah clung to Tom. Cautious, painful joy welled up in her. "I thought they'd shot you," she whispered. "I thought you were dead."

"That's what they meant for you to think. They fired into the air." He stared down at the bloodied floor. "Your father wanted it that way, wanted you to think there was no hope for us. But he didn't want my blood on his hands. Even he didn't want that."

They stood together amid the devastation of the stateroom. Bullet holes pocked the walls and shattered the lamp chimneys which lay in pieces on the floor. In the struggle the bed drapes had been ripped down, the heavy silk coverlet torn from the bed. The frightened mongrel shivered amid the ruins. And her father lay dead, the blood from his wounds already thick and cool.

She sank down beside him, touched his graying hair with trembling fingers. Then she pulled the drapes up over his ruined body and ran her hands over him, knowing that in the end, his love had been stronger than his hate.

"He knew. At the very end, he knew—about us and about Philip. But it was too late." She picked up her father's hand, wincing at the stiffness of the fingers, and pressed it to her mouth. Arthur Sinclair had been an intense, complicated man. He had done many hateful things in his life, but he had loved her in the only way he knew.

Gently she put down the lifeless hand and stood.

"Are you hurt?" asked Tom.

She shook her head. "I'm...all right now." Her voice broke, and she couldn't speak anymore.

He cradled her head against his chest. "I know, honey," he said. "I know."

She let his embrace swallow her as she grieved, while brief warm memories of the past flowed through her. She remembered her father as he would have wanted her to remember him—as a loving man whose only flaw was that he had tried to give her the world, even though that wasn't what she'd needed. In the end, he had given her the one simple thing she would cherish forever—her mother's lavaliere, and all the precious memories it evoked. In those long, quiet moments, she was seared by a powerful sense of sorrow, cleansing in its purity.

Tom regarded her with a long, searching look. "Come," he said. "Let me take you from here."

They stepped outside together, escaping the taint of gunsmoke and blood in the stateroom. The pine-scented lake wind swept over them, cold and clean, blowing steadily toward the west.

Epilogue

⸻∞⟨ઉ⟩⟨ઉ⟩∞⸻

Chicago
8 October 1872

It was the coldest October anyone could remember. The
lake made its own weather, bringing chill fog in great
hovering sheets borne on water-cooled winds. Livestock
grew thick winter coats and huddled in the windbreaks,
standing close together for warmth. The unseasonable
chill made women fire up their ovens early on baking day.
It made small children rosy-cheeked and rowdy from the
freshets blowing off the water. Laboring men paused in
their work, turned up their collars and remarked to each
other that they'd surely need to lay in extra wood chips
and scraps from the new lumber and planing mills.

It was hard to believe, folks said, that of Chicago's
three hundred thousand residents, only one hundred
eighty-seven lives had been lost in the Great Fire. Many
more found themselves homeless, but a home could be
rebuilt.

With feverish energy and bootstrap determination, Chicago had risen from the smoldering rubble. No mere pile
of brick and lumber, the city managed to retain its character despite the devastation. The lake, fringed by busy

harbors bristling with masts and smokestacks, lay open to navigation. The vital arteries of the railways came back to life. Relief money and supplies poured in from a sympathetic nation, and within days of the fire, reconstruction had begun. The city meant to make the Queen of the Prairie more regal than ever.

From her sixth-storey suite in the brand-new Hotel St. George, Deborah could see the skyline of the emerging city. She sat up in bed, her back against a bank of lace-edged pillows, and studied the remarkable skeletal ribbing of the Walker building, destined to become the tallest in the city. She admired the sight, but felt no affinity for the place. She missed the towering firs and cedars of the north woods.

A soft tapping came at the door. Smokey, who had been lazing by the fire, scrambled up and gave a yap of warning.

"Come in," Deborah said. Her face lit up as Lucy, Kathleen and Phoebe came in, their arms laden with pink-and-white parcels.

"Look at you," Lucy said, beaming. "You're absolutely blooming with health."

"Of course I am." Deborah smoothed her hand over the quilt. It looked incongruously homely in the opulent bedroom, but she insisted on taking it everywhere she went. "I haven't been sick, but—" She lifted the tiny, precious bundle in her arms so they could see.

Phoebe burst into tears. "That is so beautiful! That's the most beautiful thing I've ever seen."

"It's not a thing, you goose," Lucy scolded laughingly. "It's a baby."

"Her name is Hannah," Deborah said.

Kathleen held out her arms. "May I?"

"Of course." Deborah's friends gathered close to admire the baby. What a blessed wonder her life had turned out to be. Though she hadn't known it, she had been three months gone with child by the time she had reached the mainland the previous spring.

Like fairy godmothers, her friends bestowed their gifts on the new baby. An angora receiving blanket from Phoebe, a silver beaded crucifix from Kathleen, and from Lucy, a book of La Fontaine's fables with hand-colored illustrations.

"Something for her body, something for her soul and something for her mind," Deborah said. "Thank you."

"Well," Lucy asked, looking around the room. "Where is he?"

Her friends hadn't met Tom yet, though they'd had a reunion with Deborah a week before the baby's birth. They had hung on every word of her remarkable story, from the moment she had been taken hostage in the thick of the fire to the wrenching, terrible scene aboard the *Triumph*. She had taken grim satisfaction in relating that Philip Ascot, for all his social standing and family connections, had been hanged as a murderer three weeks after he'd shot her father. Her friends wanted to meet this Tom Silver, who had swept her away to the heart of the wilderness and transformed their friend into a wife, a mother, a woman who knew exactly who she was. With Tom and Hannah, she had found a fulfillment that had eluded her all her life.

Deborah smiled as her husband came striding into the room from the study next door.

"My God," Phoebe whispered, her awed gaze traveling slowly upward. "He *is* Paul Bunyan."

"Tom Silver," he said easily, taking each woman's hand and kissing it. "It's a pleasure to meet you at last."

Deborah watched him with a surge of pride. Though he wore a tailor-made suit of what he termed his "city clothes," he would always retain an air of wildness from the north woods. As if sensing his uncompromising, earthy maleness, Lucy, Phoebe and Kathleen blushed while congratulating him on his daughter—and his marriage.

It was an arrangement no one could have predicted for the wealthiest heiress of Chicago. Deborah and her new husband were determined to live life as it pleased them. They would spend the warm summer months on Isle Royale among the people she had come to know so well. When Hannah was older, she would run wild and free with the island children. And in the winter months, the family would return to Chicago to see old friends and tend to the affairs left behind by Arthur Sinclair. Deborah had sold her interest in most of his industries, concentrating instead on funding charitable foundations dedicated to housing the poor displaced by the fire. A special secure trust fund provided for the miners and their families on the far north island of Isle Royale, where a new church was being built.

After a half hour of visiting, Deborah couldn't stifle a yawn. New motherhood was an exhausting, exhilarating business. Taking his cue, Tom bade the three young ladies goodbye and took Hannah from Kathleen. The baby looked impossibly small in his big, rough hands, yet they were the most gentle hands Deborah had ever known.

"Come here, my love," she said, reaching for him. She felt his lips warm upon her hair, and she settled easily against him, curving her arm around the sleeping baby.

Afterword

Dear Reader,

If everything were taken from you in one night, how would you begin again? If you lost all you hold dear, what is the one thing you would fight to keep? These are the questions faced by the people of Chicago on the night of October 8, 1871, and by the fictional characters in my novels, *The Hostage, The Mistress* and *The Firebrand*.

Why does the Great Chicago Fire live on in memory? Other disasters have been more devastating, but they've been forgotten while the Great Fire endures. By destroying the heart of a city, it took away lives, property, even identities. Condemned men were set free that night. Unhappy wives left their husbands. Children were separated from their families. People reinvented themselves.

When fire sweeps everything away, the stage is set for one of the most enduring fantasies in the human imagination—Who would you become if you could start all over again?

I hope you enjoyed the story of Tom Silver and his hostage, Deborah Sinclair. Please watch for *The Mistress,* featuring Kathleen O'Leary in a very unexpected situation, in November of 2000.

Susan Wiggs
P.O. Box 4469
Rolling Bay WA 98061-0469
USA
http://www.mirastars.com/Susan/Wiggs.htm